I0685147

The Water's Edge

A Cedwynne McKenzie Novel

Book 1

The Water's Edge

A Cedwynne McKenzie Novel
Book 1

by
K. V. McMillan

Copyright © 2010-2013 by Modern Druid Incx LLC
700 East Spruce, Rogers, Arkansas
Cover Art Produced by: Alyssa May
All rights reserved. No part of this book may be reproduced, scanned, or
distributed in any printed or electronic form without permission.
First Edition: August 2013
Printed in the United States of America
ISBN: 978-0-9897213-0-1

Acknowledgments and Dedications:

I would like to thank my test readers for their input and constructive criticism.

Special Thanks to:
Miss Pete, Ashley and Kates: For the many hours of reading, rereading, coffee and conversation.
Pam, The love of my life and my life partner for her never-ending support and honest criticism.
Butch and Wayne, for giving me a male's perspective on the story.

The series itself is always dedicated to my wonderful life partner and best friend:
Pam

The Water's Edge
is dedicated to my mother, the woman who always believed in me.

To:
Beverly,
your children miss you.

The Water's Edge
Forward

After having spent a large portion of my life with my nose in a book, I found that I finally had a couple of stories to tell. Not that my stories are any more interesting or important than any other out there, they are; well.... Mine.

What, in the early part of 2010, started as a simple exercise in story telling for one person quickly became a full blown endeavor of an expanded tale. Even when the story began to take on a life of its own, never did I believe that it would get beyond a couple of modest short novels. However, my characters seemed to take on a life of their own and refused to go to sleep simply because I did. I tried on a number of occasions to wrap up the tale and put a period on it but Cedwynne, her friends and her enemies refused to go quietly. In fact they refused to shut up at all.

Now it is the spring of 2013, the book is going into the line by line editing phase to ready it for publication and I have to split my time between my normal day job, do rewrites on this book and to continue writing on the tenth volume in this series.

I originally thought that developing the characters and story then putting it on paper would be the hard parts. Boy was I wrong. I guess I should count myself lucky that my editors found the story well-constructed enough not to attack that portion of the manuscript. I had never believed I would be arguing with someone, outside of my own head, on a particular word in one sentence out of the plethora of the ones I have written so far. In a way I found it highly educational to find that what I believed was a clear and coherent thought on paper could be misconstrued simply by the usage of one word.

At this point I would really like to thank my editors for their time and patience with me when I tended to lose mine. Carl Earl, as my managing editor, has been a voice of reason as he has helped me polish the narrative and dialogue so that my wonderful line by line editor, Erika Beyer, could concentrate on fixing those pesky tenses and punctuations. Sometimes I think I missed those days in school.

If I had a glass of the Scotch, that Cedwynne likes, in hand I would raise it in a toast to those two individuals.

I would also like to express my appreciation of Alyssa May and her wonderful visual recreation of my characters and world. I hope that her artwork becomes as accepted and appreciated by those that see it as has by me. It is my hope that her visual creation of my world will become a standard on the covers of the individual books in this series, due out in the future. Her work and services, along with her husband's expertise, can be acquired through her web site at madesignimation.com. I would encourage everyone reading this to take a peek at her work.

It is my hope that this series is well received, that I can continue to offer up the storyline in subsequent volumes and that everyone involved with the actual production of this project has something that they can point to and say "I had a hand in that." All of the people that I have mentioned in my acknowledgments and forward have been more than just supportive, they have been excited about being a part of this and helping me along the way.

The Water's Edge

Prologue

The evening had turned to night as he sat at his desk going over the numerous reports and files stacked in front of him. His concentration was interrupted by the intercom on his desk.

"Mister President?" came the secretary's voice over the speaker.

"Yes, Gwen."

"Senator Stinnitt, to see you sir."

"Send him in. And Gwen?"

"Yes sir?"

"Go home. It is getting late."

"Yes sir. Good night sir."

"Good night Gwen," he replied as he clicked off the intercom and began putting away the sensitive files he had been working on.

"Jack," the President said in greeting as he came from behind his desk and offered the Senator his hand.

"Mister President," the senator responded, shaking with the President.

"Did you bring the candidate dossiers?"

"Yes sir," he said, handing over three file folders.

"Any recommendations?"

"I put them in reverse order of qualifications. We did not have a lot of candidates to choose from this time. Though the last dossier lists exceptional qualifications, age will probably play a large role in that candidate being ruled out," the senator replied.

"Between the two of us Jack. If you were picking, which one would you take?"

"I would personally say age be damned. I have not seen qualifications like that candidate before."

"Thanks Jack. I will look these over and give you a call tomorrow."

"Thank you sir. We really don't need to let District Five sit empty for too long."

"Have a good night, Jack. And say hello to Dorothy for me," the President said as he walked the other man to the door.

"Thank you sir. She will be happy to hear from you," the senator said as he walked out.

The president walked back to the couch in front of his desk, picked up the first file and began reading. It was getting fairly late into the night by the time he had gotten through the first two. Jack had been right, he thought, not really good candidates. He got up, went to the small side table and poured himself a drink. He came back to the couch, sat down, picked up the third file and began reading.

Counter Section Candidate Evaluation.

Candidate number: 23
Date Report Filed: January 3, 2248
Candidate Name:
Cedwynne Anne McKenzie
Current Assignment: United States Deputy Marshal,
Texas District 1.
Current Supervisor: Terrance James Burdock, United
States Marshal, Texas District 1.

Vital Statistics as of last Physical:

Date of Last Physical: January 15, 2247
Sex: Female
Age: 25
Height: 5' 3-3/8"
Weight: 179 lbs. ***
Body Fat: 19%
Pulse Rate, Resting: 65
Blood Pressure, Resting: 110/70
Respiration, Resting: 10
Pulse Rate, Heavy Stress: 144
Blood Pressure, Heavy Stress: 130/80
Respiration, Heavy Stress: 16-20

Attending Physician's Evaluation: All tests for Miss McKenzie fall well within the baselines established in her file upon her acceptance into the service. Neither she, nor the tests, have indicated any new health problems since her last physical a year ago. It is my opinion that Miss McKenzie is more than fit for the duties of her assignment.

Dr. William J. Kennedy, PHD. MD. 01/15/2247

*** Where normal weight at this height would tend to be in the 105-120 lbs. range, Miss McKenzie seems to have an abnormality in bone and muscle density which causes the extra weight. After extensive testing Dr. David Culiver, the attending physician at the Marshal Training Center, believes the abnormality to be an effect of her G-3 mutations. See his case file number USMS-MS-14454-2349/03/04. She shows no ill effects of the condition. On the contrary, it seems to put her in a very high percentile for strength and endurance.

Subject Background:
   Birth Date: Day: Unknown   Month: Unknown
   Year: c. 2222
      Father's Name: Unknown/ McKenzie?
            Birth Date: Unknown
            Death Date: May 25 2225*
            *See Colorado State Police Report: COSP-
TA/052525-0062
      Mother's Name: Unknown
            Birth Date: Unknown
            Death Date: Unknown

Outline of Subject's Life,
From birth to present:
   Years 1-3
   No record. Placed under the protection of Colorado
DHS at the age of three, upon the death of father.
   Years 3-6:
   Placed with Certified Foster Family. Bill and Wilma
Johnson - Ft. Collins, Colorado.
   Years 6-8:
   Placed with Certified Foster Family. David and
Jennifer Crittenden - Cheyenne Wells, Colorado.
   Years 8-9:
   Colorado DHS Protection transferred to Kansas DHS
Due to job relocation of David and Jennifer Crittenden
to Russell Kansas.
   Years 9-11:
   Placed with Certified Foster Parent: Betty Carlton,
Salina, Kansas. Due to the loss of certification of
David and Jennifer Crittenden.
   Years 11-15:
   Removed from Betty Carlton's protection due to
suspected child abuse. Placed with Certified Foster
Parents Randy and Regina Randall. Salina Kansas
   Years 15-17:
   Grandview Home for Children, Wichita Kansas. June
12, 2239, Miss McKenzie filed for and received
emancipation rights from the courts, on the basis of
age and high school education completed.
   Years 17-19:
   Wichita Community College. 2 year degree-Criminal
Justice and Constitutional Law.

Years 19-21:

Acceptance into the United States Marshals Training academy- 6/26/2241

Graduation from USM Training academy - 6/01/2243

Years 21-Present:

Accepted commission and assigned to U.S. Marshal Service Texas District 1. Presently lives in Dallas, Texas. 6/02/2243

Assessment of Candidate, Elementary through High School:

Miss McKenzie has shown average class grades, but has scored consistently in the top percentiles on all standardized tests. With two I.Q. Tests scored at 136 and 138 respectively, she is thought to be in the gifted range. Though considered to be a bit of a loner, she was never considered to be a trouble maker or outright antisocial.

At age seven Miss McKenzie was referred to Clara Team, LCSW Colorado DHS, for a psychological evaluation at the behest of her foster parents, David and Jennifer Crittenden. The session records are sealed due to Directive One, but an interview was conducted with Mrs. Clara Team, who is still in the employ of Colorado DHS. In our interview with Mrs. Team, she refused to discuss the particulars of any session. She did, however, state that she had been confused by the way Miss McKenzie presented. Mrs. Team stated that she had handled many cases such as this and the normal diagnosis from her would be a child with abandonment issues which manifested itself as an overactive imagination. However, it was her personal opinion that Miss McKenzie did not present in the same way as most of her other patients. She said she had always felt that the young Miss McKenzie was actually showing signs of a form of heightened cognizant awareness, not abandonment issues. (Layman's terminology: some form of ESP). But since that was not an accepted diagnosis then or now, she had no other choice but to labeled it as she always had. In her notes given to Colorado DHS, Mrs. Team did advise that the child be seen again in a few years for a follow up study. For some reason, when Miss McKenzie was

4

transferred from the protection of Colorado to Kansas a follow up was never attempted.

Miss McKenzie has always shown a pronounced contempt of overbearing authority. Her school records indicate a long list of rebellion against perceived unfair rules and regulations, especially when it concerned her classmates. While in her junior year of high school she completed her GED and graduated a year ahead of her scheduled matriculation. Also while in her junior year she researched and petitioned the courts for emancipation without the aid of a lawyer or legal guardian.

Assessment of Candidate, Higher Education and Beyond:

Miss McKenzie made perfect grades through her time at Wichita Community College. Her exceptional skill became apparent once she entered the training academy for the U.S. Marshal Service. She scored in the 90th percentile or above in all training, which is unheard of in a female candidate. Special note should be taken where it concerns her scores in strength/agility/endurance, marksmanship, creative/intuitive/dynamic thinking, and hand-to-hand combat/martial arts.

In strength/agility/endurance a candidate is always tested against others in their gender/height/weight class first then those results are listed among the whole class and graded against a curve to give a better overall reading of the candidate. The Marshal Service has never had a male, much less a female, in Miss McKenzie's height and weight class.

Miss McKenzie quickly became a unique problem in grading at this juncture, in that she basically set a new standard for all female cadets and a significant portion of the male cadets as well. It wasn't until she was graded against males between 6'0"-6'3" and 200-210 lbs. that she fell into a measurable percentile at 99%. Out of fairness to female cadets they are normally graded on a curve to give a better representation of where they fall in the class. In the history of the Marshal Service no female cadet has ever scored higher than the 85th percentile without the curve. Miss McKenzie, however, scored in the 94th percentile without the adjustment curve being applied to her scores.

The marksmanship portion of a Marshal's training is held as four part competition. Those being: Knife throwing, Handgun-Revolver, Handgun-Semi-Automatic, Rifle-Mid Range/No Scope and Rifle-Long Range/With Scope. As with the strength/agility/endurance portion of her training, Miss McKenzie excelled in this area also. Out of the twenty three cadets in her class her scores placed her second in her class with the third place finisher being more than fifty points behind in scoring. Miss McKenzie's finishes were as follows: Knives-1st, Handgun-Revolver-2nd, Handgun-Semi Automatic-1st, Rifle-Mid Range/no scope-2nd and Rifle-Long Range/With Scope-2nd. It should be noted here that while Miss McKenzie's score was fifty points higher than the third place finisher, the winning cadet which was a former marine sniper, only beat Miss McKenzie for the first place ribbon by two points. The final competition was on the long range rifle and Miss McKenzie did not take first place simply because the single hole in the paper target, she had sent all six of her rounds through, was one millimeter larger than that of her competitor at two hundred yards.

When it comes to her record as a U.S. Deputy Marshal, the best summation would probably be the following words taken from her last yearly review by her present supervisor, Marshal Terrance Burdock:

"There can be no argument with Deputy Marshal McKenzie's dedication to her job. Her closure rate is about 80% and of arrests resulting in prosecution, she has a 94% conviction rate. A note here: I have not found a single reference to any case where the prosecution's failure to get a conviction was due to any failure or lack of due diligence of Deputy Marshal McKenzie. I have never met a law enforcement officer that is as unshakable, diligent, loyal, and steadfast as she is. Her interpersonal skills and respect for authority, however, leave a little to be desired. Though there is not a Marshal in this district that does not beg for Deputy Marshal McKenzie to be their backup on a bust or raid; there is only one, her present partner, which is willing to put up with her on a daily basis. Where I have never known her to disregard a direct order, she is never shy about questioning those orders. Sometimes that questioning can border on insubordination. With all of that said, I personally can and do put up with her abrasive manner simply because our district would be much less without her in

it. I have never met a finer overall law enforcement officer in my life."

Assessment of Candidate Report, compiled by:
Special Agent Amelia Tenant, IBI

Mr. President,

Out of the present candidates for this position Deputy Marshal McKenzie by far has the best positive qualifications for this appointment. Her exceptional scores, training, lack of family, personality, and the hint of a special gift seems to make her ideal for a solitary and dangerous assignment. The only detraction from her candidacy would be her age. Does she lack the real world experience to be effective in this job?
Senator Jack Stinnitt.

Jack had been right; she was highly qualified for this position. But could he, in good conscience, throw someone so young to the wolves, literally? He sat for an hour thinking about the decision he had to make. Damn the age, he finally said to himself. The President picked up a pen, and across the top of Marshal McKenzie's file wrote:

Accepted for Appointment. Wednesday, March 15, 2248.
Carlton B. Bradley III,
President of The United States of America.

Chapter 1
Wednesday March 29, 2248

Most people hate Mondays; I, however, am not one of them. My day of the week to loathe would have to be Wednesday. I think the nursery rhyme got it right: Wednesday's child is full of woe. Nothing good has ever happened to me on a Wednesday. Wednesday is trash day at the apartment building where I live, every week I am awakened by the slamming of tin cans at five thirty in the morning. It always seems that all of those things in my life I hate to do, I have to do on Wednesday. Washing dishes, writing reports, getting my ass chewed by my boss, always on a Wednesday. Though I would probably have to mark today on the calendar as a Wednesday that didn't start too badly.

My hopes for a nice Wednesday started shortly after midnight when Sam and I finally made an arrest on a case we had been working for two months. Even a late bedtime did nothing to tarnish the peace and quiet between five thirty and seven this morning as I blissfully slept through the refuse collection for this week. Of course my meeting the sanitation workers last week with a badge, gun and pink fuzzy slippers might have had a hand in this morning's serenity. Another bright spot was that spring had actually arrived, somewhat, on time this year. I had to dig around and find one of my light blazers since the morning was much warmer than it had been. The day promised to be bright, sunny and warm and if it wasn't for the fact of hiding the gun I would have even left the blazer at home. For once, in a long time, I felt the score was in my favor on a Wednesday.

On the plus side; arrested someone, no trash can slamming, I got to sleep until seven and it was going to be a beautiful warm day. On the down side; I had to write the report on the arrest and do the dishes when I got home. As it stood now it was 4-2 in favor of a good day and if I wanted to tilt the scales more, I could wait until tomorrow to do dishes.

****

At eight I found myself safely behind my desk with coffee, working on the report that needed to be filed.

"McKenzie!" -came the shout through the intercom sitting on my desk.

"What?" I replied, in the general direction of the phone.

"I need to see you in my office."

"Be there in a sec," I answered, concentrating on the report I was trying to finish.

"Now, Dammit!"

I minimized the file I was working on, grabbed my coffee and headed for Captain Burdock's office. Since I had not gotten a lot of sleep last night I was tired, grumpy, two cups of coffee shy of semi-agreeable and now it looked like

Wednesday was balancing the scales back in its favor. I made my way through the maze of desks towards the Captain's office.

Captain Burdock and I had a love/hate relationship going. Though we respected each other, we rarely saw eye to eye on anything. The Captain was a holdover from the Bio-War. He had previously been Special Forces and had a very spit and polish way of doing things. Burdock was actually the Marshall of this district but his rank and reputation had preceded him so all of the Deputy Marshals just called him Captain. I was raised by a long string of foster parents and have a very deeply ingrained distrust of someone else's view of authority over me. Why I ever chose this career is beyond me, but I have been in the U.S. Marshal Service for five years. I think the only reason Burdock put up with me was my track record with closing cases. I found myself standing in front of the Captain's door. I took a deep breath and a swig of coffee, and then knocked.

"Come in!" came the shout from behind the door.

I opened the door and entered.

"Close the door," Burdock ordered.

I shut the door as I surveyed the room. Burdock sat behind his desk. There were two other men in the room, both in the nondescript gray suits that signified them as some sort of government agents. Burdock was rather short, broad chested and still in incredible shape. The two in the suits were diametrically opposed not only to Burdock, but to each other. One of the gray suits was sitting in a chair across from Burdock, while the second one stood behind. I knew in an instant that the one seated was of much higher rank than the other. The one seated was older, growing a gut, and oozed self-importance. The one standing looked like every other government agent I had come up against; tall, gaunt, ripped and lethal.

"You bellowed?" I asked.

"Take a seat," Burdock directed, giving me a look of warning.

I crossed to the other chair facing his desk and sat, waiting. I figured I had stepped on someone's toes again and this was just another ass chewing since it was a Wednesday.

"Deputy Marshal Cedwynne McKenzie, Special Agent Wallace IBI" Burdock said, introducing me to the suit that was seated.

Great. Who did I piss off that high up? The IBI was what became of the CIA and part of the FBI when the United States had been reformed. The Intercontinental Bureau of Intelligence had been formed as an intelligence gathering agency and now covered all covert affairs and intelligence gathering outside the borders of the country. The IBI was basically the repository and disseminating agent for all intelligence gathered inside the country by the other law enforcement agencies as well. Just as the CIA before them, it was still illegal for them to operate in any capacity other than informational within the borders of the United States. At that time, the law enforcement and investigative side of the

FBI was incorporated into the U.S. Marshal Service. Where before the war the Marshal Service had very distinctive responsibilities, now it was more of a national police force. Though we had jurisdiction wherever we went, our job was to enforce the national laws not the local ones. I inclined my head towards the man in the chair as he eyed me up and down stopping at my chest. I took an instant dislike to him.

"May I call you Cedwynne?" he asked, still staring at my chest.

"If you would like to look at me instead of my breasts, yes," I replied.

A twisted smile came over his face as he met my eyes.

"McKenzie!" Burdock warned me.

"What can I do for you?" I asked taking a sip of my cooling coffee.

"We have a need," he started.

I can just imagine what your need might be, I thought as I watched him go back to sizing up my breasts.

"Out of all of the services your qualifications came up as the most suited for this assignment," he said.

"What would those qualifications be?"

"Maybe it was your charming sense of humor, can't really say."

"What's the assignment?"

"Have you ever heard of Counter Section?"

Yes, I had heard of it but there had never been any real evidence that proved the existence of it. Counter Section was rumored to be an elite group of agents that worked some of the most disturbing cases across the country that local law enforcement, even some government agencies, could not explain or handle.

"I thought that was a myth?" I replied.

"Not a myth."

"So I ask again. What is the assignment?"

"Understand I can only give you generalities unless you take it."

"Fine, give me the generalities then," I said, feeling the lack of sleep and coffee.

"You will be assigned to a section of the country that you will be responsible for. You will work under your Marshal credentials but you will also carry IBI credentials. Though you will be responsible for a section, that does not mean that whatever case you might be working on at the moment won't take you to the other side of the country. The two things you need to think about are that you will have no immediate backup and closing your cases will be different than what you are now used to," he said, raising an eyebrow.

"And how are the cases closed?"

"Let's just say that normally you don't have to worry about your cases holding up in court."

"What about Directive One?" I asked surprised.

One of the things that had been put in place during the restructuring was tighter controls on the government and law enforcement where it concerned citizen's rights. Directive One became more of a basis for the new U.S. than the original Bill of Rights.

"Directive One is …. not really an issue. If you take the assignment you will understand why," Agent Wallace answered, ending the line of questioning with the same punctuation as his sentence, with the finality of a period.

"What happened to the agent that had this district?" I asked, changing the subject.

"He had to ah.... retire."

"Are you trying to say he's dead?" I asked leaning towards him.

"No not at all. He is very much still running around."

"Where will I be located?"

"Sorry. I cannot tell you that."

"Who will I answer to?"

"Your liaison will be Marshal Burdock. You will answer to three people only, the Director of the IBI, the Director of the Marshal Service, and the President. Also for your protection you cannot be removed from duty without written orders signed by at least two of the three aforementioned people," he said with some seriousness in his voice.

"Really?" I asked unbelieving.

"Yes. You will have a certain amount of autonomy."

"What about pay?"

"You will get that information if you accept the job. I will at least tell you that it will be a better deal than you have now."

"When do you need an answer?"

"By the end of the day."

I just looked at him as he stood up.

"Thank you for your time," he said to Captain Burdock.

"How do I get a hold of you to give you an answer?" I asked.

"If you accept the position, Marshal Burdock is your liaison. He will have what you need," Agent Wallace answered.

Agent Wallace nodded at the door and headed towards it with his shadow in tow. The door closed leaving Burdock and I alone in the office. I watched as Burdock's face softened when he looked at me.

"Ced, this is a very dangerous assignment," Burdock started quietly.

I was surprised at the change in the Captain. He had only called me Ced on two other occasions in the three years we had worked together and one of those we both had been a little drunk at the Marshal's banquet and ball last October. Though Burdock could be a royal pain-in-the-butt you also knew he had your back. Whether it was in a fire fight or a room full of bureaucrats, Burdock would protect his people with a tenacity that was legendary. That was the main reason that every one of the Marshals in this particular office was extremely loyal to

11

him, me included.

"Should I pass on it?" I asked.

"I can't answer that for you. Other than rumor and innuendo I don't have any real information about Counter...."

"And what are the rumors and innuendos?"

Burdock gave me a very long, hard stare. I wasn't sure if it was because I interrupted him or if he was weighing the words before he spoke them.

"Some say occult, others supernatural."

For once, since I entered this office, I couldn't think of anything to say. It took me a second to even get out the obvious.

"Occult and supernatural? Are you kidding me?"

"Just the rumors I've heard."

I had dealt with some real weirdos and losers since I became a Marshal, even had one suspect that was into Satanic rites.... But really? Fucking supernatural? *Careful Ced, you are repeating yourself-first sign of mental illness.*

"Any words of wisdom?" I finally asked.

"Ced, all I know is if you take it and survive you will be set for life. Is that a tradeoff you are willing to bet on?"

"We both know that I don't play the game of politics real well and I have very little upward motion left here unless I drastically change my ways."

"Like that is going to happen," Burdock interrupted, letting a smile start.

"True." I grinned back at him.

"What have I really got to lose? I have no family. I don't really date. The only reason I'm here is because of the job, it's not like I really like Dallas," I continued.

"Why don't you take the rest of the day off, think about it and get back with me this afternoon before five," Burdock suggested.

"What about my report from the arrest last night and my cases?"

"Make your decision first. If you decide to go, then turn everything over to Sam. If you decide to stay I'll yell at you tomorrow for it being late," he said chuckling.

"So damned if I do and damned if I don't?" I asked laughing.

"Pretty much."

"I guess I'll see you about four thirty then," I said, standing up.

"Think about it carefully, Ced," Burdock answered, standing with me and offering his hand.

I shook his hand and left the office, forgetting to shut the door as I left.

"You born in a barn McKenzie?" I heard him yell as I got about three steps away from his office.

I turned around, closed his door and headed to my desk. Okay Wednesday had officially run the gambit of bad to good, to maybe bad, to outright weird. Sam, my partner, watched me as I sat down.

"Who did you piss off this time?" Sam asked.

Out of the six partners I've had over the last five years, Sam was one of the two I liked. Grant, my first partner, was killed in the line of duty and I had not taken well to the succession of Marshals that were assigned with me until Sam. We were the polar opposites. Sam was eighty six years old and had been a Marshal now for over forty years, where I was twenty six and been on the job for only five. He was tall, skinny, and had the skin color of dark chocolate; I was only five three, curvy (especially up top), and as white as bleached bread. Where I was headstrong and unpredictable, Sam was steady and had the patience of Job. I think that was the reason we worked so well together. We complimented each other instead of mixing like oil and water.

"For a change no one," I answered, pulling my side arm out of my desk drawer.

"Did you finish that report?" Sam asked.

"Not yet."

"Burdock is going to go ballistic if we don't get it done."

"Don't worry. We have a reprieve until tomorrow. I am going to be taking some personal time until this afternoon. I will see you around four," I told him as I stood back up and shoved my gun in the holster hanging from my belt at the small of my back.

"You okay?" Sam asked, giving me a concerned look.

"Yep. I am fine. Just have a few things I have to get done before this afternoon," I said as I pulled my light cloth coat off of the back of my chair and started putting it on.

"Ced, call me if you need anything," Sam said looking worried.

"I'm fine Sam."

Sam and I had always been able to read each other so he knew something was up. He looked at me not convinced, but didn't press it.

"See ya later."

"Yep," I answered as I finished putting on my coat and headed for the door.

I walked out of the office, down the hall to the elevator, punched the button and waited on the car to get there. I began thinking about the offer I'd been given. What did I really know about it? Nothing. On the other hand what did I have holding me here? Other than Sam, and to a lesser degree Burdock, all I had was the job. If I took the new assignment I would still have the job and a bigger paycheck. I found myself walking through the park a few blocks from the office, found a bench and sat down. I wrestled with the decision until my brain thought it was going to explode.

Instead of my head exploding my stomach served notice that all it'd had this morning was a cup of black coffee. I got up and started walking to the west side of the park and the diner where most of us ate. I kept having a feeling that I was being followed and watched. I took a couple of unexpected turns and watched for anything unusual. No one seemed to take notice. I decided to stop and access my 'gift'. At a young age I learned that, for some reason, I had the capacity to see people's auras. I had only told one person in my entire life about it and that was the foster mother I was with when I was about seven. She just thought it was the ravings of a lonely child and had my head shrunk. After that I kept it as my secret and had not discussed it, even in theory, with anyone.

I scanned all of the people who were around me in the park. I couldn't discern anything that was not out of the norm. Most of them had the normal muted colors of even emotions, a couple of them had red tinges of anger but it seemed to be directed somewhere other than at me. I resumed my walk to the restaurant trying to shake the feeling I was having.

I was relieved as I opened the diner door and stepped in. It was after breakfast and before lunch so the place was empty except a couple of patrons sitting at the counter reading and nursing a drink of some type. I took a booth towards the back and faced the front of the establishment so I could watch everyone there or that might enter. Gladys, the normal day waitress, ambled over to my table.

"Hey Hun. You're in here at an odd time," she said, sitting down the glass of water she had brought.

"Taking a break, I forgot to eat this morning," I replied.

"What can I get for you?" she asked.

"Salad, oil and vinegar. Plain broiled chicken breast and coffee."

"One of these days you are going to turn into a salad and chicken breast." Gladys laughed as she wrote down my order.

"I think I'm half way there," I replied, smiling and looking down at my over developed chest.

"Honey, if I thought that yours came from what you ate, I'd follow your diet to the letter," Gladys said, grinning and moved back behind the counter to turn in my order.

****

I sat in the diner slowly eating my meal and nursing one cup of coffee after another. A few of the marshals I worked with came in for lunch and said hello, then left after their meals. I continued to sit until the lunch crowd thinned out. I made a mental list of the pros and cons of taking the job as I saw them.

Cons: I was established here. I had a life here. I had a partner that I had a bond with. I had a boss that would protect me as long as I didn't screw up too much. I knew what was expected of me. As all Marshals I could expect my seniority raises every year.

Pros: It would mean a bump in pay. If I lasted and retired from it I would be set for life.

The danger of the job was probably a wash since I faced that possibility regardless of where I was.

Other than Sam, Burdock, and the few friends I could count on one hand I had nothing holding me here. Unless someone screwed up royally, I would probably never make full Marshal. Though Sam was getting on in years, his wife wasn't and Sam had already told me he would be taking a two year leave of absence to start a family. That would mean that I would be breaking in another partner, or string of them, since Sam would probably be taking a support role when he returned. This was a definite advancement and I would not have to deal with a lot of bosses. I could see Burdock advancing to head a national district before too long and maybe even make Director of the Marshal Service, so he would ultimately be gone. So the two people that I would want to stay for would probably not be an everyday part of my life and there wasn't anyone or anything from my past that was keeping me here. What would make me stay? I had nothing. After a string of five foster families and a group home, upheaval in my life was the norm not the exception. I had been in Dallas longer than I had ever stayed anywhere before. Maybe it was time for a change and this was the opportunity that was presenting itself. There was a nagging feeling of the unknown. I might be a little apprehensive but I wasn't scared, I had not really been scared since I was seven when Jennifer had finally told me that I was an orphan. I swore that day that nothing would ever scare me again. For the most part I had kept that promise to myself.

I looked at my watch; three thirty. I paid my tab and headed back to the office. All the way there I could still not shake the feeling of being followed. I got on the elevator and hit the button for the floor our offices were on. As the door closed I realized that I was no closer to a decision than when I had left this morning. I got off the elevator, walked the short hall to the glass door and opened it to the squad room. There were a few Marshals hunched over their terminals trying to finish up the last of their reports before the end of their shift. Sam was not at his desk so I continued through the work stations until I was in front of Burdock's door. I took a deep breath and knocked.

"Come in," came Burdock's gruff voice from within.

I opened the door and entered, closing it behind me. Burdock looked up at me as I crossed the room and slumped down in the chair I had been sitting in this morning.

"So?" Burdock asked.

Even with the pro and con list I did not make up my mind until I spoke the words.

"I guess I'll take it," I said.

What it boiled down to was one question. Did I have anything to lose if I took the job? Answer: No.

"Are you sure?"

"Yep," I said in a way to try and convince myself more than Burdock.

"What made up your mind to take it?"

"I would rather face the unknown than have to listen to you yell at me about the report being late," I smarted off, smiling.

"I don't know if I am going to miss you or not," He said, grinning.

Burdock opened a drawer on his desk, pulled out a manila envelope and handed it over to me. I took it and looked at the front. It had my name on it. I opened it and poured the contents of it into my lap. I looked inside and pulled out the printed paper that was still in it. The contents that I had poured out consisted of a ring with four keys on it, a flip wallet with IBI credentials, a new U.S. Marshal identification card, and a silver necklace with an odd silver cross on it. I flipped the printed page over and read the short message.

Marshal McKenzie,

Make sure there are four (4) items in this envelope, not including this letter. You have three business days to conclude your affairs. You will be contacted sometime after that deadline. The agent that will contact you will state who he is and then ask you to get a drink, you will respond – Bottoms up. If the agent contacting you does not ask for the drink, contact your liaison immediately.

Once you have checked the contents, and committed your reply to memory destroy this message and the envelope it came in.

I finished reading the note, gathered up the things in my lap, walked over to the shredder that sat to the side of the office and fed both paper items in. I watched as it was cut and re-cut then I returned to my seat. This seemed so cloak and dagger it was funny.

"I need your old I.D." Burdock said.

I flipped open my shield, pulled out the old I.D. and replaced it with the one I had gotten in the envelope. I handed the old one to Burdock. He took it, crossed to the shredder and fed it in. He came back and actually sat down in the chair next to me.

"Ced," Burdock started, as he pulled a business card out of his pocket.

"On the back are my personal numbers. If you can't reach me on my business phones you call me at either one of those, regardless of the time of day." He said as he handed me the card. I pulled out my shield and stuck it behind my I.D.

"What about Sam?" I asked.

"That is up to you. You can tell him you got reassigned or you can tell him nothing. But you can't tell him anything about the conversations we've had. If you want I can handle it once you're gone."

"No. I like Sam. I need to tell him. So do I work here the next three days?"

"Yes, you need to get Sam and his new partner up to speed on anything

16

you're working on. I don't know what sort of personal affairs you need to take care of but you'll have to juggle the two."

"Well I guess that's it then." I said as I stood up, slipping the keys and the cross in my front jeans pocket and the IBI credentials in my back one.

"Ced. Watch your ass out there." Burdock said, with a look of real concern on his face.

I accepted the warm handshake he offered, but I got the feeling there were some things that Burdock was not telling me. I walked out of his office and headed towards my desk. Sam was back at his spot working on a file. I leaned against my desk.

"Sam?" I asked.

"Yep?" he answered, not looking up from his terminal.

"You about done?"

"Yep."

"Good. Let's go get a beer."

Sam looked up at me, I knew he suspected something. He closed down his terminal, grabbed his sport coat and got up.

"Where ya wanna go?" he asked.

"Greg's?"

"Okay," he said as he walked to the door and held it open for me.

We walked the few blocks to the bar, Sam opened the door so we could enter.

"Go find a seat, I'll get the beer," he said as he headed towards the bar.

I picked out a table in the back corner away from most of the noise and took a seat. Sam returned shortly with four bottles of beer and sat two down in front of me, and then he took a seat directly across the table.

"What's up Ced?" Sam asked.

"Right to the point, huh?" I asked, smiling.

"You have been preoccupied all day. Does this have anything to do with IBI's visit this morning?" he asked.

"What? IBI was here?" I asked, trying to put on my shocked expression.

"It's a good thing that you work on this side of the law cause you can't lie worth a shit," he said, taking a swig of beer.

"I guess that there is no other way to say this. I am being reassigned."

"Where to?"

"Honestly, I don't know. I guess you could say it is a permanent, special, assignment."

"When are you leaving?"

"I have three days to get my shit together here. Sometime after that."

"God, Ced. I'm going to miss you," he said, looking sad.

All of a sudden I felt the pangs of separation. Sam and I had shared a lot in the past two and a half years. We'd saved each others butts on numerous occasions and became much closer than friends. I wished I could tell him more. I reached across the table and took his hand. We must have made an interesting pair to the onlookers. Here was this skinny, tall dark skinned man with the beginnings of gray at his temples holding hands with a petite, young, auburn haired white girl.

"You *do* know that you and Grant are the only two that were able to put up with me," I said, trying to smile.

"If you need anything Ced, all you have to do is call."

"I'm sorry that you'll have to break in a new partner," I said, starting to tear up.

"Maybe they won't be as much of a pain in the ass as you have been," he said holding up his bottle in a toast and smiled.

I clinked the neck of my bottle against his and returned his sad smile.

Chapter 2
Monday April 3, 2248

The end of my last shift was approaching; I had worked all weekend to help Sam get his new partner halfway up to speed. I felt sorry for Sam; his new partner was ex-military and fresh out of training. But in true Sam fashion, he smiled and laughed about it. I was bummed that Sam and his new partner were transporting a prisoner to Kansas City and I wouldn't get to say a final good-bye. I had good and sad thoughts about my ex-partner as I wrote a quick good-bye note and left it on his desk. I took one last look around the squad room, picked up the only personal item from my desk. It was a very flowery and feminine coffee cup that Grant, my first partner, had given me my first week as a Deputy Marshal. I stuck it in my blazer pocket and headed for the door. I walked the five blocks to my apartment very slowly and in thought. I wondered how long I would have to wait until I was contacted by the promised agent.

I rented a small furnished apartment not far from the office. Having been raised by foster parents I learned to travel light and my apartment was an extension of that. Other than a few items that I could pack in a suitcase, everything else that I owned could be replaced if I had to leave it. I walked up the four flights of stairs instead of taking the elevator to get to my apartment. I pulled my keys out of my pocket, unlocked the door and entered what passed for home sweet home. I had a hard time wrapping my brain around what greeted me. My first thought was that I had been robbed, but I had nothing to really steal. I pulled my gun out and slipped off the safety. My apartment was immaculate, which was my first clue since I rarely cleaned it. All of the furniture was in its place but none of my personal items were anywhere to be found. I cautiously walked through the small apartment. Every room had been emptied of my personal belongings and cleaned. Even my closet was empty. I ran to the bathroom, closed the toilet lid, stood on it and took off the vent cover of the air conditioner duct near the ceiling. Damn, they took my backup pistol. I walked back into the kitchen holstering my weapon, and opened the fridge. I had to laugh that it was empty and clean except one lonely beer sitting front and center. I pulled it out, flipped the cap off and took a long swig. I looked around the apartment. If they were thieves they had to have been the most obsessive compulsive ones I had ever seen in my life since the apartment hadn't been this clean when I moved in five years ago. I took my beer back into the living room and sat down on the couch. Should I call someone? If so, who? I could just hear the conversation in my head.

"Yes I would like to report a robbery. What did they take? A couple of books, some music disks, my food, and oh yeah-they cleaned me out, literally." I think I'd pass on that conversation, even with Sam.

I was coming to the end of my beer when there was a knock at the door. I got up, sat my beer on the counter, and walked to the front door. I looked through the view hole. It was none other than Agent Wallace's shadow from the other morning wearing an identical gray suit. I opened the door.

"Yes?" I asked.

"I am Agent Gray," he said introducing himself and displaying his identification.

"Of course you are," I said as I opened the door wider and gestured him in.

He came into the room; I closed the door behind him. I went back, picked up the bottle, took a drink, and waited for him to say something.

"Would you like to go for a drink?" he asked very stiffly.

"Bottoms Up," I said as I mimicked the sentiment with my own bottle, finishing off the beer.

"Don't get many dates do you?" I asked as I sat the bottle down on the counter.

Agent Gray stood and stared at me unblinking.

"Your phone," he said as he held out his hand.

I reached into my pocket and pulled out my phone and handed it to him. He moved to the sink, popped the back off of it, and pulled the battery and SIM chip out. He sat the battery, phone, and compartment lid on the counter and the small chip down in the sink. The agent reached into his coat pocket and pulled out a small bottle with a dropper top. He screwed the top off, pulled some liquid up into the dropper, and then applied it to the chip laying in the sink. I watched as the bubbles started to smoke and reduce the once small chip into goo. He flipped on the garbage disposal and washed the mess down with a stream from the hand sprayer. He picked up the remaining pieces of the phone and stuck them in a pocket of his suit coat. He reached in the vest side of his jacket and pulled out another phone and handed it to me.

"This is your new phone. You can look in the menu to find the number. If you will turn it over," he directed.

I turned the phone over to look at the back.

"You will notice the round indention in the back. This phone cannot be tracked unless you are triangulated from towers. However, if you find yourself in your last stand press and hold that indention for ten seconds. That will activate a tracking device that will tell us where we can find the body."

"You're just Mister Happy, aren't you?"

"Give me the keys that you do not need anymore."

I pulled my ring of keys out and took the apartment and mail box key off of it and handed them over. He placed them in a pocket.

"Are you ready to go?" he asked.

"I guess so. Where?"

"To where you are supposed to be," he said as he picked up my empty beer bottle and headed for the door.

The Water's Edge

I followed him out the door, down the stairs, and out into the twilight of early evening. He pitched the bottle into a trashcan that sat on the corner as he headed down the street. I had to almost run to keep up with him.

"Hey, Goliath. You want to shorten your stride some?" I asked, making my legs work overtime.

I was about five three and my legs were considered long for my height, but he had to have been at least six three and most of him was leg. I guess he didn't want to heed my request, in fact I felt like he hastened his steps. I ran behind him for the better part of five blocks when he stopped suddenly next to a black four door sedan.

"Get in."

"Not much of a gentleman are you?" I flung at him as I opened my door and sat down in the car.

He got in the driver's side, turned the key to on, and pulled out into the street heading towards the expressway. The only noise the car made was the hum of the tires on the road and a small whine of the electric motor as it propelled us along. Since he was not being much of a conversationalist, I watched the buildings fly by until we got to the entrance of the expressway at which time he stepped down on the accelerator and flung us out on the open road at an excessive speed.

"Do they recruit you guys based on your winning personality?" I asked him.

He grunted at me and added more speed to our momentum. I shrunk down into the bucket as he passed the light traffic on the road. He took a couple of exits until we were on interstate thirty heading east. We dove for about an hour when he took an exit to a small town. He turned a couple of corners and pulled into the parking lot of an old abandoned store and flew across the parking lot towards a vehicle that was hard to describe in the fading light. He pulled up next to it.

"Here you are," he said with a sarcastic smile.

"Fine we are here. Where do I need to go?"

"I have no idea. Get out."

I sat and looked at him.

"This is your stop," he said more forcefully.

"You have got to be kidding."

"I don't kid."

"Really Mister Understatement?" I asked as I opened the door and got out into the growing darkness.

He pressed the accelerator down, jerking the door out of my hand. He made a sharp right turn, effectively closing the passenger door, and sped away back in the direction of the freeway. I should have drawn my gun and shot him, the ass. I looked at the behemoth that I was standing next to. It had the look of a camper or an old time recreational vehicle except this one had tall knobby tires and looked

21

like it was built on some sort of military chassis. It had very angular features and not one curved line to recommend style, it was totally made for function. I reached up and pulled the door handle, but it was locked. Great, I thought. I am stuck out in the middle of nowhere. At least I have a gun. Then the thought hit me. I reached into my pants pocket and pulled out the ring of keys I had gotten just five days ago. I looked closely at the four keys that were on it. One looked like a two sided vehicle key. I stuck it in the lock of the door and turned. I heard the clunk of the mechanism as the lock disengaged. I pulled on the door handle and the driver's door opened while the courtesy light illuminated the front interior of the cab. I literally had to climb up into the vehicle since the floor of it hit me about mid body. I was struck with the new smell that assailed me. There was a small envelope with my name on it sitting propped against the speedometer. I picked it up and opened it. There were two plastic cards and two thousand dollars in old style paper money. The first plastic card was a government gas/ethanol card and the other was a bank account access card, both of which had my name on it. I hoped that there were more credits in that account than in my personal one. I slid the two cards into my back pocket and put the cash back into the envelope. I noticed that there was writing on the backside of the envelope. I held it up to the light to read it.

Marshal McKenzie,
Call your liaison when you get to your destination.

So where in the fuck is my destination? I looked through the cab of the truck and found nothing else, other than the owner's manual for the vehicle. I opened the curtain separating the cab from the back. I found the light switch on the wall just inside the opening. The back was basically a camper with a bed, some built in couches, an electric stove, a chemical toilet, and a refrigerator. Of course nobody had thought to leave me a beer. I looked through every drawer, closet, nook and cranny to no avail. I sat back down in the driver's seat to think about my problem. Why would they just drop me out here with no direction? It really didn't make sense. As I sat pondering I saw a car heading towards me at a pretty good clip, I reached back for my side arm. As the car drew near; the blue lights on top started flashing. It pulled to a quick stop and one of the local cops quickly exited from the passenger side door with his flashlight drawn and the other hand on his holster. I pulled my hand from behind my back and placed it on the steering wheel.

"License and registration," the policeman ordered.

I slowly reached down to my belt where I kept my shield and pulled it out with two fingers. I flipped it open and handed it out the door to the cop.

He shined the light in my face to get a better look.

"Are you armed?" he asked.

"Yes. Small of my back. Beretta, nine mil."

"What are you doing out here, Marshal?" he asked, still a bit leery of a petite young female in an abandon parking lot.

"Came up from Dallas to pick up my camper. A friend of mine borrowed it. He had to park it and leave. I was just about to get underway."

"This is not the best neighborhood to be around in after dark," he said, handing my shield back.

"I have a phone call to make then I'll be heading back to the freeway."

"We'll drive back by here in about fifteen minutes so if you need help..." he said as he shut his flashlight off.

"Thank you officer. Have a good evening."

He tipped his hat and got back in the car. The car backed away, turned, and sped back the way it had come. I sat still thinking about my situation and that now I was under a time limit. I climbed down out of the cab, pulled my flashlight out of my belt, and began going over the outside of the vehicle as thoroughly and as quickly as I could looking for some sort of clue. As I was looking over the rear end something kept beating at my brain but I was not sure what I was looking at. Then the light went on- the policeman asked for my registration and license. The truck had a plate so it had to have a registration. I ran back to the cab of the truck, jumped up in the seat, opened the glove box, took out the owner's manual, and aimed the light down in the empty box. I was a bit perplexed that nothing else was in there. I looked at the owner's manual that I held in my hand. I turned it up, holding it by the spine, and shook. A single piece of thick paper floated to the seat. I picked it up and turned it over. I was surprised to see that it was registered to none other than me.

I read down the slip. I guess now I live in Hot Springs Arkansas, I thought as I stuck the key in the ignition and turned it on. The dash lit up. It seemed a lot more involved than most cars I had ever been in. I looked at my watch and figured I had about five minutes before the local law enforcement came back around. There were three push buttons on the dash in a row and each had a letter on it. The first one, which was depressed and lit, was marked with a 'G'. The other two were marked 'Et' and 'E'. I twisted the key and felt the rumble of the engine as it turned over and came to life. I returned the registration and manual to the glove box, hit the headlights, put it in gear and moved the lumbering monstrosity back towards the freeway. As I turned out of the parking lot and on to a surface street, I saw the police car I had seen earlier as it passed by.

I made it to the entrance ramp of the freeway and saw a diner that was still open. I whipped the truck into the lot, parked, and got out. I used the restroom then went to the counter. I pulled my coffee cup out of my blazer pocket and asked the waitress to fill it. Armed with caffeine, I went back out to the truck and climbed back in the cab. I dug out the owner's manual, moved to one of the couches in the back and sat down to begin reading. It was not long before I had a working knowledge of the vehicle I now owned. It had an internal combustion engine and an electric motor. The engine would run off of Gas or Ethanol and had two tanks for each. For speeds up to forty-five the electronic motor was viable. Hence the three push buttons. There was a large warning about not using the electric motor while in all wheel drive. I finished off my coffee and the owner's manual. Seated behind the wheel I started the engine, pulled out on the street, hit the entrance ramp, and headed east.

Now that night had officially fallen I began to mentally study what I was leaving behind since the literal view, the lights of Dallas, had long since disappeared in my mirrors. The broken white lines on the pavement of the freeway made me a bit uncomfortable since they seemed to be representing the thoughts running through my brain. Each reflective run of paint would come into view then disappear underneath the hood of the lumbering vehicle just as a thought or a face of someone I was leaving behind did the same in my mind.

I wasn't attached to Dallas or even Texas, what was making me sad was the thought of how little I was really leaving behind. Out of the five years I had been assigned to this district I had made a grand total of three friends and one solid working relationship. Other than that there was nothing, not even a house plant.

Though I would like to count Burdock among my friends, I really couldn't. A good and loyal boss? Yes. Someone that would cover your ass and be a staunch ally? Of course, but I really knew nothing about him personally and I didn't feel he had a good grasp of me either. With that said, I would still miss that relationship. That left Sam, Sam's wife Chandra, and Mitch Randolph from the information section. Though Sam and I were partners, in our off times Sam and Chandra treated me more as an adopted daughter than his partner. I spent many days breaking bread with the two of them and I was already missing those times that wouldn't come again in the near future.

Then there was Mitch-just thinking about him made me smile. Mitch had started with the Marshal Service in the information section a year before I was assigned to that district. We were close in age and where others would have been put off by his manner of speaking, and claimed it borderline sexual harassment, I found it refreshingly honest since he was rarely crude and always straightforward. Something I rarely got out of a male that wanted to get in my pants. Since I could and would sling the innuendos back, we became very good friends over the course of our time working together. It also didn't hurt that if I ever asked for anything Mitch would always find a way to get it for me. I had always been up front with Mitch when it came to the question of our dating each other. I wasn't into dating for the sake of dating and I was not going to ruin a good working relationship with the disappointments of dating a coworker. The only concessions I made were lunches and the occasional drink after work. Over time, we both became comfortable with our relationship and our friendship grew to the extent that we really could talk about anything with each other. I did, however, watch what I said about any dates I had been on or men I had been seeing. For as good of a friendship as Mitch and I had, I was not stupid about men and their sexual desires. Mitch might have been more than adequate in the bedroom, but to preserve our friendship I felt it the better part of valor not to test that theory against facts.

One of the unusual parts of our friendship was our mutual interest in history. Mitch and I could spend our lunch hour discussing nothing but history. His focus was the history of medical and technical advancement, where mine leaned towards political history and the evolution of law.

Though Mitch could recite the Presidents of the old United States, every leader of the smaller unions after The Fall, and the Presidents of the new United States in order, his real fascination was with the last two hundred and fifty years. He was always amazed that the hinge of the fate of the world could all be traced back to the development of one drug, YU-233, both the greatest advancement in medicine and the downfall of a civilization. During the early twenty-first century, life expectancy was around eighty years for most people, where now it was between one hundred and seventy five to two hundred years. He had shown me pictures from that time and I had to agree with him that now ninety was the new forty.

Though YU-233 was originally developed to combat age related diseases such as dementia and Alzheimer's, it was the testing on and usage by people in their child bearing years that brought about The Fall. Mitch's greatest fascination with that time period was the irony of it all; the idea that man would develop the means for Mother Nature to thin the herd and reclaim large parts of the world that had been misused by humanity made him laugh at our species' arrogance. I was amazed at his ability to view that era with both a clinical and humorous eye.

Once the drug was widely introduced, the problems of a longer life span with no population control became apparent very quickly. Ironically, it was the same chemical companies working on the problem of over population and shrinking food supplies that led to the final disaster. The bio companies rushed to produce quick ripening foods, based on their research with YU-233. What in the beginning looked like a successful overhaul of the immediate problem, ended in failure when the produce began to ripen so quickly that it rotted faster than it could be harvested and transported. Though many events over a number decades set the stage, historians now consider that one point in time the beginning of The Fall.

With ever increasing food riots and the pressure of an angry population looking for someone to blame, the government pulled all products of the chemical and bio companies from the shelves. That decree forced those corporations to either shut their doors or relocate. Though a few of the companies dissolved, the four major bio companies relocated to Eastern Europe and began production again.

The Water's Edge

In the space of a few short years, the states with a more rural population and less access to the genetically engineered seeds and plants found themselves with the power of heirloom variety food, abundant farmland, and a clean sustainable water supply. In contrast, the monetarily wealthy and urban sections of the country found themselves with none of those natural resources. It was that juxtaposition that started the breakup of the old United States when the federal government declared martial law to redistribute the food supplies that the rural states were producing.

With martial law in effect, those areas of the country that would become the stronger smaller unions began to organize. The first to act was what became known as the MCU or Mid-Central Union. Though the MCU was not the biggest in area of the unions, it was the strongest and ultimately the richest. The MCU made up the eastern part of Texas, eastern Oklahoma, the southern third of Missouri, and the entirety of Arkansas and Louisiana. Within the space of about three months they banded together, closed their borders, and told the federal government to essentially fuck off. The federal government sent an army to the MCU to subdue the rebels, however, the armies they sent were literally hungrier than the upstarts they were sent to quell.

In a masterfully strategic move the MCU sent a message to the invading army that they would feed them if they would surrender their arms and leave peacefully. More than three fourths of the invading force took the MCU up on its offer. The other quarter succumbed quickly to the superior might. Suddenly, the MCU was well armed and autonomous. Seeing their opportunities, other regions also banded together and formed their own unions which effectively broke the back of the federal government and ended the United States of America. Ultimately, twelve smaller unions were formed out of the old United States.

This was the final death blow for the large cities. Places like New York, Los Angeles, Chicago, Detroit, Atlanta, and Washington D.C. became nothing more than death traps of disease and falling buildings due to the mass exodus of the large cities. Most of the new unions shot any refugees who tried to cross their borders without applying for asylum. Between the food shortages and disease, the population world wide was reduced by almost half in the first twenty years of The Fall.

Though the United States was the first nation to succumb to The Fall, the rest of the world followed in short order and most of those didn't have the luxury of portions of their nation still being able to produce even a modicum of food to sustain their population. Disease, famine, and death became the devastating realities of everyday life throughout the world.

It was during this time that the relocated bio-companies, having taken control of a majority of Eastern Europe, came together and formed the United Bio-Cartel. Though made up of four smaller entities, the UBC was a formidable union in its own right with a large population and its own, well equipped, army.

The Water's Edge

When the UBC began expanding and encroaching on Western Europe, a cry for help was sent to the unions that had formed out of the old United States, Canada, and Mexico. In a meeting of the heads of state, comprising the organized entities of North America, it was agreed that the UBC would not stop at just Europe. In a unanimous vote, the Unions of North America agreed to a loose confederacy to pool resources and armies to stem the advance of the UBC. Armies were fielded on both sides, shots were fired, and The Bio-War began.

The war continued, more as a standoff than a real war, for over fifty years. It is this point that bothered Mitch the most. Though there is a lot written in the history books about particular battles and lulls in the war, there is absolutely nothing written about what the turning point of the conflict was. Though the first part of the war lasted about fifty years, it only took fifteen after the turning point for the Confederacy militias to end it.

It was in the last few months of the war that the BCU launched its final offensive. When the cartel realized the tide had turned, they recruited some of the most talented computer programers in the world and started them working on a secret project. Though the old internet of the late twentieth and early twenty-first centuries was limping along one hundred and seventy five years later, it still connected what was left of information, technology, and government. Cellular and computer technology had lagged way behind the immediate need of necessities for most people during the first years of The Fall. A few advancements still happened after the formation of the smaller unions, but the effects were not wide spread due to the lack of manufacturing that was not geared towards farming or the war.

When the wolves were at the door, the Bio-Cartel launched it's attack. A devastating virus was put out on what remained of the internet. It took less than fourteen seconds to wipe the collected data of the world into the electrical wastebasket. Though there were some closed systems that survived they were, for the most part, proprietary to their function. All at once the numerous satellites that had orbited the earth were now nothing more than man made asteroids ready to light up the night sky when their orbits decayed. With most home and government computers nothing more than boat anchors most people, after a few years, tore them apart for the metals in them or traded them for something more useful. Though cell phones and computers were now making a come back, the world had not made it back technologically to where it had been two hundred years ago.

Towards the end of the war the leaders of the MCU approached a few of the other small unions with the idea of reforming the United States. They worked for ten years to refashion the constitution. Though they based it on the original constitution of the old United States, they made major revisions to it. It took almost five years, but on July 4th 2192 the new U.S. ratified the constitution. The United States of America now covered a much larger area than it had originally.

The original forty-eight contiguous states were reformed back to their original boundaries, including Alaska and Hawaii. British Columbia and the Yukon Territories asked to join as one state now known as Yukon; likewise, most of Northern Mexico joined under the name Old Mexico. Now the United States boasted fifty two states instead of fifty.

Those thoughts about the new constitution brought up an internal question I had glossed over when I took the assignment: What had Agent Wallace really meant when he said that Directive One would no longer be an issue for me? Directive One was put in place to protect the population that hadn't been convicted of a crime. It had come about so that there was a definite investigative advantage for law enforcement if the suspect had a criminal record. The flip side of that was very stringent controls on police departments if their suspect had never been convicted of anything in the past. So did that mean everyone I was going after now had a long line of violent transgressions that would make the cases easy to research since I would not need warrants to dig into their past? I'd had Directive One hammered into my head from the moment I started at the Marshal Academy and now it was going to be a non issue? How could I just disregard a substantial part of my training and college education? I could see where it would be advantageous for me as a Marshal, but that in itself scared the hell out of me.

As I sped through Texarkana and into Arkansas my trepidation continued to build and my mind took a hard look at my own history. Where the nation had four hundred and seventy two years of history and the knowledge of where *it* had come from, I had twenty six years of not knowing anything about *my* lineage or where I had come from. My young life had been spent being shuttled between one foster home and the next until my emancipation at seventeen and escape from that part of the government system.

I guess I had grown up fairly well adjusted. Though I am sure there would be some out there that would insist that I had major psychiatric problems and needed help. Admittedly, I had a real problem with authority and the people who used it to their advantage and I also had a self-esteem issue where it concerned my height, body type, and weight. I am also sure that the few men I had dated over the last five years would tell anyone that cared to listen that I was standoffish and unable to commit to a relationship. The way I saw it, I simply hadn't met anyone worth committing to-at least not yet.

When I entered the Marshal Training Academy, the psychiatrist that did my initial psych evaluation asked me if I was overall a happy person. Of course, at the time, I answered yes since I was happy about being accepted into the Marshal Service. Thinking about that now, I probably should have answered I was neither happy nor sad-I just *was* and life is what it is. I tried to think if there had ever been a time in my life that I had been truly happy but couldn't think of one. On the other hand I could not remember any time, other than at seven years old, when I was ever sad or scared either. Even on the job I could never remember being scared. I had been shot at and taken some physical hits, but I was never anything but focused on what I was doing at the time. Even when Grant had been shot I was not necessarily sad, I was just pissed at the guy that had shot him. Yes, I cried at his funeral and I was sad not to see him everyday but it did not stop my life, even for a day.

Maybe one of the guys I dated was right, maybe I was just a cold, calculating bitch. Of course, he said that after I turned down his marriage proposal and told him we would not be going out anymore. Why was it most of the men I dated felt all I needed was a ring on my finger? Why couldn't they just be happy with the sex? I guess by society's standards I was considered cute to good looking and my chest seemed to validate that in the eyes of most men I met. But really, I was not helpless and I didn't need a bumbling fool cluttering up my house. Besides, I can make enough clutter in my own home without help from anyone. Men were curious creatures, not in their complexity but in that their main attraction was also their shortcoming, pun intended.

****

I realized my brain rambling had taken me from Dallas to Arkadelphia, but luckily I saw the sign for Hot Springs in enough time to take the exit. It was getting quite late as I made my way up the two lane highway towards my destination. Though the entities that had made up the old MCU had made out quite a lot better than the rest of the country they had still taken a population hit. I passed sign after sign denoting a town that had shrunk to miniscule inhabitants or sat deserted on the side of the road. I was getting very tired when I finally entered the city limits of Hot Springs.

This town had a long history as a bit of a wild area. In its early days it was a playground for the rich, famous, and infamous and during the early days of the war it had re-cultivated that image. I searched for a decent hotel. It was after midnight and I was tired, my final destination would have to wait until after some rest. I saw a motel that looked promising, pulled into the lot, parked, and shut the engine down. It suddenly hit me that I had nothing with me other than; the clothes on my back, some money, a side arm, and a coffee cup. Hell I didn't even have a tooth brush and my hair would be in knots by the morning. I walked across to the door of the lobby and pulled on it but it was locked. I saw a young man sitting behind the counter reading. I knocked on the door, he looked up at me and then went back to his book. I knocked again, this time rattling the door frame. He looked up again and I hammered on the door again before he could go back to his novel. With a disgusted look he got up and ambled across the small lobby and came to the door.

"I'm closed," he yelled to me through the glass.

"Is there some place else that's open?" I yelled back.

He shrugged his shoulders and started to turn around. I grabbed my shield, flipped it against the glass of the door, and pounded one more time to get his attention. He stopped and looked then came closer to study the I.D. and shield. He flipped the dead bolt and opened the door a bit but still barred my way.

"I told you we are closed."

"You are a hotel. How can you be closed?"

"We close registration at ten. It is after midnight."

"Look, I have been on the road for over six hours now. I just want a room to sleep in," I said, coming close to begging.

"Sorry, I am closed," he said sticking to his guns.

I reached in my blazer pocket and grabbed a bill from the envelope I had stuck in there. I folded it up between my fingers and stuck it in front of his face.

"Are you sure it isn't nine fifty nine?" I asked, smiling as sweetly as I could.

"Wow, you're right it is only nine fifty nine," He answered, snatching the one hundred dollar bill from my hand and opening the door enough for me to enter.

I walked in, he closed and locked the door behind me, then he led me to the counter. He slid an index sized card towards me.

"Fill in the card. How do you want to pay?"

"Do you accept credits?"

"Yep."

I pulled the Federal Bank Credits Card and slipped it across the counter. He raised an eyebrow at the black color, took it and imprinted it. I traded the registration card for a key.

"Down this side of the building, bottom floor," he said, pointing over his left shoulder.

"Is there anyplace around here open this time of night where I might be able to buy a tooth brush and tooth paste?" I asked.

He rummaged under the counter and flopped a travel sized tube and small tooth brush on the surface.

"Free," he said.

"Thanks," I answered, as I picked up the toiletries.

I turned and walked to the door and waited for him. He opened the door and let me out, I heard the distinct thunk as the deadbolt was put back in place. I turned left and walked in the direction of my room. I opened the door; the presidential suite it wasn't-but it had a fairly clean bed, hot and cold running water, and clean towels. I peeled off my clothes as I made my way to the bathroom. I sat my weapon on the counter, started the shower, relieved myself, stepped into the tub and let the hot water pelt me.

Chapter 3
Tuesday April 4, 2248

I opened my eyes to the bright light that snuck in on the sides of the curtain over the window. I looked at my watch; it was ten in the morning. I got up, dressed, brushed my teeth, and tried to put my hair in some semblance of order. I walked to the lobby to return the key. There was a mature woman behind the counter this morning. I slid the key across and pulled my notebook out of my pocket.

"Could you recommend somewhere for breakfast and give me directions to this address?" I asked as I showed her the page I had my address written on.

She looked at my notebook, and then pulled a piece of paper out from under the counter and started drawing some lines and adding street names. She slid the paper over to me.

"Well, Hun. If you take this road here and follow it around to this cross street and take that all the way out of town. The road you want will be on your left. I am not sure where the exact address is at but that is a dead end road so it should not be hard to find. The 'x' here is Grannie's Kitchen, serves the best breakfast in town and it is on your way," she answered, smiling.

****

I slowed down to check the name on the road as I started to pass it. Breakfast had been good and down home as recommended, now if I just had clean clothes to change into. The next road to the left had the right name on the sign. I turned and started the drive down. There were very few houses on the road as I drove. I came to the dead end and I noticed a mailbox with my last name sat by the gravel drive that I turned into. I pulled up to the house. It was a modest looking brick home with a carport complete with one of the new, small electric cars. The roof of the house was covered in solar panels and I could see three small wind turbines a bit behind it. On the right side of the house and a little behind was a medium-small barn with the doors closed. I pulled up to the carport, shut off the motor, and climbed out. I was struck immediately by the windows of the house, they seemed small and they were imbedded with a wire mesh. I stepped up on the porch and looked through the keys on my ring. I inserted the one that looked right into the deadbolt and turned. I pressed down on the door handle and pushed, but the door did not budge. I put my shoulder against it and shoved, nothing. I looked at the door more intently. Just to the right of the lock, in the trim, was a slot that had a faint green glow to it. I studied it. The slit was about four inches long and maybe an eighth of an inch wide. I pulled out my shield and slid the plastic encased I.D. from its sleeve. I looked at the back of it. There was a magnetic strip along the lower third. I lined up the card with the slot and pushed it in. It sank about halfway down. I heard the high hum of electricity and an audible click. I pushed down on the door lever and the door swung easily open. I pulled my card out of the slot, stepped in and closed the door behind me.

The living room was set up as a normal living room with a couch, two comfortable chairs, and end tables. Centered on the wall at the end and to my right was a fireplace. On the mantel were the few pictures that I owned, arranged as if on purpose. On the front wall, under the window, sitting on a shelf was my disk player and all of my music disks. I was glad they had made it, though I could have left them if I had been in a hurry, but they had been a bit of a bribe from an informant a few years back and I had gotten somewhat attached to all of the old music. I walked through the small archway that led into a hall with a kitchen on the opposite side. The hall led to the left with four doors, two on each side. Immediately to my right was another door. I tried it but it was locked. For later, I thought as I went into the kitchen. It was small neat and tidy. I opened the refrigerator and though this was not the same exact food from my apartment, it was the same items that had probably been thrown out. I looked through the cabinets and drawers. I had all of the plates, pots, pans, and silverware that I could need. I found the coffee and coffee maker. I started a pot, let it perk, and looked through the rest of the house. The two doors on the left side of the hall towards the front of the house were two small bedrooms. The first door on the right, behind the kitchen, was a small bathroom. The last door on the right was the master bedroom. I stepped in and looked around. This must have been a sick joke from Agent Wallace. The room was decorated in frills and flowers, not something I would have picked out for myself. I opened the closet and all of my clothes were there. Though I had taken a quick shower last night, I had not washed my hair nor been able to brush it. I took off my clothes and started the water in the shower. As I waited for the shower to warm I grabbed my phone and dialed.

"United States Marshal Service, Texas, district one," came the answer.

"Marshal Burdock," I said.

"Who may I say is calling?" The voice asked.

"Deputy Marshal McKenzie."

I heard the click of being on hold and I waited.

"Burdock," came the gruff voice I was used to.

"Hey Captain. I am in..."

"Don't tell me where you are," came the command, interrupting me.

"Fine. I'm here."

"Any problems?"

"Other than getting absolutely no information, no."

"Let me guess, you got dropped somewhere and told to find your way home?" Burdock asked, chuckling.

"Pretty much. What is that all about anyway?"

"It is a bit of a test. They want to make sure that you are self-reliant. I am not sure that you will get much help from IBI"

"Well I have a shower warming. Is there anything I need to know?"

"I have nothing, at least right now."

"Fine. I am going to go wash the road grime off."

"Be careful Ced. By the way, you need to check in weekly, just to let us know you are still breathing."

"I am still breathing. Later."

"Keep your head down," Burdock replied as he hung up.

I flipped the phone towards the bed and went to take my shower.

****

Clean and dressed comfortably in my pink fuzzy slippers and robe, I went into the kitchen, washed out my cup and filled it with the hot black liquid that sat steaming on the counter. Armed with my cup of hot courage I went to the locked door in the hall. There was no key hole on the door and the knob turned freely but the door did not move. I studied the trim around it and sure enough a glowing slot sat-this time above the door. I stuck my I.D. in and heard the same high buzz and click. The door swung away from me. I could see the beginnings of stairs heading down into the blackness. Great, I hate basements. I found the light switch on the wall and flipped it. Illumination erupted from down in the basement all the way up the stairs. I was surprised by the concrete of the walls and stairs. I stepped down and started to close the door behind me. I was struck by the thickness of the door, it had to be a good six inches. I looked at the edge of it. The side that faced the hall was a wood veneer that was a regular panel looking door, but the rest of it was solid steel and heavy. I closed it and watched as the six locking bars slid into place, silently resting in the groves on the back of the door. I continued on down the stairs.

The room at the bottom was approximately twenty feet by twenty feet. It was solid concrete; floor, walls, and ceiling. It looked as if it had been poured all at once since I could see no seams, including the stairs. Along the far wall was a row of standard five drawer file cabinets with a large heavy safe sitting next to them. A cot sat against the back wall and some canned food and water on shelves above it. A large table sat in the middle of the room with laminated maps stacked neatly on it. On the edge was a silver metal box about eighteen inches high and wide and two feet long. Other than being silver and a bit more substantial, it reminded me of a larger version of a safety deposit box. Sitting against the wall that the stairs formed as they went up, sat a regular office desk with what looked like a computer monitor sitting on it. Next to it was a thin, silver, box. On the flat wall across from the cot hung a large map of the new U.S. that seemed to have arbitrary thick black lines and colored cross hatching. In the center of the different crosshatching there was a blank space with the word "District", a two digit number, a set of initials, and a telephone number. I walked over to it and studied it closer. All of the phone numbers had the area code of eight five five which was the national government area code. I was surprised to see my initials in section zero five and what I surmised was my new telephone number. There were thirty-six sections on the map. My section ran from a straight line below Springfield Missouri that was from the western border to the Mississippi River on the north, covered lower Missouri, and included all of Arkansas and Louisiana, with the recognized borders of those states as the western edge. The Mississippi River seemed to be my eastern border until it reached the southern border of Arkansas and then continued in a direct line, east, over to Alabama to cover the lower portion of Mississippi down to the coast. Geez... that was a lot of area to be responsible for all by myself. I walked over to the table in the center of the room. I turned the box so that the lock was towards me. I pulled out my keys and tried the remaining two. The lock snapped open. I un-threaded it from the hasp and opened the lid. Inside were two envelopes, a smaller metal box and the backup weapon that had disappeared from the bathroom of my apartment in Dallas. I pulled the rolling office chair over and sat down. I opened up the first envelope and read through it.

Marshal McKenzie,

A small note of explanation: The gas card and the Bank Card are yours to use in the course of your job for both personal and work related expenses. The Bank Card has a balance of one point five million credits and will be maintained at that level from month to month. If you stay in your current position for at least five years the Bank Card will be your retirement. Your monthly pay will now be that of a full U.S. Marshal, which you now hold the rank of, plus hazard pay. That pay will be deposited monthly into your existing personal account. Get to know your surroundings. Keep your stash of printed money up. Check in at the local police station, State Police and closest Marshal's office.

In your phone you will find three pre-programed numbers listed as A, AA, AAA. These, in order listed, are direct lines to the President, the Director of the IBI and the Director of the U.S. Marshal Service. If you have a reason to call any of them you will be answered by three short beeps, input your service control number and wait. I would suggest that you program your control number into your phone to a touch key. One thing that you need to always keep in mind is that you answer to no authority other than myself, the Director of the IBI and the President of the United States. Also remember that even though you are a federal marshal you are still subject to the laws of whatever state you happen to be in at any given time.

For public information you are on special assignment. Do not discuss your cases with anyone other than fellow Counter Section agents. You will not even discuss the particulars of cases with the three people you answer to. I understand that this sounds like a lot of spook paranoia but in a very short time you will understand the reasons for it.

Miss McKenzie, I am sorry that because of the way this is set up you are very much on an island by yourself. You must be smart, resourceful, wary of everyone and above all secretive.

Yours,
Jake Perry,
Director, United States Marshal Service.

I put the letter and envelope back in the box. I pulled my I.D. card out to look closely at it, since I really hadn't payed much attention to it when I got it. Sure enough, it no longer said Deputy Marshal. I had gotten a promotion and had not noticed it. Wow, I made it to full Marshal, something I never thought I would do unless someone screwed up, and it looked like someone screwed up. I also noticed my control number had changed. My old one used to have numbers only, this one was a few spaces longer, and had both letters and numbers. I reached into the box and pulled out the next envelope. This one was bright white and was made of an expensive and heavy paper. All that was on the front were my initials. I flipped open the flap and pulled out a folded letter of the same type of paper. I was immediately struck by the embossed seal of the President of the United States at the center of the top of the page.

Marshall Cedwynne Anne McKenzie,
I would like to extend my gratitude and the gratitude of the nation upon your acceptance of this position. I would advise you to keep a very open mind and understand that all things are possible. You will be faced with things that will be trying at best and overwhelming at worst. Some of our nation's future domestic policies will be shaped by the actions and intelligence that you and the other thirty five Counter Section agents send back. I wish you safe passage and a productive future.
Yours,
Carlton B. Bradley III
President of the United States of America.

I folded up the letter and placed it back in the box. I thought it was an honor to receive it, though I hoped that President Bradley wouldn't hold it against me that I voted for one of his opponents in the last election.

I pulled out the the smaller silver box. It was about the size of a standard hard bound book though it was about four inches thick. On one surface were four sets of initials, mine being the last etched in the metal. Across the bottom, also etched, was a warning that any unauthorized entry would result in the destruction of the contents. Though I could see the small seams around the edges, I could see no way to open it. I flipped it over and noticed an indention that was vaguely cross-shaped and looked like the sun's corona scrawled by some child. The indention was probably about a quarter of an inch deep with a small round ball that seemed to be spring loaded but you could push it until it was level with the rest of the depression dead center. I put it down and ran back up to my bedroom. I came back down with the cross on the necklace I had been given. The cross I had received was made in such a way that your eye would be drawn to the block outline of the normal cross, not the unusual outline of its backing. That was the reason it hadn't been immediately apparent to me. Sure enough, when I placed it in the depression it fit perfectly, though nothing happened. I noticed that the cross would slide in all four directions and the edge of the backing would actually slide underneath the outside metal of the box. I pushed in all directions but still nothing happened. I looked in the large box on the table but there was nothing more in it. I studied the cross and the smaller box, but came up empty. I took a sip of my now cooling coffee.

Everything up to this point had been a puzzle; from getting here to getting in the door, and the only thing that hadn't been was making coffee. I guess I should be thankful for small favors. All of the puzzles had been solved by things hidden in plain sight and my ability to figure them out. The box had been left in this particular room for me, so by my reasoning the clues I need to open it were here somewhere. I leaned back in the chair and slowly rotated myself to look at the room, studying everything as I turned. I must have swiveled twice around before I stopped, looking at the large map on the wall. I stared at it from my seat. I got up and moved closer to it. Basically, it was a normal, large wall map of the country. I focused in on, not what was printed there, but what was added. All of the sections and hatch patterns had been added by hand, along with everyone's initials and phone numbers. Those, though added, were all what they appeared to be. The edge of the map had the normal numbers across top and bottom and then the letters down each side.

It was then I noticed, lightly circled, the number 3 at the top of the map. I moved closer and studied the top row of numbers. Above the 1 was written a U and other then the 3 being circled, there was nothing else unusual about the top row. I came down the side. An A was lightly circled and I continued on down the right side until I saw, next to the R, a 3 written. I continued down and started back towards the left on the bottom numbers and at the 2 there was written a D, and the 2 was also circled. I came back up the left side to where, next to the L, a 1 was written and a D was circled. I grabbed a pen and a piece of paper from the desk. I wrote these down in the positions that I had found them. I sat back down in the chair and looked at the code before me.

So I had, working clock wise, U-1 circle 3, circle A R-3, circle 2-D, L-1 circle D. I was not sure if this had anything to do with the box I was trying to open, but could it be the combination to the safe? I put all of the letters together, then the numbers. It was when I started putting the items within the circles together that the pattern started to emerge. If I used the circled letters, not as a letter representation, but as a number referenced to where it fell in the alphabet I had 1234. I rearranged everything and came up with; 1 R-3, 2 2-D, 3 U-1, and 4 1-L. I pulled the small box towards me and picked up the cross on the necklace. In the Christian religions the cross is worn with the small section up, just as it hung from the chain. I oriented the box in that way in relation to me. I sat the cross back in the indention and slowly pushed it as far as it would go to one side. I could feel it meet resistance before it would not move any farther that way. I pulled the cross out and sat it back on the table.

I looked at the code again. I had RDU and L. Seemed simple enough; Right, Down, Up and Left. I put the cross back into the indention and worked through the sequence making sure I kept downward pressure on the center and engaged the cross as far as it would go. I pulled the cross back to the center after the last one and nothing happened. Maybe this wasn't the code for this. I tried again, nothing. After the fourth or fifth try I was becoming quite frustrated. I picked up the box to look at it to see if I missed anything. I flipped it over to reread the inscriptions but they were upside down. I turned it around and read through every etching on the front, no help.

I flipped the box back over and the cross indention was upside down. Okay, what the hell. I put the cross back in and went through the sequence from that orientation. Sure enough the inside latches popped and the face I was working on popped up. Teach me to believe the Christians. I pulled the cross out of the slot and flipped the hinged lid over. Inside were two small vials of liquid attached to one long side, protected from the contents by small metal plates. I looked closer and saw small, nail like protrusions poised at each end of the vials. In the box was an old looking leather bound journal. I picked it up out of the box. The book cover was pliable and had a pliable flap that folded over with two long leather ties that wrapped around the book and tied to keep it closed. I undid the tie and opened up the front cover. There was a small scrap of paper laying on top with numbers written on it. It looked to be a normal combination. I hoped this was to the safe and it would be that easy, but probably not. I flipped through the first few pages. There were dates and what looked to be case numbers. Occasionally there would be a short note written under a day heading. The dates in the book were from almost fifty years ago. Each entry had an initial after it that corresponded to the first initial etched on the outside of the box. I turned deeper into the journal, date wise, about twelve years after the first entry and the handwriting and initials changed, but the basic content didn't. Though those initials lasted the longest, there was almost a ten year gap between the second initials and third. At the beginning of the last set of initials was a folded sheet of paper. I pulled it out and began reading.

To the next in line,

Welcome to the hardest job you will ever have. I have been in Counter Section now for five years. I have seen and experienced things that I thought were only fairy tales. Just as you are now, I sat and read the memo left for me. I had no clue what I was getting into. If I had I am not sure that I would have taken the assignment. You were chosen for your gifts and intuition, use them. When you have down time, use it. Most of your time will be spent sifting through, what others would consider, dead cases and gossip. Never overlook anything, regardless of how outlandish the claim may be. And last; choose your friends wisely and don't believe everything you are told, especially by those above you.

You are probably wondering why you were dropped here with no real backup and ties cut from your past life. This is to protect your friends and old associates, not you. This is a lesson we, as an agency, learned early on. At the bottom of this page I have listed a few files of mine and my predecessor that should help clue you in on your duties and what you will be up against. I am sure that there will be a couple of open cases when you take over. Don't feel the need to rush out and slay the dragons. Don't worry I have not had to kill any, at least yet. Get a feel for your surroundings and where you live before you go out on a case.

If your case takes you to someone else's section, call them beforehand to make sure your case is not associated with one of theirs. As far as the public should know, you are just on assignment in the area. Most of your cases will take you to the more rural areas, I hope you like the idea of camping since you will be doing a lot of it. If your case sends you in the direction of one of the dead zones, leave it open but do not attempt to follow it there. Heed this warning, your life depends on it.

My last advice. The journal you are handling needs to be kept safe and locked away. Update it weekly then put it back in a secure location. You will need to change the combination of the insurance box it is kept in, instruction to do that are etched on the inside of the box itself. Once you change the combination find a conspicuously inconspicuous place to hide the combination for the next agent. I know this might sound weird at the moment but the key to the insurance box is more than just a key for it. It just might save your life, wear it at all times. I wish you great success, safety and luck.

When you reach the point that you feel you have a small handle on your job leave your advice for the next one to follow, as all of the agents have.

Your fellow agent,
JTL.

The Water's Edge

I turned the page over to see a list of about twenty case numbers. I took the letter over to the file cabinets, went through the drawers, pulled the files out and stacked them on the center table. Most of them were fairly thick. I started to sit down when my stomach told me I needed something to eat. I looked at my watch and realized it was already four in the afternoon. I surveyed the items I had laid out over the course of the morning and early afternoon. I closed up the journal and placed it back in the insurance box. I pressed the lid down lightly and it snapped shut. I placed it and the files I had pulled in the large box, closed and locked it. I slipped the cross around my neck, picked up my backup gun and cold coffee and headed upstairs. I turned off the lights and closed the door as I stepped into the hall. I dumped the cold coffee down the sink, rinsed out the cup and sat it on the counter.

I looked into the fridge, but I had not had much to eat in the apartment when I lived in Dallas and whoever had packed and moved me had not added to the menu. Peanut butter and jelly really did not interest me this afternoon. I scoured the cabinets to no avail, though I did notice that my good bottle of Scotch had not made the move. Damn spooks. I paid good money for that, though I guess they didn't like my choice in beer since they had restocked it in my fridge. Well I guess a run to town was in the cards this afternoon, I could not do without my good Scotch. I went back to the bedroom to get out of my robe and put some clothes on.

I felt it begin as I was leaning over to tie my shoes, that ache that starts in the small of your back and then wraps around to the front like a fist squeezing. God how I hate the five days before my period and so did most of the people I worked with. It was just like clockwork, the day the moon was full I started my period and the five days before that were hell for me and everyone around me. At least once I started the PMS ended, much to the relief of those around me.

I found the key to the car on a hook in the kitchen and put it on my ring with the rest of the keys I had inherited. I walked out the front door to the carport, unplugged the little blue vehicle, got in and turned it on. It was a bit small for my taste, but I had never owned a car before and I guess that a freebie was better than nothing. I stepped on the accelerator and moved it down the driveway.

I found a grocery store and loaded up on staples for the house. Next stop a liquor store to replace my bottle of Scotch. The cramps had become worse and I was getting to be in a fairly foul mood. I drove for a while, but had not found a liquor store; maybe they didn't believe in them around here. I had yet to eat and my hunger pangs were adding to the PMS. I passed a bar that advertised food, so I did a U-turn and pulled up in the lot and parked. It didn't look like the most upscale place but it would have to do. I noticed a large number of motorcycles as I got out and headed towards the door. I opened the door and walked in. The place was dark and dingy and looked to be a bit on the rough side. A few of the guys took notice of me as I came in, but most of the clientele were busy with their drinks or their games of pool. I looked around, there were only two seats available in the entire place and those were on either side of a guy in a light plaid coat, reading, at the bar. I strode over to one of the stools.

"Is this taken?" I asked the guy over the din of the place.

Without looking up from the book he was reading he gestured with an open hand towards the bar stool. I sat down.

"Whatcha drinkin'?" the tall bartender with a pot marked face asked.

"Double Scotch, rocks, splash." I answered.

"We only take cash," he added.

I pulled a fifty out of my pocket and laid it on the bar.

"Start me a tab," I said.

He nodded, grabbed the bill, and went to pour my drink. I looked at the guy that had offered me the seat. He was hunched over a book, drinking coffee and reading. In short order my drink was in front of me.

"Hey barkeep!" I shouted over the din.

"Yeah?" he asked.

"What do you have to eat in here?" I asked.

"Burgers and fries," he replied.

"You don't want to eat here," the bookworm next to me said without looking up from his reading.

"Why?" I asked.

"Fine, your stomach," he answered.

"You want a burger or not?" the bartender finally asked.

"Let me finish my drink," I replied, as the man shrugged and walked to the other end of the bar to wait on customers.

As I took a sip of my drink I surveyed the bar. Most of the men in here did not look like they had two credits to rub together, and the few women looked as if they spent most of their nights here trying to relieve the men of the one credit they had remaining. The bikers had taken over the two pool tables in the place and were being loud and obnoxious. The only person, other than myself, that looked out of place was the professor sitting next to me reading. I turned back towards the bar and thought about all of the things I had been exposed to today. Though I had spent most of my day reading I still didn't have much of a clue as to what my job was. I decided that I would spend tomorrow pretty much holed up in my bed reading through the case files that the last agent had recommended.

I had been sitting on the stool for almost an hour when the bartender sat my third drink in front of me. I knew that this would be my last one of the evening. Anything over three, in my case, was a recipe for disaster. I had noticed earlier that the bikers seemed to be getting argumentative with the other patrons around them. I tried to tune them out and consider my options for the next few days. I sensed the man behind me before he spoke and I tensed.

"Hey sweetie. What you say I take you for a spin, then we can go for a ride on my bike?" he drunkenly slurred as he put his hand on my butt.

I was willing to play the game until he started to slide his hand up under my coat to were my gun was holstered. I reached back quickly and grabbed his wrist. I spun off of the stool taking his arm with me until I had him on his knees with his arm behind his back. I switched hands and reached back under my coat and put my hand on my weapon. It took maybe a split second longer for his buddies at the nearest pool table to start in my direction.

"What the fuck," the man I had in a wrist lock screamed as he was looking at the ground.

I moved closer into him so I could force him to the floor if the need arose.

"Hey bitch. You might want to let my friend up," the first biker spoke as he flipped his pool cue over so the butt end was up.

"You need to tell your fiend to keep his hands to himself," I replied, looking him straight in the eye.

Though the one I had a hold of and the one approaching me did not really worry me too much, the third one that stood behind the one with the cue did. He looked like a mountain and just as solid. I took a sideways glance at the bartender, he had retrieved a baseball bat from under the bar and was heading to the opening a few feet down. I was not real sure which side of the argument he would come down on. In my glance I also noticed that my partner at the bar was still reading and sipping his coffee, seemingly oblivious to what was going on around him. I was also struck by the reduction in background noise from just a few moments ago. The one with the cue took another step closer.

"Look guys, I just came in to have a couple of drinks. I understand your friend here is a bit tipsy. If you want to take him and go back to playing pool I will even buy a round for the three of you," I said trying to smooth the situation.

"You already embarrassed our friend. It's going to take a lot more than a drink, to make up for that," the cue man said, with a twisted smile on his face as he took another step closer.

At the same time I had a massive cramp that almost doubled me over, even through the anesthesia of the Scotch. Why is it a man's ability to be a prick seems to hit its peak when a woman's grasp on civility is at its lowest?

"Your friend embarrassed himself, I just kept him from getting killed," I growled back.

My patience was quickly running out. Though I was ready for the attack, I was surprised by the order of events. Cue Man started a swing with his weapon and I pushed my captive forward to block his path. I began my duck and drew my gun. I waited for either the glancing blow or the swish of the stick swinging over my head, but neither came. I came up with gun drawn but the cue stick was still hanging in the air. I followed it down and saw the hand of the professor, holding on to the wrist of the man with the weapon. When did he even stop reading, much less get off of his stool? The man I had been sitting beside was a

41

few inches taller than me and a few inches shorter than the man with the cue. I watched anxiously as they stared at each other.

"Are you sure you want to make this your fight, Pluto?" the cue man snarled down at the other.

The other one just smiled and laughed.

"You think this is funny? What do you have to laugh about?" he asked.

"Well first, I am not sure if I should be insulted that you referred to me as a former planetary body that orbits even further out than Uranus..." he started.

I laughed out loud at the pun.

"...or disgusted with your ignorance of not knowing the difference between a twentieth century cartoon canine and the great philosopher Plato," he said, staring harder at the man, though the smile never left his face.

I was beginning to worry about my casual partner since he seemed to be in a very bad defensive position. The man with the cue swung his free hand across his body aiming at the face of my erudite bar mate. It was strange to watch, it seemed like it was slow motion but also happening in the blink of an eye. Without letting go of the man's wrist, my momentary partner stepped into his assailant so that the punch went around the back of his head while, at the same time, bringing his knee up hard into the man's crotch. I watched as the man dropped the cue and began to drop to the floor. As soon as the professor felt weight on the wrist he was holding, he let go and allowed the body to drop to the floor. The one that had accosted me first had made it to his feet and he and The Mountain started to advance. I slipped the safety off of my gun. Both men stopped and eyed me, though the bartender was still coming on. I reached down to my belt, pulled out my shield and I.D., flipped it open and presented the badge out at eye level.

"Okay folks this stops here," I shouted aiming, dead center of the eyes of the man closest to me.

The two bikers stopped cold. The bartender continued coming, I pointed my weapon at him.

"Look guys, I am your worst nightmare. I'm a woman with a badge, a gun, and PMS. Are you really sure you want to piss me off any more tonight?" I snarled loudly at them.

I noticed my partner had leaned back against the bar, picked up his coffee, and was sipping and smiling. The bartender lowered his bat to his side and stared menacingly at me.

"Do I need to call the law?" he asked, snarling back.

"I *am* the fucking law. But if you would feel more comfortable with a local constable, feel free to dial the phone," I shot back.

The bartender took a step back.

"Your tab is paid, I think it's time for you to leave," the bartender said.

"Gentlemen. I think your friend could use some help," my partner said to the two bikers as he gestured to the man on the floor writhing in pain.

The Mountain and the one that started it all reached down to pick up their comrade, never taking their eyes off of me. I moved back over towards the stool I had been sitting on, never lowering my weapon. I picked up what was left of my drink and downed it in one gulp.

"You staying or going?" I asked the man that had been sitting beside me.

"I guess that I am persona non grata here now. Which is a shame since it was such a lovely place to pass the time."

He took the last sip of his coffee, threw a couple of bills on the bar, picked up his book and gestured me towards the door. I nodded my head in the direction of the door for him to start that way. I followed him, backing my way towards the door so I could keep my gun drawn and an eye on the room. He waited, holding the door open for me until I had cleared the frame then followed me out and lightly closed the door behind us. I started walking towards my car, as I put the safety back on and holstered my gun. I was about halfway across the lot when the bar door flew open and six of the bikers made the sidewalk outside, the Mountain among them.

"This isn't over bitch!" one of the bikers yelled, and took a few steps towards me as I turned around.

I pulled my weapon back out and flipped the safety off. I would catch hell if I discharged my weapon in the middle of town but I was hungry, tired, having the cramps from hell, and really starting to get pissed. The group came toward us and stopped about ten feet away.

"Gentlemen, this is a Beretta, nine millimeter. It holds twelve in the clip and one in the chamber. I hold the second highest marksmanship rating, at seventy five feet, from my graduating class. Since you are maybe ten to fifteen feet away, I can guarantee that I can drop at least three of you before you make it five feet. I can drop two more in the final distance. That will leave one of you and two of us. Which five of you do not want to ride home this evening?" I asked.

All of them stopped and considered it for a second. The one that had yelled at me decided he was stupid enough to try. He started to move; I slipped my finger to the trigger and took aim. It was the blue flashing lights and siren that stayed the shot. Two police cruisers came screeching to a halt a few feet from us. Four policemen jumped out of their cars with guns drawn. I noticed that two of them were trained on me.

"Drop your weapon!" one of them shouted at me.

I lowered, but did not let go of my weapon.

"Federal Marshal," I shouted back.

"Bullshit! Drop your weapon," he yelled.

I kept my weapon at my side and did not move.

"I have shield and I.D. on my belt. I have lowered my weapon but I cannot surrender my side arm," I said back, lowering my volume to not be shouting.

"I am only going to ask one more time. Drop the gun," the cop said.

It was a tense moment, but we had had it drilled into our heads that we never surrendered our weapon.

"Officer, I am not trying to be difficult but I cannot surrender my side arm. If you will allow me to produce my credentials we can diffuse this situation quickly," I said, looking straight at the one talking.

Everyone to a person was nervous, except my new partner who seemed to be more amused at the situation than anything. He stood there relaxed, smiling, with his right foot slightly behind his left, waiting. The officer that had been shouting at me moved closer to his partner, keeping his gun pointed at my head and his finger on the trigger. He and his partner whispered amongst themselves for a few seconds. I held statue still while they discussed the situation.

"Slowly, with two fingers of your left hand, produce your credentials," the cop said.

Suddenly I was lit with a strong beam of a flashlight. I slowly moved my left hand up to my belt where I kept my badge. I had just touched the leather case.

"Don't move," came a shout.

I froze.

"Not you, young lady," came the voice.

With the light in my eyes I could not see anything going on. But I figured, since I was the only female in the group, he meant me. I grabbed my shield, pulled it from my belt and held it out.

"Cover me," the first voice said.

I saw the light start to waver as he moved out of the line of sight of his backup and made his way to my left side. Finally the light was out of my eyes as he reached out and took my case from me.

"Stay here," he ordered.

I wanted to ask him where the fuck I was going to go. Though I was a good shot, I would be lucky to drop one of them before they had planted at least three clips in my body. I watched him move away reading my credentials with his flashlight. He sat down in the car and radioed to the dispatcher. I could not hear the conversation. After a few minutes he jumped out of the car.

"Detain those men," he ordered the other three policemen, pointing at the six bikers.

He made a beeline directly for me, this time not bothering to move out of the direct line of the other cops. He came up to me and handed my wallet back.

"I am so sorry ma'am. I hope you will accept my apology. I would never have expected someone your age to be a Deputy Marshal, much less a full U.S. Marshal," he said.

"Really, no apology necessary. May I holster my weapon?" I asked, since I had not moved my gun from my side.

"Of course, ma'am," he said.

I flipped the safety back on and slipped my gun back in the holster.

"Please, Marshal McKenzie," I said, smiling as I held out my hand.

He took it and shook.

"Officer Miller," he said.

"What brings you to Hot Springs?" he asked.

"Actually I live here now. I got here last night late. I have not had a chance to check in with local law enforcement," I answered.

"Would you like to make a statement and press charges?" he asked.

"Not unless you really want to charge these guys with something," I answered.

"Not as a going concern. It would cost more in time and money than it would really be worth," he said.

"We will hold them here for a bit if you would like to get on the road and get out of here," he added.

"I would appreciate that. Though could you give me some information?" I asked.

"Sure if I can," he answered.

"I have been starving since about four. Is there somewhere around here I could get a decent meal?" I asked.

"Sure, the Track Inn on the west side of town is open until ten. You should be able to get there in plenty of time," he answered.

"Could you give me some directions?" I asked.

"I could show you if you like?" the Professor spoke up.

I looked at him. I guess I did owe him a meal at the very least.

"Fine, as long as I don't eat alone," I answered.

"I have never been one to turn down a meal with a lovely young woman," he said, smiling back.

"Then I guess I am set. Thanks again, Officer Miller," I said, holding out my hand.

"Any time," he said as he shook it.

He tipped his hat and headed to the where the other three policemen were holding the bikers.

"Shall we?" I asked, pointing to my car.

"Sure," he said as we started walking the last few feet to where my car was parked.

He opened my door for me then went to the passenger side and got in.

"Before we go any further, can I at least know who I am riding with?" I asked.

"Hmmm... That could be a very long introduction. How about just settling for my name?" he asked, smiling.

"Great I am stuck in a car with Confucius," I flung at him.

"I would rather think that I hold a more striking, philosophical, resemblance

45

to Lao-tzu," he answered.

I laid my head on the steering wheel.

"Geez, just tell me your fucking name already," I said.

"I have been called God, a couple of times during coitus," he answered laughing.

It took all of the will power I had not to take out my gun and shoot him on the spot. I took a deep breath and worded my sentence carefully.

"Would you please tell me what your legal name is, at this particular point in time and space?" I asked with my forehead resting on the steering wheel.

"Now was that so hard? Bran Murray," he said.

"Great, now I know what to call you," I said as I sat up and stuck the key in the ignition.

"Which way to the Track Inn?" I asked.

Bran pointed, I moved the car in that direction.

"Is there a possibility of having a less than exacting conversation over dinner?" I asked as I drove.

"I guess there is always that possibility."

"But probably not likely."

"Not necessarily but we are not having dinner yet." Bran smiled.

I suddenly felt verbally defeated by the smiling professor seated in the car next to me. With everything that had happened I had not taken a good look at my passenger. He was probably between sixty and ninety. Though he was not unclean, there was a look of being unkempt and wild. His beard was not long but it was not close cropped either. He had clear blue-gray eyes and longish hair. He carried a little weight with him but not so much that he would be considered fat. I took a look at him with my gift. It was like nothing I had ever seen before. Where most people's auras were a mixture of colors over a base of orange that seemed to change brightness and veil color with mood or excitement, his was a bright light gray with strings of shiny silver that almost had a metallic look to them. Though I had seen other auras in my life that didn't have the orange base to them, they always had a color. I was deeply disturbed that it was so different than what I had seen before in either animal or human. I had no explanation for what I was seeing. I guess my shock translated to my face. I snapped off my sight at the urgency of his voice.

"Are you okay?" Bran asked.

"Yeah why?"

"You look like you have seen a ghost."

"Cramps," I said, trying to cover for my shock.

Thankfully, Bran was tactful enough to let it drop.

"Oh," was all he said.

We drove the rest of the way in silence. I had no idea what he was contemplating but I was trying to figure out what I had seen.

I parked the car; we got out and headed for the door of the restaurant. There were a few cars parked in the lot and the eatery was not really busy. We ordered our meals and Bran asked the waitress for a clean dry bowl.

"So do you prefer Marshal or McKenzie?" Bran asked from across the table.

"I guess that we don't need to stand on formality. My name is Cedwynne."

He cocked an eyebrow.

"A very old name," he said.

"Really? I have never met anyone with it other than myself."

"It is a very old Celtic name. Who was your father?"

"I figure his last name was McKenzie but other than that...."

"How about your mother?"

"Haven't a clue," I answered.

He looked at me questioningly.

"I was orphaned. The only thing that the government knew about me was my name, it was written in the tag of my clothes. They did searches, and so have I, but nothing was ever found. The only thing that anyone could piece together was that I was with my father when the accident happened. He was killed instantly, but he had no identification on him and the car he was driving was stolen. I was put in the foster care system and grew up in families from Colorado to Kansas. The doctors did a few tests and pinned my birth sometime in twenty two, twenty two. But that was the closest they could get."

Bran looked at me with real interest.

"What?" I asked, looking at him.

The waitress sat our salads, and his extra bowl, down in front of us before he could answer. I looked at the greens before me as Bran reached into his jacket pocket and pulled out four small glass containers. I watched him as he pulled the cork stoppers out of them poured different amounts out of each into the empty bowl. He mixed the contents together; I thought it had the look of some sort of cannabis since all of the ingredients looked dried and leafy for the most part.

"Here. Put this on your salad," he said, handing me the bowl.

I had only known this man for less than three hours and he thought that I would take drugs from him in the middle of a public restaurant.

"I think I will pass," I said.

"I promise that there are no illegal substances in there. It will help with the cramps," he said.

I sat looking at him.

"Really. Here," he said as he reached across the table and took a pinch out of the bowl and sprinkled it in his mouth and swallowed.

"Not poisonous either," he said and smiled.

I would have probably passed on it if I had not been hit with a massive cramp. I grabbed the bowl and sprinkled the contents over my salad. I took a tentative bite. It did not have the smell or taste of any drug I had come across in my life. In fact it actually complimented the flavor of the greens.

"Not dead yet?" Bran asked, smiling at me.

"No but I still have the cramps," I shot back.

"Give it about ten to fifteen minutes," he said and started his own salad.

I had ordered a chicken and rice dish and he an all vegetable plate. I assumed that he was a vegetarian from what he had ordered. Conversation seemed to stop as we ate. I was starving and I was paying more attention to my meal than my company. It wasn't until the after dinner coffee that I realized I had not had a cramp in a while.

"What was in that stuff?" I asked.

"Just some herbs and roots. Are you feeling better?"

"Much, thanks."

I was not only feeling better, I was feeling great. He pulled the bowl back over to him, mixed some more of the herbs, poured them into a napkin, folded it up and handed it over to me.

"This should hold you for the next few days. The benefits last for about twenty four hours, though it will work faster if you mix it in some hot water and drink it as a tea," he said as I took the napkin.

"How much at a time?" I asked.

"There should be three servings in there."

I paid the bill and we got up and walked out into the cool spring night.

"Can I drop you somewhere?" I asked.

"No, but thank you. I would prefer to walk," he said, smiling at me.

He walked me over to the car and opened my door.

"It was a pleasure to meet you, Cedwynne." He held out his hand.

"And you," I said, taking it.

He closed my door after I had sat down. He pressed a finger to his forehead as if in a casual salute, turned, and walked away towards downtown. I pressed down on the accelerator and headed to my own home.

Chapter 4
Wednesday April 5, 2248

I sat, still in my pajamas, with a cup of coffee and various case folders laid out before me on the bed. Most of the contents of the folders were massive amounts of newspaper clippings and local police reports. I could not believe the conclusions that were reached by the investigators that had come before me. In true government employee fashion, they refused to use the common terms for things, but basically they were admitting the existence of things that I had only heard about in fairy tales and horror stories. Though they used the terms; possible body shifters, night-stalkers, and viable Wiccan anomalies, I knew exactly what they were trying to say. I felt like I was wasting my time. If these things really existed everyone would know about them.

I pulled out the two files that my predecessor had considered his active cases. One was in lower Missouri and the other on the outskirts of New Orleans. I opened the Missouri folder and spread the clippings, police reports, and pictures out to study them. The general thread was violent maulings; people and animals that had been ripped open and partially eaten. The one thing common in all of them was the fact that every person and animal had had their throats ripped out perimortem. All of these had happened within a twenty mile radius of a place called Roaring River Park. There had been large animal tracks around all of the bodies and the local sheriff, a Gary Benton, had concluded they had a rogue bear. There had been four human deaths and ten cow mutilations over a fourteen month period. The last one documented was five months ago. I flipped open the journal from my predecessor and looked at the last entry of any type, it was four months ago. I studied the dates of the reports and was struck with something that seemed to register in my brain. I went into the living room, found my five year date calendar, and took it back to the bedroom. I flipped back to the dates in question. Sure enough, they all had happened on or around the time of the full moon of each month, which I knew for a fact since they coincided with my own monthly cycle. The lunatic fringe always liked the full moon for a ritual and this seemed no different to me.

I gathered up all of the things on the bed and carried them down to the basement. I sat the arm full on the table in the center. I filed the old cases, leaving out the two current ones. I walked over to the desk and looked at the computer. This one had to be one of the newest models since it had one of the flat screen monitors.

When the war ended most of the ability to mass produce miniature circuitry had been sent back to the Stone Age with the decimation of Japan and China. Though people knew what computers were and how they worked it took almost twenty years to start producing the technologies that existed back at the end of the twentieth century. They gathered the most intelligent people of the time to reverse engineer the micro circuitry that was laying around in various states of decay. Personal computers had started a comeback but they were big and bulky, especially the monitors. Most miniature manufacturing had been geared more towards communication, such as cell phones and trying to replace the communication satellites that had decayed and fallen from orbit years ago.

I found the on switch for the computer itself and pressed the button. It whirred to life. I hit the switch on the monitor as it flickered on and showed the boot up process. Compared to the computer I used to use in Dallas, this one flew. After the boot up process, the computers I was used to using would leave me at a simple command prompt that you had to type in which program you wanted to run. This one went straight to a colored screen and a white box that asked for my control number and password. I type in my control number and password and hit enter. The screen went blank for a moment then popped up with a font that said "Welcome, Marshal McKenzie", and then went back to a colored screen with little pictures and titles. I looked through the icons and found one I was looking for. I was not sure how to start it though. I moved the mouse pointer over to the icon and it changed color. I clicked the button on the mouse and another screen popped up on the monitor. I was looking at the portal for the Newsnet.

This interface was much more in-depth than any of the older ones I had worked on. I put in my search criteria and hit enter. The monitor sat unchanging for a moment then it jumped to a screen that came up with five stories around the area that fit my criteria. I began reading. Every month, over the past four, had an article on mutilations; three animal and one human. I read them twice, wrote down all of the details, and hit the X at the top of the screen. The screen went away and I was left with the colored one that had the icons on it. I searched the other icons and found one that looked promising. I clicked on it. It was a database for local and state law enforcement with a box asking for my control number and password I typed both in and pressed enter. Another criteria screen popped up. I filled in the blanks and hit enter again. Only one report came up. It was the one related to the person mauled that I had read about on Newsnet. I got all of the particulars and closed out the screen. A box came up and asked if I wanted to save the file. I clicked yes. Another box appeared and asked me to name the file and file folder I wanted it put in. Since this was an open case I copied the file number I was already working out of and pressed the enter key. After a few seconds I was back to the main page with the icons. I saw the icon that said "sign off" I clicked on that. A second later a box came up asking if I wanted to synchronize now. I was not sure what I was supposed to synchronize but I hit the yes button on the screen.

A few seconds later another box appeared that read: Synchronizing device needs to be powered up to continue. I figuratively scratched my head. What device needs to be powered up? I asked myself. I got down on hands and knees and crawled under the desk to get a better look at the computer box. I looked at the back. It had seven cables attached to it. I traced the wires. One was to the mouse, another to the screen, the third one was to the printer that sat on a stand next to the desk, the fourth was a power cable, the fifth went directly into a conduit in the wall, the sixth was for the keyboard and the last ran back up to the desktop and was attached to the slim silver box that also sat on the desk. Okay, maybe this was the device that needed to be powered up. The box was already plugged in.

I saw a small latch on the front of it. I pressed it a couple of different ways until I heard a small click. I opened the box and was surprised to find another keyboard built in to the lower half and a screen on the upper hinged lid. After a moment of thought the realization finally hit me, I had read about these. They used to be called laptops but, though strides had been made in that area, the general consensus was that they were still ten years away from mass production. I pushed the little button at the top of the keyboard, little lights came on and it whirred to life. It asked me for my control number and password; it replayed the same sequence that I had gone through on the other computer. I looked at the screen on the bigger computer and hit the continue button of the last box. A few seconds went by, the screen cleared and a message came up; Synchronization Complete. Good Day, Marshal McKenzie. Then the screen went blank and the main computer shut down. I hit the sign off icon on the laptop this time I told it not to synchronize. It told me good-bye and shut down.

I moved to the table and found the appropriate map. These maps were a mixture of road and topographical. I plotted the locations of the attacks. I marked the animal mutilations in blue and the human ones in red. I noticed that the animal mutilations were within five to ten miles of each other, where the human ones were further out and a bit more random. I pulled out a state road map and my date book. The full moon was in four days. The trip to Roaring River would be about a six hour drive.

I sat down, stared at the walls and thought. Did I really believe this? Was I sure that I was the right person to be doing this job? Was Counter Section just a cover for the government to take care of problem criminals without the hassle of Directive One? Were the names used just as code for the different crimes that they committed? Was I put here simply because I was expendable and would do anything to save my life, even disregarding Directive One? The last agent had warned me not to believe everything that those above me might tell me. What was I supposed to do if I did figure it out? I really needed someone to talk this through with.

I picked up the receiver of the land line sitting on the desk and dialed. It rang a couple of times.

"Marshal Burdock," came the answer on the line.

"Terry, this is Ced."

"You okay Ced?" he asked, knowing I didn't use his first name unless I was upset.

"Not sure. I have some questions and I need a sounding board."

"You know I cannot discuss this with you."

"You can speak hypothetically can't you?"

"I guess within reason I could."

"Why are these positions solitary posts?" I asked.

"Rumor is that the qualifications for it are very unique and there are not enough people with those qualifications to station more than one in a given area," Burdock answered.

"Are you sure that we are not just the expendable ones?"

"From what I am told you are far from expendable. In fact you and your fellow agents are more important to the government than a most of the other government officials that haven't been elected."

"I am not sure I am buying it."

"What's eating you, Ced?"

I sat thinking. My head was spinning from the unbelievability of everything. I was losing my train of thought in the maze of what I thought was true and false, based on what I had learned through my life.

"Ced?" Burdock asked after a few moments of silence.

"Okay. Do you believe in fairy tales?" I asked, in the only way I could think of.

There was silence on the other end for a few beats.

"Yes," came the quiet answer.

"Really?" I asked.

"I have lived through a couple. So yes I believe in fairy tales."

"You mean to tell me that all of the old horror novels are real? You want me to believe that?"

"You can believe or not, that is your choice. But if you refuse to believe I don't think you will last long out there."

"Did you know about this before I took the assignment?"

"Yes."

"And you didn't tell me before I took this gig?" I asked, a little put out.

"I couldn't Ced, and not because of my orders concerning you or your assignment. This goes back farther than Counter Section."

"Which means that you still won't give me any more information."

"I am afraid I can't."

"What made everyone think that a small white girl had what it takes to do this?"

"That one I can answer un-hypothetically. I have no idea. Was there anything different, that you noticed, about your training from the other Marshals in your class?"

"They had me spend a month on archaic weapons training with swords, bows and the like," I answered.

"Is there anything... ahh....physically different about you?"

"Is that a tit joke?"

"No. Legitimate question."

"Well.... I guess my weight could be one thing."

"What about your weight?"

"If you were guessing my weight what would you put it at?"

"A buck ten soaking wet."

"Try a buck seventy five to a buck eighty."

"Are you kidding me?"

"Nope. Honest."

"Now comes the tit joke."

"Hey they are not that big."

"Did anyone have an answer for you about your weight?"

"The doctors said my muscle and bone density was almost twice that of a normal human being. But since they saw no abnormalities, other than that, they chalked it up to a G-3 mutation." I answered.

"You said that was one. Are there others?"

I thought about if I really wanted to tell him about the other. I had only told one other person in my life and that person sent me straight to a therapist. I decided to keep the that one to myself for now

"Not really."

"What is it?"

"Nothing, really."

"Ced I do not have a high enough clearance to see the in-depth scores from your tests. They may have shown some things that you do not even realize yet."

"Thanks, Terry."

"You're welcome Ced. I hope you got the answers you were looking for."

"I am not sure what I got but answers were not it."

"You be careful. I meant it. If you are not prepared for this job don't do it."

"What am I supposed to do then?"

"If you don't think you can do it, pack your shit and get back to Dallas. There is always a job here for you, at least as long as I am here."

"Thank you Terry."

"Anytime. Keep your head down."

"I will try. Later."

"Later, McKenzie."

I sat looking at the phone that, a moment ago, had held the only lifeline I had left. Lost seemed like too small a word to describe what I felt. I so needed a drink. If I could find Agent Gray right now I would throttle him with my bare hands for my lost bottle of Scotch. I went upstairs, showered, and got dressed. Today I was going to go get a late lunch and a bottle of Scotch, no side trips to rough bars.

I stopped at Grannie's for a burger and directions to a liquor store. After the burger, which was quite good, and directions I drove across town to the store indicated. It took a bit of hunting but I found the label I liked, paid and started home.

****

With a fresh drink in hand I went back down to the office, pulled out the Missouri file and spread it out on the center table. I pulled out my notebook and began taking notes. All of the human deaths were women and there was no particular body type. The only thing that they had in common was that they were all found naked and had been naked when they were killed. I pulled the police reports on the four women to see if anything jumped out at me.

I studied them side by side until I noticed it. All of them, though different body types, did have one thing in common; all of them must have been in incredible shape since their weight versus their measurements meant that all of them must have been very muscular. I wasn't sure what that was telling me but it was interesting. The last agent had gotten the autopsy photos of two of the women. I looked closely at them. I had never seen stomachs like theirs that were not on body builders. Maybe there was a gym connection here. I found that all of them lived in different towns and not close enough to share that connection. I had seen many serial killers over the last five years and could always find something in the victims that could tie everything together, but this one did not seem to have that connection.

I took a sip of my drink and studied the table. I kept out the police reports of the human maulings, pushed the rest aside and laid out the topo map I had marked earlier. I placed the police reports of the women next to the spots where they were found and drew a line from that spot to the towns they were from. The first victim was from a town called Fairview, the second from Wheaton, the third from Butterfield, and the last from Jenkins. All four of them had been found within ten miles of each other, over the course of fourteen months. I added in the fifth, the one I had found on line, who was from Shell Knob. All of the bodies had been discovered in heavily wooded areas slightly northeast of a town called Cassville.

When I added in the livestock mutilation I found an anomaly. Though the human and animal deaths were tied together by cause of death, all of the animal deaths were in an area on the southeast side of Cassville. There was a good thirty miles between center of the animal mutilations and the center of the human ones. Maybe the place to start should be in the center of the livestock mutilations.

I had two theories going. One: All the mutilations were being done by one person and they were traveling further out of their area to kill the humans. Two:

The livestock mutilations were being done by an animal or one human and the human ones were being perpetrated by someone nearby to make it look like the livestock deaths. If there was only one suspect then why did they travel that much further south to mutilate livestock? Could it be it was closer to where they lived? I decided to leave the human deaths out of the investigation for the moment to see if there was some rhyme or reason to the animal ones. I began drawing lines connecting all of the livestock sites. I connected them around, then across from each other. I studied the map to find a common area where most of the lines crossed. It was a spot about ten miles directly southeast of Cassville. I got in close to the map and looked at the area. There was a fire road that led through the mountains and forest that all of the lines crossed. If this was just a bear or a wolf I didn't think that the mutilations would be this scattered around a central point. It seemed too thought out to be an animal. I could not say it wasn't, but... I picked up my drink and took another sip.

What was I going to do? Now that was the question wasn't it? Did I buy the myth or did I approach this as I always had? Regardless of myth or fact all of this still tied together in some way. Even if the animal deaths were by a different person, my job was to catch the person or persons responsible for the human ones. If the animal deaths led me to that then I was ahead of the game. If they didn't lead to anything but a dead end, I at least ruled that suspect out. Investigation one oh one, narrow down the suspect list.

I pulled my date book off of the pile and opened it. Today was Wednesday the fifth and the full moon would be this Saturday night into Sunday morning. I looked at the map again and marked the road that all of the lines crossed. I had always found that when you went to the center of things you would find the cause. I knew it was a shot in the dark but I had to start somewhere. I would go up and take a look. I would probably not find anything, but I needed to do something or I would go nuts just sitting here trying to make up my mind on what to do. I had made up my mind in that instant. I would go up this Saturday, find a place and camp out for the evening. If I found something, fine. If not I would continue to watch the area and see if a pattern emerged. I found the name of the local sheriff and wrote his name and office number in my notebook. I straightened all of the papers and maps and put them in their places except for the map I had drawn on.

I sat looking across the room at the safe. I had not opened it yet. I pulled out the combination and went to the large dial on the front. It took me two tries but I finally opened it. I am not sure what I expected but what I found was not it. Inside were two long rifles with night scopes, a large quantity of ammunition a couple of miniature crossbows, a large quantity of quarrels, a sheathed sword, two medium sized flashlights, and a few large envelopes. I looked closer at the ammunition. There were various calibers, including nine mil and thirty eight, which would fit both of my personal weapons. They were also unusual in that the bullets were not just lead, but laced with what looked like silver lines. Could these really be silver bullets? There was a printed page taped to the inside door of the safe. I opened the door a bit farther so the light would fall on the writing.

Shape-shifters: Aim for the brain or the heart to take them down instantly. The silver will poison them fatally but if it is just a wounding shot you may be in mortal danger, or worse. What could be worse than mortal danger? I asked the person who had written this. *Keep all weapons loaded with the ammunition from this safe. Throw out all standard bullets so there will be no mistakes. Also, folklore is wrong about them not being able to touch silver. It is only fatal or poisonous if introduced into their blood stream. Most travel in packs.*

Night-stalkers: Stake to the heart or separate head from body. Crosses and full spectrum flashlights will offer a modicum of protection. Have not found anything else that is useful. Word of warning: Night-stalkers seem to come in three types; those that have passed, those that have been turned, and those that have yet to pass. Those that have yet to pass can be neutralized by any conventional weapon, however, if they are not cremated or decapitated, they will just have to be neutralized a second time after resurrection.

Viable Wiccans: Can be neutralized with any conventional weapon. Be warned their defensive and offensive powers can me quite formidable. This section of beings are the least studied and as such have the least amount of information available on them. It is widely believed that Wiccans are pretty much respectful of others and do not crave notoriety. However, instances have been noted of blatant aggression by some.

I grabbed a couple of boxes of shells for both my weapons, sat at the table, and traded them for the ammunition I had in both guns and my spare clips. I sat my weapons down on the table and looked at the maps again. I felt the twinges of a cramp begin. I went upstairs, closed the basement door behind me, and poured another stiff one.

Chapter 5
Saturday April 8, 2248

I loaded my behemoth for the day, locked up and headed out for Missouri. I'd spent the last two days curled up in bed, nursing my cramps, drinking the tea I had gotten from Bran, and reading all of the old fantasy novels I picked up at a local book store. I thought about the stories that I'd read as I drove. I found it quite interesting that each of the authors had written their stories from the perspective of another species and that wheirwolves, vampires, and witches were the protagonists. Though I would have preferred my lead characters in the form of a stronger human hero, I will admit I was sucked into a couple of the stories and had become invested in those lead characters. I'd bought and read the novels hoping they'd give me some sort of insight as to the myths and legends behind them. A fun story to go along with it was just a plus, though I was a little miffed at the writers for making all of their heroines tall, proportional, and beautiful. Being short, over endowed, and weighing too much for my frame ensured that I would never be a heroine in one of their fantasies.

I had always been told that there was a grain of truth in all myths and legends. If what the other agents had left for me in their reports were true, I was hoping the myths in those books might prove informative. Hopefully, there was at least one useful fact in there somewhere. I wasn't buying it but..... If, and I capitalized that if a few times, I gave any credence to the reports and/or the novels, then I could reason that the person or persons I was after was strong, fast, had exceptional hearing and olfactory sense, possibly traveled in packs, and could be killed with silver. To a certain extent I was willing to buy the grain of truth where it came to heightened senses and strength, since I could point to my own gift of sight as a substantiation of that train of thought. I knew that everyone, even the President of the United States, had told me to keep an open mind and I was trying to do that with this trip to Missouri. But turning into a wolf? *Sorry, still not buying it.*

I had been going over the realities versus the mythical possibilities so many times in the past hundred miles that the line between fantasy and reality was starting to blur. I forced my thoughts to other areas to try and regain my focus and my loosening grip on my sanity. I looked down at the dash to check my speed and thought about the lumbering monstrosity I was driving. I was finding the longer I drove it the more comfortable I was becoming with it and in it. So I guess insulting the vehicle in my thought process wasn't very nice.

"So what should I call you?" I asked the dashboard.

I looked at the dashboard with all of the switches and dials. It seemed very involved and complicated.

"Definitely female...," I started, actually vocalizing my thoughts.

"Though even you'd have to admit that you're a bit unusual and quite the behemoth."

"Well then, how do you feel about Behemoth and I will call you Bee for short?" I asked.

I actually waited a few seconds, thinking that I would hear an answer come from the whine of the tires on pavement.

"Fine, since I hear no objections, Bee it is," I said to the dash.

Great. Here I was talking to a vehicle and asking it if it liked its name. I felt another finger start to let go of the sanity rope. If Freud were here he'd have a field day with this part of my psyche; "You hate your father and want acceptance from your mother, so you identify with inanimate objects." Screw you and the cigar you rode in on Sigmund.

Okay, enough Ced. Time for a break and some coffee. I stopped in Springdale to gas up, get some coffee, and try to find enough sanity to say "fuck this", pack my bags, and get my ass back to Dallas. Evidently I didn't find my sanity since by the bottom of my coffee cup I found myself back on the road and still heading north.

****

I bounced along in Bee on the small back roads looking for the fire road I had marked on the map. With the massive loss of population, especially around the old forests, Mother Nature had reclaimed what was hers with a vengeance. I turned down a dirt road, which was more of a two lane path than anything else, and traveled for a couple of bone jarring miles looking for a suitable place to camp. I passed a few small clearings but nothing that was big enough for Bee. I was probably four or five miles into the forest and mountains before I found what I was looking for. I turned into a large clearing, parked in the middle of it, and shut the engine down. I had never been much of a nature girl and deep woods camping had never been on my list of to-dos. Luckily, I would not be stuck in a tent. I looked at my watch; it would be about two more hours until nightfall. I knew that this was a stab in the dark and I had to giggle at my own unintended pun, but this was dead center of all of the animal mutilations over the past year or so. I had no clue what I would find or if I would find anything, but this was a place to start. I was sure to arrive at the last minute, so to speak, so that I would maintain some element of surprise. I brewed some coffee and poured a cup. I opened the door and jumped down to the ground to look around the glade I had parked in. After surveying the area, I retreated to the comfort of Behemoth to catch a little sleep before night fall.

****

My eyes popped open when I heard the first howl from a distance outside. Though it was dark, the moonlight flooded through the two small windows of the camper. I grabbed the night vision binoculars and my gun, making sure to chamber a round as quietly as I could and replace the round in the chamber with another bullet. I clicked the safety on and slid my side arm back in its holster. I silently made my way to the small door in the back of the camper and cracked it to look outside. I tried to calm myself with the knowledge that it was probably just a real wolf or coyote, but there was something in my brain that didn't want to buy it. Too many fantasy novels in the past couple of days. I eased the door open, stuck my head out and looked around. I listened intently as I heard the sounds of something slowly moving in the underbrush beyond the tree line perpendicular to the side of Bee. I slowly stepped down to the ground and moved to the passenger side, listened closely to the sounds, and hid in shadows. I froze when I heard the definite sounds of canine sniffing at the tree line. I almost peed myself when the howl came from the same spot. I could see four shadows at the edge of the clearing a little off to my left. I raised my binoculars to my eyes. I could see four wolves of large proportion, though one was perceptively smaller than the other three. As I was watching them pace I noticed that the biggest one had stopped and seemed to be looking directly at me or more exactly sniffing at me.

I let my binoculars fall down to my chest which hung from their strap around my neck. I looked at the shadows and opened up my gift. There were four distinct, sentient auras. I was shocked. When I was younger and first realized that I had a gift, I would practice looking at auras by watching the wildlife around the property where I grew up. What I found was that any animal, other than human, only had a faint silver glow around them and not a full-fledged aura. I reasoned for myself that it was a life force glow and it took a soul or sentient being to produce a real aura.

The one that had been sniffing at me let out three short yips and started slowly inching in my direction. I noticed that two of the four had moved back into the tree line and disappeared from the view of my gift. I could see the largest of the bunch was coming straight towards me and the smallest of them had moved a few yards to its right and was making an advancement from there. I scanned the tree line and could see the other two had gone in opposite directions and were circling quickly to gain my flank on both sides as their auras blinked in and out of the underbrush. I started moving back towards the rear of Behemoth to get to the safety of its interior, since I had been stupid and locked the front doors to the cab. I reached behind me and pulled my gun, switching off the safety as it cleared the holster. I could barely see the one to my left in the trees, since he had made it to the line that was cut off by the front of the truck. The other one was at the edge of the clearing which was in line with the back of Bee. The two in front of me were moving a bit quicker now in my direction. I dropped my sight and made a dash for the end of the camper and was drawn up short by a fifth one I had not seen. It was just sitting in front of the back door like a pet waiting on its master to let it in. His coat was a deep brown; he lifted his lips in a snarl and stood. This wolf was bigger than the other four. I tried to hold my fear down but it was not working real well. I glanced around quickly. I had been outflanked and surrounded. The other four were closing in at a very leisurely pace. It was like they knew they had their quarry dead to rights. *Did I just think the words dead? Gotta stop that.* I assessed my situation, I was fucked and I knew it.

I knew I could get two of them before I went down, so I switched my pistol to my left hand and used the back corner of Behemoth as some protection from the largest wolf that was there. I raised my pistol and sighted, using my eyes and not my gift, at the biggest wolf at the back door of Bee. I froze for a second as I looked in its eyes; they weren't the eyes of a mere animal. The orbs staring at me were deep green and intelligent. That lost second cost me the battle and probably the war.

The first wolf that had yipped sprung and slammed my arm, and me, back into the side of the camper. My hand hit so hard that the gun discharged then dropped from my grasp and went flying. I dropped to the ground and rolled back in the direction of the attack since he had careened off to the left after hitting me. I hopped up into a squatting position and went for my backup weapon strapped to my calf. Before I could get the safety strap unsnapped, I was hit by the smallest of the wolves on my upper right shoulder and slammed back to the ground on my left side. Even with the quick glance I got, I had time enough to realize the smallest one had blue eyes and its coat, for lack of a better description, was blonde. I started to roll towards Bee and get beneath her for some protection. As I rolled to my back the biggest of the wolves landed on my chest, growling at me. Score one for the fantasy novels; they *were* fast and strong. He must have been all of two hundred and fifty pounds, and I could feel most of it crushing my chest. I tried to reach my backup by reaching down with my right hand and pulling my knee up in the belly of the monster on top of me. He snapped at my face so I put my left forearm up to ward off the attack. He snapped and caught my arm. I was frightened that this was going to be it but he surprised me by not biting down. He held my arm, looked down at me, and shook his head lightly as if he were telling me no. I almost had my gun when another set of teeth had a hold of my right wrist, but like the set around my arm they didn't even break the skin.

They had me. I might be able to get in a good kick, but really there was nothing I could do. I felt the teeth on my left arm lighten up and let go. I removed my arm from his maw and slowly let it fall to my side. I also lowered my right leg so the gun was out of reach of my hand. As soon as I did, the other set of teeth let go of my wrist. I was having a hard time breathing because of the two paws that were bearing down on my ribcage. He seemed to sense it and moved them so he was straddling and looking straight down at me. I started to try and move to crawl out from underneath him when he let go a menacing growl. I froze in my spot.

He moved his muzzle down and took a long sniff of my body. He looked back at me and cocked his head like it was a smell he could not figure out. I lay there while he continued his assessment of me. My shield hung from belt and he sniffed it and let out a small growl. It was when he stuck his nose in my crotch that I had enough. He could kill me for all I cared but that was off limits. I put all of the power I had in the open hand slap I placed upside his head. His neck snapped away from me but his teeth came back snapping at my hand. He growled at me so I growled back. He put his nose right up to mine and stared at me. I stared back at him; he really did have very pretty green eyes. I was not sure how long we stayed in that position but eventually he slowly drew back. He made a few yips in the direction of the others then moved back off of me. I sat up slowly. The smallest of the five of them was standing to my left and cutting off any escape that way. The rest of them had set up a line that allowed me safe passage to the back of the camper but nowhere else. I rose slowly, keeping my hands down, and started towards the back of Behemoth. The one that had been sitting on my chest was standing a few feet directly behind the door looking at it. I moved towards the back of Bee and opened the door. I heard a growl from behind me. I took that as motivation to get in the safety of my camper. I crawled up inside and closed the door quickly behind me. I heard a few yips and a howl then all went silent.

I ran to the tall cabinet next to the stove and pulled out the rifle with night scope. They had made their mistake; I could pick them off from the safety of the camper. I chambered a round in the rifle as I tore the screen off of the window on the side of Bee facing the tree line. I cranked open the small panes of the window and stuck the muzzle of the rifle out between the small sections of glass. I looked through the scope at three of them, including the one that had been on my chest. I put him in the crosshairs, flipped the safety off, and laid my finger on the trigger. I knew I could take down all three of them before they could make the tree line. I had thoughtfully worked through the progression of my shots; I had my finger on the trigger but I just could not make myself squeeze it.

A fight had started in my brain. I worked through what I knew about just plain wolves in the wild and watched as the three in my scope started to walk to the tree line. Wolves were pack animals, had territories and defended them, just as any human would protect and defend their homes. Even if they were wheirwolves, which in my head was still a big if, I didn't know if any one of them was the one I was after. I had no proof to justify killing them. They had done nothing harmful to me other than scare the pee out of me. They could have torn me to shreds but they didn't. Other than dirty clothes, a few bumps, bruises, and scratches I was no worse off than when I went out into the clearing. I had to admit to myself that I was the interloper into their territory. Would I have acted any different if they would have come into my home? Actually yes, I would have shot first and waited on the coroner. I would not have let a person breaking into my house off scott free.

I flipped the safety back on the rifle, pulled it from the window, slid down the wall of Bee, and sat shaking on the couch. I sat for a few minutes to try and collect my shattered nerves and emotions; needless to say, all I could collect was enough of my nerve to stow the rifle and sit down on the bed and shiver. It took me almost fifteen minutes to work up enough mental strength to get up, close the window, and replace the screen. What was my next move? I had no real idea what to do. I realized that my side arm was still outside. I found the flashlight in the closet, grabbed it, and went to the back door of the camper. I looked out and lying a few yards away was one of the wolves. I moved to the front cab and looked out the windshield, and sure enough another one was guarding about the same distance in front. I looked at my watch; it was one thirty in the morning. I sat back down on the bed. I was going nowhere unless I drove out and I wasn't leaving without my gun. I could probably shoot my way out to it but, outside of my first partner's murderer, I didn't kill for the sake of killing, even if it was just a wolf. From the myths I remembered, by the light of the next day they would be back in human form. If that was the case with the five wolves I had come up against, then I was sure that the two still left guarding me would be gone or naked and on two legs. I at least knew how to handle a naked man. I lay back on the bed to try and rest and wait for the light of day.

Chapter 6
Sunday April 9, 2248

I could feel every bruise and scrape as I opened my eyes. It was still dark outside and I needed to pee. I fumbled around in the dark until I found the closet that represented the bathroom. God, it hurt to move. I finished and found the bed again. I was cold so I wrapped up in the bedspread and tried to drift back to sleep. All that I could see when I closed my eyes were green eyes looking at me. I lay there and felt the pains that told me I had been tossed around. As much as I tried I could not relax enough to fall into a slumber. I gave up, turned on one of the small lights mounted on the wall, and made some fresh coffee. I made sure the door in the back was locked and moved to the cab and started the truck to produce some heat. I flicked on the headlights. My front guard was not there anymore, or at least he was nowhere I could see. I turned off the headlights since it made no difference if he was there or not, I was not going outside to check on him. I poured myself a cup of coffee even though the brewer was still percolating, and tried to get comfortable on one of the couches. For only the second time in my short life I felt alone and helpless. God, I hated that feeling.

I was just finishing my second cup of coffee when I saw the first rays of light start streaking the sky. I went to the back door, unlocked and opened it. I saw my weapon, lying in the weeds, a few yards from the back of Behemoth. I sat my coffee cup down, took a breath and sprung out the door, hitting the ground running. I made it to my gun, picked it up, quickly surveyed the clearing, and sprinted back to the camper. I closed the door, picked up my coffee, and studied my pistol to make sure it was okay. A little clean up and it was as good as new. I popped the clip out and replaced the spent round so I had a full complement and reseated the clip in the grip of my side arm.

The sun, shining through the windows, made me feel a lot better than I had all night. Now what did I do? I had my gun; I could drive back to Hot Springs, pack, and go back to Dallas. Yes, that was a viable option, probably the preferable one, but something in me would not let this be. I'd overcome my fear and helplessness when I was seven. It was nineteen years later and I wasn't going to disappoint that little girl looking across time at me by tucking my tail and running away now, when she hadn't years ago. Fine, I was going to have to admit to myself that I saw something last night that I had never seen before. I saw it, experienced it, and had the bumps and bruises to prove to myself that it had happened. *So dammit, Ced, deal with it.* I found my resolve and strength from my seven year old self. Since I had taken this job all I had were questions, I wanted answers now and I wasn't going to leave until I had some.

I rummaged through the small closet and pulled out the backpack I had thrown in there before leaving. I pulled six bottles of water out of the fridge and stuffed them in the bottom. I grabbed the topo map off of the front seat, folded it, and placed it in the front pocket. I pulled my compass out of the glove box and placed it in next to the map. I zipped up the pockets and shouldered the pack. Grabbing the keys out of the ignition, I walked back through the camper and exited the back door. I locked everything up and began a systematic search working out from the camper.

Every federal law enforcement officer, from military police to U.S. Marshals to Secret Service, had a part of their training in common. All of us had to complete a portion of the military special forces training in survival and evasion. I had spent two weeks in the woods and mountains, and another two weeks in the desert, learning how to survive, track, and evade. Though I would rather evade the sample pusher at the local supermarket to track down my peanut butter and bread, the forest of Missouri was an element I wasn't incapable of handling.

I started following tracks through the clearing and just inside the tree line trying to find a trail to follow. I found the single tracks in front and behind Bee, but I was really after the ones that had taken me to the ground and my night guards had not been among those three. I finally found what I was looking for; three sets of tracks that left the clearing together. I took a drink of water and started in that direction.

The trail was fairly easy to follow since there was a lot of undergrowth and the twigs and small branches bent or broke easily. I had been hiking almost a mile and a half when the trail split. By the looks of it two of them went one way while the other took off by himself. I took the map out and checked my bearings marking where I was at, as I had done periodically since I left the clearing. I took a drink of water and decided I would play a hunch and follow the two that were traveling together.

The spring day was turning quite warm and I was hot and sweaty, even with the downward slope of the terrain. I broke out of the trees at the top of a sloping bank of a swift stream. I looked down to see exactly what I was hoping for. There were two sets of tracks. I bent down and looked closely at them. One set of paw prints was much smaller than the other. That's what I'd hoped for. The smaller wolf was smaller because it was a female and she was traveling with her mate. I looked to the other shore and found where they had exited the stream and started up the other bank.

It was getting to be around noon and I'd been following the trail for about five hours now. I was amazed at how convoluted it had been. I'd probably hiked for about seven miles, but according to the map I was no more than a couple away from Bee. They must have gone out hunting after their little excursion with me since I found a couple of rabbit carcasses along the way. I was getting no closer to an answer than when I'd left the glade this morning at sunrise. I found a shady spot, sat down, opened another bottle of water, and contemplated returning to Bee and coming back in a month to try again. No, dammit. This trail had to end up somewhere and if they were truly shape-shifters, they would have shifted back by now. This meant that they were walking around on two legs and as such they would probably be doing human things.

I forced myself to get up and start again. I couldn't have walked more than a few hundred feet when the trail went into a thicket so dense I couldn't just walk into it. I had to get down on my hands and knees and crawl through the opening in the underbrush. I was surprised when I emerged from the wall of briars and small trees into a small opening that had been trampled down for about eight foot around. I stood up and looked at the four or five spots that were flatter than the rest, about the size of an adult body. Opposite from where I stood was another opening in the underbrush, but this one was tall enough to admit a standing person. I walked through the larger opening and out the other side where I found myself standing on a fairly worn path that led in two directions.

I pulled out the map and plotted where I was at. If I took a right on the path it would lead back down towards the stream I crossed a while ago. If I went left it would take me towards one of the secondary roads that was about six miles away. I decided I would head left, that way if nothing else, I might be able to catch a ride back down in the direction of Bee. I was beginning to think that the path would go on forever when I came to a tree line and an open field before me. The clearing was probably eight to ten acres, and across the field was a split rail fence enclosing a house and a small barn. I thought about the one that had sniffed at me last night. If their smell was that delicate, then I would use it to my advantage. I wasn't going to make the same mistake I'd made last night. I'd been discovered outside of Bee because of smell. If their noses worked in human form like they did in that of a wolf, I would need all the cover I could get. I paused to make sure the wind was blowing towards me. The path I was on, for the most part, led directly to the house. I readjusted my pack and started walking.

I was a few feet from the fence when I saw her. She was working in the garden in back of the house. The woman was a few inches taller than I was with blonde hair, and wore a cut off tee shirt and shorts. Though I kept myself in excellent physical shape, she was perfect. There didn't seem to be an ounce of body fat on her. I'd never seen abs so defined on a living woman before, though she did have that in common with the two women in the autopsy photos. With every movement, you could see her muscles moving effortlessly.

I gave her a hard look with my gift. In the past I'd simply used my gift to track people in the dark, see the color of their mood, or the intent of a stranger I'd never had a reason to look more than once at someone. In that moment I realized that a person's aura was as unique to them as their fingerprints. My God, I'd never noticed that before. That was a mistake I would never make again. She was the small blonde wolf with blue eyes I encountered last night. I came up quietly to the fence and leaned against the top rail.

"Excuse me," I called to the young woman in the garden.

I watched her flinch in surprise, but she caught herself quickly and slowly raised her eyes in my direction. It was the same blue eyes that knocked me to the ground last night. Where the blue eyes I looked into last night seemed unusually human and intelligent, those same eyes, now in a human, seemed wild and deadly.

"May I help you?" she asked suspiciously as she rose from her kneeling position and took a few steps towards me.

I could see her nostrils flair as if she were trying to get a good whiff of me.

"Yes. I met up with five strangers last night and they left me with a few questions I would like to ask and was wondering if you might be able to point me in the right direction?"

"Not many people live around here. Not sure I can really help you," she answered.

"For the most part I am looking for a man, probably between two hundred and fifty to sixty pounds, dark brown hair, and bright green eyes."

She eyed me for a moment without answering.

"Willis," she shouted towards the house.

We stood eying each other for a few beats until the back door on the house opened and a man walked out wearing jeans and a tee shirt. He was around six foot one or so and, like the woman staring at me, was ripped from head to toe. I checked his aura and sure enough, he'd been the one that had taken me to the ground first. He walked the distance from the house to were the woman stood. He looked at me and stepped towards the fence in a definite show of strength. The woman, though staying behind him, moved with him and out a bit from his left side.

"Who are you?" he asked me intently.

"Marshal Cedwynne McKenzie," I said, and produced my credentials from my belt.

"You're out of your jurisdiction here," he said, stressing the word here.

Though I did not want to get into a pissing contest with him about my jurisdiction being the entire United States, technically he was probably right if I was standing on private property. Unless I had a warrant or subpoena or was working under another article of Directive One, I had no jurisdiction. I thought quickly.

"I am looking for a man between two hundred and fifty to sixty pounds, dark brown hair and bright green eyes."

"Not sure I know him," he replied.

"Interesting since you both were with him last night."

I was surprised by the reaction. All of us had been in pretty close quarters last night I was sure that he would recognize me on sight, but he seemed not to. He stepped much closer to me, his nostrils flared, and the look of recognition showed on his face. His eyebrows knotted together as he eyed me. We stood silently looking at each other for a few tense moments. He reached down into his jeans pocket, while still looking at me, and produced a phone. It took all of the will power I had to not ask him where he kept that thing when he was on all fours. He flipped it open and dialed a number and put the phone to his ear.

"Yes, Sheriff Benton please," he said into the receiver.

Sheriff Benton... Where did I know that name from? Oh, yeah, he was the local Sheriff. I read his reports on the maulings. Great, he was calling the cops. Maybe this would get uglier than I thought.

"Gary? I think you need to get over here, now," he said in the phone as he walked away to get out of ear shot.

Though Willis had moved away and turned his back on me, the young blonde stood, steadfast, watching me closely. After a few moments he started walking back in my direction.

"Okay, bye," he said, hung up and stuck the phone back in his pocket.

"You look a little rough around the edges. Would you like to come sit down and have some lemonade or water?" he asked, softening a bit and actually smiling.

I was wary of his quick change in mood. Though even if the cops came, the worse thing that would probably happen is they would ask me to leave.

"Yes, some lemonade sounds lovely." I smiled back.

He stepped away from the fence.

"Greta, would you get our guest a glass of lemonade?"

I thought it sounded more like an order than a request. She looked at him for a second then turned and went in the house. I jumped over the barricade between us and landed a few feet away from him.

"Let's get out of the sun," he said as he gestured towards the house.

He stepped back, effectively forcing me to proceed him up on the porch. He pulled open the back door for me to enter. I am not sure what I expected as I walked into the kitchen, maybe grass beds and mounted wildlife heads? What was there looked to be a well-kept home complete with female touches, evident from the ruffled kitchen curtains to the floral print on the couch I could see in the living room.

"Have a seat," he said as he pulled out a chair from the table.

I pulled off my pack and sat down as Greta put a large glass of lemonade in front of me. I took a sip; it was very cool and refreshing.

"Thank you," I said to Greta who had not said a word since Willis had come outside.

She nodded her head as she sat on the other side of the table from me. Willis pulled out a chair, angling it towards me and sat down. I was beginning to believe my hosts weren't stellar conversationalist, since they seemed to be content to sit quietly, watching me drink my lemonade. It was then I felt it start. Damn, why does everything annoying happen during my period?

"May I use the restroom?" I asked.

"By all means. Greta, would you show her where it is at?" he asked her.

"This way," Greta said, rising from her seat.

I unzipped the front pouch on my backpack and pulled out a tampon. Willis seemed very intent on me until he saw the paper wrapper and smiled. I got up and followed Greta through the living room and down a hall. She opened up a door and gestured me in.

"No feminine products in the toilet please. We're on a septic system here. Wrap them up well and put them in the trashcan," she said as she shut the door behind me.

I went to the toilet, relieved myself, and performed the function I had come into the room for. I went to the sink to wash up. I was shocked at the reflection that greeted me from the mirror. My blazer was filthy and torn. My hair was tangled and unruly while my face was smeared with dirt, sweat, and scratches. Willis had been right, I was a little rough around the edges. I washed up and tried to put my hair back in some sort of order, which was hard since I was not taking a shower and had no brush to attack it with. I dried my hands and opened the door. Greta was leaning against the opposite wall waiting on me. She allowed me to go first as she followed me back in the kitchen.

"Better?" Willis asked.

"Yes, much. Thank you," I answered and sat back down.

I took a long drink of the lemonade in front of me.

"This is wonderful lemonade," I said.

"Greta is a great cook," Willis said with a note of pride in his voice.

"Thank you, Greta," I said in her direction.

She just inclined her head. Our tense, intermittent, conversation was interrupted by a knock at the door. Willis got up, went through the living room, and opened the front door. He came back into the kitchen followed by a uniform of the local sheriff's department. The uniform was filled out by a man that was a good six four, chiseled features, a thick head of dark brown hair, a mouth full of white teeth, and bright green eyes. I didn't have to switch to my gift, I would know them anywhere. I had a momentary fantasy of having his babies. I would have a litter; they would have four legs and be snapping to chew their way out. Then the shiver ran up my spine when I thought about breast feeding. Though he was still gorgeous, thoughts of offspring ruined the first part of the fantasy, not to mention that he was now a suspect. That was compounded by the fact that he was also the local law, the same law that had written the reports that I was basing my case on. Damn... But suspect or not I had no trouble looking at him.

"Sheriff Gary Benton," said the uniform as he bent slightly and offered me his hand.

"Marshal Cedwynne McKenzie," I replied as I accepted it.

"May I ask for your credentials?" he asked politely.

"As long as I can ask for yours," I replied, smiling.

He smiled and pulled his wallet out of his back pocket, opened it to his identification, and handed it to me. I pulled my shield from my belt and exchanged credentials. Though I only glanced at his, he studied mine for a few beats, took out a small notebook, and wrote down my badge number, name, and control number before handing it back to me.

"What district are you out of?" he asked.

"I'm on special assignment and located in Arkansas," I answered, not telling him where I was from.

"Isn't that a bit unusual?"

"I guess. But I do what I am told, for the most part," I replied, smiling.

"What brings you to our neck of the woods?"

I was getting tired of the chit chat game.

"I'm working a string of murders."

"Really?" he said, cocking an eyebrow at me.

"Yes, Really."

"If you'll tell me about them maybe I can help."

"Maybe. But, not to be rude to my hosts, I really can't discuss it with civilians," I said.

"Willis, Greta. Would you be kind enough to give me and the Marshal a little bit of privacy for a moment?"

Though it was phrased as a request I knew that it wasn't.

"Sure, Gary," Willis said as he got up and motioned Greta to the back door.

Once the door had closed behind the two, the sheriff looked at me and his demeanor changed.

"Marshal, let's cut the crap. What are you doing here?" he asked accusingly, doing his best to make me defensive.

"I wasn't lying. I am working a string of murders and maulings that seem to be connected. The last two police reports were written by you and you know a lot more than you put in them. We both know that they were not the result of a rogue bear," I said, staring straight at him, which seemed to anger him even more.

Though he was now a suspect, as far as my investigation went, my gut told me he wasn't the person I was after. Or I really hoped it was my gut telling me that and not a region a bit lower.

"Fucking Counter Section," I heard him say under his breath with a bit of disgust.

"What did you say?" I asked a little heated.

"Did last night not teach you anything?"

"Actually a lot," I replied, though I was surprised that he beat me to the punch.

"This is going to get you killed."

"Are you threatening me?"

"Heavens no. But even if you do catch the responsible parties, what are you going to do with them?"

"I figure it will have a very unpleasant outcome for one of us involved."

"You really are out of your jurisdiction on this."

"Then whose jurisdiction do you think it is?" I asked, getting a little more hot under the collar.

This was the second time today that I had been told I was out of my jurisdiction and I was getting tired of hearing it.

"Those that are better prepared to deal with it," he said, angrily.

"This has been going on for almost two years, at least. Are you waiting for the second coming of Christ for someone who is prepared to deal with it?" I asked him.

I had pissed him off and I could see it in his eyes.

"Marshal, you are in way over your head."

"I may be, but it's my job."

He sat staring at me for a few minutes. Then it hit me.

"You know who it is, don't you?" I asked.

"What makes you think that?" he asked gruffly.

"Your body language and your irritation."

"Marshal, you should let this one go," he said, softening a bit.

"I can't. This is the whole reason I was reassigned."

"Marshal, you cannot hope to bring this to a conclusion under the terms of Directive One."

"Let me worry about that."

"So you're just here to commit genocide?" he asked, spitting the question at me.

"What do you mean, genocide?" I asked, truly confused.

"You're here to eradicate anybody different than the norm. Why didn't you just start firing last night? Or why didn't you just wait and come back with an army next month?" he asked, openly disgusted with me.

"Why didn't you rip me to pieces last night?" I countered, rhetorically and angrily.

Even through our mutual distrust and anger, we both knew why the other one acted as they had.

"I am not here to do anything but catch the person or persons responsible for the murders that I am investigating. After last night I understand that the responsible party will probably never stand trial and that I need to be damn sure of my evidence before I play judge and jury."

"That may be what they told you. But the moment you have your evidence your supervisor will have an army out here combing the woods and taking out anything that moves," he said, pressing his point.

I began to laugh.

70

"You find this funny?" he asked, leaning towards me menacingly.

"I doubt very seriously that the President of the United States is going to do anything since he will not get any report until long after it is over. I answer to three people and all of them are in Washington City. For all intents and purposes I'm autonomous."

"That in itself is pretty fucking scary."

"And a rogue shape-shifter isn't?"

"Please if you are going to hunt us, then at least don't insult us by calling us that."

I had never stopped to think that anyone would find that insulting.

"Then what's your preference?" I asked.

"The term is wheir or wheirwolf," he spit at me.

"Then let me restate my question: A rogue wheirwolf isn't as scary as me being autonomous?"

"Maybe. What I can't understand is why one of your kind would be a hunter."

"My kind?" I asked, really confused.

"Yes, your kind," he answered condescendingly.

"Really, I don't know what you are talking about."

He looked hard at me. His nostrils flared and he cocked his head to one side like he had last night.

"You don't know, do you?" he asked, openly perplexed.

"No. I have no idea what you are talking about."

"You don't smell human."

"What do I smell like?" I asked, hoping he wouldn't say: "Someone that has not used deodorant".

"I'm not sure. I've never encountered anything like it. Very salty but earthy at the same time. But definitely not human."

"Look, I'm not special other than my tracking abilities and marksmanship."

He was looking at me in disbelief and I was trying my hardest to not let him see the indecision created by what he'd just told me.

"Be careful Marshal. There may be things in your life that come up and bite you in the ass," he said, genuinely warning me.

"I'll have to cross that bridge when I get to it. But for now I have a job to do and I'm intent on doing it," I said with all of the conviction I could muster.

"What do you really know about the wheir community?" he asked.

"To be honest, very little outside of folklore."

He snorted in disgust.

"Then why don't you educate me?" I asked in challenge.

"Why? So you can write it all down and pass it on to the people who will come after us?"

"Look, we are on the same side here. I just want to keep *everyone* safe. If that means taking out a killer, be it a regular human, shape-shi...Wheirwolf, or a fucking *fairy*, I will do it," I said.

"I've never heard of a fairy killing anyone."

"Don't tell me..."

"There are a lot of things out there," he said with a twisted smile.

"Great. Now I have visions of a howitzer-toting, three inch, winged psychopath." I laughed sadly.

"I doubt they could come close to lifting the howitzer, so you should be pretty safe," he said smiling.

"Sheriff, please tell me what you know," I halfway pleaded with him.

He stopped for a second and thought.

"I can't leave your hosts standing outside their own home while you and I argue," he said as he stood up.

"Then what's your suggestion?"

"Let me take you back to your vehicle. I will decide what I want to say on the way," he said as he went to the back door and opened it.

I had a twinge of distrust, but if anything happened to me there would probably be an exhaustive investigation in this area and I was pretty sure that Sheriff Benton wanted none of that.

"Fine," I answered.

"Willis?" he called out the door.

I didn't hear an answer but the Sheriff closed the door, came back to the table, and sat down. A few moments later Willis came through the same door.

"Yeah, Gary?" Willis asked.

"I am going to give the Marshal a ride back to her vehicle. I will see you and Greta later."

I stood up with Sheriff Benton, grabbing my pack as I rose.

"Thank you for your hospitality and please tell Greta thank you for the lemonade," I said to Willis.

Willis inclined his head in my direction.

"Shall we," the Sheriff said, gesturing in the direction of the front door.

I walked through the living room and out on the front porch with the Sheriff close on my heels. He ushered me to his patrol car, opened the front door, and let me sit down. He closed the door, went around and got in, started it and pointed it down the driveway. He asked for no directions as he pulled out onto a secondary road and gunned it. We both sat in silence as he sped down the two-lane. He took a few turns and I realized where we were as he turned on the path that led to the clearing where Bee was parked. He pulled up behind my camper and turned off his cruiser.

"You're not going to leave this alone are you?" he asked after we had sat there in silence for a few minutes.

"No. I'll be up here every month until the killing stops or I catch someone."

We sat through another silence. I decided I would take a less confrontational approach.

"Sheriff. I understand, now, that I was an unwanted guest in your home last night. I admit that you handled it a lot differently than I would have, had someone entered my home uninvited. May I invite you into my home and we try this again?" I asked, gesturing toward the camper through the windshield.

"Okay."

We both got out of his cruiser. I rummaged through my pocket, took out my keys, walked to the door, and unlocked it. I struggled up into the camper as he followed me in and closed the door.

"I can offer you coffee or water. I am afraid that's the choice of beverages here," I said as I opened the door.

"Coffee," he said.

I put a pot on to perk, grabbed my brush, and started working some of the knots and debris out of my hair.

"If you'd like to have a seat," I said, nodding towards one of the couches.

He took a seat as I sat down on the one opposite him.

"Marshal, as a professional courtesy, I will help you to a point."

"But?"

"But what?"

"There was a but at the end of that sentence."

"But if at any point in time I feel like you are lying to me or playing me for a fool, our conversation is over."

"I'll accept that."

"Why'd you pick this spot?" he asked.

"What?"

"Why did you pick this particular spot to come to?"

I got up and sat my brush down on the counter, got the topo map out of my pack and laid it out on the bed. He got up to come look at it.

"These five circles here are the human murders. These are the animal mutilations here." I started pointing at the map.

"If you leave out the human murders and just take the animal mutilations and draw connecting lines between all of them they all cross this fire road and most of them intersect right about here. The only reason I picked this particular clearing is that it was big enough for my camper," I explained.

"I think I'm going to kill him," he said under his breath.

"Who?"

"Don't worry about it. I can assure you it has nothing to do with the human murders. I can also assure you that the person responsible for the animal mutilations is not responsible for the human murders"

"Okay, fine but that is how I picked this area and this place."

"Natural investigator aren't you?"

73

"I don't know about that but I like puzzles and I'm very good at my job."

"What do you want to know?" he asked, sitting back down.

"First, who is the person I am looking for?" I asked as I poured two cups of coffee.

"I don't know."

I stood looking at him. He stared back.

"All I have is some sugar," I said, breaking eye contact.

"Black is fine."

"Was asking you who the suspect is a hard question?" I asked sarcastically, handing him a cup of coffee.

"I can't give you a name. The problem I have tracking this guy is that I don't think I've ever run into him in person."

"I am not sure I understand."

"I can tell you what he smells like. But I don't think that would do you any good. I've never, in the six years that I've been Sheriff, run into him in two legged form. And I've never seen him in his wheir form. I know that he's heavier than I am and I believe he's a turned wheir."

"I thought all wheirwolves were turned."

"No. Part of the folklore that is only partially right. There are biological wheirs and turned wheirs."

"I guess it kind of makes this hard in that there is only one chance a month to really catch this guy."

"Also a bit of a misnomer."

"How so?" I asked.

"The full moon is the time of the month that all wheirs *have* to turn. But as a wheir becomes older and more in control of themselves they can extend that," he answered.

I looked quizzically at him.

"It starts gradually. We learn that we can still change within a few nights of the full moon. Over the course of time we learn that we can affect the change more at will. Though, it will usually take an intense emotion to start it. The problem is that once the change is made we cannot change back as readily. Biological wheirs have a bit of a head start, especially if their parents have raised them right; they've been dealing with it from puberty." He said.

"So puberty is the start for biological wheirs?"

"Yes," he answered.

He sat contemplating his coffee cup. I watched him intently as he made some sort of decision.

"Which maulings are you looking at?" he asked.

I got up and went to the closet and pulled out the file I'd brought from home with everything listed and handed it to him. He flipped through the clippings and police reports, including the ones he had written.

"Smart tack, including reported animal mutilations in it. But this is not a complete list," he said.

"What do you mean?"

"I know of two other murders in the Kansas City outskirts and one just north of Springfield that were committed by the same man. There's also one between Joplin and Kansas City, but I don't know if he was involved. Why did you only include these five?"

"I tightened my search to this area, since north of Joplin is someone else's responsibility."

He looked hard at me.

"What do you mean 'someone else's responsibility'? How many Counter Section Agents do I have to contend with around here?"

"I never said I was Counter Section."

"You didn't have to. Are you working with the last one that was up here bothering me?"

"What other one?"

"About five or six months ago. Tall, military looking type. He said he was from somewhere in Arkansas or Louisiana. I think he said his name was James."

JTL was the initials of the agent I took over for, James could be the first initial.

"No I am not working with him."

"You still didn't answer my question."

"Which question?"

"How many Counter Section Agents do I have to deal with on this?"

"Counter Section is a myth. I am a U.S. Marshal."

"If that's the way it's going to be then I've given you all of the information I can," he said accusingly and stood.

I needed information and he had it. If I let him leave I would be butting my head against a wall for months, if not years, trying to close this case. He already knew I was Counter Section. What real harm would it do if I admitted to what he already knew as fact? He wasn't dumb by any stretch of the imagination. I took a deep breath and played a gut feeling.

"You're on the border of two Districts. The agent you met before was my predecessor. From Joplin down to the coast is my District and you have another one just north of you. You shouldn't have to deal with any other agent but me without my knowledge." I answered his original question looking straight at him.

He had a shocked look on his face as he sat back down.

"Are all of you U.S. Marshals?"

"Honestly, I have no clue. There are a number of us out here working under the same rules and looking for the same things. We all have an area we are responsible for. Though we are free to move about the country, as our cases dictate, we are based in a smaller area. All I have are initials and phone numbers.

It has to do with protecting each of us from reprisals. I understand it but it makes the job that much harder."

"How long have you been doing this?"

"I've been a Marshal for almost six years now. I have had this assignment for all of about a week."

"You told Willis that he and Greta had been with me, here last night. Was that just an educated bluff or did you know?"

"I knew," I answered honestly.

"How?"

Seeing an aura was not something I was ready to admit to people I knew, much less someone I had just met.

"Your eyes," I answered, with a half-truth.

"Our eyes?"

"Yes. I got a good look at yours and Greta's last night. This morning I followed two sets of tracks from here to a small glade just south of Willis and Greta's house. Tracking them back to their house was time consuming and a pain, but it wasn't really hard. When I saw her eyes I knew she was the smaller blonde wolf with blue eyes I'd seen last night. Just by association and hair color I connected Willis. Who was the first person he called? You. Before you got there I thought he'd just called the local law on me, but when I saw your eyes I had you. I couldn't forget those green eyes, they're a dead giveaway," I said, smiling.

He actually blushed. I was surprised at that.

"The only ones who are halfway safe are the other two that were with you and stood guard outside of my camper last night. But give me a couple of days up here and I'll bet you I can find them. Why is it Greta and Willis didn't know me on sight?"

"There's a bit of difference in how we perceive the world as human and wolf. There are certain senses we rely on in either state and there is some cross over. As a human, we rely on the senses all humans rely on, especially our brains, but being wheir our sense of smell and hearing are extremely heightened over that of a normal human. As a wolf, we're still able to rationalize and problem solve, but our sense of smell and hearing become our most potent senses and our vision becomes secondary. Wolf priorities are much different than human. As a wolf, our bodily needs become so powerful we have a hard time holding on to human boundaries," he answered.

"You said that there were murders north of here. Did you track him there?"

"No. Outside of my territory. Most packs don't take lightly to invasion of their territory, even if it is to hunt a rogue."

"So it's true that wheirs travel in packs?"

"For the most part, yes. Though there are solitary wheirs, most prefer the safety and hierarchy of a pack. But you need to realize that as unique and varied as the human race is, so are wheirs. As a going concern wheirs prefer to be left alone and will not initiate contact with anyone but their own kind. The trouble happens when someone refuses to leave them alone," he said, stressing the end of his sentence and staring at me.

"You can trust me or not, that's your choice. My only goal is to stop the murders. I don't want to disrupt your pack, or any others' for that matter, I just want to close this case and move on to the next."

"And how do you plan to do that?"

"Unless they are an innocent bystander, all victims of a serial killer will share some trait that makes them a target. I will have to study the files I already have and the new ones you mentioned and see if I can figure out what that trait is. Once I have it I will know what he is looking for, give it to him, and catch him. I have a month."

"One thing you might want to know then is that his hunting has changed. He is learning that he can change at times other than the full moon. The reports you have only list a date that it was reported or a time of death declared by a coroner. Not when it might have really happened. So are you going to just park out in the woods and wait, hoping you are in the right area?"

"If that's what it takes," I said defiantly.

"Foolish waste of time."

"Maybe. But do you have a better idea?"

"Go home. Start another case and let me handle this."

"We both know, as officers of the law, I can't do that."

"It was worth a shot. Marshal, you are going to get yourself killed. I personally think it would be a shame since you are so young and seem to have a gift for putting a case together."

"Then help me," I said staring at him.

"How am I supposed to do that? The only way I can track him down is as a wheir and you would be unable to keep up."

"You already have a plan, don't you?"

It took him a beat to answer.

"What do you know about the dead women you already have files on?"

"That all of them had their throats ripped out perimortem. All of them were naked when they were killed, all of them were in good shape if you look at the ratio of weight to height and measurements, and the two I have autopsy photos of look like they worked out a lot more than a regular person. They had abs from hell just... like... Greta." I finished the sentence, making the leap for myself.

"You mean they were all wheirs?"

"Yes. They weren't naked when they were killed; they were just not wearing clothes"

He stood there weighing something.

"What is it?" I asked.

"Though your research was pretty good. Your assumption was wrong as to location. His center of operations is more north of here. If he's a solitary, as I believe he is, one of his driving forces will be sexual. In the wheir community the possibility of a female wheir being born is about one in five so most females are turned and members of the pack that turned them. As a solitary wheir there's a good possibility he doesn't have access to that...ah... release. The murdered females fought to the death to keep him away," he started.

"Greta is the bait," I said more to myself, skipping ahead of his thought process and interrupting him.

He didn't say anything but I knew by the look on his face I had nailed it.

"So you're going to dangle Greta out there. That is your plan isn't it?" I asked, pushing him.

"He switches areas about every three to four months to keep both the human and wheir community guessing. He hasn't been around here for about two months and I believe he'll be back, probably next month since he wasn't here last night or before. We have a plan for the next month. If it does not pan out then we'll keep trying. We'll let Greta go out a bit on her own and lead him back to a spot that we've picked so we can take care of the matter."

"Take me along."

"I can't do that."

"Why not?"

"Two reasons. First, my pack comes first and if it's a choice between them or you, they come first. Second, I don't want you to get trigger happy. Silver is a horrible way to die and I don't want any of my pack to have to endure that," he said, leveling his eyes at me.

"I have better reactions and recognition than that and as far as my safety is concerned I understood the dangers of my job when I signed up to be a Marshal."

"Still..." he started.

"You already told me what my mistake was, do you think I won't get closer, just in the limited time I have between now and next month, especially knowing what you plan to do?" I asked, pushing.

"You know you're a pain in the butt?"

"You have no idea," I said being serious.

He stood thinking for a moment.

"You'll be up here following everyone around for the next month if I don't acquiesce to this, won't you?" he asked.

"I'll be on all of you daily."

"You stick to my plan and stay out of the way."

"I'll stick to the plan but if I get a clean shot I'm taking him down."

"You hurt one of my pack and no one will find your body."

He was being dead serious and it was my death he was being serious about. I swallowed hard and nodded my head.

"He's learned to change ahead of the moon by a few days. It may take us two or three nights, if at all, next month. The full moon next month is the eighth, which is a Monday. Be here Friday the fifth and I will lay out everything for you."

"Okay, I will be back by the fifth of next month. Is there a hotel around here I can stay at?"

"Don't worry about that we will put you up at Greta and Willis'."

"Maybe they would prefer not to have a house guest."

"Not their decision."

I looked at him and understood; it wasn't their decision. *Careful, Ced, you're playing with fire where this Sheriff is concerned.*

"So, now can I get you to go home and rethink your decision?"

"I'll go home but I won't change my mind."

"Your neck," he said, standing up and handing me his coffee cup.

"That it is," I said, smiling and taking the mug.

"I assume you have my number, Marshal?"

"Yes, but can I ask a favor?"

"What now?" he asked, exasperated.

"This Marshal, Sheriff shit is starting to wear on my nerves. My name is Cedwynne or I prefer Ced," I said, offering my hand.

"Gary," he said, taking my hand and shaking it.

"You know how to get out of here, Ced?"

"Yes. I'm pretty good with directions."

"Well, I have a job that I need to get back to. Call me next month before you come up. I'll meet you at my office and we'll take it from there."

"I will. It was good to meet you Gary," I said as he opened the door and stepped out into the afternoon sun.

"You might not think that after next month," he said as he started for his cruiser.

I watched his strong back as he walked away and got in his car. He gave me a polite wave, started the engine, backed around and headed out. I closed the door, locked it, rinsed out the cups and coffee pot, stowed everything, and took my spot behind the wheel of Bee.

****

It had been a long drive and I was tired, sore, and relieved that the trip was about over as I approached the turn to the road that led to my house. I had driven a few hundred feet down the road when I noticed a man walking towards me on the opposite side of the street. It took me a minute to realize I knew him. It was Bran. I was surprised to find him on my road. I slowed to a stop and rolled down my window. He looked up and recognized me.

"What are you doing out this way?" I asked.

"Looking for you."

"Well, you found me."

"I left my book in your car the other night, wanted to get it back. I would like to finish it."

"How did you know where to find me?"

"I have a friend at the city utility. Not hard to find an address if you have a name."

"Have you ever thought about being a cop?" I asked, laughing.

"Not in the least."

"Hop in. I'll take you back to the house and give you your book."

I popped the lock on the passenger side of the cab as he walked around. He got in and looked at my scratches, and rumpled, dirty clothes.

"Run into some trouble?" he asked.

"Took a bit of a tumble but I'm fine."

He cocked an eyebrow. I put Bee in gear and headed to my house. I had failed to notice that he was wearing a jacket. I had a full complement of them for different seasons to cover the weapon I carried. I thought it strange he would be wearing one with the weather having turned quite warm lately.

"Are you carrying a weapon on you?" I asked as I pulled up to my mailbox and stopped.

He looked at me for a second.

"I am carrying a pretty good sized pocket knife that could be considered a weapon and a farm implement that I guess could be used as one if a person were versed in Kama. But then, almost anything can be used as a weapon if you think about it," he said.

I was intrigued, to some extent, having studied archaic weapons during my training.

"Then I guess a good follow up question is: Are *you* versed in Kama?" I asked.

"Only what I've read."

If someone can concentrate enough in a loud rough bar to read, then he had probably read a lot about it. I reached down to open the mailbox. It was empty so I closed it, then drove up my drive and pulled up to the outside of the carport. I noticed the grass was getting high and there was a stack of newspapers on my porch. I didn't understand the newspapers since I hadn't subscribed to any of them. I shut off the engine and opened the door.

"Locked or unlocked?" he asked as he opened his.

"Locked," I answered as I jumped down from the cab.

I walked over to the little car in the carport, unlocked the door, and opened it. Sure enough, a book was tucked down between the passenger seat and the center console.

"Right there," I said as I stood back to let him get it.

He walked over, reached in, and pulled it out.

"Thanks," he said.

"You're welcome. I am sorry you had to wait so long to get it back."

"Not to worry, I have other books."

"Looks like you have a lot of yard work to get to," he said, indicating the overgrown mess of the front lawn.

I looked around the yard. The grass would need cutting in short order and there seemed to be a lot of limbs and natural debris that needed picked up. The moment I'd gotten out of foster services, I moved to the nearest city, got a job and rented an apartment. I had lived in apartments ever since. I hadn't touched a yard implement in years.

"You wouldn't happen to know anybody around here that might be interested in making a few credits or bucks on the side?" I asked.

"I do some handyman work if you would be interested?"

"What do you charge?"

He looked around the yard.

"Fifty bucks a month to keep the lawn mowed and fed, the flowerbeds in good order, trim the hedges, and deal with the yard waste. Raking the leaves in the fall, and any other handiwork you might need would be per job," he said.

I snuck a look at his aura. It was the same one I had seen the night I had met him. There were absolutely no tinges of red or black. He was at least a decent conversationalist and I liked him for some reason, so what the hell.

"Deal," I said, holding out my hand to seal the deal.

He took it, shook, and smiled.

"I can get back out here on Tuesday afternoon," he said.

"Works for me."

"Do you have a mower and yard implements?" he asked.

"Don't know. I got this place furnished and sight unseen. You could look in the barn, I haven't even been out there yet.

"I will bring mine Tuesday, just in case."

"Okay."

"Did you have a productive trip?"

I thought it odd he phrased the question that way.

"Yes. Very productive," I answered as I closed and locked the door on the car.

"Well, I need to be heading. Is there anything you need help getting in the house before I leave?"

"No, but thanks. I didn't pack a suitcase. Besides I am ready to take a nap after my trip. The few items I need to get out of the camper can wait until tomorrow morning."

"Okay then. You have a nice day," he said, inclining his head and started walking down the drive.

"Bran?" I called after him.

He turned around expectantly.

"Can I give you a lift somewhere?"

"No thanks, besides I would just leave my book in your car again and have to walk all the way back out here to get it. Better safe than sorry. Besides, I like to walk," he said as he shot me a wave and walked on down the drive.

I shook my head and smiled, waving back. I walked to the front door, unlocked it, then stuck my identification in the slot and opened the door. I pushed the piles of papers through with my foot, kicking the straggler hard enough to end up almost in the kitchen. I entered and closed the door behind me, locking it. It was hot, muggy, and stale in the house. I found the thermostat and kicked the air conditioner on. I went to the fridge, got a beer, and sat on the couch. I felt different inside than when I left. I wasn't sure what it was, maybe a little older and wiser. I opened the beer and took a sip as the air conditioner started moving the air and I could feel the first wisps of cool. By the time I'd finished my beer the house was finally feeling cool. I decided that the nap I had mentioned earlier was definitely in order. I went to my bedroom, kicked off my shoes and took the much needed shower. I lay down and was out before my head hit the pillow.

Chapter 7
Monday April 10, 2248

The sunlight streaming through my bedroom window woke me. It took me a second to realize that, without meaning to, I had slept through the night. My stomach also informed me that I hadn't anything to eat, except for the beer when I got home, since the burger around three yesterday afternoon. I crawled out of bed, dressed, and went to the kitchen to feed my stomach and my caffeine addiction. I picked up the paper that I had kicked into the hall yesterday, and sat it on the counter as I fixed a pot of coffee. I started scrambling eggs and frying some sausage, and my eyes were drawn to the pile of rolled newspapers littering the entryway in front of the door. I had not subscribed to any of them, so why were they here? I dished up my breakfast, poured a cup of coffee, grabbed the newspaper from the counter, and sat down at the table. I opened the paper and noticed that it was from Gulf Port Mississippi. I got up and went to the door, collected a couple more of the rolled logs, and brought them back to the kitchen. Every one of them was from someplace different, ranging from Missouri to Louisiana. It finally made sense. All of the files I'd read had a large number of newspaper clippings along with police reports and printed materials from Newsnet. This was where I was supposed to get my leads; the papers. I spread the first one out and began to peruse it. After the third paper and second cup of coffee, I realized that I did not need to read every word in every section. I could hold my scanning to the news section and maybe the front page and local op-ed sections if it was a city or county paper. I'd gotten through all of the papers that I brought into the kitchen, though a pile still resided in front of the door. They would just have to wait for a while.

I refilled my cup, started another pot, and walked over to the small window that looked out on the back yard. The weekend had been a very scary, long and learning experience. I had a lot of my preconceived notions about life, and even myself, shattered. I had also come close to having my sanity shattered in the process. Was this a job that I thought I could do? That was the final question, wasn't it: could I accept what I had seen? I guess I would have to since I'd sat down and talked with three wheirwolves. Could I survive this or did I need to call Burdock and tell him I was coming back? In these thoughts, something Sheriff Benton had said to me kept hammering at my brain: *You don't smell human. I'm not sure. I've never encountered anything like it. Very salty but earthy at the same time. But definitely not human.* Now what the fuck was I supposed to do with that? I had never considered myself different, other than the G-3 anomaly. Yes, I was stronger than most women my size, hell I was stronger than most women period, and a lot of men. I always had exceptional endurance but I figured that was just from being in good shape. *So Ced, what are you going to do?*

The Water's Edge

If I went back to Dallas I knew I could have my old job, old partner and old life, probably including my old apartment. But if I went back I would have things nagging at me for the rest of my life. Could I live with myself knowing I had been too scared or lazy to face what was out there and what was in me? If I stayed, and lived... Now there was the caveat. If it hadn't been for the wheirwolves I'd met up with last weekend *not* killing me, I wouldn't be asking myself that question now. What would've happened if I'd come up against the one I was looking for to begin with? I would've been totally unprepared to react in time to save my life. Did the government not realize how stupid this was? Giving us no real training on what to expect. No wonder the life expectancy of a Counter Section agent was short.

I knew I could do this all day. It was a never ending loop of what was bad about everything and the self-doubt that accompanied it. If Sheriff Benton was not lying about my not being human, would I ever be able to find out anything about myself if I wasn't in this job? The answer to that one was fairly simple: probably not. Did I really want to know? Deep down the answer was yes. What everything boiled down to was this: *yes, the horror movies were right- deal with it, Ced.* Yes, there was a good chance I would not live to see the retirement account that was waiting for me. But was that really any different than my old assignment, other than having a large retirement account to look forward to? Not really. Yes, I was alone out here and needed to use my strengths better. No, I wasn't going back.

I raised my coffee cup to the view of the back yard through the window. To all of the wheirwolves, vampires, witches, and howitzer toting fairies out there: I'm not going anywhere, so deal with it. I took a drink to seal my singular toast.

So now that I'd made my decision to stay and tough this out, what was the first order of business? I thought about the supernatural population and thought of Bran. He would be working around here on a regular basis. Though my gut had not warned me about him and his aura had not raised a red flag, I still needed to check out his background. I refilled my coffee and headed down to my office.

I fired up the computer and waited. After all of the log-on procedures, I pulled up a general police nationwide search. I typed in "Bran Murray" and waited. It took a few seconds. There were one hundred and three. I guessed him to be around eighty to a hundred so I eliminated all of them under the age of fifty, which left me about forty. I narrowed my search to Hot Springs and, sure enough, it left me one. I opened up the file. He had no criminal record and the only reason he had a file at all was that he had worked off and on for the park service as a landscaper. He currently held a valid Tennessee driver's license and was now listed as working for the park service around Hot Springs. I looked at the birth date and it read c. 2160. We came across this a lot in our searches. A lot of people who were born before the U.S. was put back together again were born at home and, unless there was a family bible or a relative that kept detailed records of the family, there was usually not a record of a birth. That would put him somewhere between eighty and ninety. From his employment records he had worked throughout the south over the past forty years. He never seemed to spend more than two or three years in one spot before he would show up somewhere else. There seemed to be a gap in time between 2220 and 2229. I assumed he had been working in the private sector and there would be no record of that. I jumped over to the government files and pulled up his record of service with the parks. Though he did not stay more than a couple of years at a place, every former supervisor had given him glowing recommendations for his next position. Almost every one of them finished up by saying they'd been sad to see him go. I found out his present position was as part-time head grounds keeper at one of the local parks. I also searched the U.S. Marshal and IBI Databases, but I found nothing else. Well that wipes out one personal worry. He may be a supernatural of some sort, but my gift and my gut had been pretty much on target.

While I had my computer up I redid the search on maulings in lower Missouri, widening my search to include Kansas City and below. I found the other cases that Sheriff Benton had told me about. I printed off the documents I needed, filed the electronic ones in the case folder I had started, and closed down the computer. So what now? What did agents do in their down time? I pulled out a piece of paper and started writing a to-do list. I hadn't checked in with the local police yet, so I put that at the top of my list. After a few minutes I had a fairly lengthy list that would take me a couple of days to accomplish. I looked at my watch; it was just about eight thirty. I picked up my empty coffee cup and headed upstairs. I unloaded Bee and put things away, adding the things I had printed off this morning to the existing file I had gotten out of Bee, which I left on my desk. I even washed the dishes and it wasn't even Wednesday. I guessed that I would have more time in my day to keep up with such things than I used to. I freshened up, grabbed some of the unread newspapers, and drove towards town.

In the short time that I've been here, the amount of people and traffic in this small town still amazed me. I knew that the actual population for Hot Springs was right around forty thousand but with the horse track, historic downtown, hot springs baths, the three lakes in the region, and the parks to go along with them, it was a tourists' mecca. After I had checked in at the police station and introduced myself I decided to drive around the town and learn it. After an hour of getting a feel for the place, I went to the downtown strip to find someplace for lunch. I parked the car, retrieved the newspapers from the small back seat, and went in search of food. I found an interesting little coffee shop on one of the side streets. It had food and coffee; two of my favorites things. I entered, ordered, and found a nice place in the back to spread out. My order finally came and the young man was paying so much attention to my chest he almost spilled my coffee on me.

The Water's Edge

I was blissfully reading my paper, which had nothing in it that would interest me on a professional level, and nibbling on my sandwich when I was interrupted by a voice from above me.

"Cedwynne?"

"Bran? What are you doing here?" I asked, looking up.

"Lunch break. I come here to read and eat."

"Well, you are welcome to join me if you don't mind my company," I said, pointing to the chair across from me.

"Don't mind if I do," he said as he took the old, large canvas bag off his shoulder and placed it in the chair.

"I will be back in a sec," he said and walked to the counter to order.

He was back in a few moments, picked up his bag, and sat down.

"By the way, I meant to give this to you yesterday but forgot," he said as he rummaged around in his bag.

He pulled out a brown bottle that was square, the size of about two of my fists and was sealed with a cork stopper. He handed it to me.

"A gift. There should be enough for the next three months. Use about a tablespoon per dose," he said.

"Thanks. It really worked. I was wondering if I'd be able to talk you out of some more."

"Consider me your personal dealer," he said, smiling.

I placed the bottle on the table. His order came and we started talking. The thing that I liked about him was that he was easy to talk to, a good conversationalist, and by the end of the time you were with him you had had a good time and not been too personal on either side. All of a sudden we had finished an hour, our sandwiches, our drinks, and he was standing up to head back to work.

"It is always a pleasure, Cedwynne," he said, giving me a small bow.

"Please, my friends call me Ced," I said, holding out my hand.

He took my small, soft hand in his large, calloused one.

"I am honored to be considered among your friends, Ced," he said, smiling.

"I will see you tomorrow at the house." I smiled back.

"Tomorrow afternoon," he corrected me politely, slipped his bag back on his shoulder, and walked out into the growing heat of the day.

I watched him leave the shop and head off down the street. He had to be one of the most unusual and interesting people I had ever met. I would love to know his history. When I was doing background on him, I found nothing that would indicate he had ever been to school, much less college, but he seemed to be quite intelligent and extremely well read.

Chapter 8
Tuesday April 11, 2248

Tuesday morning began almost the same as Monday; I slept until the sun woke me, I got up, putting on my robe and pink fuzzy slippers found the kitchen, got a coffee, and began my day reading the paper looking for leads. I was really getting used to this schedule very quickly. It beat the hell out of having to dress and be at an office by a particular time.

I spent the morning drinking coffee and pouring over the never ending line of newspapers that seemed to show up on my doorstep every day. Shortly before lunch, I found the motivation to actually get dressed. After a quick meal, I went back to the papers; I was determined to get through all of papers in the house so I could just be responsible for those that came every morning. I found a few articles that I cut out and put in folders I'd started for possible cases. I was interrupted from my reading by the doorbell. It startled me since I didn't know I even had one. I opened the door to Bran standing there.

"Hey. Is it afternoon already?"

"Yes it is," he said, smiling.

"Would you like something to drink before you start?"

"That would be great."

"Not to be rude, but I need to put some things up right quick. Could you stay here for a minute?"

"Sure. I am glued to this spot."

I hurried back in the kitchen, stacked the read papers neatly on the end of the table, put the clippings laying about back into their folders, and stuck them in a drawer. I went back to the door and invited Bran in. He followed me to the kitchen.

"Have a seat. Juice, coffee and water are about all I have to offer," I said.

"Coffee is fine, black."

I pulled down another mug, filled it, topped mine off, and took both back to the table. I handed Bran his mug and sat down across from him. He took a sip then looked at my mug and smiled.

"What?" I asked.

"Your mug seems to be a bit out of character for you."

"How so?"

"Not to be rude but the clothes you wear are very utilitarian, the personal items that I noticed in the living room show no real flair for the feminine, you dress to downplay your female features, and you are in a vocation that is dominated by men. The only thing that would speak to femininity would be your walk and your bust, but you can really do nothing about those since that is just the way you are built. The mug you handed me is basic white and belongs to a set of dishes that was purchased strictly for their functionality. But in all of this neutrality and utilitarianism, you have this coffee cup that would be delicate in any feminine hand that held it. I will even bet that it is the one you use every day," Bran said.

I looked at him for a moment.

"Your powers of observation are exceptional. Are you sure you're not a cop?" I asked.

He shook his head and smiled.

"This cup was a gift from my first partner. He thought I needed some color and female touches to my life," I explained, starting to have a warm feeling about Grant.

"What happened to him?"

"I had a protection detail that I had to be on. The woman the Marshal Service was protecting insisted a female Marshal be in the apartment with her. Being the only female in our district not in the middle of a pressing case, I was elected. My partner, Grant, got a tip on a case we were watching and decided not to wait for me to finish up the assignment. Thinking he had enough to make an arrest, he went in with no backup and got shot. I wasn't there to cover his ass," I said sadly.

"There are things we can affect and things we can't. You cannot be responsible for others decisions," Bran said.

"Thanks, Buddha."

"What happened to the guy that killed your partner?"

"That was the first suspect I ever killed in the line of duty," I answered, looking into the black liquid in my cup.

"Was it justified?"

"The first bullet was, but the rest of the clip was pure revenge. If I would have stopped after the first round, the suspect would have stood trial. But that's not how my supervisor wrote up the shooting."

Bran cocked an eyebrow at me.

"Though my supervisor wrote it up as justifiable, he assigned me to a desk for eight months and made me go to therapy that whole time," I said.

"Loyalty is an interesting trait in people," he said, more to himself than me.

"Are you expecting an attack?" he asked, changing the subject.

"Not that I know of. Why?"

"Well, the outside walls on this place are a good eighteen inches thick. You have steel reinforced doors, windows that are small with safety wire embedded in glass that is a good three to four inches thick."

"Like I said. I took the house sight unseen."

Bran smiled like he knew something.

"Okay, enough of me being on the hot seat. How old are you?" I asked.

"Hmm. How to answer that?"

"How about your real age?" I asked.

The Water's Edge

"Well, if you are one to believe in past lives, then that number could increase substantially into the hundreds or thousands. If you are one to believe in the existence of a soul, then it could be anywhere from double digits to millions of years. If we take the date on my drivers license, which was a best guess estimate, I am eighty eight which would be, ah, six hundred and sixteen in dog years," he said, smiling.

I laid my forehead down on the table.

"Can you ever give a short and succinct answer?" I asked from the fake wood of the table.

"The right answer to a question could be different from situation to situation. Ced, a better question to ask someone would be: How old do you feel today?"

"Fine. How old do you feel today?" I asked with my head still down.

"Today I am feeling like I am about twenty. How about you?"

"One million."

"Nice round number. I guess in a cosmic setting that would be relatively young," he said and I could hear the laughter in his voice.

"Don't you have a lawn to mow?"

"I have many."

I sat back up and looked at him.

"There is no winning with you," I said, exasperated.

"Is there really a winner or a loser? I have found there is only knowledge."

"I'm going to regret this. What do you mean by that?"

"At some point in time our bodies will die. So in that aspect we all lose. It is what we learn on the way that marks our accomplishments," he answered, finished his coffee, and stood up.

"Ced, it is the things that we think we know that will kill us, not the things we do or don't know," he said as he walked towards the door.

I got up and followed him. He smiled at me and opened the door. I watched him walk out to his old, beat up pickup. He opened the camper shell on the back and started to unload equipment. I closed the door and went back to my newspapers.

****

Eventually I grew tired of research, made a couple of glasses of ice water, and went out on the front porch. I watched Bran working in the yard. He had taken off his jacket and shirt and was down to his tee shirt. He was in incredible shape for his age. Though he had a small midlife paunch, his arms and chest were well defined. He cut the grass with one of the very old style push mowers that had a series of blades on a cylinder that rotated when pushed and cut as it turned. I noticed an old, beat up, semi-circular scabbard that hung from the middle of his back with a hilt coming out of it. It looked like a sickle. It must

89

have been the farm implement that he had referred to when I picked him up on Sunday. I walked across the large yard to where he was working.

"Thought you could use some water," I said as I approached.

"Thank you." He stopped pushing the mower and took the offered glass.

"I'm not much of a cook but if you would like, you can join me this evening."

"Will the offer be good on another day?"

"Sure. Why?"

"Tonight is music night."

"Music night?"

"I get together with a few people every week and we play music for the evening. So I have a prior commitment."

"You play an instrument?"

"I play mandolin and guitar."

"Interesting."

"We all have talents," he said, grinning.

"Mine seems to be killing people."

"Don't sell yourself short. You have a lot of life ahead of you to find yours."

"We'll just have to see."

"Yes, we will," he replied with an odd look in his eyes.

"If you need more water, just hit the doorbell," I said and turned to go back in the house.

As I was walking back to the porch I heard the mower start again. There was something soothing about the rhythmic clicking and swooshing sound it made.

****

I had just opened a can of soup for dinner when the doorbell rang. I walked over and opened it.

"I am leaving for the day. I will be back on Friday to do some maintenance," Bran said.

I pulled a fifty out of my pocket and handed it to him.

"I have not completed my month."

"I am a pretty good judge of character. I believe you'll honor your word and handshake, so I have no problem with paying my debts early," I said.

He took the bill, put it in his pocket, tipped his non-existent hat, and walked towards his truck. I stood by my first assessment of him: he had to be one of the most interesting and unusual people I'd ever met. I closed the door and went back to the dinner I was warming on the stove.

Chapter 9
Friday May 5, 2248

I spent most of the morning packing Bee with everything I thought I would need for the next few days. I was becoming a little apprehensive about the upcoming weekend. Would I really be able to handle this? I needed to; that was the only answer I could give myself.

I had just locked the door and stood on the front porch looking out over the well cared for front yard. Bran had been amazing with how he kept it. The lawn almost made the house look shabby since it would be something one would expect to see in front of something a bit more upscale.

The things that I had learned about Bran this past month had also surprised me. Though I knew he could sit still for hours reading in the middle of a war zone, he had a hard time not working on something. I also learned that he wasn't a vegetarian like I had thought after our first meal together. The first week he had worked on the yard he found a pile of old bricks that had been left after the building of the house. As opposed to stacking them somewhere, or giving them to someone who might need them, he decided that a brick grill on the small back patio was in order. He came back during the weekend and had one built in less than an afternoon. I tried to pay him for his time but he flatly refused, though he accepted a steak or grilled burger dinner every Friday evening after he did the maintenance on the lawn for the week. It actually became something of a habit for us. Every Friday he would get off of his normal job, come over to water and feed the grass. Then we would grill something and sit out in the back yard, eat, drink a beer or two, and talk until he needed to head back to where he was staying. I was beginning to really like him. He was starting to become a friend that I could talk to.

I walked over and climbed up into Bee, started the engine, and headed out towards Missouri. I had been quite productive over the past four weeks. I had checked in with the local police and county sheriff. I had even taken a day to go to Little Rock and check in with the Marshal over Arkansas and the state police. I'd gotten in the habit of running every morning for a few miles, going through my martial arts forms, and reading through all of the papers on my doorstep by lunch. The afternoons I spent adding to or studying the four possible cases I had started on my own. But the thing that I was finding I liked the most about my job now was that I was not shaken out of bed by an alarm clock, and I could work all day in my robe and slippers if I wanted to. In just a little over a month I'd made a life for myself and if I answered the psychiatrist's question now I would have to say that I was becoming happy with where I was.

I called Sheriff Benton when I was about an hour away, he told me to meet him at his office, which was at the courthouse in Cassville. I finally made it to the downtown square, found a place to park, walked across to the courthouse and up the front stairs. I followed the signs in the main hall back to his office. I asked for him at the counter and waited until he emerged from the door in back. He took a few seconds to leave some instructions to the deputy on duty, then walked through the old style half glass door at the end of the counter.

"Marshal," he said in a not so happy greeting.

"Sheriff."

"Are you sure you won't go home?"

"No," I answered succinctly.

"Then follow me," he sighed as he went to the door and held it open for me.

I followed him through the halls to the front door and down the steps where we split and went to our separate vehicles. I backed out of my space and waited for him to pull up beside me. He pointed in a direction, I nodded, and he took off with me following. He turned off of the main two lane highway, took a few back roads until he was turning into the drive for the house I remembered. I was shocked at the number of cars parked around the front yard; Bran would kill me if I had people park on the lawn. I waited until Sheriff Benton had parked and gotten out of his cruiser. He pointed me to a spot towards the end of the Willis' house. He met me at my door as I jumped down out of the cab.

"Do you have luggage?" he asked.

"A suitcase in the back," I answered as I headed towards the back door of Bee.

I opened up the door and pulled the suitcase out. He immediately took it from me.

"Does Willis run a used car business?" I asked, pointing at the full front yard.

"No. Just a little get-together," he said as he led me up onto the porch.

He knocked and we waited. Willis opened the door. He looked at me and then looked questioningly at Sheriff Benton.

"Can we come in?" the Sheriff asked.

Willis moved back, opening the door so the two of us could enter. We went inside where Willis gestured to the couch and I sat down.

"Where is Greta?" Sheriff Benton asked.

"Out back. I will get her," Willis answered.

Willis went through the kitchen and out the back door. We waited a few minutes before the two of them entered the living room. Greta gave me an evil look as she sat down. I could tell by the look in both Willis and Greta's eyes that they were a long way from being sold on this idea or me.

"Greta, Willis, you remember Marshal McKenzie," Sheriff Benton started.

I got a stiffly polite nod from both of them.

"As far as the rest of the pack is concerned she is my guest up here for the weekend. She and I would both prefer that you introduce her as Cedwynne, not as Marshal McKenzie. Marshal, for the next few days do not brush your teeth with toothpaste, wash with soaps that have any scent to them, and do not use deodorant. Give Greta all of the clothes you will be wearing out for the next couple of days so she can wash them and get any artificial scents out of them. I expect Miss McKenzie to be treated well and with a modicum of respect. If anyone asks this evening, she is my date and nothing more needs to be said," he finished.

I knew his short monologue was a mandate, not a request.

"Greta, if you will show Cedwynne where she will be staying for the next few days, I would appreciate it. I am going to run back to the house, change, and get my jeep. I will be back in a few minutes," he said as he turned and went towards the door.

"Gary, are you sure about this?" Willis asked, as he walked the Sheriff to the door.

"No, but if she gets the shot fine. If she gets in the way, it's her hide," the Sheriff said as he turned and walked out the door.

Willis shut the door and turned to look at me.

"Marshal, if any one of us gets harmed by your actions..." he started.

"I know, no one will find the body," I finished for him.

"Greta. Would you show our guest where she will be staying and can freshen up," he said, getting up and walking out the door.

"This way," Greta said as she moved to the hall.

I picked up my suitcase, followed her to a door across from the bathroom I had used before. She opened the door and led me into the bedroom.

"This will be your room for the next couple of days. The bathroom across the hall will be yours. I will put out towels and soap for you to use. If you will give me your clothes tomorrow morning, I will make sure they get rinsed out. Once you freshen up everyone will be in the back yard," she said and started to leave.

"Greta?" I asked.

"Yes?" she said stopping in the doorway.

"Thank you for the place to stay."

She nodded, turned, left the room, and closed the door without saying another word. Great, pissing off your host was not good manners in any society. I wish Sheriff Benton would have just let me stay at a local hotel. I flipped my suitcase on the bed and opened it. I pulled out the clothes I had brought to go out in and laid them out on the bed with my underwear. I grabbed my hairbrush and walked across to the bathroom to freshen up. After putting my hair in order I went back to the bedroom, flipped it in the suitcase, and sat down on the bed. I could hear the voices from the back yard as I sat there. Did I really want to be a part of this party? Not really. I reached into my suitcase, pulled out the novel I had been reading, and laid back on the pillows. Maybe I should just read until I fell asleep. I flipped to the bookmark and began reading. I had probably been reading for about an hour when there was a knock at my door.

"Just a minute," I called out as I put the mark back in, sat the book on the bedside table, and went to open the door.

I opened the door to Sheriff Benton in a fairly tight tee shirt and jeans-God, he was gorgeous.

"Yes?" I asked, openly blushing.

"Are you not going to eat with us?"

"I thought it would be better all the way around if I holed up in here for the evening."

"Nonsense. You are our guest. We may have a different way of doing things than you are used to but we are a hospitable pack. Just think of me as your date for the evening that you do not have to give a good night kiss to," he said, holding out his hand.

"But..,"

"I insist," he said, leaning towards me to have his palm closer.

If he keeps this up he just might get a good night kiss. Down girl. I took his hand and he smiled at me.

"Not so bad?" he asked.

"Sheriff, really. You don't have to make me feel welcome."

"First off, I am off duty so the name is Gary. Tonight is a normal get-together of the pack. It's nothing official and you need to eat so come on," he said, wrapping his large hand around mine and gently pulling me out into the hall.

"A bit of warning though," he said as I closed the door.

"What?"

"Stay relatively close to me tonight. The unattached males would love to move in on you, which unfortunately is most of the pack," he said, chuckling.

"Got it. Stay close. That should be easy enough," I answered as he led me down the hall, through the kitchen and out onto the back porch.

Counting myself, there were twenty-two people in the large back yard; sixteen men and six women.

"Beer?" Greta asked as Gary and I stepped off of the porch.

"Yes, thanks," I answered.

Greta reached into a cooler she was standing by, pulled two bottles out, opened them and handed them to Gary and I. Gary started introducing me around. It took a good three or four introductions before I got used to all of the sniffing and cocked heads as the pack met me. I had always considered it a bit of an invasion of privacy to look at people with my sight. But since those around me felt the need to meet me by sniffing me, I figured I would use my natural gift as they were using theirs. I brought up my sight and took a look. Something hit me right off the bat. Everyone there had the same base color of a very dark green. Was it just that wheirs had a unique color or did every species? Most of the other people I had looked at with my sight, outside of Bran, had the muted orange-red as a base. Well you learn something new every day. I was brought to an abrupt stop by one of the men standing towards the back of the people milling about. I had seen those black snakes and that red veil in auras before. I dropped my sight to take a better, normal, look at him. He was relatively average, if someone with cut muscles could be considered average. He seemed very ill at ease and he was taking particular note of me. I would keep my eye on him.

"Gary?" I whispered.

"Yes?" he whispered back, getting closer.

"Is the whole pack going out on this excursion?" I asked, keeping my voice low.

"No. There will only be four or five of us going. Why?"

"Just wondering how many of you I need to be able to recognize."

"You will meet the ones going tomorrow evening when we get ready to leave."

"Okay," I replied as we walked up to another two that Gary started to introduce me to.

I knew them immediately from a month ago.

"Ced, this is Thomas and Craig," he said, introducing the two large men standing in front of us.

"I believe the three of us have already met," I said, shaking their hands.

I saw the look of surprise in both of them.

"Really? When?" Craig asked me.

"About a month ago under much different circumstances but yes, we have met," I answered.

Gary laughed, the other two just looked at me. Gary moved me away towards one of the picnic tables that were set out in the yard.

"That was a test wasn't it?" I asked him as we sat down.

"Guilty," he said, taking a drink.

"Did I pass?"

"Surprisingly, yes."

Once Gary had sat down everyone else began following suit. Greta and the other women went back into the house and started bringing out platters of food and setting them on the tables. The table that Gary was sitting at was placed first. Once all of the food was out on the tables, everyone waited for Gary to begin putting food on his plate and no one took a bite before he did. I was beginning to see the hierarchy of the pack as the dinner went along. Gary was the leader, I knew the books called it the Alpha but I wasn't sure what Gary would call it. It seemed that next in line was Willis, then Thomas, and Craig. Greta seemed to be the head of all of the females and treated as such. One of the things I noticed very quickly was that none of the men lifted one of their fingers or asses to get anything for themselves. I would just love for one of them to tell me I needed to get them another beer. Wheirwolf or not, it would not end well for them. Thankfully, after the meal started the tension towards me eased some; even Greta seemed to be a little warmer.

The evening ran into night and then late. It was well after midnight and I was getting sleepy. I was standing in a small group with Gary, Willis, and Craig as they were discussing something to do with the local city government.

"Gentlemen," I started when there was a break in their conversation.

"I do not want to seem rude but I have had a long day and I need to get some sleep."

"Let me walk you in," Gary said as he gestured towards the porch and the back door.

He walked me up on the porch, through the kitchen, and to my bedroom.

"You might want to try and stay up as late as you can," he said.

"Why?"

"Because there is a good chance you will be staying up later than this the next few nights. Unless that is going to be too much for you and you want to go home."

"Dream on Sheriff."

"You can't fault me for trying," He said gruffly.

"I guess I can't."

"Like I said. Try and stay awake as long as you can. I don't need a sleepy Marshal with a gun taking pot shots at anything that moves."

"I have been on my share of overnight stakeouts, I will be fine," I said as I opened the door.

"See you tomorrow."

"Good night Gary," I said as I closed the door behind me.

I got ready for bed and crawled between the sheets. I opened my book and began reading. I could hear the voices from the back yard as I lay there. I made myself stay awake, reading, until the party broke up and people started leaving. I looked at my watch. Geez, it was four thirty in the morning. I closed my book, sat it on the nightstand, and turned off the light.

****

My cramps woke me. The room was fairly light, even with the curtains drawn. I looked at my watch; two thirty. If it wasn't for the fact I had to pee and my cramps were killing me, I would roll over and go back to sleep. I forced myself up, threw on some clothes, and went to the bathroom. I went back to the bedroom, grabbed my brush and my brown jar of miracle root, and went to find a teakettle. When I walked into the kitchen, Greta was sitting at the table working on some sort of needlework.

"Did you sleep okay?" she asked not looking up.

"Yes, thank you. Do you have a teakettle I can use?"

She put her needlework down and started to get up.

"I can get it if you will tell me where it is," I said.

"Lower cabinet, left of the stove," she said and sat back down.

I went to where she directed, found the kettle, filled it with water and sat it on the stove to warm. I sat my bottle on the counter and began brushing my hair to get the night's tangles out.

"If you will bring me your clothes, I will rinse them out and dry them," she said from the table.

I walked back to the bedroom, got my clothes and brought them back to her. She picked all of them up, threw them in the washer that stood in the corner of the kitchen, and started them. On her way back she stopped at one of the cupboards, pulled out a mug and sat it on the counter. She reached in a drawer and pulled out a spoon, setting it next to the mug. She went back to the table and resumed her sewing. By the time I got back from the bedroom after putting my brush away, the teakettle was singing. I turned off the flame and poured the hot water into the mug. I spooned out a serving of the mixture in the jar and dropped it in the water. I gave it a good stir, sat the spoon in the sink, and went to sit at the table.

"That is an interesting smell, what sort of tea is it?" Greta asked.

"It is an herb mixture a friend of mine gave me for my cramps."

"Does it work?"

"Like a charm," I answered, taking a sip.

"I guess I should count myself lucky that I never had bad cramps."

"I know I count myself lucky to have Bran as my friend to keep me supplied with this," I said, taking a long sip.

"Where's Willis?" I asked, changing the subject.

"He had to run into town for a little bit."

"Oh," I said and took another sip.

The conversation lagged. I did not know what to talk to her about and she seemed uninterested in starting a conversation with me.

"Thank you for the use of your mug," I said as I stood up to put it in the sink.

"Why are you doing this?" she asked, to my surprise.

"Doing what?"

"Going out with us. Gary says we don't need you."

"Because it is my job to catch this guy."

"And what gift does your kind have that makes you think you can catch him?"

"My kind? I am a U.S. Marshal and I am good at my job."

"Not what you do for a living. I mean your kind. You aren't human and you're not wheir. What is the gift you have that makes you think you can take on

97

a wheir?"

"The only gift, as you call it, that I have is my skill with weapons and my reaction times."

"And you want me to trust you with my life based on that?" she asked, openly distrustful.

"I have people who have trusted me with their life based on less."

"I am not those people."

"Would it make a difference to you if we went out back, you set up targets, and I show you how good I am?"

"What good would that do? Still targets in bright daylight are nothing; you will be shooting moving targets in the dark."

She had a point and I could not think of any rebuttal.

"That's what I thought," she said after I didn't answer.

"Are you afraid of going out?" I asked.

"Doesn't make a difference whether I am afraid or not."

"Why's that?"

"I've been told this is what I have to do for the pack. I don't have a choice so fear isn't an option."

It hit me all of a sudden that I had been so intent on catching this guy I had not thought some of this through. I had been so self-involved that I had taken Greta's participation in this for granted. She was the fucking bait. What if the others didn't get there in time? She would end up just like the other women that had fought and died. I stared at the herbs, that refused to dissolve, in the bottom of the mug looking for an answer.

"Greta?" I asked softly, moving back to the table and retaking my seat.

"Yes?" she asked, still pulling the thread through the material on her hoop.

"Greta, look at me," I prompted quietly.

She sat down her hoop and looked me in the eye.

"I'm sorry. If it was up to me I would never put you in that type of danger," I said.

"You aren't putting me in the danger, you're just adding to it," she said as she picked her material back up and started working on it again.

I could see the tears welling up in her eyes. I could think of nothing else to say to ease her mind. I stood up, sat my mug in the sink, and went back to the bedroom. I lay back on the bed and thought about Greta and the real danger she was in. The herb tea had started to work and I could feel my eyes closing.

****

Voices drifting down the hallway woke me, and I opened my eyes. It took me a second to realize where I was at. My clothes lay folded on the end of the bed. I got up, got dressed, and remade the bed. I looked at my watch and noticed it was almost four. I went back into the hall and followed the voices to the kitchen. I came in on the end of a conversation between Gary and Willis.

"Willis, could you get a hold of Casey, fill him in on our plans, and get him over here?" Gary asked.

"Are you sure he is ready for this?" Willis asked.

"I feel we need one more and he's the one that's closest to being ready, plus he's the fastest one in the pack. We just might need his speed," Gary answered.

The conversation stopped when I came in. Willis pulled his phone out of his pocket and went into the living room to make the call.

"Did you sleep okay?" Gary asked me, pushing a seat out at the table for me.

"Yes. I slept very well, thank you. So when are we leaving?" I asked distractedly as I sat down.

"About five."

There was a knock at the door. I heard Willis finish his phone conversation and answer it. Willis led Craig and Thomas back into the kitchen.

"Casey will be here in about ten minutes," Willis said as Craig and Thomas took a seat at the table.

"Cedwynne, would you like something to drink?" Greta asked me.

"Yes, please. May I have some of your lemonade?" I asked.

Greta went to the cupboard, took out a glass filled it with ice and liquid, and sat it in front of me. The rest of them talked for awhile until another knock came at the door. Willis led Casey into the kitchen after letting him in. I had met Casey briefly last night. Casey was probably around my age but I could tell by the way he looked at me that he did not think much of me.

"We are going to eat before we go, would you care for something?" Gary asked me.

"Sure."

"What would you like?" Greta asked.

"I'll just have what you're having."

It was Greta that openly laughed as if I missed the joke.

"How about some scrambled eggs with mushrooms and cheese?" she asked.

"Sure that would be fine. Can I also get another glass of your lemonade?"

"Yes," she answered, went to the fridge, refilled my glass and sat it in front of me.

I took a drink as she got out a frying pan and began making my meal. I noticed that Casey was eying me. It gave me the shivers; I couldn't tell if it was lust or hunger that was in the stare.

"Casey. Focus," Gary barked at him, also noticing the look.

Greta sat a plate and silverware in front of me. She went back to the counter and picked up plates that I had not noticed when I came in, and brought them to the table where the other place settings were. I was surprised at what was on the plates she sat down. Each one had a very large slab of raw meat. No wonder

Greta had laughed at my ignorance earlier. She sat down with her own plate after she had served everyone else. I was getting to see first-hand one of the crossover traits. I found it interesting that, though each one of them ate their steaks with some gusto, it was very civilized in that knives, forks, and good manners were used.

"Excellent eggs," I complimented Greta.

She gave me a small smile and went back to her meal. As we were eating I got a handle on the dynamic of the pack that was around the table. I already knew that Gary was in charge, but where everyone else thanked Greta for the meal she had served them, Gary didn't. I deduced that Willis was the next honored since everyone acquiesced to him after Gary. Greta, Thomas, and Craig seemed to be on the same level and bringing up the rear was Casey. This was a study that would probably come in useful later.

"Gary? What's the plan this evening?" I asked.

"We'll leave here in about twenty minutes and take three vehicles. Willis, Thomas, and Casey will head north and east of our picked spot, myself and Craig will head further north. You and Greta will travel together and she will find you a place near our trap. She'll start working her way out as if she's hunting by herself. If we get lucky she'll hook our prey and pull him back where we can surround him and do what needs to be done. You need to make sure that you stay hidden and out of the way," he said seriously.

"Okay," I said as I took another bite of my meal.

"Would you mind taking that monster you drive? I don't think Greta's car will make it where we need to go," Gary asked me.

"Sure."

After we finished our meals I helped Greta do dishes, since none of the men seemed interested in being helpful.

"You don't have to do this," Greta said as she started the dishwater.

"Yes I do. You have opened up your home and I will repay in whatever way I can."

She shrugged her shoulders and went to work.

****

Greta and I were seated in Bee heading roughly north following the two cars in front of us. It was beginning to get dark and Greta gave me directions to turn as the other two cars continued on their way. I had to put Bee in four wheel drive for the last couple of miles.

"Okay stop here. We'll have to walk the rest of the way," Greta said.

I stopped, put it in park, and shut down the motor. I made sure I had an extra clip in my pocket for my nine mil, I grabbed the rifle with the scope out of the back, got out of the camper and locked it up. I followed Greta through the underbrush for a few hundred yards when she stopped.

"You need to continue on due north for another couple of hundred feet and you'll get to a small clearing. The wind is out of the southwest this evening so stay on the eastern edge of the tree line. There is a large oak with low branches on the eastern edge. Get up in it and find a comfortable spot. This could take a while or all night," she said.

"I thought you were starting from there," I said.

"I am, but I need to change first and I need to come around the western edge and enter from the north so my scent will be there. He does not need to smell both of us together. Especially since you are around your period. Get up high and above the direct wind," Greta told me.

"Greta," I said as she started to turn and go.

"Yes?"

"Be careful."

"I will," she said, turned and disappeared into the underbrush to my left.

I continued on the way she'd told me. The moon had risen and produced enough light for me to see. I finally came out on a clearing that was mostly to my left. I circled to the right of the clearing, found the tree she had said would be there and climbed up. I went a few branches up, found a fork facing the clearing that I thought I could tolerate for an extended period, and got as comfortable as I could. I pulled my gun from the holster and chambered a round then replaced it in the clip from an extra I had in my pocket; I would have a full thirteen rounds. I put it back in the holster, not setting the safety. I was not going to lose precious seconds making sure the safety was off. That, as I had learned last month, could cost me my life. I checked the rounds in the rifle and made sure the scope was working and sighted well in the low light level.

I had been sitting in my perch for about fifteen minutes when I heard some rustling in the bushes off to my right at the other end of the clearing. I looked for an aura and could see Greta as she made her way, almost haphazardly, into the clearing. She loped around the edge of the clearing until she got to the tree I was in. She sat down, looked up into the foliage, and gave a small yip.

"Yes, I'm here Greta," I whispered down at her.

She seemed to understand. She got up and started moving about the clearing, with her nose to the ground taking in the scents that presented themselves. I focused on her aura. I had never tested my gift to see how far reaching it was, but I kept watching as she moved into the underbrush on the west side of the clearing. My special sight worked in the way my normal vision would; the more substantial the object between us the less I saw of her. Though if it hadn't been dark, my gift wouldn't have given me the advantage of seeing the glow of her aura through the breaks in the underbrush. By my calculations, I lost all sight of her when she was about thirty to forty yards away from the clearing. I could hear her making her way through the underbrush for another fifteen minutes or so.

Then the sounds of her movement blended into the normal insect and night noises.

As the din of the night sounds became background, I gripped my precarious perch and thought of what I'd learned in the last month. All of a sudden my life in Dallas seemed ages away. I mused about Sam and his new partner and hoped he was doing well and keeping his head down. I needed to give him a call when I got back home. I knew I couldn't tell him where I was or what I was doing, but no one had told me it was against the rules to stay in contact with him.

I also gave some thought to what Greta had said earlier today, echoing what Gary had, about me and what my kind had as a gift. Maybe she and Gary were wrong about me belonging to some "kind" of different species or even that "kind" having any gifts. There was something inside that wasn't willing to just let their assessments of me go that easily. I forced my mind to turn to the project at hand. I sat intent on what my ears were telling me. Right now, however, they weren't telling me anything new.

The dew had settled and I was cold and damp as the sky started to lighten in the east. I heard rustling in the underbrush; I brought my sight up and could see Greta's aura blinking in and out of the breaks in the foliage. She broke the tree line, came to the center of the clearing, yipped a couple of times in my direction, then headed the way she had entered earlier in the night. This had been a very uncomfortable stakeout. Most others I'd been on I'd at least had coffee. I climbed down out of the tree, stretched to get my muscles working again and started in the direction of Bee. I put my rifle away and started the engine to get some heat going. It wasn't long before a very tired looking Greta climbed up in the passenger seat.

"I remember how to get back to your house once I'm on the main road, so if you'll give me directions on how to get there you can take the bed in the back and get some sleep," I said as she got in.

"Are you sure?"

"Yes."

"Thank you. I'm exhausted."

Greta gave me some quick directions, which I jotted down, then went to the back of the camper to sleep. I put Bee in gear and headed back to the main road. Once I was on the black top, I headed south. I found a diner near a small town, whipped in, got some coffee and an egg sandwich, climbed back in Bee, and resumed my driving.

Gary and Willis were waiting on the porch as I drove up and parked. Gary walked over to my door and opened it for me.

"Where is Greta?" he asked not seeing her in the cab.

"I told her to take the bed in back and get some sleep," I answered as I hopped down to the ground.

"Do you mind if she stays there?" Willis asked coming up.

"Of course not, but I'm sure she'd be more comfortable in her own bed."

"Once a wheir goes to sleep after a change you might lose an arm waking them before they are ready," Gary informed me.

"I like my arms; she can sleep in there as long as she wants. I, however, am going to take a hot shower and go to bed," I said as I started towards the house.

"I take it our friend didn't show up," I said to Gary as we stepped up on the porch.

"No, he didn't. I'll check the police wires this afternoon to see if he did something somewhere else."

"Then good night or morning or whatever," I said as Willis opened the door and I entered.

I went straight to the bathroom, took a hot shower, and crawled into bed.

Chapter 10
Monday May 8, 2248

Sunday night had been almost a carbon copy of Saturday. The only difference was a change of location. Gary had moved the trap to a different clearing a few miles west of the one before. He left Casey at the original site just in case but nothing came of it. Yet again we were heading north for our third and final night of the month. I had a feeling that I would be back up here next month doing exactly the same thing. I parked, checked my guns, and walked with Greta towards the glade we had been at Saturday. I found my tree, climbed up, and got comfortable-okay not comfortable, but set. Greta came out of the tree line, already morphed, made sure I was where I was supposed to be, and started her tracking.

****

I must have been sitting for almost four hours, wishing I had coffee, when I heard what sounded like an angry howl followed by a couple of startled yips. I waited for a few minutes and heard nothing more. God, I hope Greta had not fallen prey before she could make it back here. It was then I heard noises coming, fairly far off, due north of me. I heard a short howl, now closer, that was answered further off to the north, then answered again off to the northwest. I instinctively knew that the last two howls were Gary and Willis. Then I heard what sounded like a dog fight from the north.

My attention was brought closer with massive rustling in the underbrush. I looked for Greta's aura in the direction of the noise. I could just barely see it to the north heading going at a pretty good clip and heading directly for the clearing. I looked a bit further behind her and saw the other aura heading in the same direction and gaining on her. It looked as if she would reach the clearing before the wheir chasing her would. The wheir following her had that same dark green base color in its aura as Greta. However, he had the red veil and black snakes in his which I knew from experience meant nothing but trouble. I leveled my rifle but I knew that if they entered the clearing at the angle they were on I wouldn't have a clear shot, especially if the wheir following her kept gaining on her as much as he seemed to be. I sat helpless for the moment.

I could hear the fight still happening further out to the north. It was a split second between seeing Greta break the tree line at a full run, and the flying form that tackled her a few yards inside. They rolled together on the ground, snapping at each other, Greta trying her best to keep him off of her and maneuver him closer to my side of the clearing. I quickly lowered myself a couple of branches to get a better shooting position. I was just taking aim, trying to find an opening, when Greta let out a sorrowful howl as he bit down on her right shoulder. She rolled on her back to break the hold. I could see the wound, even in the moonlight, as she was able to dislodge his teeth.

The other wheir that had followed her in was huge. He had to have outweighed Gary by a good forty pounds. I had to find an opening because I knew Greta could not hold her own against him. Greta was still between him and I as she came to her feet facing him. It was like he knew I was there as he went down in a spring stance to keep Greta between us as she started to retreat to the center of the clearing. He lunged low at her and caught her in the side, landing on her as they both rolled over. I could hear the pop of her rib all the way from where I sat. Where in the fuck was her backup? I couldn't hear anything other than the snarls from her assailant and her pained whimpering as he sank his teeth into her side to hold her. I could tell what he was trying to do even from here.

I remembered back to the foster mother I had been placed with after David and Jennifer Crittenden had lost their certification. She would take in young women from the foster system and use them as in-home prostitutes, luckily I had not been old enough yet to help her in her endeavors, but I would hear my foster sisters cry themselves to sleep at night after what was done to them. Since that time, as a woman, I had always felt that rape was as bad as or worse than death. I was unable to do anything back then, but now I could and I was not going to let it happen to Greta.

Fuck it; I was the only backup she had. I swung my feet over the limb I was on and dropped the eight feet or so to the ground. I dropped the rifle, pulled my side arm, and started running. I let out a banshee yell and let fly a round close enough to them to get his attention but making sure I didn't hit Greta in the process.

Greta lay across the ground between us. Without letting go of the hold he had on her side he lowered himself behind her keeping her between us. I could hear her labored breathing as she whimpered in pain. I slowly moved closer and to my right to try and get a shot. He knew what I was doing and drug her around to keep her between us. I could see the evil laughter in his eyes as he bit down harder on her side, making her whimper louder.

I froze for a second. We were about twenty to thirty feet apart. If it were daylight I would have probably taken the shot. But the light and shadows playing across the clearing made it hard to see where one of them started and the other one ended. I hoped that Willis and Gary were getting close since what I was about to do was probably going to cost me. Keeping my weapon raised I took a step closer. This garnered Greta another bite.

"Fine, asshole!" I yelled at the wheir hiding behind her.

I stopped for a second and faked taking a step back then kicked with that foot and took off running directly at him. It registered in his brain that if he took another bite out of Greta, I would have more than a clear shot. However, he did something I hadn't planned on. He let go of Greta and put everything he had in a lunge towards me. I got off a shot but it only grazed his side. He growled savagely as he hit me with his front legs full force. Even though I had built up some momentum and power, his was more.

I felt the wind go out of me as he hit me full force and I landed on my back with him on top of me. Instinctively I put my left arm up to ward off the teeth. Which he took full advantage of and bit down, hard. The bite brought my breath back as I felt the excruciating pain of his teeth sinking in and muscle and skin tearing. The agony I felt also cleared my brain. I realized I still had my gun in my right hand. As he started to shake my arm, I felt my shoulder dislocate and send fireworks to the inside of my eyes. With all of the strength I had left I raised my right hand and forced the barrel of my gun up underneath his jaw and into the underside of his his throat. As he jerked his head back to my right to finish off my arm I pulled the trigger for the first round. Then I emptied the rest of the clip into the underside of his brain. By the time I got to the forth or fifth shot there was nothing left of his skull to stop the other six bullets that traveled that path. I felt the blood and brain matter saturate my face and upper body. His jaw went slack and he collapsed down on the right side of me.

I lay there for a second trying to make my body work. I looked over at Greta, she was not really moving, though I could see she was breathing. I tried to get up but the searing pain in my left shoulder made me lay back for a moment more. I took a deep breath and rolled over so my right arm would be in a position to push up and get me on my feet. I stumbled over to where Greta lay.

She was pretty beat up but the thing that worried me most was the wound in her side. She was losing a lot of blood. I knew what I had to do and I knew it was going to be excruciating. I peeled out of my coat, and I thought I would pass out from the pain. It was then I noticed the hamburger that used to be my arm. She wasn't the only one losing blood. I popped all of the buttons on the front of my shirt and, as quickly as the pain would let me, removed it too. I wrapped the shirt tightly around my injured arm and tied it on using the sleeves, as best I could. I dumped everything out of my coat pockets, folded it up and applied it as a pressure bandage to Greta's side. I ran my fingers through the thick fur of her neck and tried to sooth her.

I heard the rustle of the underbrush from the way she had come out of the woods. I put my injured arm on Greta's side to hold the bandage in place. I grabbed my gun, sprung the clip and let it fall to the ground. I felt around, keeping my eyes on the tree line and found the extra clip I had emptied out of my coat pocket. I laid the gun down, so I could line the clip up with the opening and using the ground, snapped it into place. I placed it between my thighs and with a little difficulty chambered a round. I raised it and aimed in the direction of the noise that was coming towards me.

I looked for an aura; I saw it a few seconds before it broke the tree line. It was not an aura of any of the wheirs I had traveled up here with. I was just

106

aiming for my shot when I saw in my left peripheral vision an aura I knew. Casey left the ground and hit the charging wheir with a powerful lunge that took both of them to the ground. Casey rolled up on his feet and quickly put himself between Greta and I and the new threat. I kept my gun trained on the spot where the two of them were. If I had been on the top of my game it would have been an easy shot. But with my own loss of blood and the pain, I wasn't sure I could hit the broad side of a barn in bright daylight.

I watched the two square off and was worried about Casey since the other wheir seemed to have about fifty pounds on him. The aggressive wheir lunged at Casey. For what Casey lacked in size, he made up for with speed. He easily sidestepped the lunge and latched on to the back of the others' neck. The larger wheir rolled over on Casey, breaking the hold. Casey moved out of the way as the larger wheir snapped at his back leg.

All hell broke loose as Craig and Gary broke the tree line and headed straight for the other two. It didn't take long for it to end with another carcass laying in the grass. I looked up to see Thomas and Willis break the tree line from the other side. Willis and Thomas slowed to a walk as they got closer to the group standing around the body of the last one. I noticed Willis finally take a look in my direction. It dawned on him that Greta was not standing. He sniffed the air since he was upwind of us and started coming in our direction. He got within a few feet of us and gave out a nasty snarl that seemed aimed at me.

"Back off, Willis," I yelled at him.

He kept coming and I could see the anger in his eyes. He was almost at a run when Gary hit him full side and rolled him to the ground. Willis came up snapping. Gary stood his ground. Willis charged him. Gary met Willis' charge with his own. They wrestled for a bit until Gary got the upper hand and had Willis on his back with Willis' throat in his teeth. Willis went limp and whimpered. Gary lightly shook him to get his attention then let go and moved off. Willis got up, his tail between his legs, and slowly made his way towards Greta and I, not looking at me. I guess I couldn't blame him. I would've probably wanted to kill someone if my mate was laying injured in the middle of nowhere. He came over to where Greta was, nudged her with his muzzle then licked hers in a show of care and affection. She licked his back in answer. He lay down with his muzzle on top of hers and whined. I was having a hard time focusing and was starting to see auras mix with the bodies they belonged to. I applied all of the focus I had left to keeping pressure on the bandage on Greta's side. Gary came over and sniffed me and licked the hand on my injured arm that I had on Greta's side. I laid my gun down and scratched his head between his ears. He walked away and I focused my attention on Greta.

I wasn't sure how long I was sitting there when I heard what sounded like a painful scream issue from the tree line off to my right. My vision was starting to get cloudy as I turned to look at what the noise was. I figured I'd started hallucinating when I saw a naked man emerge from the woods and start walking in my direction. As he came closer I reached for my gun. The image stopped a few feet away.

"Ced," the figure said.

I knew the voice but I could not place it. The pain in my arm was becoming such that I couldn't block it out anymore. There were black edges around the corners of my vision.

"Ced. You're hurt. Put down the gun," The waving figure was saying.

I tried to concentrate as the black on both sides of my vision started creeping in to meet each other. I saw the bare arms reach for me as the sides met and everything went black.

Chapter 11
Wednesday May 10, 2248

I opened my eyes; my head was hurting. I was in the room I went to sleep in after my shower Monday morning. Fuck, what a bad dream. I hoped the evening would not go as bad as the dream had. I tried to move and felt the pain run down my back from my arm. I looked down at my left arm. My forearm was bandaged tightly and my upper arm was held to my torso with an elastic bandage keeping it in place. I also realized that I was naked. I started to panic and looked to my right. Gary was sitting in a chair smiling at me. Shit, it wasn't a dream. All I could think about was Greta laying on the ground, not moving, and bleeding.

"How's Greta?" I asked worried.

"She's fine. The better question is how are you?" he asked gently.

"Great, now you're sounding like a friend of mine; always pointing out the better questions. I feel like I've been run over by a train," I answered, suddenly becoming aware of my bare chest in front of a man in my room.

I reached for the sheet and brought it up under my chin. This garnered a small chuckle from him.

"What day is it?" I asked.

"You've been out for two days."

"Shit; that means its Wednesday. Nothing good ever happens on a Wednesday."

"Actually it was Monday that something bad happened. You waking up is a good thing. Are you up for a little company?" he asked, smiling.

"Sure, I guess."

"Don't go anywhere," he said, getting up.

"Like where the fuck am I going to go?" I asked, rhetorically.

He laughed and left the room. I looked at the bedside table. All of my personal belongings were arranged neatly there. I closed my eyes for a second. When I opened them Greta was standing next to the bed. She was wearing one of her cut off tees and shorts. I could see the larger bandage taped to her shoulder, and the elastic one wrapped around her ribs, peeking out from the cut off bottom of the shirt.

"Hey," she said softly, smiling down at me.

"Are you okay?" I asked.

"Thanks to you," she said as she sat down softly on the side of the bed.

She reached up and brushed the hair from my face.

"You could have been killed. Why didn't you stay in the tree?"

"I couldn't get a clear shot and though you were holding your own, he was going to take you and do things I did not want to watch. We ladies have to stick together," I said, trying to smile but that hurt too.

"Can I get you anything? Something to eat or drink?"

"Some of your world famous lemonade would be heaven."

"Coming right up," she said as she got up to leave the room.

"I'm sorry, Ced." she said from the doorway.

"About what?"

"Ever doubting you would take the shot."

"I was there to do whatever I could to protect you. I haven't lost a person I was protecting yet and you weren't going to be my first."

"You know, Ced, for a non-wheir you're great to have around," she said as she opened the door.

I smiled at her as she left.

She came back a few minutes later carrying a glass of lemonade and sat it on the nightstand. She was followed in the room by Willis.

"Would you like to try and prop up?" Greta asked.

"That would be nice."

"Willis, will you help me?"

They moved to each side of the bed. Greta grabbed me around the middle from my right so I could hook my good arm around her neck and support myself, as she lifted me to a sitting position. Willis put more pillows behind me. Greta gently laid me back letting me situate myself using my good arm to lower myself back on the pillows. She took the sheet and gently tucked it in behind my left shoulder, running it across me, above my breast, and tucked the other edge under my right side so my right arm was above it. She handed me my drink which I took a long sip of. She sat on the bed at my feet as Willis came over and stood next to me where she had been.

"Ced, I want to apologize," he started.

"For what?" I asked, surprised.

"I thought you'd shot Greta by mistake. I didn't think..."

He had his hands in his pockets and didn't seem able to look me in the eye.

"Willis, I can't say I would have acted differently if the situation had been reversed."

"But you risked your own life to save someone that you really didn't know and who hadn't treated you very well. I should have acted better."

"Look. I've had partners in my time I didn't get along with socially. That didn't mean we didn't have each others' backs when push came to shove. That night I was part of a team and one of the team members needed me. Besides, we all survived and we got the bad guy," I said, trying to put him at ease.

I knew that apologizing cost him a lot, and apologizing to a woman cost him that much more.

"Ced, I don't care where or for what, if ever you need help or a place to stay all you have to do is call me or Greta and we'll be there for you."

"Thank you."

He nodded his head in acknowledgment. All of a sudden I had to go.

"Willis, would you mind leaving for a minute?" I asked.

"Not at all. Why?"

"I really need to go to the bathroom and I have no clothes on," I answered, a little embarrassed.

"Oh. Sure," he said smiling, then turned and left the room.

"Greta. Do you think you could help me to the bathroom?"

"Yes, but it's going to hurt."

"I would prefer to suffer the pain than mess up the bed."

Greta came to the right side of the bed and grabbed me like she had before. I put my arm over her shoulder. She let me put my weight there as she helped me get my legs out of the bed and on the floor. She stood me up slowly. My head began to swim and my knees started to get weak. Greta felt the added weight and quickly wrapped her arms around my waist to hold me up.

"Stand still for a second and catch your breath."

I closed my eyes and concentrated on not fainting. After a few seconds the room quit spinning and I found my equilibrium. We walked slowly towards the door. Each step sent shock waves up my arm. I gritted my teeth as we crossed the hall and she helped me sit down on the toilet.

"Do you want me to stay or go?" she asked.

"If you could wait just outside the door, I would appreciate it. The only thing is I need a tampon."

Greta leaned over and pulled a couple out from under the sink and sat them on the windowsill.

"Here are a few extra. Leave them there so they are easier to get to. Yell if you feel lightheaded again," she said as she left me there and went out the door.

I felt like I hadn't peed in a week. I finished up everything I needed to do and, using the windowsill that was next to the toilet, I managed to get myself to a standing position. My head did not swim near as much as the first time. I made it to the bathroom door and opened it slowly. Greta was standing right there to offer me her arm, which I took immediately. We slowly made our way to the bed and Greta tucked me back in. I took a small sip of the lemonade. I realized that just that short walk had worn me out.

"Greta, I think I am going to nap for a while."

"Okay, Ced. Just call out if you need anything," she said as she touched me on the forehead, and left the room.

I closed my eyes and let the tired take me.

****

I tended to wake for a while, then go back to sleep. Each time I woke there seemed to be someone different in the room. I guessed they were taking turns sitting with me. In one of my more lucid moments I realized Gary was sitting next to the bed reading a book. I took a long look at him. He was still gorgeous. If I could have moved right then, I'd have pulled him over in the bed with me-offspring be damned. He looked up from his book with those deep green eyes, and smiled at me.

"What time is it?" I asked.

"It is a little after midnight."

"What day?"

"Thursday morning."

"Can I get a glass of water?"

"Sure," he said as he got up and went to the dresser.

There was a pitcher and glasses that had been set there ready for just this scenario. He filled the glass and came back over, handing it to me as he sat down on the side of the bed.

"Can I ask a couple of questions, not meaning any disrespect?" I asked lowly.

"Sure."

"Did we get the right guy?"

"Yes."

"How do you know for sure?"

"A couple of those cases were in my jurisdiction. I did more than just look at the scene," he said, pointing at his nose.

"Your second question?"

"What the fuck took you guys so long?"

"Evidently, our friend had started his own traveling pack. There were actually four of them, not one. Willis, Thomas, and Casey were intercepted by one. Willis and Thomas sent Casey on, since he's the fastest runner of all of us, while they finished off the one that had stopped them. Craig and I met up with two more on the north side of the glade. They held us off for a bit, then split up. It took Craig and I both to put an end to the one that stayed. By the time the rest of us got there, you'd killed the Alpha and Casey was taking on the last one. Needless to say, it ended quickly from there," he answered, touching my forehead as if to check for fever.

Something had started gnawing at my brain, and I sat quietly. Of all of the things that could have been running through my head, it was the fact that the wheir I had shot seemed to know I was there.

"Did I say something to disturb you?" Gary asked, lifting my chin so he could look in my eyes.

"No. Not as such. But something got me to thinking. We went out in three separate groups. I was pretty high up in the tree when the Alpha arrived, but it was like he knew exactly where I was and always kept Greta between us so I couldn't get a shot. I know that you and Craig were upwind of the Alpha and

Greta the whole time, so you could smell them. Then conveniently both you and the other group ran into resistance. As a going concern I don't like coincidences. So you tell me, what are the odds of all of that happening?"

Gary sat for a moment very much in deep thought.

"Do you know what you are suggesting?" he asked.

"Yes. It isn't pretty when you come to the realization a friend isn't a friend. I know the hard part of this: which friend is not a friend?"

"You keep proving you're more than just your good looks."

"I'm not sure if I should be flattered or not."

"Trust me. It's a hard earned compliment," he replied, softly.

He sat quietly for a long time.

"Did you realize this at the time?" he finally asked.

"Not about the others that you ran into but that he knew where I was, yes."

"Then why did you get out of the tree if you knew it might be a trap?"

"I don't know how it is in the wheir community, but I witnessed enough rape and abuse in my younger days. I wasn't going to sit by and watch it again."

"Were you.. ah.. when you were younger?" he asked, not wanting to say the word.

"No. But I probably would've been if I'd stayed in that foster home," I answered.

"If it helps, wheirs take a dim view of forced copulation when it deals with an interloper coming into our pack. We also feel the same about one of our own stepping out of the pack for an attack like that."

I think I understood what he was saying, but I wasn't sure. All of a sudden I was wide awake and my brain was starting to work.

"There is something I need to know," Gary started.

"What?"

"There was some cloud cover Monday night and there was a lot of fur walking around."

"Is there a question in there somewhere?"

"I know you didn't have time to look at eyes."

I could hear Bran in my head telling me *that* still wasn't a question, but I knew what he meant. I thought long and hard about what I wanted to say. Did I owe him an explanation? No, I didn't. I could come up with something about just getting lucky, but I knew he wouldn't buy it. I'd been carrying this secret with me for most of my life. I'd refrained from telling anyone because the last person I had confided in thought I was losing it. Maybe he would understand. Even better, maybe he could help, or at least believe me.

"I'll answer that unasked question if you'll answer one for me first," I replied.

"Okay. What's your question?"

"You've told me that you know people by smell. You can identify them down to a personal level right?"

"Yes."

"I've only told one person in my life about this and she sent me to a shrink. If this comes back to haunt me, I will wait for you one night and you will not tell another soul," I said, staring at him.

"Fine, I accept your terms," he said, smiling at me.

"I see auras."

"So that's how you knew us last month," he muttered.

It surprised me that he just accepted it.

"Yes and no. Normal wildlife has a small glow, but only sentient beings have a full-fledged aura. And those auras, as I've recently found out, are as unique as fingerprints. You keep your aura even after you shift. When I came upon Greta the next day it was her eyes, like I told you, that gave her away. It wasn't until after I had seen them that I even checked her aura against what I'd seen the night before. Willis, Craig, and Thomas I recognized after I saw their auras. With you, however, I didn't have to look at your aura. I'd gotten up close and personal with those green orbs; hard to forget."

I could swear I saw him blush again.

"What do you see when you look at auras?" he asked.

I thought for a minute to figure out how to explain it.

"Well, it's like looking at the sun in a way. They're quite bright and I can see them in the light of day or the dark of night just the same. Your aura outlines your body like the corona of the sun. There seems to be a base color with spikes of color on top. Then over that is like a sheer curtain of color that changes shades based on the mood of the person. I am still learning about it since I've never had a mentor to learn from. I learned just recently that each aura is unique to each person and that each species, for lack of a better word, seems to have its own base color with individual colors making up the spikes in the corona. For example, all the wheirs I've seen so far, even the ones we killed, have a base of a very deep green though the shade of it might be a bit different from person to person. Humans seem to have an orange-red base, but everything else is pretty much the same other than the colors of their spikes seem to be a bit more muted than wheirs'. I've met someone recently that doesn't fall in either of those categories, and I have no idea if he is human or not," I explained.

"What does your aura look like?"

"I don't know. I've tried to look at it in the mirror but it doesn't show up. But since I've seen other auras in a mirror, I suppose I don't have one or can't see my own," I answered, shrugging my one good shoulder.

"Has your gift ever been wrong?"

"Not for what I use it for. I knew who everyone was the other night. When anyone, wheirs included, have their sheer curtain turn a deep red it seems to denote anger, or I guess a better word would be evil intent. If there are black snakes in it, it usually means this is not the first time they have been mean or evil to someone. The two wheirwolves that I saw alive, other than you and your pack, had a bright red curtain and lots of black snakes."

"So it could've been pitch black out there and you could've taken the shot?"

"If I could've gotten around Greta, I could've hit him between the eyes using only his aura. I've done it before," I answered seriously.

"You and Greta have alluded to me not smelling human. I need a definite answer on this. Are you saying I'm not human or are you saying I don't smell like a normal human?" I asked.

"I'd say you're not human," he stated honestly and flatly.

"Then what am I?"

"I have no clue. I've never run across anyone like you before in my life."

I sat thinking about it. Was he telling me I wasn't human for some weird reason that only he knew? What could be the answer? This wasn't like seeing a doctor; I'd have a hard time asking for a second opinion. What was I going to do, find all the wheirwolves I could and ask them to smell me? I could just see where that would lead. I could think of no reason he would lie to me. Fuck, if I wasn't human what was I?

"Ced, are you okay?" he asked.

"Yes, I guess. It is hard to learn that the last twenty six years of your life have been a bit of a lie."

"My God, I knew you were young but I had no idea that you were that young. How did you make full Marshal?"

"Just unlucky I guess."

He could tell that I was a bit down now. As awake as I felt a few moments ago, I was now very tired and sleepy.

"I think I'd like to sleep for a while," I said.

"I didn't mean to make you upset."

"You didn't. I just need to close my eyes."

"I'll be right here if you need anything," he said as he sat back down in his chair.

I closed my eyes and tried not to think about what sort of monster I would turn into one day.

****

I opened my eyes again, wide awake, and immediately my brain started working on my problems. I looked over and Gary was still in his chair reading. I reached over on the nightstand for the water that I'd sat there. Gary looked at me

"What time is it?" I asked.

"You've been asleep for about two and a half hours. What is it with you and time?"

"I've already lost two days this week, I'm trying not to lose any more," I answered, taking a drink. "May I ask a few questions about wheirs?"

He looked at me for a second, deciding.

"Okay, shoot," he said as he closed the book in his lap.

"When we spoke last month, you said that only one in five biological wheirs were female and the rest were turned. Why is that?"

"Not real sure, could be a genetic thing, environmental, or maybe both. It could also be an evolutionary thing seeing as how it is the male that becomes Alpha and defends the pack."

"I'd assume that it takes two biological wheirs to have a biological offspring."

"Not necessarily. All it means to be biological is that you have two parents that are wheir. A turned wheir happens when the saliva of any wheir is introduced into the blood stream of a non-wheir. And no being scratched by their nails will not turn someone. A turned wheir, if they are of child bearing years, can have a biological offspring. If a wheir mates with a normal human their offspring won't be able to shift, and they're known as half-wheirs. However, if a half-wheir were to mate with a full blooded wheir, then the offspring produced would be able to morph. If two half-wheirs were to mate, then there is a one in four chance their offspring would be a full blooded wheir. There's an interesting piece of trivia about half-wheirs mating. Just as they have a one in four chance of having a biological wheir, they also have a one in four chance of having an offspring that is totally human." Gary was explaining.

"That isn't trivia, that's just genetics."

"The trivia is this: If a two half-wheirs have a human child it is always a female and if they have a biological wheir it is always male."

"Wow, that is interesting."

"I have a handle on what a wolf pack is like in the wild. What's it like with wheirs, if that's not too personal?"

"Packs are as different as the Alphas that run them. But one thing they all have in common is that they're not democracies. They can't be. Ours is a probably a bit different in that we have a chosen succession if something happens to any of us."

"I assume you are the Alpha?"

"For now."

"Are you planning on going somewhere?"

"Not on my own," he answered.

I looked questioningly at him.

"At some time I will take a mate. If she's human then the end won't be as near. If she's wheir the fight will start."

"Why will a wheir mate start a fight?"

"Because Greta is the alpha female but she's not my mate. But, my mate, if I had one, would be considered the alpha female just by my status. Neither Willis nor Greta would probably take kindly to that. If the pack splits, most of the females would follow her if not all. That would give Willis the power base to challenge me. A fight over leadership gets pretty bloody. The only female that Greta would let usurp her position in the pack, without a fight, would be you."

"Why me?"

"You did something she couldn't do, plus in doing it you saved her life."

"But I'm not wheir."

"Let's hope it stays that way," he said a little sadly.

"What?"

"I was going to wait until you were stronger to talk to you about this, but since we're on this subject I guess we should discuss it. Wheir saliva was introduced into your bloodstream," he said bluntly.

The meaning of that hit me like a ton of bricks. "If I'm right and you're not human you should have nothing to worry about. One species can't turn another."

"Shit. What am I going to do if you are wrong?" I asked, looking at my bandaged arm, on the verge of tears.

"You'll deal with it. You're one of the strongest people I've met in my life. Just in the short amount of time I've known you, you've faced down challenge after challenge and beat each one. Maybe you should talk to Greta about this."

"Why?" I asked dejectedly.

"She's not biological; she's been through what you are going through. I was born to this; it's all I have ever known."

"But what about my job and my life?"

"What about it?"

I looked at him.

"You mean you can't take one day a month off?"

It hit me what he was saying. I'd have one day a month that I wouldn't be able to do my job. Most people got two or three days a week that they didn't have to work. But that didn't make me feel any better.

"I think it would be wise if you come back up the next couple of full moons. The pack can help you learn about it if you turn. It won't be like your gift of seeing auras. You won't be in this alone," he said, trying to sooth me the same way I had tried with Greta.

"Would you mind leaving me alone for a while?" I asked.

"I'm sorry, Ced."

"Really, I'll be fine. I'd just like a bit of a pity party for a little while."

"Okay, Do you want the light on or off?"

"Off."

He got up, flipped off the bedside lamp, and left. I cried until I fell asleep.

****

117

The rising of the sun brought a new determination in me and a decision to get my ass out of this bed and go home sometime in the near future. I was laying there thinking about what Gary and I had talked about last night and deciding if I could get up and go to the bathroom by myself when Greta opened the door silently and poked her head in.

"You awake?" she asked softly.

"Yes, come in."

Greta entered followed closely by Gary.

"Mary's here to check your wounds. Would you like some breakfast after that?" she asked.

"Yes to the breakfast, but who's Mary?"

"You met her the other night at the cookout. She's actually a registered nurse and the one that sewed you up. She's been coming by every morning to check on you," Greta explained.

"Oh."

I thought I remembered another female roaming around in the haze that had been the last three days but I just couldn't pin a face to it.

"I'll be back with breakfast in a little while," Greta said as she left the room.

"Since you have people looking after you, I'm going to go get cleaned up and go to work. I'll drop back by later and check on you," Gary said as he started to go.

"Gary?" I asked.

"Yes?" He turned back to me.

"Thank you."

"For what?"

"For sitting with me and talking to me."

"Ced, you protected my pack and in essence you protected me. I would have been nowhere else but here," he said smiling at me, and started to leave.

"Keep your head down," I said, smiling back at him.

"What?" he asked, turning around.

"Sorry. It's something the Marshals say to each other. Basically, it means when the bullets are flying, keep your head down so we can talk again."

"Oh. I'll do my best," he said, smiling at me from the door way.

"May I take a look at the patient?" a female voice asked from behind Gary.

"By all means. Ced, try and have a good day," Gary said as he went out the door and Mary came in.

"How are you feeling today?" Mary asked as she came to my bedside and began gently unwrapping my arm.

"Getting better every day," I replied, even though I was not sure it was true.

"Let's see how the arm is doing."

During our light conversation I found Mary to be an interesting mix. She was part of the pack and a wheir, but her day job was as a pediatric nurse. After having seen what wheirs were capable of, it seemed to me that she was very much the oxymoron. I watched closely as she tended to my injuries. There were stitches crisscrossing my lower arm, I would have a hell of a scar to tell my kids about, if I ever had any. Maybe I would just give birth around here and let Mary tell them. That would put the fear of God in them.

"What is so funny?" Mary asked me.

I guess I'd been chuckling out loud.

"Was just having a thought about what I would tell my kids about the massive scar on mommy's arm," I replied.

"Well it's looking pretty good. You are one lucky woman."

"How so?"

"Gary told me how big the guy was that did this. The bite itself would have shattered the bones in the arm of most people. And the shaking would have ripped it right off. But other than the gouges and flesh tears, the only real damage you suffered were a few small cracks in one bone and a dislocated shoulder. What are you?"

"I wish I knew. Up until Gary told me I smelled funny, I had no indication I was much different from any other human out there."

"Did he actually say you smelled funny?"

"No, my words not his."

"Funny, wouldn't be the words I would've used either," she said as she started re-wrapping my arm.

"What sort of care should I be giving it over the next few weeks?"

"Keep it clean and dry. Make sure that you eat things that are high in iron and protein you lost a lot of blood."

"So cans of soup won't do it. I guess I'll have to do a lot of shopping when I get home."

"You leaving?" Mary asked, somewhat shocked.

"I'm planning on going home Sunday morning, unless Willis and Greta kick me out before then."

"Does Gary know about your plans?"

"Not yet. I really don't have a handle on how this wheir thing works. Do I need his permission to leave?."

"No. I just know he's very much taken with you, as is most of the pack, and I've never seen Greta show as much affection to another female as she has with you."

"How so?"

"As soon as Greta was patched up and bandaged she immediately came in here with you. She never really left your side for two days. It took a direct order from Gary and a promise that he would not leave your side, for them to get her to go to bed last night and get some sleep."

119

"Really?" I asked, a little confused at that.

Greta had not really liked me when we first met and I knew she had never trusted me.

"You've become somewhat feared and awed around here. And in Greta and Gary's case somewhat loved."

"I don't know why. I just did my job."

"Killing an Alpha is a feat in itself, but it's what came later that really awed the pack."

"What came later?"

"Casey really didn't like you when he first met you," Mary started.

"I got that feeling."

"He was the one that got back first. But he was there right before the last one came at you. He was actually watching, from the tree line, as you tended to Greta and struggled with one arm to get your gun reloaded, cocked and aimed, while the whole time keeping a pressure bandage to her side, never moving, and with no fear that he could detect. He told everyone that you would've probably taken down the other one without ever moving from Greta's side. But he didn't want to take a chance on the wheir getting both of you, so he interceded. You won him over then."

"I didn't think that wheirs had that good of sight in their wolf state."

"It isn't that it's bad it's just that it helps if we can smell what we're seeing. Casey was downwind of you and what he was scenting and seeing made sense."

"Oh."

"He even said you took aim at Gary to keep him away from Greta after he had morphed back. Is that true?" she asked.

"I think so. I kind of remember getting ready to fire at this naked man approaching me, but I was very fuzzy by then and things went to black shortly after that," I answered.

Mary smiled at me.

"Are you coming back up next moon?"

"Probably. I'll need to get a handle on this but I have work to get done and a house of my own to take care of. Which leaves me only about three weeks to do that."

"Then just keep the arm clean and bandaged. I'm not sure what your healing time will be. Wheirs heal very fast. Sometimes, depending on the injury, it can be overnight. You seem to be healing quicker than a normal human but not as fast as a wheir. The stitches should probably come out in another week but if they start to itch so bad you can't stand it, use a pair of small sharp scissors to cut them and tweezers to pull them out. Remember to pull from the knot side. You need to start trying to move your left arm pretty soon but don't overdo it. If you don't see improvement in your shoulder over the next week you might want to see a doctor. Gary didn't want to take you to a doctor unless it was life threatening. It would have been hard to explain."

"Okay."

"Well, I got to get to work. I'll look in on you every morning 'til you leave," Mary said as she got up, collected the used bandages, and left.

I lay there thinking about how I would write this case up. Though I needed to give some sort of accurate description on how I closed the case, I needed to keep the identities of the members of the pack out of it. Gary would have to be mentioned as a local authority. I was interrupted in my thoughts by a knock at the door.

"Come in."

Greta opened the door and brought in some breakfast. She placed the tray on the chair, helped me to a lounging position, and then placed the tray across my lap.

"I bet you'll be so glad when I go home and stop being an anchor around your neck." I smiled and took a bite of my eggs.

"You've been no bother at all. Though I wish you felt better," she said, sitting down in the chair as I ate. "I made a run to the store yesterday and got you some clothes that will be easier for you to get on and off."

"Do you think we can get me up, showered, and dressed this morning?"

"Are you sure you're up to that much exertion?"

"No, not sure at all. But if I don't get out of this bed pretty soon, I'm going to go nuts."

"Well, after you finish breakfast, we'll get you to the shower and see how you feel after that."

"Works for me," I said as I took a sip of coffee.

****

I finished my breakfast and Greta took it out of the bedroom. She returned with a plastic trash bag and some surgical tape.

"You ready for a shower?"

"Yep."

She helped me to the side of the bed and let me stand up in my own time frame. My head didn't swim nearly as much as it had yesterday. My equilibrium was better from the start and I found I could walk on my own, still rather slowly, without feeling like I was going to fall over. We made it to the bathroom in record time, at least for me considering the past couple of days. Greta left me to use the toilet then returned with the plastic bag and tape. She folded the bag so it was a bit wider than the bandage on my arm. She carefully wrapped it around my arm, taping it down so that it would hold out the water.

"You need to hold your left arm as still as you can while you are in the shower," Greta said as she started unwinding the elastic bandage that kept my upper arm to my torso.

She finished unwrapping me and I stood naked in the middle of the bath.

"Do you prefer cool, warm, or hot water?" she asked as she started the shower.

"Between warm and hot."

"Are you going to want to wash your hair?"

"Probably. Why?"

"With hair that long you won't be able to wash it with one hand," she answered as she started pulling off her shirt.

I was surprised by the fact that the large bandage that was on her shoulder, just yesterday, was gone and the only visual sign that she'd ever needed one was a scar that looked relatively new. She no longer had an elastic bandage around her side for her rib and the wound she had suffered there, and again a relatively newer looking scar, along with a few fading bruises, were all that showed. She took off her shorts and panties then pulled the curtain back and held out her hand to me. I took it as I stepped in the shower. She stepped in behind me and pulled the curtain closed.

I stepped up into the spray and let the warm water wash over me. Though my shoulder hurt with almost every little movement, it was more of a dull ache and stiffness than the massive shooting pain from yesterday. Greta handed me a regular, store bought, bar of soap. I started on my front and lathered to my heart's content. Washing my left arm and pit was a bit painful but I managed to do it.

"Hand me the soap," I heard from behind me.

I held the soap back over my shoulder. Greta took it and began washing my back and places that would be impossible for me to reach. Only a few short days ago I would've been more than embarrassed by what was happening. Now it felt like one of the most natural things in the world. I felt her gentle hands up and down my back, on my butt, and down my thighs. I felt a shiver run up my back. Though the moment was erotic, there was a larger feeling of belonging that I didn't understand. I felt her move closer to me. She reached around me putting one arm over my injured one and the other under my right and pulled me to her. She held me in an embrace and nuzzled her face into the curve of my neck. I felt warm and accepted. I leaned back into her and accepted the embrace. We stood like that for a moment. She finally let her arms drop away from me.

"Get your hair wet so I can wash it."

I turned around and leaned back into the water to wet my hair.

"Can I ask a question?" I asked her.

"Sure."

"How did you handle being turned?"

"I can't really say I ever handled it. I finally became resigned to it," she answered and did a twirling motion with her finger to make me turn around.

"I was turned twelve years ago, when I was eighteen. The first couple of years I was frightened and alone. Then I met Willis. He explained some things to me and spent a few full moons with me to make me understand that it wasn't as scary as I thought it was," Greta began as she poured shampoo on my head and began to lather it up.

"I mated with him after about six months, then we married about eight months after that. He introduced me to the small pack he was with after we mated. At the time I was the only female so naturally I had status. I've come to find, over the years, that living this life has its benefits and its pitfalls."

"What are the pitfalls?" I asked as she massaged my scalp.

"There is the constant threat of outside packs and Alphas moving into our pack's territory. Also, the hierarchy of wheir society and the constant balance you have to keep between your human and wheir side, regardless of that hierarchy. There's also the constant danger of being outed by humans. But the worst, for me anyway, is how good I feel after we kill something. In my human form I'd never think about hunting, but in my wheir form that's pretty much half of what I think about."

"What are the benefits?"

"The pack. There's nothing like the feeling of togetherness that you get. The wild feeling that you get to let out every time you change; to run free through the forest and the fields is quite liberating. Your metabolism changes drastically and there's no such thing as a diet. Most days I can't eat enough to make me feel full. Your physical endurance becomes incredible. And your strength almost doubles in your human form. Sex becomes a very rough and tumble sport whether you have it as a human or a wheir; it's one of the few times the animal human meets the wheir and both are happy at the same time. You heal at incredible rates, and my favorite is my period," she said as she gently spun me around so I could rinse my hair.

"What about your period?"

"It lasts for all of about fifteen minutes. From the start of my change to wheir until it's complete. Incredibly quick," she said as she leaned over me to get some soap I had missed.

"That would be lovely; one tampon and you're done."

"Spin back around and let me put some conditioner on. Do you think you're going to turn?"

"I don't know. I've always thought I was human but everyone here has been saying I'm not, even you. Gary said that one species couldn't turn another, but he didn't seem sure of how that applied to me."

"You're an interesting mix," she agreed as she moved in closer to me and took a deep breath.

"You have the most wonderful smell."

"I've heard my odor mentioned on more than one occasion since I got up here. Could you describe it to me?"

"Hmm. Other than your female smell, you smell like a mixture of fresh cool ocean wind and warm fresh earth. That's the best way I can describe it."

"So I smell like a salty mud puddle in the middle of June?" I asked, laughing.

"You don't take compliments well do you?"

"No. Never have. Gary said something to me about the pack expecting you to abdicate so I would be alpha female. Why?" I asked, changing the subject.

"Because you've earned it."

"I understand the feeling of indebtedness from you. I've had those same feelings, on more than one occasion, about partners that have saved my life, but I don't understand those feelings from people I've really had no interaction with," I said as Greta applied the conditioner.

"You don't understand what you did for the pack the other night. Trade places with me while the conditioner sets."

"Then explain it to me," I said as we switched places and Greta started to take a shower herself.

"We both know you were just working on a case, as you see it. But by killing an Alpha and most of his pack just outside our northern border, the pack to our north will see us as a very strong pack and pretty much leave us alone. You strengthened Gary's position as the Alpha male in this pack, since he was the one to make the decision to take you along. You not only protected the pack you protected me. That says volumes to the others here. Whether you become wheir or not, you will still be considered a valued friend of this pack. I'm sure Gary has already told you as much," she said as she started washing her hair.

"I guess it's good to have friends," I said lightheartedly, smiling.

"I don't think you understand that you made twenty-one friends the other day that would fight to the death to protect you."

"What?" I asked, surprised at the statement.

"A pack views loyalty as the highest commitment. You showed your loyalty; regardless of if you view it that way. They are willing to repay that loyalty with their own, up to and including death, defending you just as you did me," she said as she finished washing and moved me back under the spray to rinse the conditioner out.

I was speechless. I'd never thought about how my closing a case would affect others.

"You ready to get out?" she asked.

"I guess so. The warm water just feels so good."

"Then stay in for a bit longer. I'll get out and get dressed."

I nodded at her and stepped back into the warm water as she got out and closed the curtain. I let my mind wander on what we'd been talking about as I listened to Greta moving about the bathroom. I heard the hair dryer kick on for a bit and then shut down. I heard the rustling of the curtain behind me.

"You're gonna become a prune. I'm turning the water off now," she said, laughing.

I felt the water cease. I turned to her and pouted.

"God, you'd think you were six years old," she said, laughing.

She offered me her hand and helped me out of the tub. She handed me a towel to start drying myself. She took another one and started on my back and my hair. After we had me toweled dry, she handed me a new tooth brush and a tube of toothpaste. She got out a hair brush and started untangling my hair. I was brushing my teeth when I thought about what Gary and I had talked about last night. I concentrated my sight on the mirror. Greta's aura popped into view behind me. I started to shut it off when I noticed something in hers. I concentrated harder and realized that I did have an aura-it was just clear, for the lack of a better term. I cocked my head to get a better understanding of what I was seeing.

"What's wrong?" Greta asked.

"Could you do me a favor?" I asked, concentrating as hard as I could on the outline around my own body.

"Sure."

"Go out to my camper. In the drawer directly to the right of the cook stove is a flashlight. Could you bring it in here?"

"We have a flashlight in the kitchen."

"Mine's a full spectrum flashlight. I need that one."

"Okay. I'll be back in a minute," she said as she put the brush down and left the bathroom.

I studied the mirror. Though I could see something around my body that looked like the shimmer of heat that rises off the pavement on a hot day, I couldn't really make anything else out. Greta returned with the flashlight.

"Close the door, turn off the lights, close the curtain, and then sit on the edge of the tub so you are below the mirror. Turn the flashlight on and aim the center of the beam at my shoulders."

"What's going on?"

"I'm not sure yet," I answered, still concentrating on the mirror.

Though the curtain on the window still let in some outside light, the room was relatively dark. I concentrated on the mirror and Greta hit the button on the flashlight. All of a sudden I could see the shimmering corona that was my aura. It was like every other I had seen only devoid of color; no that wasn't right. It had a very light blue tint to it. The blue was more like a wash as opposed to a base color. I stared at myself for a few minutes. Then shut my sight down.

"Okay. You can turn the light back on," I said, already preoccupied with what it all meant.

"What was that all about?" Greta asked as she picked up the brush and went back to my hair.

125

I thought about what I could or should tell her. I had spent years with this as my own secret, and I'd let Gary in on it. Was I going to tell the whole world now? No, but after the last few days I figured that if anybody deserved to know, it should be Greta.

"I see auras," I said after a few moments.

"You see what?" she asked a little disbelieving.

"I can see anyone's aura when I want to. Day, night, and anything in between."

"So I never needed to worry about you being able to take a shot in the dark?"

"No."

"Why didn't you tell me?"

"The only person I ever told when I was younger thought I was nuts and sent me to a psychiatrist. I would much rather you underestimated me then have you worry about being out with a crazy woman. I hope this doesn't lower your estimation of me."

"No. It only makes my trust stronger," she said.

"Have you always seen them?"

"For as long as I can remember. Where you use your sense of smell and hearing to track and locate, I use my sight."

"Did Gary know?"

"Not until last night. When I told him last night, he asked me about seeing my own. I never have before, but I thought I saw something when I was brushing my teeth."

"So, what did you see?"

"When you were standing behind me earlier I found I did have one; it is just, for lack of a better term, clear. It took an active light behind it, your aura, for me to be able to see it. With the full spectrum flashlight it showed up distinctively and well defined."

"You are a very interesting person, Ced," Greta said as she started the hairdryer.

Greta finished with the hairdryer and we started to get me dressed. She'd bought me a light short sleeved blouse, panties, and gym shorts to wear. I opted for a sling to hold my arm instead of having it taped to my torso. I quickly understood the wisdom behind the gym shorts. They allowed me to go to the bathroom by myself and not have to worry about zippers and buttons. I felt much better cleaned and clothed.

Greta picked up the used towels, put the bathroom back in order, and walked to the door.

"Back to bed?" she asked.

"No. I think I'd like to go sit on the back porch and sun myself if that's okay with you."

"I think that would be a good idea," she said as she held the door open for me.

I walked, slowly, into the kitchen with Greta.

"Do you want something to drink? Maybe some of your tea?" she asked.

"That's just for the week before my period. I'm a coffee junkie and would prefer that, if you have some made."

"Why don't you go outside, find a chair, and I'll bring you some."

"I'm tired of feeling helpless. Tell me where the mugs are and I'll get it myself."

"Upper cabinet left of the sink."

I went to the cabinet, pulled down a mug, poured my coffee, and went to the back door. I found an Adirondack chair and sat down. It felt wonderful to let the sun and breeze wash over me. I took a sip of my coffee and surveyed the back yard and the field beyond to the tree line.

****

I guess I'd fallen asleep because the next thing that I knew I heard a voice next to me.

"Ced," came the male voice into my fuzzy state.

"Ced," came Gary's voice again.

"Can a girl not get her beauty sleep?" I asked without opening my eyes.

"I think you're a woman that doesn't need it," he said, chuckling.

"Does that mean I'm so ugly that it won't do me any good?" I asked, looking up at him.

"This is the reason I'm single. There's just no complimenting your gender and no those pants don't make your butt look too big," he replied, laughing.

He was dressed in his uniform. He had a cup of coffee in one hand and a newspaper in the other. By the look of the sun, I guessed it was shortly before noon.

"Don't you have a job to do?" I asked as he took a chair next to me.

"Hey, even us low level law enforcement types get lunch," he said as he took a sip of his coffee.

"Okay, granted. I thought you weren't coming by until this evening. To what do I owe the honor of this early visit?"

"Came by to check on you and to give you this. I thought you might need it."

"A newspaper? Oh, how thoughtful," I replied sarcastically.

"You must be feeling better," he said, laughing.

I looked at the paper; it was a local one out of Kansas City. He flipped it over in my hand and pointed at the article at the bottom of the page he had it folded to. There were black and white photos of four men. I read the article underneath. It was about a local businessman and three of his employees that had gone on a fishing trip and had not returned by Tuesday for work.

"And?" I asked.

"Identification of two people you met this past Monday."

"Are you sure?"

"Yes. One thing you did not stay conscious long enough to see is; once a wheir is killed, he morphs back to his human form. I could positively I.D. three of the four from their pictures, and by process of elimination I would assume the fourth one to be the other, since someone blew most of his head and face away, but his body structure was the same."

I pointed at the businessman's picture and looked questioningly at him. He nodded his head. I turned to another page and read the rest of the story. I was surprised to learn that the three men with him all had records and were considered small time thugs. The businessman had been questioned in three sexual assaults around the Kansas City area but nothing was ever proven. Then something else caught my eye. The person he worked for was also under investigation by local police on various criminal activities. Something started working in my brain.

"Gary. Did you read the whole article?"

"No. Why?" I handed the paper back to him and pointed at the last few paragraphs.

He read through them and handed the paper back to me.

"And?" he asked.

"This might not be over."

"Why do you say that?"

"It may be just that criminals were working for criminals, but what do you know about a Mister George Greyson?" I asked reading from the paper.

"What are you getting at?"

"What if Mister Greyson is more than just a crooked human?"

Gary looked at me and cocked his head. I looked at Gary as he worked through what I had postulated. One of the things that had changed in the new union from the old was that all law enforcement officials that were elected or appointed had to take the same training that all regular enforcement officers did. If they did not pass the tests, they could not hold the office. Though there was still corruption out there, it had cut down on the number of officials that had no business being there. In a way, it was a comfort to know that even the Director of the Marshall service had the same basic training as I had. I had the same comfort in that knowledge where Gary was concerned.

"Then we may still have a very real problem in our own pack," Gary said, more to himself than me.

"I'm not sure if I like your mind or not."

"Ignorance is bliss?" I asked.

"Sometimes."

"Gary. There is something I need to discuss with you."

"That being?" he asked, turning his attention to me.

"I'll be leaving Sunday morning to head back home. And now after reading that I really need to get back."

"What? You're in no condition to travel."

"Maybe. But I need to look into this and without my computer I can't."

"You could come to my office and use one of ours."

"No, I can't."

"Why not?"

"One: I was dropped out in the middle of nowhere, and something is still bothering me about that. I've had to cut most ties with my friends from where I used to be for their protection and I don't need a path that leads back to the pack's doorstep. Two: my setup gives me access to things yours won't."

"I'll miss you," he said, looking at me with those beautiful, sad, green eyes.

"Hey, I'll be back in about three weeks," I said, smiling.

"Oh. You'll be coming back up for the next moon?"

"I think that would be the best plan. I would hate to be sitting in a bar and slobber into my drink after nightfall," I said, smiling.

"Have you always been such a smart-ass?" he asked.

"Pretty much."

"I have a favor to ask though," I said.

"What would that be?"

"I need a phone that's not connected to me. I'd like to keep in touch with you and the pack, but I want no connection between my official phone and anyone up here. If you have anyone that could disable the tracking device in it, that would be a plus. I have cash so it would be untraceable, and it can't be in your name either since you'll be listed in my report as a local contact I used when I came up here. I wish I could leave your name out of it, but you wrote a few of the reports that this case was based on and a requirement of my job is that I have to notify local police if I'm in their area."

"Yeah, I think we can get that done."

"By the way. What are you going to do if someone finds the bodies?"

"The only thing that someone might find will be wherever they left their clothes. Unless they are a wheir, they would have to know exactly where to look to even find a trace of them, and what's left of the actual bodies will never be identified."

"How can you be so sure?"

"Having a mortician that also runs the local crematorium in the pack is a plus," he said, smiling.

I thought of something he said to me the first day I really met him.

"So you weren't lying to me when you told me that they wouldn't find my body."

"Nope."

"Ouch, that hurts," I said, smiling

"Well, my lunch is over and I need to get back to work. I'll come by this evening to check on you," he said as he got up.

"Keep your head down."

"You too," he answered as he went back into the house.

I closed my eyes and let the sun bake me.

Chapter 12
Saturday May 13, 2248

It was Saturday night. Gary, Willis, and Greta had put together a party, sort of a going away thing, though I truly believed this little community would use any excuse for a get-together.

I was getting around a lot better and though my shoulder and forearm still hurt excessively, I was able to dress myself. I could hear people starting to arrive as I was in my bedroom getting ready. Over the last few days I'd learned a lot about wheirs and pack dynamics. I made sure that I didn't use anything with a lot of scents in it since, even in human form, the wheir sense of smell was so keen a lot of smells added together tended to assail them to such a degree as to be offensive. I came out of my room and went to the kitchen to see if Greta needed any help, but she just shooed me out into the back yard where everyone was gathered. I'd learned from the last party and from Gary there were twenty wheirs, not including him, in his pack. Out of those, five were female and only two of those were unattached. I stepped out on the porch. Gary glued himself to my side. I removed myself from the group to cook my own steak, since all of them thought I was barbaric to not eat mine raw. But as soon as I returned to the group, Gary reinstalled himself at my side.

"Do I still need a bodyguard?" I whispered to him.

"In a way. If the unattached males think you're fair game they'll be fighting amongst themselves to try and court you and gain your status. I'm just trying to keep peace in my pack and protect you from having to deal with that this evening," he whispered back.

"Marking your territory?" I asked smiling.

Damned if he didn't blush.

"Not in such a crass term," he said.

"Sheriff Benton, If I did not know better I'd say you're sweet on the new schoolmarm," I picked at him.

He stuck another bite of steak in his mouth to cover up his own awkwardness. I searched the crowd of people. I noticed Mary sitting at one of the picnic tables. There was a guy sitting next to her that seemed to be trying too hard. She seemed very uninterested but it wasn't dawning on him that she wanted nothing to do with him. His name was Phillip; he was the one I remembered having the red and black in his aura from the last get-together.

Gary had explained to me how he'd set up his pack. There were three very strong males with alpha traits. He'd split the pack up so that each sub-Alpha basically had a smaller pack under them and a portion of the overall territory that they were responsible for. He'd told me that at some point in the future he'd be challenged by one of them for leadership of the whole pack. I understood the wisdom of his thought process. If the other Alphas had to worry about challenges from below them, his position was relatively safe. He admitted that the major risk he ran would be that one of them would basically break his pack away from the rest of the group and establish themselves as independent. But the whole pack realized that Gary was a strong and fair leader as a wheir, and the protection he offered as a human, being the local law enforcement, was a combination that was too good to challenge.

I'd been uncomfortable, at first, with the constant sniffing of me, and that had not changed. I understood it was basically their way of shaking hands but it was still unnerving for me when they would take a good whiff of me as they literally shook my hand. I sat and watched them as a group. I knew that, even in human form, scent was identification for them just as faces and names were for me. It hit me then, other than the six of them I'd gone out with, I'd not really identified each one of them with my gift. I'd always felt that extended aura viewing was an invasion of privacy, but why should I be limited in my knowledge of them by stunting my gift around them when they used all of their senses to identify me? I let my sight wander from guest to guest to identify them in my own way. I was brought up short when I got to Philip. His aura seemed even deeper red than the last time I'd looked and the black was even more pronounced. Those same black lines were in the aura of every criminal I'd ever arrested.

"Tell me about Philip."

"A relatively new member of the pack. He's a CPA that moved here about five years ago, shortly after he was turned. He stayed solitary for about a year, we kept an eye on him and other than killing a domestic cow or two he made no trouble. Though, evidently we haven't broken him of that habit since that's what you caught onto when you came up last month."

"Ah... So that was the person you wanted to kill," I said, smiling.

"Yes it was. We brought him into the pack for his own protection, and other than not being much help in a fight, he seems to have come to some sort of grip with what he is. In the human world he's helpful with money matters and in the pack he's not a hindrance. Why?"

"Just wondering. He seems to be very awkward in a social setting," I said, nodding my head in Phillip and Mary's direction.

"Yes. Doesn't take hints very well," Gary acknowledged.

"Will you excuse me for a minute? I'd like to talk to Mary," I said as I got up.

"Sure."

I picked up my beer and headed in the direction of the picnic table where Mary and Philip sat.

"Can I join you?" I asked Mary as I approached the table, keeping my sight on Philip.

"Sure," she said, openly relieved that I had sat down.

"How are you feeling?" she asked.

"Much better than a few days ago."

"Have you been able to start moving that arm?"

"Some, but it gets achy and tired quickly," I said, indicating the sling.

"Keep moving it."

"I will," I told her.

"Philip, isn't it?" I politely asked the man seated next to her.

"Yes," he replied, not meeting my gaze.

I didn't need my sight to tell me that he feared and hated me. But my sight showed me the red and black streaks getting deeper with the polite conversation we were having. I stayed for an acceptable amount of time, excused myself, and went back to my place to finish my meal.

"What are you up to?" Gary asked me as I sat down.

"Just getting some medical advice before I head home."

He looked at me. We both knew I was lying through my teeth but he let it drop. The party went late and I was exhausted when I finally fell into bed for the night.

Chapter 13
Sunday May 14, 2248

I was saying my good-byes to Greta and Willis when Gary drove up in his cruiser. He got out and came towards me.

"Gonna leave without saying good-bye?" he asked, smiling.

"You snooze you lose," I said, matching his smile.

"You loaded and ready to hit the road?"

"Yep."

"Let me walk you to your monstrosity," he said as he offered me his arm.

"Her name is Bee," I said to him with a fake sense of the insulted.

"What?"

"Her name is Bee and she'll be very upset with you if you slight her."

"Are you kidding me?"

I just stood there and looked at him.

"Women...." he said, shaking his head.

"Willis, Greta. Thanks again for everything. I'll see you in a couple of weeks. I hope you won't mind if I crash here for a couple of days," I said, turning my attention back to my hosts.

"You're always welcome and you can stay for as long as you like. Maybe next time it won't be as hectic," Willis said, smiling.

Greta came over, put her arms around me, and gave me a kiss on the cheek.

"You call me if you need anything," she said.

I thought I saw a very large crack in her normally reserved exterior.

"I will. I promise," I said as we broke apart and Willis came up to her and put his arm around her waist.

I smiled at them and Gary walked me out to Bee. He opened the door then turned to face me. He took my good hand in his and covered it with his other.

"You be careful and keep in touch," he said.

"Don't worry, I will," I said, smiling up at all six four of him and ending with those wonderful green eyes.

"Here. As requested, tracking turned off. It's paid for a year and it's in a friend of Casey's name," he said as he reached in his pocket, pulled out a cellphone and charger, and handed it to me.

I took the items and tossed them up on the dash.

"You have the number?" I asked.

He nodded his head.

"Give the number to Greta and Willis but for right now keep it between the three of you," I said.

"Okay. Will do," he said, looking at me quizzically.

"I'll see you in a few weeks," I said as I reached up with my good arm and pulled him down in a hug.

He reached around me with both of his strong arms and lifted me off the ground and sat me up in the cab of the camper. I closed the door and rolled the window down.

"Drive safe," he said as I started the engine.

"Will do, keep your head down," I replied as I stuck it in reverse, backed around, and headed down the drive to the road.

****

It was a long and emotional drive. For, as high as I was about going home having closed my first case, I was just as apprehensive about the next full moon and the new knowledge of not being human. I repeatedly went from high to low in a matter of seconds thinking about the past week. I was exhausted by the time I turned onto the road to my house. It took me a second to recognize Bran walking towards my house. *Deja vu*, I thought. I rolled down the window and pulled up next to him.

"Haven't we met like this before?" I asked.

I seemed to have startled him out of a serious train of thought.

"Cedwynne!" He said, surprised.

"What are you doing out this way on foot? Leave a book again or did you just miss me?"

"May I get in?"

"Sure," I said as I stuck the shifter in park and unlocked the passenger door.

He crossed over in front of the truck and climbed in. Though I'd worn long sleeves I still wore the sling and he noticed that.

"What happened to you?"

"I took a hard fall, I'll be fine."

"You seem to do a lot of that when you go out of town."

I'd forgotten I was a bit rough around the edges last month when I'd found him on my road.

"Hazards of the job. What are you doing out this way on a Sunday?"

"Checking on your house."

"Checking on the house, why?"

"I didn't get out here to cut the grass until Tuesday afternoon this week. When I got there a dark sedan with tinted windows was sitting in front of your house. A man in a dark suit asked me what I was doing there."

"What did you tell him?"

"The truth. I told him that I was taking care of the lawn. He seemed very intent on not answering any question I posed to him."

"What did he look like?"

"Tall, in good shape, sunglasses, brown hair, and serious. Very government. I asked him if he wanted to leave a message for the owner of the house. He seemed very nervous, said no, and left. I just figured it had something to do with your job so I did the lawn and headed back to town. I thought it odd that the same sedan was parked at the Dairy Bar across from this road when I left. So I have been walking back out here every day to check on things."

"You didn't happen to get a plate number did you?"

"No, but it was a government tag."

Great, what was this all about? I didn't need something else on my plate right now; I had enough to worry about. Maybe it was just someone sending me some information but that seemed unlikely since the only people who'd need to get in touch with me had my phone number. I was having a sinking feeling in my stomach.

"Thanks for keeping an eye on the place," I said, still thinking.

"Any time."

"Can I drop you somewhere?"

"No, my truck is parked on a side road not far from here. I can get to it by cutting through the woods over there," he said, pointing to the woods to my left.

"Do you need help getting anything in the house today?" he asked, indicating my arm.

"I have a suitcase in the back that I'd appreciate the help with."

"Then drive on."

I put Bee in gear and drove on to my house. This was nagging at me more and more just in the short distance to my carport. I stopped, put it in park, and shut the engine off. I grabbed the phone and charger off of the dash and we both climbed out of the cab. Bran met me by the back door of the camper. I opened it up and let him get my suitcase out. I opened the house and we both entered, stepping over the mountain of papers that had accumulated over the past week. I'd left the AC on so it wasn't hot or stuffy this time. Something was nagging at my attention but I couldn't put a finger on it.

"My bedroom's the last door on the right down the hall. If you'd put that on the bed, I'd appreciate it," I said as I crossed into the kitchen to plug in my phone.

It was then I noticed it. I couldn't see out the front windows. I hadn't remembered closing the curtains. In fact in the whole month I'd been here the only curtains that I remember closing were the ones in my bedroom. I'd never closed the ones in the living room, because I could see out those windows into the front yard while I was cooking or doing dishes. Had someone been in here or was I being overly suspicious and had closed them before I left? Regardless, I was now paranoid and my brain began to run with it.

"Are you okay?" Bran asked.

"What?"

"Are you okay? You seem off somewhere."

What if someone was listening in on our conversation? *Come on, Ced.*

Really? Now you're just being paranoid.

"No. I'm fine. I was just thinking about something. We've missed a couple of Fridays, would you like to stick around and have a steak or burger?"

"As long as it includes a beer," he answered, smiling.

"Would you mind cooking this evening? I seem to be a little handicapped."

"It would be my pleasure," he replied as he went to the back door, removed the bar, unlocked it, and went out on the back porch to start the fire.

I pulled two beers out of the fridge and followed him out on the porch to hand him one. I came back inside to wash up a little. I pulled two steaks out of the fridge, sat them on a plate to come to room temperature, and went back to my bathroom to wash my hands and face. My mind would not let go of the curtains as I stood at the sink. I decided to do a walk-through of the house and see if anything else was off. I dried my hands and face and began a stroll through the house. I walked slowly, going through each room, paying attention to everything I thought important. Not dusting was a bad habit of mine, but I looked around to see if any of the dust that had accumulated over the past month had been disturbed. I found nothing in the three bedrooms or the two baths. I moved out to the living room. I inspected the curtains and windowsill. I couldn't see anything that seemed out of place. Nothing seemed moved. *Okay, Ced, you're being nuts.* I went back into the kitchen, grabbed my beer, and went out to the back to enjoy my Friday habit on a Sunday.

Chapter 14
Monday May 15, 2248

The clock next to the bed read almost ten in the morning by the time I motivated myself to get up. I took a shower, taking extra care with my arm, and got dressed for the day. I reapplied a dressing to my forearm and sat it gently back in the sling. I started a pot of coffee and made some breakfast.

I sat down at the table, with breakfast in hand, and thought about what I needed to get done today. I needed to do a closing report on the case. I needed to do some follow up research on George Greyson and see what that revealed and if it was just a coincidence that all four wheirs worked for him or not. I wanted to do some checking on Philip just in case he had something to do with this. I also needed to contact the agent that had the section that included Kansas City and inform them that the case I had just closed extended into their district and that it possibly closed cases that they were watching. I finished up my meal, rinsed off the plate, got a cup of coffee, and headed down to the basement.

I fired up both computers and pulled up a template of our official report. First things first, close the case. I began typing, although hampered by my disability. I defined my terms of proven, probable, and possible for the cases that this report would be closing, including the four around Kansas City that Gary had pointed out to me. I found references to three of them in open cases from the section above mine. It took me a full forty-five minutes to type the report with one hand. I finished the report, printed a copy off for my own files, and then filed the electronic one to the master case file on the Counter Section server started by my predecessor.

I got a new file folder out of the desk, assigned a case number to it, though I didn't start one on the server just yet. I placed the newspaper article that Gary had given me in the folder and set it aside for whatever information I might find in my search today. I looked up at the map to find the section that included Kansas City. I copied the phone number and the initials 'TTZ' on a piece of paper.

I ran upstairs to refill my cup and went back to my computers. I started with the police database for George Greyson. It took a while to return an exorbitant number of hits. I began systematically going through them, printing them off, and filing them to my computer. As I got about halfway through the list, I finally got smart and pulled up the U.S. Marshal database on the laptop and did the same search. Though there were no cases open or closed in the Marshal database, it did list as references all of the cases I was printing out from the other computer. I was almost done printing, collating, and stapling the printed matter. As the last couple of files printed off I pulled up the IBI database on the laptop and repeated my search. It pretty much returned the same information and case files as the police search but with the addition of one last case number. It was an

Army Intelligence case file. I'd run across a few of these before. If you were lucky enough to get into the file, most of it would be redacted because of classified information, and very little would be of use. All of the other files had printed from the main computer so I went to the portal for Army Intelligence and after putting in my control number and password about three times, it sent me to a search page. I typed in the case number. A box came up asking for my password. I'd come across this before. I'd put in my password and it would just say I wasn't authorized to view the file. I typed it in anyway and hit enter. To my elated surprise it popped the file up. Other than some names here and there that were redacted, the file was complete. I hit print and save and waited. The printer spit out the four pages and the file saved to my computer. I had just closed out of the Army Intelligence server when the phone on my desk rang.

"Hello?" I asked in the receiver.

"Marshal McKenzie?" The voice speaking asked.

"Yes."

"Have you been on the Army Intelligence server?"

"Unless you identify yourself, this conversation is at an end," I said into the phone.

"This is Jeremy Pinter, Director, IBI," the voice almost yelled into the phone.

Though the person on the other end of the phone was probably who he said he was, I couldn't just take a voice's say so.

"What may I do for you today?"

"You can answer the question."

"I will call you back on the number I have listed for you and I will discuss this with you."

"You hang up on me it'll mean your job."

I was liking IBI less and less as time went by.

"One: you can't fire me on your own. Two: I'm protecting myself and you by the rules that were spelled out to me by not only your agency, but my other two supervisors and my predecessor. If you cannot abide by the rules you helped develop, then I suggest that you start the process to relieve me of my post," I said and immediately hung up.

I picked up my official cell, flipped it open, located the programed number, and hit dial. I waited for the beeps then pressed the key I'd programed for my control number. It rang a couple of times.

"Hello," a gruff angry voice answered.

"Director Pinter?" I asked as sweetly as I could.

"You're on very thin ice, Marshal."

I figured I should smooth some ruffled feathers since at some point in time I might need the man on the other end of the call as an ally.

"Director Pinter. Please understand I meant no insult. I had to make sure that protocol was followed. This was the only way I could guarantee I was validating your identity. I read everything available to me where it came to safeguarding not only information, but identities as well. And if I say no, or refuse to answer something, I'm staying strictly within the job as I understand it. I hope you will accept my apology for any slight or insubordination you might have perceived," I said, laying it on as thick as I thought I could get away with.

"My apologies also. The Secretary of The Army just called me and chewed my ass. It seems you accessed a case that was red flagged because of national security. I need to know what you were looking for," a calmer voice spoke to me.

"Last Monday I closed case number CS05-2047/0511-0021/JTL and in so doing, another case may be connected, or at least it might be a loose end since it crosses over into another agent's district. I am running down a lead on a suspect before I either continue on with it, turn it over to the other section agent, turn what information I can over to the local authorities, or trash it as a dead lead. One of the case files that was listed under his name in the IBI database was the one that belonged to Army Intelligence. I figured since my control number opened up the file that I had clearance to view it. I was just collecting information on my subject and as far as I know the two cases are not connected. I don't know if it's even a case that needs to remain in my purview. I was just trying to be thorough before I called everything closed and went to my next case."

"I can't blame you for being thorough. Can you give me the name you were researching?"

I figured I could give him a tidbit since his clearance level was as high as or higher than mine.

"George Greyson," I answered.

"What makes you think he's tied to the case you closed?"

"The threat I neutralized held a low level posting in his company. When I did a search on Mister Greyson I found a trail of investigation records that led back forty-five years. But his transgressions, as far as I can tell, don't fall in the realm of my job. I'm just making sure he isn't the same type of threat as the perpetrator I just dealt with. If he looks like he might be, I'll probably hand it over to the agent whose district he resides in."

"Oh. So that's the reason for all of this?"

"I am afraid so and I'm sorry about that."

"Not your fault and I apologize again for my behavior. How long have you been on the job?"

"A little over a month."

"That's impressive, closing a case in that short of amount of time. I think I understand why you were chosen. Have you spoken with the other agent yet?"

"No sir. I just got back home late yesterday. It's taken me most of the morning to write my reports. I decided I'd call that agent tomorrow after I checked in with my liaison," I answered.

"Okay fine. I'll deal with the Secretary. Good-bye."

"Goodbye, sir. I promise I'm through poking around Military Intelligence."

I heard a small chuckle as the phone went dead. I folded up my phone and put it on the desk. I finished collating and stapling the files I'd printed, and put them in the folder I'd started. I'd read these more in depth, later.

Now to do some checking into Philip. I went to the U.S. Marshal database and typed in Philip Allen Andrews, Joplin. Other than his driver's license, nothing else came back. I saved the file to my computer after I copied down his birth date and license number. I jumped over to a general search of records. I got a hit on his birth certificate, his CPA license, a marriage certificate from fifteen years ago, and a divorce listing from a Kansas City paper from five years ago. I figured that would've been about the time he was turned. I went back to the general police database. His name came up in reference to another file. I followed that lead and was shocked that his name was in a report of an investigation involving none other than George Greyson almost twenty years ago. I read the report. It listed him as a low level accountant working for Greyson's company who was questioned in connection with an ongoing investigation concerning a racketeering allegation against Greyson. Philip wasn't held or listed as a suspect after the initial interview. The allegation was never proven and there were discrepancies in statements, the investigating officer noted as much, and the investigation was closed. So now the person I thought to be the mole in Gary's pack was also connected to Greyson. With Philip being tied to Greyson, I printed out two copies of that report and saved an electronic one to the file I'd made for Philips driver's license on my computer. I placed one of the printouts in the file folder laying on the desk and sat the other one aside for Gary.

Did Greyson have anything to do with it, or was he just the owner of the company and the wheirs involved knew each other from having worked for him? That seemed to be an excellent theory: the Alpha I'd killed had wanted Gary's territory and possibly his pack, and he knew Phillip from when they worked at Greyson's company. Phillip had given him information on Gary's movements so that the Alpha could attack. Though it was a good theory it was a little too cut and dried and there was one thing that bothered me about it. Where was Philip getting his information? Gary didn't include him in any of the inner workings of the pack. In fact I got the impression the only reason Phillip was in the pack at all was that Gary wanted to protect him from himself. Still a loose end there.

I was interrupted by the doorbell. I went upstairs to answer the door; Bran stood in the doorway. I'd forgotten that he would be out today to cut the lawn.

"Are you ever going to do anything about this mountain of dead trees?" he asked, indicating the enormous pile of papers that had collected there.

"One of these years."

"Just wanted to tell you I was here."

"Need anything to drink before you start?"

"No. I have a jug of water with me."

"Ring the bell if you need anything I have to get back to work."

"Will do," he replied as he turned and walked off the porch and I closed the door behind him already back to the thoughts I was working through before he got there.

Loose ends: who was Philip getting his information from?

Another thing that was bothering me was that I'd been the wild card in the mix, yet the Alpha knew I was there and didn't seem worried about it. But if the Alpha knew I was there then he would've had to have newer information. That could mean that one of the six wheirwolves I went out with last weekend was feeding Philip information to pass on. So that meant that I'd have to add Gary, Willis, Craig, Thomas, Greta, and Casey to the suspect list. *So let's look at their reasons to feed information to Philip.*

What did Gary have to gain? Defeating four males on his northern border would make him look stronger to the packs around him. I found it a little far-fetched that he would go to all that trouble and risk losing a female. Unless taking out his major competition in the three sub-Alphas and the alpha female in the pack was part of his plan.

Willis, Craig, Thomas, and Greta all had the same motive. Get rid of Gary.

Casey was a last minute addition and didn't know the plan. Okay, one suspect eliminated. I felt the need to eliminate Greta also. Even if she knew about a coup, I doubted she was strong enough to overtake the sub-Alphas and impress her will on them to pull it off as her own plan.

So I was down to four. Could I bring that number down some? I was still the wild card in this. If, whoever was feeding the information to Philip had hoped that I'd be a casualty; then Gary was looking a little less like a suspect. If it was Gary, why'd he let me live? I wasn't sure how quickly the rest of them could morph back to two legs but Gary had already turned back to human when I passed out. It would've been very easy for him to open one of my arteries and let me bleed the rest of the way out. It would've been an easy cover for him to tell everyone that I just lost too much blood and died. Hell, as far as that went he could have just killed me outright and no one would have cared since what the Alpha says, goes. For right now Gary went to the list that included Greta and Casey.

Willis, Thomas, and Craig. Why would Willis risk Greta? With the number of males to females in the wheir community that would just be stupid, and I didn't think Willis was stupid. Besides Willis was willing to charge me when I had a drawn gun loaded with silver to save her. Not to mention his attention to her when he settled down. Nope; Willis to the other list.

Thomas and Craig; very viable. Get rid of Gary and Greta, the two main alphas in the pack. Plausible. However Craig was with Gary when they ran into two rogue wheirs. It would've been very easy for Craig to switch sides and the three of them take Gary down. He didn't do that; he helped Gary kill the one that stayed then came on to kill the last one in the clearing.

Now, that I was down to Thomas, he seemed to look guiltier. I had no argument or facts that I could even construe to clear him.

Only one thing to do. Run everyone and see if there were any connections between them and the four wheirs we killed last Monday. I started at the top and worked my way down. After most of the afternoon I'd worked my way through Gary, Willis, Thomas, and Craig. Though I'd found out a few interesting tidbits about them, I found nothing linking them to the other four wheirs, or even Philip, other than being in the same pack. That left me with Greta and Casey. I ran both of them. Casey had very little out there and Greta had even less. No helpful conclusions there. My stomach, however, made a conclusion of its own: it was hungry and I'd not had anything since this morning.

I went upstairs and quickly made a sandwich. As I took a bite it hit me that Bran hadn't been back for water or anything. I went to the front window and looked out. His truck was gone. I was surprised that he hadn't said good-bye.

With sandwich in hand I sat back down at the computers. I sat looking at the doodles and lines I'd been making from one name to another. Though Thomas was looking like my best suspect, I had one thing left I really had to take notice of; my sight. I had eaten a meal with the whole pack on Friday before we went out and then again a couple of days ago. At both those times I'd looked at everyone in the pack with my sight and not a one of them, except Philip, had anything in their auras coming anywhere close to anger or aggression; no red, no black snakes.

Great, I had another never ending loop with Philip at the center of it. The wheirs that were killed knew where we were going to be. Philip had to be the mole since he was connected to the outside wheirs via Greyson. But who was giving Philip his information?

I'd like to talk to Gary about this, but if by some chance he was involved that would be a bad idea. If he wasn't involved and I told him, he'd rip out Philip's throat before I could find out who was pulling the strings. I decided I'd had enough of this mental masturbation. It would have to wait until tomorrow, since I was getting sleepy and tired of being down here.

I grabbed my coffee cup, the folder, my phone, and headed up the stairs. I turned off the coffee pot, rinsed my cup, and headed back to my bedroom with file folder in hand. I put the folder on the bed, my two phones on the nightstand next to my gun, pulled off my clothes, and went to the bathroom to get ready for bed.

I crawled into the bed clean and ready to read. I arranged the files on George

Greyson chronologically, except the one from Army Intelligence which I placed last. Over the next three hours I found out more about the shady life of one George Greyson than I cared to know. The most interesting thing I learned about him was that he must have been made out of Teflon since nothing had ever really stuck to him. He went to trial two times. One had been a hung jury twice and the statute of limitations had run out before the prosecution could bring him before the court a third time. The other one had the charges dropped when two of the three key witnesses recanted their testimony and the third disappeared. He now owned a string of restaurants and coffee shops in west central Missouri along with an import/export business that seemed awfully small for the amount of funds that went through it.

I turned my attention to the final file, the one from Army Intelligence, in the folder. I began reading it. Evidently, a ranking officer of the army had sold or tried to sell some sensitive information about some project. One of the names that was listed as a suspected buyer was George Greyson. A lot of investigation went into the case; including wiretaps and in home listening devices, but nothing solid had been produced. After about a year the Special Agent in charge of the case was replaced. The investigation continued under the new Special Agent for another year. Though promising leads appeared, they petered out and since the sensitive material that had been thought to be leaked became obsolete, the case, though still open, was put on the back burner. I was about to flip the other three pages over and put the file back in the folder, when I noticed the signature and name of the last Special Agent. There below his signature was his printed name. Special Agent in charge, Terrence T. Zahn.

Was this just a coincidence? Or was it one more in a long line of coincidences that ended up not being coincidences? The agent in charge of Section 10, the one above mine, was TTZ. I knew there were many people throughout the country with a last name that began with a Z. But let's face it, the only other two letters in the alphabet that would have as few or fewer would be Q and X, and for someone to have the same initials was possible, but the the possible was becoming less probable when you started adding in the other similarities. Both were in a form of law enforcement, and both were in close proximity to the subject. The army file was from West Virginia when George Greyson was there and George Greyson now lived and worked in the same district as the other TTZ. I so wanted to run downstairs and see if I could pull up a picture of Special Agent Zahn, but I knew that if he was the agent above me I'd probably be breaking protocol, big time. And if he wasn't, I'd be opening up a whole can of worms that had nothing to do with this case. I'd been able to close the last can with Director Pinter but I wasn't sure I could do it again. I had to satisfy myself with the puzzle. It was a good thing I always liked puzzles. I stuffed all of the files back into the folder and placed it on the nightstand and turned out the light.

The Water's Edge

I'm always annoyed and amazed when my brain works the most just as I'm trying to shut it down. Tonight was no different. It laid out three scenarios before me. One: everything with TTZ was actually a coincidence period. Two: Special Agent Terrence Zahn had been jerked out of his assignment and thrown to the wolves, like I had, and since he'd been working the case against Greyson they put him in that area so he could also keep an eye on Greyson. Three: TTZ was in bed with Greyson and was part of the reason things didn't stick to him. For the most part I ruled out number one. When it came to this case, I didn't believe there were any coincidences. Number two was highly probable and I could accept the reasoning, knowing the way our government worked. I was having a hard time with number three. I would think that the research that went into picking Counter Section agents would be very in depth and thorough, but then again I had no idea what criteria they used to find us. There would be one way, at least in my mind, to rule out number three. Which came first; the chicken or the egg? If Greyson was in Kansas City before TTZ was assigned to that district, I would lay my money on number two. If TTZ was in the district first, then my money would be on; however far-fetched, number three or number one. But it couldn't be number one since I'd already ruled it out. It took about another hour before my brain let my body sleep.

Chapter 15
Tuesday May 16, 2248

I woke up early, threw some clothes on, gathered up all of the things on my nightstand, and went to the kitchen to start coffee. As I waited for the coffee pot to fill I thought about the best way I could find out when TTZ took over without raising any flags. As the last drops from the brew fell into the full pot, I had it. I filled my cup and with file in hand, went down to the basement.

I looked at the last date on the file from Army Intelligence. I went to the Counter Section server and searched on all files from District ten one year before the last date on the AI file. Once I had those files I had the initials of the agent prior to TTZ, an ATB. I searched all files for district ten opened by ATB and closed within the year after the Army Intelligence file. I picked the last three of that agent's files to be closed and opened them one at a time. In the second one I found what I was looking for. Just as I'd done yesterday, he'd closed his predecessor's case with a date and his initials. I wrote that date down. If that was the first case he closed, which it might not have been, I would back up the date by six months just to be on the safe side and use that as a start date for TTZ as a Section agent. I looked through the file folder and picked out dates until I could find Greyson in Kansas City. I was shocked. When TTZ was closing a case in district ten, Greyson was around Lexington Kentucky. He didn't get to Kansas City until a year after TTZ closed that old case of his predecessor. I picked up my mug, took a drink, and stared at the screen. For some reason this was bothering me. If, and I'd admit that was a big if, it was true that TTZ was working with or for Greyson, what else could be hinky about Counter Section? I know it could just be a coincidence, but government cars in front of my house and the curtains that I never close being closed, was really coloring my thoughts on this.

Okay, Reality Check time: Come on, Ced, do you really think that TTZ is dirty? Do you really think that the Government is watching you and interfering in your home based on a moved piece of fabric and a car? Do you really think Greyson is out to get you because his name came up tied to some thugs that you took out and his connection with an old military intelligence agent that has the same initials as the Counter Section agent in the district above yours?

Hey girl, the other side of the argument spoke up: *two months ago Counter Section was just a myth, you were a human with a gift that helped you catch the bad guys, and wheirwolves didn't exist outside of horror and fantasy novels.*

I looked down at my bandaged arm. I was probably not human and I'd been out with, and bitten by, one of the fantasy creatures. I closed down the computer, put the file in the top drawer of my desk, and went upstairs for more coffee and breakfast. As I crunched on my dry cereal I started to plan out my day. I needed to go for a run and clear my head. But first things first. I grabbed my official phone and dialed Burdock's office number.

"Burdock," came the answer after a couple of rings.

"Hey Captain," I said as cheerfully as I could.

"Ced! I was beginning to get worried; it's been over a week."

"I'm fine. I was working a case and was away for a bit. Didn't think it was prudent to call you last week."

"Everything going okay?"

"Yep. Closed my first case. That was an experience."

"Damn, McKenzie, that was quick."

"I think I got a little lucky on that one."

"Anything you need to tell me?"

"Nope. Just a check in."

"Well then, some of us have to work in an office for a living. I'll talk to you next week."

"Will do. Have a good one," I said as we both hung up.

I thought about my arm as I started to get dressed to go running. Maybe running wasn't the best option. Mary had told me I needed to start using it, but maybe the pounding of a run wasn't in its best interest. I had woods on my property and it backed up to a state forest; maybe a hike through the forest would be a better idea. I dug my hiking boots out of the closet, put them on, and headed towards the front door. As I started to turn the knob I had the thought that I knew nothing about the property that I lived on. I went back down to my computer, turned it on, waited for the boot up process, and found a search icon of the national property database. I typed in my address and waited. While it was searching, I found a topo map of Hot Springs and the surrounding area. The plot listing came up and I wrote down the coordinates of the property and traced it on the map. I searched for the last title transfer and the abstract that went along with it. The property was roughly ten acres, basically square, butted up to the national forest on the northern side, and until March thirtieth had been owned by the federal government. Now, however, it was titled to one Cedwynne Anne McKenzie. Wow, just like the two vehicles outside, it seemed I also owned my house and property. I shut down the computers, picked up the map, and headed out to walk the property.

The sun was bright and the day was warming up quickly. I walked out into the woods and headed towards the national forest. I left my arm out of the sling to try and give it some exercise. I ran over everything I had going on in my head: Greyson, the Pack, Philip, Zahn, TTZ, closed curtains, dark cars with government plates, dark suited men around my house, not being human, and a wheir bite that may or may not change me. If I didn't know better, I'd say it was Wednesday. My mind started talking to itself. I'd closed the case so why did I need to take it any further? Was any of this really my problem? Warring packs were not under my purview as long as bodies didn't start showing up. Were

Greyson and TTZ my worry? Not really; out of my district and probably should be handled by another agency, if at all.

I found the old fence line and began to follow it. I turned over my decisions in my head as I counted fence posts. I'd been hiking for almost two hours when I reached my driveway, all the way around the property from where I started. I made my decisions as I approached my home. Greyson and TTZ/Zahn would go on the back burner and stay there unless it reared its ugly head. I'd call TTZ about the cases I'd closed in his area. Where the pack was concerned, I would need a little more involvement. They were in my district and I, as a U.S. Marshal, was sworn to protect them. As a whole, the pack saved my life and I just might need them more than I wanted to admit about right now. I would talk to Gary about Philip when I went back up in a couple of weeks, and I'd try and find out where Philip had gotten his information. As far as the government vehicle went, I'd keep an eye out and see if there were any more clues I could come up with. So until the next full moon on June seventh, I'd continue to build my cases, clean up the dead trees on my porch, and work with my arm to get it back in shape.

****

It took me five trips to move all of the papers off the porch and pile them in the living room so that I could go through them later. I went downstairs got TTZ's phone number, made a few notes about files on the same piece of paper, and went back outside to be in the sunshine. I'd spent the last two days in the basement and I needed a break.

I dialed the number I had written down. I waited a few rings when a male voice answered.

"Hello?" it said.

"Agent TTZ, District ten?"

"Who is this?" he asked suspiciously.

"CAM, District five."

"Yeah right."

"Are you near your map?"

"Yes," he said, still suspicious.

"Call me back on the number listed under my initials," I said and hung up.

I waited a few minutes. I was beginning to believe he thought it was a prank call. A few seconds later my phone rang.

"Hello."

"Still not sure."

"If you're near your map, you're near a computer. Get on the Counter Section Server. Look up case number CS05-2047/0511-0021/JTL," I said, reading the case number to him.

"Okay. Hold on a moment," he answered.

"Got it," he said after a few seconds.

"I closed that case last week. There are four police cases referenced in your area. I know you were watching three of them; I'm not sure about the fourth. I listed three of those cases as probably closed and the fourth one as a possible. I thought I'd let you know so you wouldn't spend a lot of time on them other than to make sure the last one was or wasn't associated," I said.

"Great. Thanks. But you should have called me before you went after them. I could've helped."

"I ran across those cases from Kansas City very late in the game and really didn't have time. By the time I even thought about calling you it was over."

"You're the new kid on the block, aren't you?"

"I guess so," I said as cheerfully as I could.

"You've only been there for what, about a month now?"

"About that."

"Impressive. It says here there were four altogether that you neutralized?"

"Yes. The one I listed as the threat is the one responsible, the other three were his backup were basically willing collateral damage."

"And you got all three of them?"

"Yes. It just lined up right."

"You also state that you came upon them in the commission of another crime?"

"Yes, why?"

"You didn't mention the victim's name."

"She escaped unharmed and I felt it was better to protect her identity since she was not injured and needed no medical attention. Luckily, she thought she'd been attacked by a pack of wolves."

"You didn't put down coordinates for your neutralization."

I was beginning to get suspicious of the length of the conversation and all of the questions about my report.

"I'd tracked them a long way. I took a bit of a spill, broke my compass, and lost my map. I am not sure I could find the place again if I tried."

I knew it was a bit of a weak answer and he didn't buy it, but it was all he was going to get. I was starting to dislike him.

"Sounds like a harrowing experience. What was the woman doing out that far?"

"She was into deep woods camping. Not my cup of tea, but to each their own. She probably won't be doing it again anytime soon."

"What was his tell?"

"I beg your pardon?"

"His tell. What did you use to identify him as your killer?"

I had never, in all of the cases I had come across, seen anywhere that any

149

agent ever justified their identification in their report. This was becoming more
hinky as the conversation went along. I had to think quickly. I'd seen the picture
of the Alpha I had killed in the paper and I remembered that he had a severely
chipped front tooth.

"He had a chipped tooth and it showed up in his bite."

"That was convenient, wasn't it?" he asked, and I didn't like the way he
asked it.

"It wasn't convenient for the women he killed," I shot back, annoyed.

"I guess not."

"I really need to get going..."

"Hold on a sec."

I heard some drawers open and close, then some rustling of paper.

"Here it is. I have a hefty file of some border line cases that you'll probably
want to file with the hard copy one you have. There are also some leads to other
things in your district that you'll probably want to follow up on."

"Can you put it in my transfer file on the server?"

"Nothing in it is in electronic form. Do you have a post office box
somewhere I could send it to, or could we meet somewhere between the two of
us so you could get it?"

I thought for a minute. Something didn't seem right about this but not
knowing what the protocol was, I wasn't sure what to do. I needed time to think
this over.

"I don't have a post office box yet. I'm out getting some groceries right now
and am away from my calendar. I know I'll be down in Louisiana over the next
few weeks doing some leg work on a couple of cases. Can I give you a call back
when I return from there?"

"Sure. That will be fine."

"Great. I'll call you back then."

"Okay. Later," he said and hung up.

How is it I could lie well to someone I didn't like or distrusted, but couldn't
keep a birthday present secret if I liked the recipient? I thought about the
conversation and the questions TTZ asked. Okay maybe TTZ wouldn't go on the
back burner, but he'd wait until tomorrow. I was done sitting in the basement for
the day.

Chapter 16
Friday June 2, 2248

I'd started doing more research on TTZ over the last two weeks. I pulled up cases from every district that touched mine so it would look as if I was studying past cases from different agents. What I found interesting about TTZ was that he'd been assigned to that area for about eight years and in that time, though he closed plenty of cases, the number of cases around Kansas City were few and far between. I focused in on them. I found it frightening that every case he closed seemed to be in areas that were around something owned by George Greyson, but none of the suspects could be tied to Greyson. On two of them, I found the threats he neutralized were actually competitors of Greyson. Coincidence? Not buying it. The more I looked at TTZ, the more I was convinced that he was in bed with Greyson. I should probably walk away from this until I knew exactly who I could trust, or turn it over to another agency that might be better equipped to handle a bad agent, and I probably would, if it weren't for Gary's pack. Gary's pack sat right on the agent's border. Something clicked in my brain. Most of the murders in the case I'd closed were on the northern edge of Gary's territory. The wheir responsible, and the three with him, worked for Greyson. Philip had worked for Greyson at one time. Had Gary's pack been the target? What was so special about Gary's pack or his territory? There weren't any large cities around there, except maybe Joplin or Springfield, but Gary's territory didn't extend that far. Were the murders planted there as a flag to get my attention, or not necessarily mine, but the agent of district five? That would be quite a bit of planning, sending in wheirs to attack wheirs, but make it noticeable enough to get a Counter Section agent there to take all of them out. Two weeks ago I thought these were probably two or three separate things with most of it leading back to Philip. The longer I looked at this, the more it looked like this case wasn't closed and everything revolved around one George Greyson. I was beginning to agree with Gary; my logic was becoming a pain in the butt.

The question now was who did I trust? Burdock and Sam? Too far away. Bran to a certain extent, but he wasn't someone I could count on in this. TTZ? Not on my life. The Pack? Not really, but who else did I have? I was going to have to make a leap of faith here. If not the whole pack, then who in the pack? I felt deep down that I could count on Greta, but I wasn't sure how much help she would be. Gary? I could probably count on him unless it put the pack in danger. But then again his pack seemed to be in danger already. I'd have to be very careful about the way I did this. Okay, Gary was my best bet.

I needed a sounding board. I picked up my personal phone and dialed Burdock's private cellphone.

"Hello?" Burdock's unsure voice answered.

"Hey, Terry."

"McKenzie?"

"Yes."

"Sorry, didn't know the number."

"I am calling on a personal phone."

"Oh, Okay. What can I do for you?"

"I need a sounding board I trust."

"I'll do what I can. Shoot."

"I think I've fallen into something that may be bigger than I can handle and I need some advice."

"Okay. Let's work through it. Remember no specifics."

"It's about closing my first case."

"I'd think that would be a good thing."

"On the surface it is."

"But?"

"Closing the case has opened more questions than it answered. I'm running into coincidences that are turning out not to be coincidences. Out of the people that are supposedly on my side, I don't know who I can trust. I am feeling quite paranoid about some things and I am beginning to question the impetus behind Counter Section."

"What about it?" he asked.

"When I first got here and looked through all of the files and information at my disposal, I felt I was doing what was right and I'd be saving lives. I'm not so sure of that anymore and it's only been a couple of months. I got a feeling after reading through some recommended case files that the agents before me felt the same way in the beginning, and then found out things that jaded them. It is almost like we do a job and for the most part we do the right thing, but we feel like we have to hold back so much information from the government to protect the general public. I believe those agents and I learned something from the Bio-Wars; too many secrets in the hands of people with power are a bad thing.

I think I was surprised when I found out the fairy tale characters have feelings, wants, and needs. They live productive lives for themselves, their families, communities, and their country. They laugh, they love, and they expect no more or no less than you or I would from our lives. There is a nagging thing in me that feels if I were to tell any of what I've really learned in the past month to the nameless and faceless people on the other side of my computer screen, it would all come crashing down around their heads. When I was in Dallas it was easy; if people broke the law, I caught them. Simple. Out here it's a whole different ballgame. I feel that the prosecution of criminals may turn into persecution of smaller societies that have to live by different rules," I replied.

"That's a lot to get from one case, but what do you mean by different rules?"

"Like needing one particular day off a month, or only being able to come out at night; hell, name your restriction."

152

"What are you really trying to say?" he asked.

"I have made allies over the past month, that I can explain absolutely nothing to, who would seem to do more for me as backup than most of the Deputy Marshals under your watch would ever do. This isn't what I bargained for," I said.

"Do you want to come in?" Burdock asked.

"Now there's the dilemma isn't it?" I asked, chuckling sadly.

"How so?"

"If I resign my position: First, would they let me come back in? Second, if I come in how would I be able to try and protect those allies I've made and the larger portion of that society that's done nothing more wrong than being born different. This kind of reminds me of the racial problems the old United States had."

"Ced. Not to seem unfeeling, but do you think the stress of your first case has sent you over the edge?"

"I don't think so. I think it opened my eyes."

"Just remember, Ced, that in a hostage situation nine out of ten times, even if the demands are met, the hostage dies if we don't take action. Sometimes even when we do take action, the hostage still dies. Don't become so focused on the plight of the hostage that you miss your opportunity to affect an end to the situation on the hope this will be the tenth time."

"Maybe I'm too young and idealistic."

"Ced. As much as you want to, you cannot save them all," he said sadly.

"I know Terry, I just don't want to lose friends."

"You did get too close didn't you?"

"I'm not sure I understand what you mean," I answered a bit too slowly.

"If I understand you correctly, then I'll answer one of your earlier questions. You might as well stay out there because they won't let you come back in."

"What is that supposed to mean?" I asked.

"You know exactly what I mean. You need to learn to fight dirty, even with the people who are supposed to be on your side. You'll need to become more than a exceptional cop. You'll need to use every trick you know, and then learn some more to keep them off balance. I wish I could offer you physical help but that isn't going to happen. I can give you some advice that will be helpful. Stand by the allies you trust 'til the end. I didn't and it cost me a lot more than my life. Don't make my mistake. And, Ced, you need to get very mean."

"Sometime, if we ever get the chance, you and I will have to share a keg and swap stories."

"It's going to have to be more than a keg. Now, what are the rest of your difficulties?"

"First; is it unusual for an agent from one district to request a meeting of an agent from another?"

"It's highly unusual, but not unheard of. One of the reasons there's only one of you in each section is numbers. If someone that wants you dead gets lucky and catches two agents at the same time, that could be devastating for a large chunk of the country. Does this have anything to do with the AI file Director Perry told me about?"

"Not directly."

"Which means yes. Did you hack your way in?"

"No, I didn't hack it. I was doing a search on someone and that file came up. I put in my control number and it just opened."

"Was there anything useful in it?"

"Not really, I understood the gist of the file but the particulars had been redacted. What I was looking for was background on a suspect but the file provided very little information on him."

"Were you meddling in national security?"

"I couldn't have given a shit about the national security element of it. That was basically what I told the Director of IBI, when he called me."

"You always did like to step on toes. You said that was first, are there others?" Burdock asked.

"Yeah, what happens if your evidence leads to corrupt agents and officials?"

There was dead silence on his end of the phone.

"Are you sure?" he asked quietly.

"I don't have solid proof yet. But early indications are pointing in that direction."

"Maybe you should talk to one of your supervisors."

"Not sure I can," I said quietly.

"Shit."

"What?"

"Then, Ced, you are going to have to get very, very, mean," Burdock said lowly.

"I will Terry."

"Ced I mean it. Like a rattlesnake."

"So I'm alone on this?"

"I'm afraid so Ced."

"Keep your head down Captain."

"You too, Ced," He replied sadly as the phone went dead

I went over what I got out of the conversation. Basically, I needed to grow up a little bit and keep my focus on what I needed to do. Now Burdock knew that I had been bitten. Unless I wanted to cash out and run, he was right, I wouldn't be allowed back. One of the things that struck me as strange was that Burdock had no answers for me where it came to TTZ and what to do. So I really was on my own.

The Water's Edge
****

I was just closing a few files down when I was hit with the first cramp. Damn, that hurt more than I remembered. I went upstairs and made some of Bran's special tea, drank it, and went to lay down for a few minutes.

I was walking along a beach looking out at the waves of the ocean. I could hear the waves slapping the shore and the wind, blowing in from the sea, lightly calling my name. I took off all of my clothes and walked into the water until it was over my head. I began to swim under the surface. It was odd that I didn't swim to the surface, but went further down. I didn't feel the need to gulp for air; it was like I could breathe the water itself. The ocean was warm and teaming with life. I swam with an unfettered joy. The further from shore I got, the less concerned I became with the worries I'd left on land. I understood the water, the tides, and waves above me as they were whipped up by the air. I could sense a storm brewing overhead as the turbulence of the surface made its way deeper and deeper until it reached me and started to toss me around. I tried to dive deeper, but couldn't break the pull of the riptide. I was tossed and shoved by unseen hands until I focused on a large, almost formless sea creature that had large evil red eyes. It opened its gaping maw to consume me whole, but the tides of the ocean ripped me from its presence and spit me back out on to the shore. I hit with such force that every joint in my body hurt.

I woke up screaming, drenched in sweat, and sick at my stomach. I ran to the bathroom and vomited up everything I'd eaten so far today. I lay my cheek on the cool porcelain of the toilet seat as I tried to catch my breath. I could feel the fever that was burning me up and every joint in my body hurt. Though my cramps had stopped, they had been replaced by something else. I knelt there with my head resting on my arm for what felt like hours. I finally got up, washed my face, and brushed my teeth. I looked at myself in the mirror and could see the red tinge of fever in my cheeks. I had never really been sick in my life and this was a new experience; not a pleasant one either.

I went to the kitchen to get a glass of water. I filled the glass and went to sit in the living room. As I sat on the couch, thinking I would prefer to die, I saw the picture I'd taken almost nine years ago of the red and gold sunset reflecting off of the Gulf. The foster home I lived in had taken a short trip down to the gulf for a weekend. It was the first time I had ever seen the ocean and when I got my photos developed, I was entranced by that picture and framed it. It was one of the few items in my life I felt I would be poorer for if it were lost. It always sat on top of the volume of Hans Christian Anderson fairy tales, one of the two things I had left from my father. I could barely remember sitting on his lap while he would read to me from it.

I got up, went to the mantle, and pulled down the framed picture of the ocean. I turned it over and removed the back. In the thick cardboard of the back I checked to see if the other item my father had left me was still there. It was. I was told it was around my neck as a necklace as I enter the foster system. Everyone thought it was odd that a child would have a safety deposit box key as a locket. I had tried every bank I could get into, both present and those that had fallen many years ago, but I'd never found box 2290, and probably never would. I replaced the back on the picture and reinstalled the frame in its place of honor. I was hit by another round of stomach cramps. I made it to the small bath in the hall before I let the water I had just consumed back out. I returned to bed, sweated, and hoped the end of either my sickness or my life would come soon.

****

The doorbell rang and woke me out of the fitful sleep I'd fallen into. I got up and felt worse than earlier. I stumbled to the door and opened it. I watched Bran's smile fade into a frown as he got a look at me.

"Damn. I forgot you were coming today," I said.

"Ced, you don't look good."

"I bet you get all the girls with lines like that," I said, trying my best to smile.

He reached out his hand and felt my head.

"Ced, you're burning up. Back to bed," he said as he backed me up and entered.

He spun me around, which almost started another round of heaves, and gently pushed me in the direction of the hall. He pushed me down the hall and into the bedroom.

"You have been holding out on me. You do have a feminine side," he said as he walked around and flipped back the covers.

"I didn't decorate it. It came this way," I said, as I sat down on the bed, flipped my slippers off, and laid back.

He covered me up and went to the bathroom. He returned with a cool washcloth that he laid on my forehead.

"Does it feel like the flu?"

"Don't know, never had it."

"Then describe how you feel."

"Vomiting, fever, and it feels like every joint in my body's going to explode."

"Could be the flu. I will be back in minute," he said as he got up and walked out of the room.

I could hear him go down the hall, open the door, and go outside. I lay there, miserable, for a few minutes. I was surprised when the doorbell rang again. Then it hit me he'd closed the door behind him. I forced myself up and back to the front door.

"Forget your key?" I asked as I opened it.

"I could have sworn I made sure it was unlocked," he said, checking the door knob as he closed it.

"It has a secondary electronic lock," I partially explained as I stumbled back to the bedroom and fell into bed.

Bran covered me back up and went to the kitchen. He returned with some warm water and a small vial of blackish colored liquid.

"Sit up," he said.

I propped myself up. He handed me the vial and the glass of warm water.

"Drink the entire vial and wait a few moments, then sip some of the warm water. Just a warning, the medicine is not very tasty," he instructed and warned.

I took a deep breath and downed the liquid. Not tasty was an understatement. It tasted like I was drinking ode to used sweat socks. My stomach did a couple of rolls but settled back down. I took a couple of sips of the water and handed him back the glass.

"There's a reason they call these things vials," I said as I handed him back the small glass container.

"And what is that reason?"

"Because everything that comes out of it is vile."

"You can't be too sick; your tongue is still working."

"If I had the energy, I'd flip you off too," I said and laid back down.

"What have you eaten today?"

"Some cereal and an apple, though it didn't stay down long."

"Rest for a bit. I am going to rummage and see if I can find anything worth feeding you," he said as he turned and left the room.

I closed my eyes and let the blah run over my body. I could hear cabinet doors closing. It wasn't long before Bran was back in the bedroom.

"Geez, Ced, do you always eat this badly?"

"Hey, it's my beauty secret."

"I am going to run into town and pick up a few things for you. You want to tell me how to disengage the electronic lock?" he asked.

I rolled over, opened the drawer on the nightstand, and took out my Marshal Shield and my IBI wallet.

"Bran, I hope I can trust you," I said seriously.

"Of course, Ced."

I pulled out both identification cards and looked at the backs. Both of them had the same magnetic strip at the same distance from the bottom of the card.

"When you are coming up to the door on the outside of the house, with your fingers feel the outside of the trim around the door. Even with the doorknob, you should feel a small slit that is as long as my identification card. Slip it in with the magnetic strip facing down towards the wall and my photo away from the door and facing out. Make sure it is all the way down; you will hear a high buzz and a small click, and before you pull the identification card out, open the door. Take both of these right now and see if both of them work. Then come back here before you leave," I said and handed him both cards.

Bran was back rather quickly.

"They both open the door," he said, handing them back to me.

"Take this one," I said, handing him my IBI identification.

"What are you? Marshal or IBI?"

"It's too long of a story to explain. I was trained as, and have always been, a Marshal. The IBI credentials are backup for my current assignment. I essentially answer to both departments," I said, feeling I'd said too much as it was.

He gave me a weird look, shrugged his shoulders, turned around and started walking towards the door.

"I will be back in a little bit," He said as he left the bedroom.

I lay there drifting in and out of sleep. The nasty stuff that Bran had forced down my throat seemed to calm my stomach, but hadn't done anything for the aches and fever.

I sat calmly on the beach as the woman knelt in front of me. She had a very beautiful face with big dark eyes and long black hair. At first I thought her eyes were also black, but on closer look they were so dark blue that they just seemed to be. I felt her cup my face in her hands and look hard at me.

"Remember, Winnie. I will always love you," She said as she kissed me on the forehead. She stood up and smiled down at me.

As she walked away, I found that her hair wasn't black either but such a deep red that it was almost maroon in the bright sun of the beach. I felt the tear roll down my cheek as she went to the car that was waiting. I watched her get in and the last sound I remember was the slamming of the car door.

"Ced. Ced. Cedwynne," Bran was saying as I woke looking at him.

"Are you okay?" He asked.

"Yeah, why?" I asked, blinking to wake up fully.

"You were mumbling something and crying."

I felt my cheeks and could feel the wetness of the tears that were still on them.

"I keep having these weird realistic dreams," I explained.

"It's the fever," He said as he placed his hand on my forehead.

"Is the tincture helping?" He asked.

"My stomach feels much better, but the aches and the fever feel about the same."

"I am going to go make you something to eat. We need to get something in your system."

"While you do that, I'm going to lay here and die. I hope you won't think I'm rude."

"Not at all." He smiled at me and left the room.

I felt nasty. My shirt was sticking to me and the sheets were wet where I'd been laying. I lay there and drifted in and out, thankfully without any more dreams. I could smell the aromas coming out of the kitchen. Even in my state, my stomach started to growl at me. I was starving by the time Bran came back in with a bowl on a plate, a sandwich cut in half, and a glass of water.

"You think you can eat?" he asked.

I propped myself up with pillows behind me.

"You did not have a bed tray so you will have to balance it," he said as he put the plate in my lap and sat the water glass on the bedside table.

It smelled wonderful.

"What is it?" I asked.

"It is chicken soup, old family recipe, and a simple grilled cheese sandwich. Eat what you can," he said, as he sat on the foot of the bed watching me.

I was in love the moment I put the first bite in my mouth. It wasn't like any chicken soup I'd had before. But then again most of the chicken soup I'd eaten in my life had come from a can.

"This is fantastic. What are the large green things in here?" I asked.

"Seaweed."

I stopped with the spoon halfway to my mouth.

"Really?" I asked surprised.

"Yes, really. It is good for you," he said, and motioned me to continue eating.

I shrugged my shoulders and took the bite.

I finished most of the soup and half the sandwich before I was full. I handed the plate back to him, which he took back to the kitchen. I was feeling a little better. I felt like my fever was lower, but my joints were feeling worse and my left arm was starting to hurt. I hadn't really thought about my arm for the better part of the last week. Other than a twinge in my shoulder occasionally when I moved wrong, it hadn't bothered me. My forearm had healed, though it still had a road map of white scars that looked like they didn't know where they were going, but I hadn't had any trouble out of it. I'd taken to wearing long sleeved shirts and blouses to cover the scars but other than cosmetic there didn't seem to be any lasting damage.

"Bran, I am going to take a shower. I've sweated through my clothes and the sheets and feel nasty," I said as he came back in the room.

"Are you sure you want to get up?"

"Yes," I said as I started to stand.

My head swam and I grabbed the side of the bed to steady myself. I found my equilibrium and slowly made my way to the bathroom.

"Where are your extra sheets?"

"Hall bath in the linen closet," I said as I closed the door to my bath.

I started the water in the shower and got undressed. I really focused more on staying standing than anything else. It wasn't until I got in the shower; I looked down at my left arm. Where there had been, just that morning, the delicate white lines of a spider web, now there was a nasty nest of red snakes. My first thought was infection. I looked closely at my arm. Only the scars were red and ugly, there were no red streaks radiating out or up my arm. Then I understood. This wasn't the flu or infection. The full moon was only five days away; it was beginning. I washed as quickly as the fever, joint pain, and woozy head would let me. I got out, dried off, closed the bedroom door, and got dressed. I grabbed my personal phone off the nightstand, sat down on the bed, dialed the phone, and waited.

"Hello?" I heard Greta's voice from the receiver.

"Greta, this is Ced."

"You okay?"

"Yes and no."

"What's going on?" she asked, openly worried.

"Vomiting, excessive joint pain, fever, and a can of angry red snakes on my arm."

"Shit."

"When were you planning on coming up?" she asked.

"Monday, midday."

"Damn. Where are you?"

"Home."

"Give me directions, I'll come get you."

"You know I can't do that."

"You'll be in no shape to drive by Monday. We need to get you back up here, now."

"Fuck Monday, I'm in no shape to drive today."

"Can you take a bus or something? I can pick you up somewhere."

"Can I call you back in a couple of minutes?"

"Sure, whatever you need."

"Okay, talk to you in a sec," I said as I hung up.

I got up from the bed and went to the kitchen, stopping a couple of times to steady myself. Bran was cleaning up the kitchen from cooking.

"Do you have anything planned for the rest of your day and evening?" I asked.

"No. I was going to do my lawn maintenance here then spend my evening reading."

"Will your truck make it to Russellville?"

160

"Yes, why?"

"I need to get there to meet someone."

"Ced, you are in no condition to go anywhere."

"I know, but either someone takes me or I have to drive myself."

"You are going whether I take you are not. Aren't you?"

I nodded my head slowly.

"Okay fine," he said agreeing.

"I'll pay for your fuel and time."

"Pay for the gas. I donate the time."

Holding onto his arm, I flipped my phone open and hit redial.

"Ced?" Greta asked after the first ring.

"Yes. Can you meet me in Russellville, Arkansas?"

"Sure. You aren't driving are you?"

"No, a friend is going to bring me."

"When are you leaving?"

"As soon as I get some things packed and loaded."

"Okay. I'm going to call Willis and Gary and tell them I'm coming to pick you up, then I'm leaving."

"Okay. I'll call you when I get closer and we can find a place to meet."

"That will be fine. Ced, drink a lot of water. Even if you feel like you have to stop and pee every ten miles, keep yourself hydrated."

"I will. I'll see you in a couple of hours. Greta?"

"Yes?"

"Thank you."

"Shut up and get on the road," she said and hung up.

"Help me get packed?" I asked Bran as I folded my phone and stuck it in my pocket.

"Sure, Ced. But I don't understand."

"I'll tell you as much as I can when I get back. But it isn't the flu and Greta knows how to help me. Though I must admit that the vile vial pretty much cured the stomach portion, and the soup was incredible," I told him, squeezing his arm.

"Let's get you packed," he said as he steered me towards the bedroom.

It ended up being more Bran packing my suitcases and me telling him what I wanted in them, more than anything. I picked up my official phone, turned it over and took the battery out of it. If there was a tracking device in it, it would have to work on any small battery it might have as a backup, which I hoped would go dead if I left the main battery out of it long enough. I knew it was a paranoid thing but if I did change, like it looked like I was going to, I wanted nothing that would lead back to the pack. Especially, if they ended up being the only ones I could trust. I threw that phone in one open suitcase along with my backup weapon. I grabbed my identification, gun, and keys and put them where they normally lived on my body.

"Do you still have my IBI card?"

Bran pulled it out of his pocket and handed it to me. I put it back in its wallet and stuck it in my back pocket.

"Could I ask you to go ahead and take the suitcases out to your truck? I need to lock up some things and get a large glass of water to take with me. I'll be out in a minute."

"Sure. Do you want to take a pillow along also?"

"That probably wouldn't be a bad idea."

Bran picked up both suitcases, stuck my pillow under his arm, and headed out of the room. I stood carefully and made my way to the basement door. I pulled my IBI card out since it was easiest to get to the way I was feeling. I stuck it in the slot but nothing happened. I reinserted it, still nothing happened. I was beginning to get worried. I pulled out my other card and it opened as normal. I thought it odd that one card would work but the other one wouldn't. I slowly made my way down to my desk, pulled the file I had printed off about Philip out of the drawer, folded it and stuck it in my back pocket.

I stood in the kitchen after making the slow climb up from the basement, and made sure everything was turned off. I found the largest glass I had and filled it with water, walked to the front door and opened it. I closed it again and made sure that both of my cards worked; they did. I locked the knob and the deadbolt and walked to the truck where Bran stood holding the door open for me. He helped me up into the cab, closed the door, and got in behind the wheel on the other side. As beat up as the outside of the truck was, the inside was clean and well kept. The engine roared to life when Bran turned the key. He headed down the drive, drove back into town, and turned north onto highway seven.

"Is your stomach okay?" he asked.

"Yes, it's fine. It's the rest of me that wants to die."

"Just checking. This is a twisting road and I wanted to make sure your stomach could take it. It is the shortest way to Russellville from Hot Springs."

I nodded my head and took a drink of water. I finished my water, put my pillow behind my head, laid back, and closed my eyes.

****

"Ced, we are here," Bran said and woke me from my light sleep.

I pulled my phone out of my pocket and dialed.

"Hello?" Greta answered.

"Greta where are you?"

"Just left a town called ... ah Clarksville."

"Okay you're about twenty minutes away. Get off on the exit that says Old College Avenue, I think it is the third Russellville exit. Turn right at the end of the ramp and there should be a fuel station immediately on your left. I'll meet you there."

"Okay, talk to you in a bit. Bye," she said and hung up.

Bran had heard my directions and started for the rendezvous. It took about ten minutes for us to get there.

I let Bran have my fuel card so he could fuel up. About the time he'd finished, I saw Greta pull into the station. I crawled out of the cab of the truck and waved at her. She pulled around next to Bran's truck. I had my pillow in my arms as I walked towards her car.

"Sweetie, let's get you in the car. Do you want to sit in front or lay down in back?" she asked.

"Front."

She took hold of me and led me to the door, opened it, and made me sit down.

"Trunk or backseat?" Bran said, coming up behind her.

"Backseat." Greta pointed and opened up the back door.

Bran put the luggage in the car and close the door.

"Ced, are you going to be okay?" he asked, squatting down to be eye to eye with me.

"Yes. I'll probably be back sometime next weekend. Can you look in on the house?"

"Sure," he said and stood up.

"By the way. Bran Murray, Greta Shaw," I said, introducing them.

"Thanks for bringing her," Greta said.

"Not a problem. Well, I have a yard to mow before the sun goes down. If I don't get it done, the old lady that owns the place becomes a real pain," Bran said, squeezing my hand on the window edge.

"Thanks, Bran. I owe you at least a nice meal."

"I would prefer a little knowledge."

"I'll see what I can do."

"Greta, nice to meet you. Get her somewhere she will be comfortable."

"That's my intent," Greta said as she sat down behind the steering wheel and turned the key on.

She had one of the newer, larger electric cars and it quietly eased its way back out on the road and towards the freeway.

"You have the strangest smelling friends," Greta said, once we were up to speed on the freeway.

"What do you mean?"

"Well, he doesn't smell totally human. He has the human smell about him, but he also has half of your smell."

"What do you mean half of my smell?"

"He has that earthy smell that makes up part of yours only his is much stronger, though he doesn't have any of the salty breeze smell that you have mixed in," she answered, trying to explain.

"There's going to have to be a knowledge trade," I said, not realizing I had said it out loud.

"What?"

"Nothing. I was thinking out loud."

"Oh. Here," Greta said, handing me a plastic bag with some plant leaves in it.

"What is it?"

"Something to help with the fever. Chew on two of the leaves, but don't swallow the leaves themselves."

"How long?" I asked as I pulled two of the leaves out of the bag.

"Until the taste is gone; here is some water to help," Greta said, handing me a quart jar with a lid on it.

I stuck the leaves in my mouth and started chewing. I thought I would retch from the taste.

"I know it doesn't taste good but it'll break your fever," she said.

I continued to chew and take small amounts of water to swallow the juice with. I'd finally come to the end of the flavor in the leaves and tossed them out the window. I finished off the water in the jar and screwed the lid back on it. I put my pillow in the corner of the seat and the door, and closed my eyes.

****

"Ced," Greta's voice came to me and I felt her light touch on my arm.

"Yes?" I asked with my eyes closed.

"We're here."

I opened my eyes in time to see Gary and Willis leave the porch and head in our direction. Willis went to Greta side of the car and opened the door. Gary came directly to mine and opened it.

"How are you feeling?" he asked, squatting down.

"I've kicked three of the four symptoms today."

"So the train didn't hit you as hard this time?"

"No, it was only a small truck. I was just confused and a bit scared by myself."

"Shall we get you inside?" he asked, standing up and offering a hand.

I took it, swung my legs out of the car, and stood up. Big mistake. I felt my knees buckle the moment I reached full height. The next thing I knew, I was being carried into the house and laid on the bed in the room I'd stayed in before.

"Sure it was just a truck?" Gary asked.

"Yes, I'm sure. I just stood up too quick," I answered, working my way up, slowly, into a seated position against the pillows.

"Greta?" I asked.

"Yes?"

I patted the bed next to me. She came over and sat down.

"Walk me through what is going on and what I can expect."

"Remember some of the things I tell you may or may not apply to you. I was alone for the first two years and was trying things on my own. When I was turned, about a week before my first moon, I had severe pain in my joints, intense vomiting, and a fever that was around a hundred and four. As the day of the moon got closer the vomiting lessened, but the fever and joint pain got worse. I thought I was going to die until the night of the moon. I fought it every month with everything I had in me. I think, after talking to others who were turned, if I'd have accepted what was going on sooner it would've resolved itself sooner. Others have said that after their first month they no longer had the vomiting and their fever would begin to rise but not hit the one hundred and four mark until the day of the moon; that's a normal body temperature for a canine. The joint pain will lessen over time with the number of moons you live through, to a point where it is just an achy feeling for a few days before. My joint pain was horrible until I had Willis to show me how to change. Yours will be what it'll be depending on how you approach it."

"Do you have any aspirin around here?"

"Doesn't help. I tried everything I could get my hands on. One time I even scored some morphine; though it never touched the pain, it at least made me feel like I didn't care."

"Great! I already have nasty human PMS. I get to add nasty wheir PMS to it. What should we call it? Hell?"

Greta smiled and giggled at me.

"If you can keep your humor, you'll do fine. Though I have to ask: why aren't you throwing up? Other than when you were chewing the leaves, I haven't even seen you retch."

"Bran gave me something earlier today. He's a life saver with his homemade mixtures."

"You'll have to see if he'll give up the recipe. All I've been able to find is something that helps with the fever."

"So what do I have to look forward to the next few days and the full moon?"

"Your joint pain will increase to the point you'll think your joints are going to explode. Hopefully, the stuff Bran gave you will keep your stomach healthy. Your temperature should do a steady climb to one oh four by Tuesday. Feel free to crawl in a tub of cold water any time you feel the need."

"Does that help?"

"It's soothing and you don't feel like you're going to burst into flame."

"What about the change itself?"

Greta looked at Willis.

"Gary, would you like to step out on the back porch with me for a beer?"

Willis asked.

"Sure. That sounds good."

They left the room leaving Greta and I alone.

"When the first change happens your muscles will feel like they are tightening so much that you'll be convinced that your bones will break from the constriction. I think that has something to do with your muscle mass changing, since after your first time your muscles will look more like mine than what you have now. You'll feel a cramp around your midsection that will be more intense than any menstrual cramp you've ever had in your life. When you feel that coming on, let it happen. Let the body do what it's going to do anyway. The longer you fight it the longer it'll take for the change to happen. Trust me, the more you accept it the easier and more painless it becomes.

When the change starts, don't run from the pain. You'll only make it hurt worse. Accept what's happening. The first few times it will be hard to do because you're going to be scared and the pain will seem unbearable. Female wheirs have a couple of different changes than the males. One, as I told you when you were up last, is that your period will last only as long as it takes you to change. My first time, I fought it for so long it took an hour. Now it only takes a few minutes. You should instinctively know to find a stream, pond, or snow-bank to clean yourself in. Also, you'll let off a scent that will make the males want to mount you. The longer you're in a pack and the higher your rank, the higher ranking your suitors will become also.

On this one issue, and this one alone, you can fight back regardless of who the advances are from, even the Alpha. But be forewarned if you lose the fight you belong, for that time, to the male that pins you. Sorry, that's just the way it is. Those of us that are mated have nothing to worry about except from our own mates and the Alpha of the pack. Gary has always kept himself in check when it comes to that. Though he'll play with all of us, he's never aggressively tried to pin one of the mated females in the pack. As the night wears on your scent will fade quickly and the pack will form, run, play, and hunt until it is time to bed down for the night and wait for the change back. Surprisingly, the change back is usually painless since you'll be asleep. That covers the change process, but there's one more thing we need to discuss."

"What's that?"

"Once you turn, though you're accepted around this pack, you're not a member of it. You'll have a high status from the get go but be careful, especially with the males. It's how you need to act around Gary that you need to pay real close attention to. In your human form you can get away with a lot more around him than any of us can simply because you're just a friend. In the pack what he says goes, no argument, unless you're prepared to fight him for the pack. Even after your change, since the pack's helping you, you will be allowed some leeway. But if Gary approaches, you don't look him in the eye. You never initiate contact with him, he'll do that with you if he so chooses. Don't take an aggressive stance with him. And finally stay out of his way. You won't be expected to be subservient to him, but don't push your autonomy either. Once the group forms, stay close to me. I'll help you and try to keep you out of trouble."

"Thanks, Greta," I said as I leaned into her and nuzzled her neck as she had done me before.

She wrapped me in her arms, smoothed the back of my head and kissed me on the cheek.

"I need to talk to Gary for a bit in private," I told her.

"I'll go get him for you," she said as she got up and went out the door.

A few moments later Gary came in.

"Greta said you wanted to talk to me?"

"Would you sit down?" I asked, pointing to the bed next to me.

Gary sat down where Greta had been earlier.

"After I got home last month, I wrote up my report and closed the case but loose ends kept popping up. I've worked through them every which way I can think of, and I'm up against a few things that I'm not sure how to deal with."

"What are you trying to say?"

"Two months ago you were a name on a piece of paper for me and for you I didn't even exist. From what everyone here has told me and the way I am treated now I feel that I'm at least accepted here."

"Of course you're accepted here," Gary interrupted, smiling.

"I'm taking a leap of faith here and I am putting all of my hope in the belief that I can at least trust and count on you personally."

Gary looked at me. I knew he was working it through. He understood what I was saying, but he needed to apply it to his own responsibilities.

"I believe that you can trust me," he finally said.

"In Counter Section we're thrown out here with no real backup. I have no one I can really count on to even bounce things off of, much less expect to pick up a weapon and follow me into a dangerous situation. What I am about to talk to you about, I need you to look at it as a fellow cop and not an Alpha."

"Do you know what you are asking?"

"Yes, a cop is what you do for a living, being an Alpha is your life, and the pack is your family."

"As long as you understand what you're asking of me."

"Yes I do. I need to know that once we finish this conversation that you will act, at least right now, as a cop. You can go all big dog Alpha later. But for the next month you'll need to be an investigator so that we can get to the bottom of this so it doesn't rear its ugly head ever again," I said.

"I thought you closed the case?"

"I closed the case of the murdered female wheirs. I did nothing about how far out this goes, who's pulling the strings, and the mole or moles you have in your pack."

"You know who the mole is, don't you?"

I nodded my head and dug the file out of my back pocket. I unfolded the sheet.

"You promise me you'll be a cop?"

"Yes, I promise," he said with a flash of anger in his eyes.

I handed him the report I had about Philip.

"Philip? Are you kidding me? He has to be told to raise his leg when he pees every month. And how does this prove he is the mole?" Gary asked, pointing at the paper.

"Follow me on this."

He folded his arms in that "convince me" way.

"Last month we went out in three groups. Willis, Thomas, and Casey in group one. You and Craig in group two, and Greta and I in group three. Greta found the Alpha and led him back to the clearing. The whole time he knew exactly where I was. Meanwhile, Willis, Thomas, and Casey just happen to run into a wheir prepared to take them on. Then, you and Craig also just happen to run into two wheirs ready to do battle with you. Any of those things itself and I'd say it was just a coincidence. But all three at once, and it just so happens that two wheirs were sent against an Alpha of the established pack? Not buying the coincidence angle here. I find out that all four of the dead wheirs work for a Mister George Greyson, who by chance has a rap sheet longer than your arm. It also turns out that Philip used to work for Greyson around the time he was bitten and turned," I said, pointing to the paper in Gary's hand.

"Then I find out that the Agent in the section above mine also has a history with Greyson. Are you buying the coincidences here?"

"No, but all of this is circumstantial at best," he answered.

"How long had you been going out looking for that Alpha?"

"About three months. Why?"

"Because I was the wild card in all of this. The Alpha that we killed knew exactly where *I* was." I said, looking straight at Gary.

"But Philip didn't know about any of this."

"My thoughts exactly, unless someone was feeding him information."

"Are you trying to tell me that someone that high up in the pack is behind this?" he asked, starting to get angry with me.

"That's exactly what I thought originally."

"But you don't think that now?" he asked confused.

"In the beginning I had six suspects, including you."

"You really think I'd do something like that?"

I walked him through my thought processes on him, Willis, Craig, Thomas, Greta, and Casey. I also worked him through how I eliminated all of them but Thomas.

"So you're saying Thomas is behind all of this?"

"I thought that, until I added in my last piece of evidence."

"What's that?"

"My sight."

"What does your sight have to do with this?"

"One of the things that I can see when I look at auras is mood or intent and past indiscretions. Anger and evil intent shows up as this overall red mist, and the past indiscretions show up as these black snake-like lines in their coronas. I've seen this in every criminal I've caught in my law enforcement career. Philip is the only member of your pack that has those snakes and they are very much defined, he also has a lot of anger mixed in with that. From my experience that's an explosive combination. I got the opportunity to watch all of you together on two separate occasions. No one in the group, but Philip, showed any anger whatsoever especially towards you," I explained.

"So you're saying that Philip's the one inside the pack, but you don't know where he's getting his information and that for some reason my pack is being targeted by either the Greyson or the Agent in the district above you?"

"That's pretty much it in a nutshell."

Gary sat fuming. I knew he wanted to get his hands on Philip and put an end to his life.

"Gary, you and I both need to be smart in how we deal with this. You can't just eliminate a mole. If you do we might never find out where he is getting his information from and who he's giving it to."

"I take it you have a plan?"

"Yes, but it's going to piss you off."

"Then let's get it over with."

"I think I have a way to get Philip out of here with no bloodshed or bodies to hide."

"Okay, I am listening."

"Let me handle most of it. I'm not a small county sheriff, no offense, and have a much farther reach than you do. I have a feeling he knows I'm a Counter Section agent and as far as he knows I can do what I like and nothing will be said. I'm going to use that. If it doesn't work, then you can take more drastic measures and I will help clean up the mess. If Philip is tied to Greyson in the way I think he is, then the information he has will eventually make it to someone else who can cause a lot more problems for you, the pack, and even me. I'm afraid at some point it's going to get bloody; I just want the pack safe and out of the way. I need you to keep an eye on Philip. Also keep an eye out for anyone who's spending too much time with him. I have a few leads outside the pack that I'd like to work on over the next month. When we both have something more solid we can deal with it then."

"Do you think Greyson's pulling the strings?" he asked.

"I don't know. He has a rap sheet that goes back forty years with no convictions. It makes me think someone pretty high up the food chain is sweeping away the shit for him, since he's never landed in jail."

"Do you have an idea who that could be?"

"Not yet."

"Ced, just as you can't stand by and watch people get hurt, I can't stand by and watch you try and tackle this alone. You can't expect me to."

"Gary, there's a big difference if I lose my job or become a casualty than if you do."

"And that would be?"

"I have a place to retreat to if I lose my job, you...."

"Where would that place be?" he asked, interrupting.

"Here... I hope," I said, smiling.

I got a wide smile and a nod from Gary.

"If I'm a casualty, I hope that someone will miss me, but then again I'm not protecting twenty other people every day. If something happens to you or any member of your pack you, or they, will be mourned greatly. But how deep an investigation will result from that? I've read case files of other agents being killed on the job, when that happens the districts bordering the dead agent's toss all of their resources into that one case until it is solved. Do you know there's not one open case involving the death of an agent in the line of duty? We as agents have a lot of power and a lot of resources. And if others out there have been as smart as I have, I'm sure they have an army of allies that would help them in a moment's notice to add to our legal resources," I said, cocking an eyebrow in his direction, hoping he would get my meaning.

"God, Ced. I hate your stubborn, well thought out reasoning. I wish I could find a hole in it but I can't."

"I can only see one hole in it."

"What's that?"

"I'm wrong about it all and this is just a bunch of weird coincidences."

"You going to be this much trouble come Tuesday?"

"Probably. You know I won't be a good follower," I said with a sad smile.

"Yes. You'll be as much of a stubborn pain in the ass as a wheir as you are now," he said with a chuckle.

"By the way, I want to apologize now."

"For what?" he asked.

"For the bitch I am going to be over the next few days," I said, smiling.

"You need to apologize for the real bitch you're going to be on Tuesday," he said, laughing.

It took me a second to get the joke. I looked at him hard.

"I have broken many a man's fingers for less," I said, trying to keep a straight face but it wasn't working real well.

We both went into a staring contest that lasted a grand total of about five seconds before both of us started laughing.

"If the pain is going to get worse before it gets better, can we get a beer and go outside and sit?"

"Sure, if you think your stomach is up for it."

I nodded. He got up and offered me a hand and then his arm. It hurt to move but I gritted my teeth as we walked to the kitchen. He grabbed two beers out of the fridge on the way outside to join Greta and Willis on the back porch. Night had fallen and the stars were out. I shoved all of the worries about Greyson, Philip, Zahn, and whoever else out of my head and decided that they could wait a few days. For the next five days all I needed to concentrate on was the one thing that was going to change my life forever.

Chapter 17
Tuesday June 6, 2248

I hadn't been much help around the household for the past couple of days. There were times that it had hurt to even move my eyes. I'd gotten very little sleep and kept to myself to try and not be too much of a bitch. I was beginning to wonder if I'd make it through the next few hours. I could hear the voices in the kitchen as the pack started to gather. I forced myself up from the bed, got dressed, and slowly made my way into the kitchen. Wills, Greta, Gary, and Casey were sitting around the table having some lemonade and talking.

"Hey, Ced," Casey greeted me as I came in the door.

I tried the best I could to grunt nicely in his direction.

"Ced. Sit down and let me get you something to drink," Greta said as she pulled out a chair for me.

I sat down, hating my life and body, and a glass of yellow sweetness appeared in front of me.

"You doing okay?" Gary asked.

I looked at him, with my bloodshot eyes.

"I guess that's my answer," he said, smiling.

"If I didn't like you so much I'd rip your eyes out," I said flatly.

"It'll be over in a couple of hours."

"If not, I'm going to shoot myself."

I felt like I was a young girl again going through my first period. I remember my foster mother and my two older foster sisters being somewhat comforting but basically telling me: you get a pass this first month so you'd better enjoy it, 'cause after that you'll be no different than the rest of us.

We sat around the table drinking and talking, well... everyone else was talking, I was only partially listening. Gary got up from the table and everyone else followed, except me.

"It's time," he said, leaning down towards me.

I slowly stood up. He offered me a hand, which I took immediately. The five of us made our way to his jeep. Gary was driving and Willis sat in the front passenger seat. I was put in the middle, in the back, between Casey and Greta. The jeep pulled out and started down the road. Until now I'd been so concerned with the pain I hadn't really thought of anything else. Now I felt like a condemned prisoner walking to my execution. As the miles and time rolled by, my trepidation built to a fever pitch. We took a few back roads until Gary pulled up to a clearing. Everyone got out and Greta helped me to my feet. I looked around the clearing. There were a few tents set up and scattered around. Gary started off in the direction of the tents and everyone followed. I was surprised when we passed the tents and went straight into the tree line.

I felt like we'd hiked for miles when we came to another small clearing and

Gary stopped. I could hear running water off to my right. The rest of the group started to get undressed as I stood looking at them, frozen to my spot. Greta came over to me after she'd disrobed.

"Ced. You will want to get undressed, unless you want to go home naked tomorrow," she reminded me.

I pulled the two plastic bags I'd brought out of my pocket. I placed my gun and credentials in one, sealed it up, and then stuffed it inside the other one. I looked around for a place to hide it. I saw a good sized rock I thought I could move. I went over to it and tried to lift up one side of it but the pain was so intense that I couldn't budge it. Greta came over and lifted it for me. I found a spot underneath where the rock had a bit of an indention. I placed my package on the ground in the corresponding place and let Greta lower it. We'd just stood back up when Gary came over and took a sniff. Then he actually peed on the rock. I had to laugh.

"Why?" I asked, still giggling.

"I could still smell the metal and gunpowder. I didn't want someone to find it before we got back," he said and walked away.

"You really need to get undressed, it's about time," Greta said.

She led me back over to where she had folded and hidden her clothes. I took mine off and handed them to her as she folded and hid them in the bushes. Once I was naked, she stood up and offered me her hand. I took it and she led me out of the clearing and down the slope a little way so we were only a couple of yards from the stream. Even with my normal human nose, I could smell it. She lowered herself to her knees and sat back on her heels, I slowly did the same.

"Where is everybody?" I asked.

"We go out to different spots. The whole pack will meet up about two hours after we change. We will run and hunt for a while and then they'll break up into their smaller packs and head back to their crash points."

I had to quit talking. The joint pain was getting worse and it grew like a crescendo until I thought my joints would pop open. Where I had been just scared before, now I was terrified. I'd never felt such pain. People say the worst pain a woman can ever feel and endure is childbirth. Based on what I felt then, I'd never be adding to the world population. I tried my best to let it happen but I found a part of me trying to stop it. I took a deep breath to try and calm myself. My muscles felt like they were rippling and tightening around me. The pressure and the pain got to the point of unbearable, then the cramp that Greta had warned me about closed in around my middle. I felt myself double over and sink to the ground. Then everything went black.

****

I felt something nudging me; I didn't want to open my eyes. I lay there for a moment to collect myself. There was no joint pain or cramps. I took in a deep breath and realized I could smell everything. I could smell, yes smell, Greta. I could also hear everything around me from the smallest insect to things crashing around in the bushes further away. I opened my eyes slowly. I saw Greta sitting on her haunches, her blonde fur glowing in the moonlight, looking at me with her head cocked to one side like she was trying to figure something out. I took another deep breath and smiled, I think. I wasn't sure wolves could smile. I sat up but something, intellectually, wasn't right. I was taller than Greta, and I shouldn't be. I reached out to touch her and that's when I noticed it. My hand and arm were still a hand and an arm. No fur, no paw. I looked down at myself and saw the white skin of my legs and thighs. I felt my face; same face I'd always had. I was physically the same now as I had been when I sat down except for the blood that coated the inside of my thighs.

Greta was still looking at me hard. I reached out and touched her head, between her ears.

"Greta, I am fine," I said, staring at her.

She sniffed me, nudged me, and started walking towards the stream. I got up and followed her. We both cleaned ourselves in the cold water. I found it strange that the temperature of the water really didn't bother me. As I was standing there watching Greta, something came over me. I took a running start at Greta, as she was getting out of the water, and landed on her back, biting at her ear. I rolled her over and lay there as she licked my face. God, I felt good. I could smell and hear everything around me. I could hear and smell the two rabbits that were off to my right. I could smell Gary as he came down the bank to where Greta and I were. Greta got up, lowered her tail, and kept her head below his. I rolled over and came up to my knees. I made sure I kept my eyes away from his. He came towards me. I offered out my hand palm up to show no aggression. He sniffed it then came in towards me. He placed his nose under my chin and raised it so I was looking directly at him.

"I'm fine. In fact, I've never felt this great in my life," I said, smiling at him.

I wasn't sure if he understood the words but he understood my intent. He licked me on the cheek, turned, and headed up the bank. I stood up. Greta turned as if she were going, then stopped and looked at me. Even though my sense of smell was heightened, my hearing was outstanding, and I was sure I was probably stronger than I used to be, there would be no way that I could keep up with any of them. I knew, instinctively, where we were going to meet up at the end of the night so I was fine on my own. I looked at Greta and smiled. She was being a loyal and protective friend.

"Go, Greta. I'll be just fine," I said, making a shooing motion with my hand.

She cocked her head at me as if to ask me if I were sure.

"Go, Greta. Run, hunt, and play with your mate. I will be fine," I said.

Greta came over to me and nuzzled against my leg, then turned and took off towards the howling that had started off in the distance. I walked back up the bank to where we'd left our clothes. I got redressed, though it felt like my bra and shirt was tighter and my belt wouldn't tighten down on my waist like it used to. My pants were annoying me a little since they were sitting further down on my hips than I was used to. I found my rock and with one hand, and very little exertion, lifted it and got my things out from under it. I put my gun in its holster and my credentials in my back pocket, folded up the bags, and stuffed them in one of my front pockets. I stood motionless with my eyes closed, listening and smelling everything around me. It was quite the new experience. I could hear the pack howling and yipping in the distance as they were running. I even knew which howl was whose. There was a large part of me that wanted to be running with them. I felt a little sad about it but I was more intent on what new things had become a part of me. I wondered if I would retain this heightened awareness after tonight. I hoped so. Then it hit me. Did I still have my sight when I was like this? I listened and heard a deer not far away. I looked in its direction and switched to my sight. Sure enough, the silver glow was there but it was different than it had been before. For lack of a better explanation, it was brighter and more well defined than it had been before tonight. I'd have to try it with the pack when they got back later.

Then it hit me; I was starving. I hadn't had a lot to eat over the past few days. I wondered if the tent village was just for show or if there were drinks and food there. I set out in the direction we'd come. Though I got side tracked a couple of times and needed to run and chase a rabbit and a deer, I finally got close enough to the camp to smell it. It was downwind of me and I could smell the tents, the car, the fading scents of the people that had been there, and something else. I could smell the scent of two others. I took a good whiff again to see if my new heightened senses were playing tricks on me. Nope, two distinctive scents. Not wheir, but human and there was the smell of gunpowder and metal. I stopped and pulled my weapon. I felt in my pocket for my third clip, the one I'd loaded with normal ammunition. I exchanged clips and quietly chambered a round. I stuck one extra clip in my back pocket where I could reach it quickly. If I got to a second or third clip, it wouldn't make a difference if they were lead or silver.

I started making my way to the camping area. As I got closer I could tell that the two scents were on opposite sides of the clearing. I lay on my stomach, pressing myself to the ground, and crept forward until I was next to the edge of the clearing. I switched to my sight and could see both their auras more than plainly. Their auras were more intense and focused than I'd ever seen before. One of the things that bothered me was that one of them was up in a tree on the right side. I wished I had my night vision binoculars. The one on the ground was pacing back and forth; the moon hadn't come anywhere near its zenith, so the glade was in light and shadow, and he kept blinking in and out of focus for me. Then he made his mistake. He stopped in an area that was fully lit from the moon. He was about six foot, had a rifle on his shoulder, and a holster on his hip. Though he seemed to be in normal hunter's regalia, the boots, belt, and holster gave him away as military or ex-military.

As I lay there for a while watching and deciding what to do, my mind went back to the last conversation Burdock and I had a couple of weeks ago. He'd talked about hostage situations. I realized I was in one. Though I wasn't sure the two men standing out there weren't some sort of law enforcement or ranger, they were setting a trap for the people who were with the tents; in effect the people and tents were hostages. I needed to focus on the situation and not on the hostages. I had one thing going for me; I was a wild card yet again. Burdock had also told me I needed to get very mean.

Mean was a term Burdock used from his military background when he would brief the Marshals going into a dangerous situation. It was Burdock's code for: bullets would be flying in our direction and we needed to be prepared to use deadly force to bring the suspects down.

In our phone conversation he'd told me to get "very mean" and he stressed the word "very" in his sentence. I wished I knew the things he wasn't telling me. While I was playing brain tag, the one in the clearing took something out of his pocket and held it at his side. I heard two distinctive clicks, then shortly after I heard two from the tree. The man in the clearing stuck whatever it was back in his pocket.

The wheir in me was starting to get antsy and mad. No mad wasn't it; a better phrase would be very interested. Great, just one more thing I had to control right now. I was at an impasse. I couldn't just start shooting if they had a legitimate reason for being here, yet I couldn't just stroll into the clearing, identify myself, and bank on a theory that they wouldn't shoot me on sight. I knew the pack was probably a good four or five hours from getting back to this spot. I inched my way back the way I'd come until I was far enough back into the forest to stand up. Gary had parked his jeep on the edge of the clearing and I could see it from the vantage point I'd just left. There was only an old firebreak road to this spot and the two men in the clearing had to get there somehow. I started quietly making my way around the clearing keeping a pretty good buffer between me and it. I went around the right side so it would put me up the fire road a bit above where we were parked. I could see the wide, cleared area of the road shimmering in the moonlight through the breaks in the underbrush and trees. I found a large oak near the edge of the road and the dense forest and stood behind it. I snuck a peek around the left side of it towards where we had parked. I could just barely see the tail lights of the jeep just off of the road, but saw no other vehicles that way. I slowly inched my head around the other side and peered back up the road. There it sat about two hundred yards down. I couldn't make out much about it. I was just ready to step out and take the road to it when a face lit up behind the wheel from the cigarette lighter. I stopped. *Almost stupid,*

The Water's Edge

Ced. You think there is only two of them? Silly girl. I was somewhat upwind of him and the vehicle, so I opened my sight-human.

I slipped back into the forest. I hoped there were only three of them. I started making my way through the underbrush, keeping parallel to the road. I knew when I was about even with the vehicle, since I could smell him and his cigarette. I could also smell traces of old food and the two humans I'd smelled back in the clearing. My stomach gave off a small growl, reminding me of the whole reason I'd come back to the camp. I concentrated on what I smelled; I smiled to myself that I was learning about my new senses. There were only three of them. I could tell with the aromas that found me from the inside of the vehicle. I continued on past the car for a good fifty yards and made my way back to the road. I was burning time and I needed to hurry. Staying in the shadow of the tree line I moved quickly a few yards further up. Though the road was lit rather well, I hoped that his attention would be to where his buddies were and not intent on the rear view mirrors. If I sprinted fast enough he probably wouldn't even notice and if he did he might just think it was some wildlife. I was just getting up the courage to run when he opened the door and got out. I froze. Had he seen me? I watched intently as he casually strode across the road and a short way into the underbrush. I smiled as I heard his urine steam hit the ground. I took my chance and ran.

I crouched down in the trees on the other side and watched. A few seconds later he came out of the woods and headed back to his vehicle, lighting another cigarette. The underbrush on this side of the road cleared out pretty well a couple of yards from the tree line. I made excellent time to where I was roughly even with him. I crept back towards the tree line, staying low, and inched up to where I could see the front of his vehicle. It was one of the government types, built on a military frame. It sort of reminded me of a smaller version of Bee. Though it did not sit as high off the ground as mine and was not as tall, it still looked like you could take it into battle. It had four doors, a storage space behind the back seat, and a back hatch. The windows were tinted and I couldn't see in, but both front windows were rolled down to allow a cross breeze. I looked at the driver with my sight. His aura, like his buddies, was normal human. What took me off guard was the lack of black. Yes, there was black but it was more like what I had seen in most of the Marshals and police officers I'd met. It was as if they'd done things that deep in their heart they knew might be wrong, but they'd done them for a higher purpose that they believed in. My question was why were they here?

I was even with the front tire on the passenger side. I crept over the small berm and snaked my way to the front wheel. I made sure I stayed crouched out of the view of the outside mirrors. I slowly pulled my weapon from my holster and switched the safety off. I had to watch where I sprung up on him. I did not want to take out my shoulder with the mirror itself. I took a quiet deep breath and stood quickly with my gun through the open window on the passenger side.

177

"Move and it'll be the last thing you ever do," I said barely above a whisper.

I heard the intake of breath at the surprise and I could actually hear his heartbeat start racing.

"Say nothing and put your hands on the wheel where I can see them," I instructed.

He looked at me as he did as he was told. I could hear him start to regulate his breathing and slow his heart rate.

"Keep your hands right there. You move one finger and it will be the last time. Do I make myself clear?" I asked him.

He nodded his head. I quickly moved around the front of the vehicle until I had a clear shot at him from the front of the driver's side.

"Take your left hand off of the steering wheel and reach out the window and open your door. Do not exit the vehicle until I tell you," I instructed him.

He reached slowly out the window and pulled up on the latch, the door sprung open slightly.

"Put both hands on the window frame. Push the door open and slowly get out of the car, but leave your hands on the door."

He did as he was told.

"Slowly close the door quietly with both hands."

He shut the door.

"Move out from the vehicle with your hands in front at shoulder height."

He moved two steps away from the vehicle. He had a side arm in a military issue holster with a solid flap that snapped over the weapon. I looked at his face. He couldn't be any older than I was.

"Right or left handed?" I asked.

"Right," he answered quietly.

"Slow wide circular motion with your right arm and hand. Pull your identification and place it on the hood of the vehicle," I said.

He put his flip wallet on the hood near the door.

"Back two paces," I instructed.

As he moved I moved to where I could reach the wallet on the hood. I opened it and glanced down. I grabbed the ID and shook it loose from the sleeve it was in. In the moonlight it looked just like mine. The name read Agent Thomas R. Smith, IBI. Really, couldn't these morons be any more creative that that? I flipped it over and looked at it. Seemed official. I was about to hand it back to him when my thumb ran across the picture that was on it. My identification from both agencies had the picture printed directly to the plastic then laminated between two more sheets of thin clear plastic. There was a bump around his picture. Fucking fake.

"How many of you are out here?" I asked.

"Just me."

"Wrong. Wanna try this again? This time include your buddies about two hundred yards down the road. How many of you are out here?"

"Who's asking?"

I reached into my pocket and pulled out my shield, depositing his ID in my pocket at the same time. I flipped the wallet open and held it up.

"U.S. Marshal McKenzie," I said.

I saw a look of surprise cross his face.

"Three," he said, answering the question.

"One point for honesty. Who's in charge?"

"Me."

I knew it was another lie.

"Why are you in my jurisdiction and fucking up a stakeout I have going?"

"Didn't know it was your jurisdiction."

"Bullshit."

I was getting tired of the game. I guess he was too, since I saw him start to reach for his gun. It took me less time to cross the three steps between us and land a well-aimed hiking boot into his crotch than it took him to get his hand halfway down his body. It was like both his arms had minds of their own. They forgot what they were doing and went straight for his manhood. I watched him drop to his knees in pain. He got his breath and started to open his mouth to yell. I put everything I had into the backhand across his face. Everything I had was more than I thought. His head whipped to his right from the force of my left hand across it. I heard the crack in his neck. He was on his knees upright for what seemed like a couple of seconds. I could hear his heart beating then it skipped a few beats and stopped. He dropped to the ground on his side. Damn. I'd wanted information, not a dead body.

Before that, anytime I'd killed someone I'd been distraught over it and played the scenario over and over in my brain to see if I could've handled it any differently. Tonight I just felt like it was a game and he'd lost. Oh shit, the wheir was hunting. I thought about the war going on inside of me for a moment until I heard the howls off in the distance. It wouldn't be long until they'd start heading back. I holstered my pistol as I went to the body. I rolled him over and started going through his pockets. His pants pockets had a small knife and some loose change. I felt down his legs until I got to something on his right calf. I jerked up his pants leg and saw the two throwing knives stuffed in a sheath and stuck down in his boot. I popped the strap, took out the sheath and stuck it down in my own boot. Fastening the strap around the outside of my pants leg. I moved up his body quickly. He had a small flashlight on his belt; I stuck it in my pocket. I checked the chest pockets on his shirt and found a slick piece of paper. I pulled it out and stuck it in my back pocket.

I got up and headed for the door of the vehicle. I reached for the door latch and thought better of it. I pulled the two plastic bags out of my pocket and put them over my hands like gloves. I opened the door. The keys were in the seat and a small pair of binoculars sat on the dash. I picked them up and looked through them– night vision. I slung the strap around my neck. Other than paper sacks that had held sandwiches and cold cups of coffee, there was nothing in the front or the back seats. I moved to the back and opened the hatch. There were three military issue blankets, a body bag, a small black canvas bag, and three rifle cases. I grabbed the bag and opened the zipper. I clicked on the small flashlight and looked through it. I smiled. Inside were three cellphones that were turned off and three wallets. In their endeavor to be organized and neat, they had rubber banded each cellphone to a wallet. I took a sniff of the three. I put the one that belonged to the body on the ground back in the bag and set the other two down. I opened up the wallets. One belonged to a Johnathan Pierce from Maryland and the other one belonged to William Strathmore of Kentucky. I looked at the endorsements on the licenses. Johnathan was a retired army captain in the reserves and William was a retired major, also in the reserves. William Strathmore was the one pacing on the ground and I figured he was also in charge. I threw the wallets and phones back in the bag and zipped it up. While I had the light on, I looked behind the seat and pulled out the slick piece of paper I had taken out of the young man's pocket and unfolded it. I was shocked. It was a picture of me. Really? Of me? The puzzle would have to wait until later. I folded the paper up and stuck it in the bag with the wallets.

I turned my attention to the rifle cases. I'd only seen two rifles. I hoped I hadn't screwed up and missed a fourth person. The top two cases were empty but just by the heft I could tell the third one wasn't. I opened it and found an older model sniper rifle with a muzzle silencer and a night scope. It was designed to hold six shots, one of those in the chamber. I checked it. It was fully loaded. I took it out of the case and slung it over my shoulder. I silently closed the hatch. I walked to the side of the vehicle and propped the rifle up against the side. I grabbed the body and drug it around to behind the car. I ran back around, grabbed the rifle, and jogged towards the clearing.

I entered the tree line about fifty yards from Gary's jeep. I made my way to where I had a clear shot at the sniper in the tree and the one in the clearing. I thought everything through and measured everything out. I was amazed and shocked at myself. I was having no emotional or ethical issues with what I was about to do. Something in me was just finding this a fun hunt. *Really, Ced? Nothing? Nope – nothing.* I took off the bags I'd been using for gloves and placed them in my pocket. I steadied the rifle on the back side of a large oak, away from the guy in the clearing. There was no second guessing myself when I heard Burdock's voice in my mind giving me permission: *you need to get **VERY** mean.*

I sighted through the scope, it was an easy shot, and squeezed the trigger slowly. Though to a normal human the sound out of the muzzle would have been a quiet puff, to a wheir it sounded like a small explosion. I knew the muzzle flash would give me away if the guy in the clearing was looking in the general direction. I heard the bullet hit its target as I twirled, took two steps, and dove for the spot I'd picked out earlier. The guy in the clearing was good but misguided. I heard his bullet strike a tree a few paces to my right from where I lay. I caught a break when the body of my latest victim hit the ground with a thump. It took the man's attention away from me for a split second. I aimed and fired. The bones in his knee shattered with the impact of the bullet. I bolted another round into the chamber and sighted. Though he'd fallen to the ground, he'd held onto his rifle. He tried to roll over, dragging his useless leg around, to get on his stomach. As he put his right hand down, I fired. The bullet busted up his hand pretty good. I heard him scream in pain and saw him lay over on his back and hold his right hand with his left. I chambered another round and got up, keeping an eye on him as I made my way out of the tree line and into the clearing. Keeping my finger on the trigger and the barrel aimed at him, I walked slowly towards him.

"I know it hurts but you need to keep very still," I said to him.

I could hear about half a mile out a group of wheirs making a beeline for my location. I quickly circled the guy and kicked his rifle almost out of the clearing. I switched trigger hands and reached for my own side arm. I pulled my gun and keeping it aimed at him, I laid the rifle in the grass way out of his reach. I bent down, unsnapped the flap on his holster, pulled out his side arm and tossed it next to his rifle.

"Major Strathmore?" I asked, not lowering my weapon.

"What?" came the disbelief that I would know his name.

"You have about three minutes before four, very angry, wheirwolves break the tree line. The question is, do you want to talk to me or do I walk away?"

"You're full of shit. You're in as much danger as I am."

"Suit yourself," I said as I backed up a little so I could watch most of the clearing.

"Do you know what it is like to be bitten by a wheir?" I asked.

He didn't say anything.

"It hurts like hell," I said, showing him the angry red snakes that actually looked like they were slithering up my arm in the bright moonlight.

"Then you get to be one for the rest of your life, if they don't tear you to shreds first. You're lucky though the ones that are coming have eaten, so they'll just probably play with you for a while before they rip your guts and throat out," I said.

I could see from the auras coming towards me that Casey was going to far outdistance the rest of the pack; I was glad it wasn't Gary. The rest of the pack I could challenge. I needed this guy alive and if Gary got here first, he'd kill first and ask questions later. Casey stopped just outside of the tree line I watched him as he sniffed the air and look at me. He made his entrance with teeth bared, growling, and was making a direct line for the man on the ground. I angled towards him, keeping an eye on the man. Casey wasn't stopping. I looked him directly in the eye and growled at him. He stopped and looked at me and started to change course. I stared directly at him and took an aggressive step towards him. He stopped, looked at me, lowered his tail, and started pacing. He would look at the guy on the ground occasionally and growl. I smiled since I knew it was more for show than anything. I turned to the guy on the ground.

"Believe me now?"

Still no answer.

"You have about a minute before the Alpha gets here. If I'm not going to get any information out of you, I'm not going to go to the trouble to try and stop him. Just be forewarned, I may not be able to stop him anyway. You lost your safety net about two minutes ago," I said and waited.

Gary didn't even slow down, neither did Willis or Greta. All three burst into the clearing and had a pretty good head of steam going. I stepped into the path of Willis and Greta, who I hoped wouldn't run me over to protect me. Willis and Greta slowed, but Gary kept coming.

"Gary, please I need him alive," I said in the most pleading voice I could without directly looking at him.

The man threw up his good arm to protect himself as Gary came to an abrupt stop snapping at his face. I knew Gary had understood me or the man would be dead by now. Gary blustered for a few more minutes, showing his teeth and snapping at the man. He finally growled at him, moved a few feet off, sat down, and stared at him. I had to admire him. He had full control of himself. Where the others were pacing back and forth he sat stock still and watched. Greta came over to me and took a good sniff to make sure I was all right.

"I'm fine Greta. Nothing broken, no blood," I said as I scratched her behind the ears.

She nuzzled me once, growled at the man, than went back to pacing with Willis.

"I'm quickly running out of time. You ready to talk?" I asked.

"What are you?" he asked.

"I'm a U.S. Marshal. And you?"

"You're what?"

"Didn't know who you were going after?"

"All we had was a picture and intel on where you were going to be around dawn."

"Who sent you?"

"I got the orders via special envoy. The packet contained your picture and a dossier on your espionage and the secrets you stole from the army. It said you were an Irish national and were working for a couple of South American governments. The orders had the proper signatures," he said.

"You didn't question an army mission within the U.S.?"

"Are you that naïve?" he asked in return.

"Not anymore. You know what is sad? You and your team were probably excellent soldiers and did many good things for the government and the people of the United States. You were all probably a credit to your uniforms and to your units. But you weren't good citizens. You forgot what this nation was originally formed and reformed on. There's a reason for Directive One," I said.

I holstered my weapon, pulled out my shield, and walked towards him.

"Do you want to know who you were really after?" I asked.

He nodded his head. I flipped open my identification, shined the flashlight on it so he could read, and showed it to him.

"Have you ever heard of Counter Section?"

His eyes got wide.

"That's a myth."

"Now whose turn is it to be naïve?" I asked rhetorically.

"Welcome to the myth," I added.

He looked intently at my identification and badge.

"What was your objective?" I asked.

"To neutralize you and dispose of the evidence."

"How were you going to contact someone to tell them your mission was accomplished?"

"I was to receive a call today at oh nine hundred."

"What was to happen if you didn't complete it?"

"Our orders were for for this excursion only. If we didn't accomplish our mission we were to return home and await further orders."

"Is there any sort of code to be used?"

"Affirmative or negative. Nothing more."

I figured he was telling the truth since he'd answered quickly. He'd lost a lot of blood and was becoming woozy.

"Where are your orders?"

"They were destroyed, per operational procedures."

I figured as much but I had to ask. I walked a few feet away from him to think for a moment. When did this get to the point that someone wanted me dead personally? The only names I had were Philip, Greyson, and Zahn. What the fuck did I ever do to any of them? I didn't know what I'd done, but there was something in me that was going to really fuck them up now. I walked back over to where the Major was laying.

"One more question and the interview is done. Do you remember the name of the special envoy?"

He thought for a moment.

"A Special Agent Zahn, Military Intelligence."

GET VERY MEAN. Burdock's voice came to me. I found his side arm in the grass. I put the plastic bags back over my hands, picked it up, made sure there was a round in the chamber, and pulled the clip out. I pushed the safety back on and walked towards him.

"You have a choice. The nearest hospital is so far away that you'll bleed out before I can get you there. There is one shot in here. You can either finish your mission and get torn to shreds, or you can have a quick end. If you choose the quick end, I'll make sure your bodies are found and you and your team will be buried with the honors that you and every good soldier deserves. If not...." I said, letting the last of the sentence trail off, placed the gun on his lap and started to walk away.

I heard his labored breathing and the small click of the safety being snapped off. I walked a few more feet with my back turned to him. Casey let out a small growl. The shot sounded like a Howitzer going off to my new hearing. Since I didn't feel a bullet pierce my body and I was still walking, I knew what choice he'd made. I reached down and picked up the two rifles. Gary came to me and nudged me. I looked down at him. He turned to the pack, yipped a couple of times, and headed to the place they'd left their clothes.

****

I think I was running on total adrenaline. I didn't stop to think I just did. I sprinted back down the road to where the soldier's vehicle was at. I wasn't even winded by the time I got there but my stomach was starting to cramp from hunger. I wrestled the body laying behind it up in the hatch, put the plastic bags on my hands, closed the door, got in the driver's seat, and drove it up to the campsite. I could see the bloodied body lying in the clearing as I pulled around Gary's jeep. I shut off the lights and engine, and got out. The adrenaline had just worn off. I sat down in the grass and shook.

What the fuck did I ever do to Zahn? If they would have left me alone, I'd have let it lie. Hell, I would've had no reason to pursue it any further than Philip. The sun was starting to lighten the eastern sky. I felt something happening to me. I wanted to sleep but I had to stay awake. I felt a small loosening of my muscles and a relaxing of my joints, but nothing else. I took a deep breath. I could still smell the forest around me in minute detail. I listened and could hear the small family of rodents off to my right. I stood up. God, I could use a steak and some coffee. I smelled Gary before I saw him. He came through the tree line and headed directly over to me. He didn't say a word. He gathered me up in his arms and held me. I took a deep breath and started crying. By the time I'd cried myself out Greta, Willis, and Casey had joined us. Greta came over and touched me on the shoulder.

"You going to be okay?" she asked softly.

I broke from Gary, wiping my eyes and nodding my head.

"Is this camp just for show or is there something to eat around here?" I asked as my stomach second the motion.

"No, there's actually food here," Gary said.

Greta headed for one of the tents.

"What the fuck happened last night?" Willis asked.

"I'll explain it all later. Right now I have a lot to do before I can leave," I said.

"Why don't we just get Albert out here and they'll never be found?" Gary said.

"No. I made a promise that they would get the honors they deserved from serving their country. They weren't bad men they were just put in a very bad position," I said, starting to feel the gravity of what I'd done.

"I'd suggest that all of you break your camp down and get out of here so you won't be anywhere near this. I am going to eat something and get to work," I said.

Not a one of them moved. They all stood and looked at me.

"What?" I asked.

"What's your plan?" Gary asked.

"I can't involve you more than you already are. Get out of here while you have the chance," I said.

"Ced. We're going to help," Gary said.

I went over to the government vehicle, popped the hatch, pulled out the picture, unfolded it, and brought it back over so all of them could see it.

"This was their objective and if you look in the back of their vehicle, under the body, you will see they had one body bag, and it was mine.

Someone's been pissed at me for a while because that picture was taken before I even took this assignment. In fact it was taken the day the assignment was offered to me. This isn't your fight. I get a funny feeling that pretty soon people I know will start becoming collateral damage. Or you might be targeted just to get to me," I stopped, realizing I had begun ranting a bit.

Gary came to me and put both of his strong hands on my shoulders, held me still, and looked me in the eyes. I almost got lost in the green until he started talking.

"We're going to help you, so get over yourself. So you'd better tell me what your plan is before it gets too late."

Greta came back from the tent with a large ham steak for each of us. I took mine from her and started to eat. Once my stomach quit acting like it would use me for food, I started trying to tell them my plan without letting too much out.

"First, do we have more plastic bags like these?" I asked, holding up the two I had been using.

"Yes, a whole box of them in the tent," Greta said.

"Each one of you will need them to go over your hands. Do not touch anything or anyone associated with them," I said pointing at the body that lay on the ground.

I pulled my IBI card out of my back pocket along with the one that I had taken from the first of my victims.

"There will be another one of them over there in the trees. We need to go through their pockets and pull out anything that might be associated with me or the pack. The one over there in the trees and the other one here in the clearing will have an identification card on them. Probably an IBI card like this one," I said holding up the fake one.

"You shot three IBI agents?" Willis asked in disbelief.

"They're fake. If you feel the difference around the picture on this one and mine, you can tell," I said, passing the two cards around.

"I thought you were a U.S. Marshal," Willis said as he checked the difference in the cards.

"I am. It's a long story. Gary understands," I said.

They all looked at Gary. He nodded his head.

"In the back of their car is a black bag with their real identification in it," I added.

Gary handed the two ID's back to me. I stuck them both in my back pocket.

"They were working on intelligence that I'd be here at dawn this morning. If I'd changed, we all would've walked into the trap and it wouldn't have been pretty."

"I'm going to fucking kill him," Gary said.

I knew Philip was a marked man. If I could keep Gary focused, I might have a chance to get Philip out of here and get some information from him. But the longer this went on, the more I was about ready to let Gary have at him.

"Gary, he's the least of my worries. And not real high on yours right now either. We have more immediate problems and they go a lot higher," I said.

"Who are we talking about?" Willis asked.

"Nobody right now," Gary said and Willis dropped it.

"How do I smell?" I asked out of the blue.

"What?" Greta asked.

"Has my smell changed?" I asked.

"Well, Yes. Your underlying smell is still the same, but it is like it is covered with wheir. Which, I must say, the mixture is quite odd but you're still you," she said.

"Since my smell has changed, I need a promise from you that, for right now, you tell the rest of the pack that I did morph, but I didn't want to go out as far as the rest of you and I stayed close to the stream. Okay?"

All of them nodded their heads.

"For the next few months I would stay as far away from this site as you can, especially during the moons. And when you break down the tents today, make damn sure you get everything. As far as the vehicle goes, I would like to stick that last guy in the body bag since he was the one that got the bloodiest. Then we put all of them in the back cargo space and cover them with the blankets that are back there. I will clean up the gun I used, police all of the brass, and pack them up."

They nodded again.

"Gary? Is there someone we can call to come out and pickup Willis, Greta, and Casey?" I asked.

"Sure, I can get Craig out here in about an hour."

"That should give us time to get this place cleaned and packed."

"I want to go with you," Greta said.

"I need Gary to come pick me up after I've dumped the truck. We need to be very inconspicuous and having a carload following a government vehicle wouldn't be good. Besides, if I get caught with three bodies in the car, Gary can tell the authorities that I looked suspicious and he was checking me out. Since he's a county sheriff, his word will go a long way," I explained.

"Well then. Willis, if you and Casey will get the body from over in the woods and drag him over here. Greta, if you will search pockets and pull what might be needed out of them, I'll help Ced Police brass and tear down tents," Gary said.

Everyone scattered and started their jobs. Gary pulled his phone out of his pocket as I rolled the one body around and got everything out of the back but him. I tossed the body bag in the direction of the guy in the clearing that Greta was searching. I put the black canvass bag to the side and started wiping down the rifle I'd used.

* *

I had all of the rifles put away and stowed in the back seat. Once Greta had finished with the first body, she began on the one Willis and Casey had brought back from the tree line. Willis and Casey loaded the Major in the body bag as Greta finished searching through all the pockets of the tree sniper. We loaded all of the bodies in the cargo space with the full body bag on top. I spread out the blankets, covered them up, and shut the hatch. I took all of the things that Greta had pulled out of pockets, along with the ID and picture I already had, and stuck them in the black bag. It didn't take that much longer to have everything, including tents, packed and ready to go. I begged another slab of ham from Greta as we waited on Craig to come pick up the other three. I looked at my watch; it was just now six thirty. I sat in the grass and pigged out--God, I was hungry.

"There doesn't seem to be anything wrong with your appetite," Gary said as he sat down next to me.

"I can't seem to get full," I said as I took another bite.

"What happened last night?"

"I'll fill you in when we're alone."

"No, I didn't mean that. I meant earlier."

"You tell me. I felt everything Greta said I would feel. I can even hear and smell better now. But when I opened my eyes I was still in this form."

"I've never encountered this before. But it's done wonders for your hands," he said.

I looked at my hands. My fingernails had always been so thin, they would chip and break at the least provocation and with the type of work I did, I had to keep them short anyway. I looked at the nails that ended my fingers now; they were longer than I'd ever had them in my life. They were perfectly rounded and strong. I hadn't noticed in the excitement and activity of last night.

I'd been envious of Greta's from the moment I met her. Hers were long and one of the few things in the makeup department she indulged in. She always kept them perfectly manicured and painted.

"Wow, these are wonderful. Maybe I can keep them," I said, staring at my hands.

"You'll have to work to keep them short," Greta said from a few feet away. Damn wheir hearing.

Craig pulled into the clearing. Gary got up to meet him, but I was too intent on my food to be social. They loaded the camping gear into Craig's car along with Willis, Greta, and Casey. Greta admonished me to stay safe as they left.

"Do you have a map?" I asked Gary.

"Sure. He said as he got it out of his car and laid it on the hood.

I opened it up and spread it out.

"Where are we right now?"

He pointed to a spot on the map. I looked over the roads and saw the destination I needed. There was an interchange on the highway between Joplin and Springfield which would put me into TTZ's territory about the right time.

"I'm figuring about an hour from where we are to here." I pointed on the map.

"More like an hour fifteen," Gary corrected me.

I went over and picked up the canvass bag. I pulled out the cellphones and the wallets. I grabbed the Major's phone and set it aside. I pulled all of their driver's licenses out then their retired and reserve military IDs. I folded up the wallets bundled them back with their phones, except the major's. I pulled the batteries out of the cellphones, keeping the majors handy. I put all of the articles I was going to keep back in the bag. I grabbed the three wallets and two cellphones and batteries, walked back to their vehicle and put them under the blankets in the back next to the bodies.

"Do you have a regular screwdriver and pair of wire cutters or a very sharp knife?" I asked as I closed the hatch.

"I think so," he said as he went to the back of his jeep.

The Water's Edge

He came back over and handed me the tools. I got down on my back and crawled under the back of the vehicle.

"What are you doing?"

"All government vehicles have passive/active tracking devices. I need to deal with this one," I said as I located the little black box riveted to the back of the frame in front of the back bumper.

The little red light was blinking every few seconds or so. I was happy to see that it was not solid red, which would mean that the tracking was active. I found the little slot for the plastic lid, slid the blade of the screwdriver underneath and popped off the top. I looked through the wiring and electronics and found the small battery that was its backup power. I had to do this right. In passive mode all it was doing was recording mileage, speed, and turns. If the main battery line was cut, it would go active and send out a distress call and upload all of its information to whoever was listening. If you popped the backup battery, it would send a warning that it needed to be replaced which would result in a phone call to someone. I positioned the cutters to get all of the power wires leading to it and the screwdriver ready at the edge of the backup battery. Keeping a steady eye on the little red light, I took a deep breath, cut and popped at the same time. There were no out of sequence red flashes and it never lit again. I used the cutters and the screwdriver to remove all of the electronics from the inside of the box and popped the lid back on a now empty and useless case.

I walked back to where Gary was standing with the tools in one hand and the guts of a tracking device in the other.

"I'm always amazed that you're not just a pretty face and a sexy body," Gary said, smiling at me as he leaned against the car.

"I hope you don't have a lot planned today; it's going to be very busy for a lot of it," I said, blushing and changing the subject.

"Nope. Nothing going on," he answered.

I looked at my watch; it was going on seven thirty. I handed the tools back to Gary.

"Is there a diner or something between here and there?"

"Yes, about a half an hour from here."

"Fine, will you lead until we get there?"

"Sure. You ready to go?"

I nodded my head. I threw the major's phone, battery, and the guts of the tracking device in the bag and put it in Gary's jeep. I went to the government vehicle, put two more bags on my feet and got in. I turned the thing around as Gary backed out onto the fire road. I followed him as he led us back out to pavement.

I was starving again by the time Gary turned into the diner. I drove on past and found a side road to pull off in. If the car was found before we finished breakfast, then so be it. I walked back to the diner.

The Water's Edge

After my stomach seemed somewhat sated, we were back on the road and heading to the freeway. I found the area I was looking for. Off the interchange there was a state road maintenance area. I pulled the truck back among the equipment that had been parked there. I got out, locked the door with the keys in it, and walked back to the interchange where Gary was waiting.

"Let me drive for a bit," I said.

Gary got out, got in the passenger side, and I sat behind the wheel.

"At nine the major's phone is going to ring. I need you to answer it. You'll be asked if you accomplished your mission. Say negative and hang up."

"Okay."

I drove a few miles back to a rest area I'd seen near a pond. I pulled in and shut off the engine. I put a bag back over my hand, grabbed the cellphone and battery out of the bag, and got out. We found a picnic table near the pond. I installed the battery, turned the phone on, and we sat and waited. It rang at nine oh one. I handed the bag to Gary. He slipped it on and answered the phone. He waited a second then answered "Negative" and hung up. I took the phone from him. Flipped it over, popped the back cover, pulled the battery out then closed it back up. I got up, walked to the edge of the pond, and threw both the phone and the battery as far as I could, into the deep part of the water.

"Shall we go back to Greta's?" I asked.

We walked back to the jeep. Gary opened my door for me and I sat down. I was really beginning to get tired. Gary put the jeep in gear and headed back towards Cassville.

"Do you have a color copy machine at the office?" I asked.

"Yes."

"Can I use it a little later?"

"Of course."

"Thanks."

"Are you going to tell me what happened last night?"

It took most of the drive back to Willis and Greta's to tell him about finding the people in the camp area when I went back to find something to eat. I related as much of the story as I could to him, making sure I said nothing about TTZ or how far up I was beginning to suspect things went.

We pulled into the drive. Willis, Greta, and Casey were sitting on the front porch waiting for us. Gary stopped the jeep and we got out. I reached back in and grabbed the bag.

"Greta, can I use your table?" I asked as I got up on the porch.

"Sure," Greta said as she got up from the chair and led everybody back into the house.

I sat down at the table and noticed I had an audience that sat with me.

"What? Am I going to have a cheering section too?" I asked.

Casey looked around at the others at the table who weren't saying anything. I guess he decided that if no one else was going to speak up, he would.

"Ced. How much trouble are you in?" he asked.

"More than you will ever know."

"And why is that?" he asked forcefully.

I was beginning to like him a lot. He had that inquisitive and fearless nature of the young. He reminded me a lot of me.

"Casey, I understand that you feel left out and that I owe you an explanation. If I could fill you in on everything I would. I will at least explain a few things. Up until a little over a month ago I was a happy Deputy U.S. Marshal with a desk, a great partner, a pain in the butt supervisor that covered everyone's ass, and a very uncomplicated life. I was offered a permanent special assignment that I took. I closed my first case last month. I found things, while finishing my report that led me to believe that the case I thought was just a rogue wheir was much more and was more involved. Evidently, I stepped on someone's toes and they're very unhappy about it. I've tried my damnedest to keep the pack out of it but I'm not sure I succeeded. The less everyone knows about me and what I do, the better for all of you. I know it's hard to accept but this is my job. The next few days will decide whether this becomes very bloody or goes away."

I reached across and touched Casey's hand and looked him in the eye. He tried to look away.

"Casey, look at me," I said forcefully.

He brought his eyes back up to mine.

"Hopefully you have a very long life ahead of you. You don't need to cut it short on something I've unwittingly gotten you into. I appreciate and am thankful to have the support of the friends I've made here and I'm trying my hardest to protect that."

"I am here to help if you need it," he said.

"I know and I'll probably take you up on that offer from time to time. But right now I need you to stay out of the way of the flying glass."

"Would everyone like some lunch?" Greta asked, breaking the tension.

Everyone said yes, including me. As Greta busied herself with a meal. I dumped the contents of the bag out on the table. I went through everything and started organizing it. There were three copies of the picture of me, I flipped one over and was surprised to find a name on it. Clair McDuff was hand written across it. Greta had pulled things out of pockets that could just as well have been left and I placed them to the side. One thing that caught my attention was a folded piece of paper. I opened it up and smoothed it out. The major was covering his ass, I thought as I read what was written.

Clair McDuff.
Age: 26-27
Hair: Auburn/red – Shoulder blade length.

Eyes: Lt. Blue/Gray
Height: 5'-3"
Weight: Aprox. 110-115 lbs
Measurements: *34-D*
                             24
                             35
Distinguishing Features:
Small scar above right eyebrow, very light complexion, smaller than average feet (size three shoe), usually wears no makeup of any kind, Right handed, excellent marksman, advanced training in hand to hand and martial arts (Favors left foot beginning attack).

MI-SO/2248-997-433/A
Col. J.T. May

Well, so I did have an order number to follow, though they were way off on my weight.

"Greta, do you have a sharp knife, clear tape, and some paper clips?" I asked.

"Sure. I'll get them after I finish making lunch."

I looked at the things I had; three pictures of me, three drivers' licenses, three military IDs, three fake IBI credentials, and a handwritten paper of my traits that also listed a file number and an actual Colonel's name. Greta sat plates down for everybody and stepped out of the room for a moment. I took a bite of the very large sandwich Greta had given me. She came back into the kitchen and handed me the things I'd asked for. Everybody ate and watched as I went to work. I delicately cut around the plastic covering above the picture on the IBI credentials of the first victim. I pulled the picture off to reveal the picture underneath. I took the clear tape and taped it down next to the real one so both could be seen. I clipped the ID's of each individual together so I had three stacks. I folded the paper back up and stacked everything neatly, set it aside and continued with my lunch.

"Gary, can I use that copier in your office later?"

"Yes. Why?"

"I have a friend that gave me some advice and I'm taking it. If they want to take me on, I am going to show them how much of a bitch I can be, human or wheir."

"I don't think I want to touch that" Willis said, smiling around his sandwich.

We finished our lunch. I put everything I was keeping in the bag and zipped it up.

"I'm going to take a shower and get a nap in. Is anybody going to be up for a while?" I asked.

"I'll set an alarm. What time do you need up?" Greta asked.

"No later than two thirty."

I got clean clothes out of my suitcase and went to take a shower. With the shower warming, I started to run a brush through my hair and found it more difficult than normal. I took a good look at my hair and face in the mirror. It seemed different. I ran my fingers through my hair. I'd always had relatively normal hair that was fairly straight. What I ran my fingers through now was thick and wavy. My face looked a little thinner and more defined. Well, let's see: better hearing, better sense of smell, fingernails to die for, a one day period, no changing shape and growing hair all over my body? Fine, I'd take the week of Goliath PMS as an exchange. I felt the exhaustion build as my clothes hit the floor, and I stepped into the deliciously hot shower. I finished up quickly, dried off, finished my hair, and stepped into some panties and oversized shirt. Comatose took me somewhere between the bathroom door and the bed.

****

"Ced?" I heard Greta calling my name and shaking me.

"What?" I asked not opening my eyes.

"It's two thirty."

It took me a minute to realize I'd asked someone to wake me.

"Okay. I'm awake."

I lay there for a minute to get the motivation to get out of bed. I forced myself up, grabbed my suitcase and opened it on the bed. My pants hadn't fit real well this morning so I pulled out a girl's worst nightmare, the dreaded, tight, skinny jeans. I slid them on and up. They weren't tight, they were loose in fact. *Geez, did I lose that much weight overnight?* I stuck my head out the door.

"Greta?" I said just above a whisper, knowing she could hear it if she were in the house.

Greta came down the hall from the kitchen.

"What?"

"Do you have a scale?"

"In the closet in the bathroom. Why?

"My clothes don't fit."

She just smiled and pointed towards the door of the bath. I went in, with her following, found the scales and drug them out into the floor and stepped on them.

"Your scales have to be wrong."

She stepped on the scales.

"Nope they're right."

"They can't be," I said as I stepped back on them.

"I weighed one seventy six just two days ago. There's no way in hell I gained seventeen pounds in two days. Not with the way my jeans fit."

"You weigh one ninety two?" Greta asked, shocked.

"I've always been heavy because of my bone and muscle density, but this is more than I've weighed in my life." I stood there looking down at the dial in disbelief.

"Do you have a cloth tape measure?" I asked her.

"Yeah, hold on a minute," she said as she left the bath.

She came back in a second and handed it to me. I dropped my pants and took off my shirt so I was just standing there in my panties. I ran the tape around my waist. It measured twenty-two inches.

"Okay this is nuts. I gain weight and lose inches? I've had a twenty-four inch waist for years," I said as I put the tape around my hips and sure enough, I had lost an inch there.

"Would you?" I asked, handing her the tape and pointing at my chest.

She took the tape and ran it around my chest under my breasts.

"What is it?"

"Thirty-six."

"Damn, no wonder my bra felt uncomfortable. I have always been a thirty-four."

She held out her hand to me. I took it and she led me back to the bedroom I was using and opened the closet door. On the back was a full length mirror. I was shocked. My body had changed; where I had always kept myself in pretty good shape, I would never have been called ripped. Though my stomach muscles weren't as ripped as Greta's, they stood out in rows, very defined. My arms were well defined as were my shoulders. My legs and thighs, though still shapely, were tight and muscular. And the girls seemed to stick out farther than they ever had before like they were waving to anyone that wanted the attention.

"The effects of your change," Greta said.

"If I'm seeing all these effects, then why didn't I change last night?"

Greta shrugged her shoulders.

"Maybe you will next month or maybe because of what you are, you won't. I don't know."

I looked at myself again in the mirror and still couldn't believe that it was the same person that I saw only two or three days ago.

"Gary will be here in a few minutes. You need to get moving."

"Okay," I said, stepping back to find my clothes but still looking at the mirror.

"Hmm. Bad case of narcissism going on here," Greta laughed.

"Okay, I quit," I said, crossing to the closet door and closing it.

I got dressed quickly as Greta left to go finish what she was doing before I interrupted her. I was just putting my side arm in its holster when I heard Gary in the living room. I walked out of the bedroom and down the hall.

"You ready?" Gary asked as I came in.

"Yep. Let me get the stuff from the table," I said as I went to the kitchen.

I grabbed the black bag and headed to the front door where Gary was waiting. He escorted me to his cruiser and installed me in the passenger side, got in behind the wheel, and headed down the drive.

****

I was sitting at the typewriter as Gary made color copies of the ID's and pictures of me, then normal copies of the folded piece of paper with the order number on it. I finished the two letters I was writing. I made copies of those and sat down at a desk to put things together.

"Can I have three envelopes and two file folders?" I asked.

Gary went to a small closet and returned with the items I asked for. I addressed the three envelopes, put a copy of the IDs, a copy of the letter with my personal information on it, a copy of the picture that they'd been carrying, and a copy of the first letter I'd written in each and sealed them.

"Do you have someone that you trust to leave these with that can mail them if something happens to either me or you?" I asked.

"Yes, I have a lawyer," he said, taking the envelopes I'd given him.

He looked down at the top one.

"The President? Are you serious?"

"Yep."

I took the original IDs, pictures and information page and placed it in a file folder and taped it up; that would be going back home with me.

In the last folder I put the final copies and the last page I'd typed. On that page I put every case number and referenced every article I'd found so far that mentioned George Greyson and Terrence Zahn. I even included what the last mercenary had told me about the special envoy.

"Okay, I'm done."

We went back out to his car and he drove back out to Willis and Greta's.

Gary cut the engine and got out. He met me at the front of the car and offered his hand, which I took with enjoyment. He felt it and smiled at me. We walked up the front steps and onto the porch where Greta was sitting waiting on us.

"Something to drink?" She asked us both.

"Scotch if you have it or a beer will do," I said.

"Beer," Gary said.

"I think Willis has some Scotch socked away somewhere," she said, smiling at me and opened the door to the house for us to enter.

I went to the bedroom and put the files I had with me in one of my suitcases. Greta came in, handed me my drink and sat down on my bed.

"How much trouble are you in?" she asked.

"A lot, Greta."

She seemed very disturbed by that. I'd seen a much softer side of her since I had been bitten. Greta was only four years older than I was, but she seemed more than that. Not in her looks but in her demeanor. I wasn't sure if she wanted children but I knew deep down she would make the perfect mother. She'd really started to mother me since that night a month ago. Maybe mother wasn't the right word, but at least a very protective older sister.

"When are you going back home?"

"Ready to get rid of me?" I asked, smiling.

"You know better than that. I was hoping you'd stay through Saturday and join the pack for our cookout."

I knew that the longer I stayed, the more time whoever was after me had to make another attempt while I was out of my comfort zone.

"I'm not sure that would be such a good idea. I don't know who's after me or if they'll try to use the pack to get to me."

"The pack is going to want to see you after this moon."

"Don't you mean that the pack is going to want to sniff me after this moon?" I asked, laughing.

"Potato, Patato," she replied, smiling back.

"I really need to be heading out tomorrow. They will get their chance next month."

"So you're coming back?" She asked surprised.

"Of course. Until I know that my full moons are going to be like this all the time, minus people trying to kill me, I'm not going to take the chance of not being near a pack that accepts me. Provided Gary is okay with it."

You would have thought I'd just given her a Christmas gift.

"He'd be pissed at you if you didn't come up."

"Really?"

"He's quite taken with you."

"I haven't gotten that from him."

"If you'd quit being a Marshal for a day and just be a woman you might find out," she said, winking at me.

"Great, just what I need; a big dog Alpha sniffing after me."

"You're horrible, Ced," she laughed.

I raised my glass to her, smiled and took a sip.

"So do you mind if I stay tonight?

"You can be such a pain in the butt. Let's go out on the porch with Willis and Gary," she said, standing up and going to the door.

I followed her to the kitchen where she stopped and got fresh beers. We walked outside into the fading light of the day. I took a seat next to Gary as Greta took hers next to Willis and handed out the beers.

I sat there and listened to the night sounds and the conversation. I could smell Gary sitting next to me. Through the excitement of the day I felt like I had missed out on something and that something was a feeling that was growing deep between my thighs. *God, Ced, you went through hell the past few days, you have someone trying to kill you, and all you can think about is sex?* Yes, that was all I seemed to be thinking about. It was a good thing I'd be leaving tomorrow since I didn't think I'd be able to stay around here any longer and not jump Gary's bones. *Look at it logically girl. You don't know him and you don't know what can of worms you might open up by doing it.* I had myself almost talked down when Gary looked at me and smiled. God, it was like he knew exactly what I was thinking. *Remember, Ced; snapping four legged babies trying to nurse.* Nope, didn't make a dent in my sexual need. It took me a second to realize someone was talking to me.

"What?" I asked Willis.

"Are you staying until the weekend?"

"No, not this month. I have to get home."

"Really, you aren't staying?" Gary asked.

It took all the will power I had to say the next sentence.

"No. You and I both know why I need to get back," I said, smiling at him.

"But I'll be back next full moon," I added.

"Then I guess I'll forgive you," he said, smiling back.

God, I about melted looking into those green eyes. *No, wait, I was lying. I'll stay here as long as you will let me. Geez, Ced, quit being such a sniveling mush brain.*

"I'm glad you forgive me," I said as I reached over and touch his hand that was resting on the arm of the chair.

I think I will throw up now.

"It isn't hard to do," he said as he wrapped his large strong hand around mine.

I melted and smiled like a silly school girl. Any pretense I ever had to a rough and tumble law enforcement professional was gone after that one moment.

We sat on the back porch through a paper plate dinner Greta fixed and on into the night. The adrenaline that I'd been running on most of the day was finally giving out and any sexual thoughts were quickly dissipating.

"Guys, you may be adjusted to this wheir thing of staying up all day and night but I'm exhausted. I need to go to bed," I said as I stood up.

"How are you getting home tomorrow?" Willis asked.

Shit. I forgot I had no transportation here.

"I was going to see if Greta could take me to the bus station in Springdale."

"Do you want her to take you home?" Gary asked.

"You know the answer to that. The bus will be fine."

"Wouldn't a train be more comfortable?" he asked.

"Maybe, but I don't have to give my name or ID for a bus ticket."

"Are you sure.....?" he started to ask, but quit while he was ahead.

"Let me walk you in," he said, getting up.

"Good night Greta, Willis."

"Night sweetie," Greta replied for both of them.

I still had a hold of Gary's hand and led him back to the door of my bedroom. He looked down at me and smiled. In a flash he had me in his arms kissing me. Though I kissed back wholeheartedly I pulled back from him and slapped him across the face. I wasn't sure why and really wasn't sure why I laughed after doing it. He looked down at me with an evil grin and kissed me again. This time he caught me by the wrist before my palm found his cheek. He grabbed my other wrist and pined them both behind me at the small of my back. This time, without the worry of a slap he picked me up off of the floor and kissed me hard. We came up for air and I smiled.

"Mister Benton, is that anyway to treat the new bitch on the block?" I asked.

"I could think of better ways, but even I wouldn't do that in Willis' house," he said, smiling at me, kissing me again but more gently.

He sat me back on solid ground and let my wrists go. I wrapped my arms around his neck and pulled him down to me. After a good five minutes I found enough will power to come up for air.

"I really need to get to bed," I said.

"Alone," I added as he opened his mouth to say something.

"Me too. I have to work tomorrow. What time are you leaving?"

"As soon as is convenient for Greta."

"I'll try and get out in the morning and at least have a cup of coffee."

"I'd like that."

"Good night, Ced," he said as he cupped my cheek in his palm and kissed me very gently good night.

"Night Gary," I said as I opened the door behind me and slipped into my room.

I heard him walk away, humming.

Chapter 18
Thursday June 8, 2248

I sat at the kitchen table sipping my coffee as Willis left for work. I had to admit that he was quite handsome in his suit and tie. I watched with a little envy as Greta handed him his lunch and kissed him good-bye. Greta turned on the radio she had over the sink and started to clean up the kitchen after the morning meal. The radio was low and Greta and I talked as she worked. It was something in the lead in that caught my attention.

"Greta, could you turn that up a little?"

Greta hit the volume and the newsman's voice came through.

"A gruesome triple homicide was discovered at a Highway Department marshaling yard on the Joplin-Springfield expressway Saturday evening. A source said that the three bodies were found in a government vehicle. Three bodies were dumped in the back hatch access and foul play is suspected. No witnesses have come forwarded. It is believed that the victims were military since the Department of Defense has taken over the investigation.

Now, your weather....."

I got up and turned it down. I stood looking out of the sink window into the back yard at a loss for what I should feel.

****

Gary finally got to the house after I was already packed and had about thirty minutes before Greta was to take me to the bus station in Springdale.

"I didn't think you were going to make it," I said as he kissed me quickly, got a cup of coffee, and sat down.

"Seemed to be a lot going on this morning. I wish we could schedule the full moons on weekends."

"Weekends *would* be a plus. I'll be glad when I get this stuff straightened out and things quiet down in this neck of the woods."

"I'm not sure I want that."

"Why?" I asked, surprised.

"Well, if it gets too quiet here, I'm not sure my favorite Marshal will even bother coming to this small burg anymore."

I slid my chair around the corner of the table next to him. I put my head on his shoulder.

"Nah, too much fun. Besides from what I understand they have a wonderful bed and breakfast here and it has great amenities," I laughed.

I caught a look at his watch.

"Damn."

"What?" he asked.

"I've got to get going to catch my bus."

"I don't know why you won't let one of us drive you home or at least closer to where you live."

"You know why."

"Yeah."

Gary got up with me. We gathered my suitcases and other personal items out of my room. I stuck my holster on the back of my belt and Gary helped me on with my blazer. We walked quietly out to Greta's car and loaded everything in. He kissed me hard as he held the door open.

"I'll see you in a few weeks and who knows? I might have something else that brings me up here before then," I said as I sat down in the car.

"Stay safe, Ced," he told me as he shut the door.

"Keep your head down," I answered as he walked away to his own car.

"You ready to go?" Greta asked.

"Not really but I don't have a choice."

Greta put the car in gear and headed down the drive.

****

The moment I boarded the bus, I knew I'd made a mistake. Even though this was an express from Springdale to Little Rock, I wasn't sure I'd be able to stand it for the four hours it would take to get there. Then I'd have another hour and a half from Little Rock to Hot Springs.

The stale smell of hundreds of people who had ridden it in the last few days, the bio-diesel smell, and the horrible cologne of the man that decided to sit next to me brought to the forefront the drawbacks of wheir smell and enclosed places.

I don't know if it was the cacophony of smells and conversations, the distance from the full moon, the lack of adrenaline that was no longer pumping through my veins, or a combination of all of it, but my mind turned quickly to the past few days. I was flooded with thoughts of Zahn, Greyson, Philip, the pack, of who wanted me dead and the three bodies I had stuffed into the back of a vehicle and left on the side of the road. I'd become a cold heartless killing bitch. As much as I tried to work up some sort of guilt over what I'd done Tuesday night, I just couldn't and that bothered me more than killing the three men. Had I really lost any empathy for the world and people in it? I tried to sleep to get away from it but my mind wouldn't shut off and the man beside me wouldn't shut up. If I was really a cold heartless killer, I would have pulled out both of my side arms and lowered the population of this traveling hell hole by one.

Come on, Ced, work the puzzle. I forced myself to start looking at who was after me and what I could have done to make them hate me this much. The longer I looked at it, I knew that Gary's pack was not and had never been the target. I was. But how could anyone know that this particular case would be the first one I would go after? Knowing Zahn had been the envoy to send the kill orders out on me and that they had pictures of me from that day in Dallas made this a conspiracy, that went way up and across departments. *Ced, you should really think about packing your bags when you get home and running to the darkest corner of the world.* Great thought but, with my luck, I would get there and it would be filled with vampires. What the hell was I going to do? Was it just a matter of time before snipers would be taking shots at me going in and out of my house? Was this job really worth this? If I was forced to answer that question right now it would be an resounding NO.

I thought about Gary, Greta, and the rest of the pack. Would they be left alone if I disappeared or would Zahn be vindictive and take them out? Did I care? Could I care? The tears that started rolling down my cheeks answered that question. How many Garys and Gretas were out there that had absolutely no protection simply because no one cared. What about all of the population that would be at the mercy of any thug with a gun if all of the police in the country felt the way I did right now and walked? If they couldn't grow a backbone, screw em. I knew deep down I didn't really feel that way but it was a great fantasy.

I wasn't the cold heartless killing bitch I imagined myself to be. I'd had three trained killers waiting to take me out. The wheir in me had known that, and I did what they would have done to me before they could. Would I have found a different way out if I hadn't been bitten? If I was the old me would I have tried to capture or disarm them? Maybe, but I get a bit vengeful at times. Just ask Grant's killer--oh wait--he is rotting in a grave somewhere because I put thirteen slugs in him, hard to ask him now. I'd have probably put a second clip in him if someone hadn't stopped me. *So what do you do now, Ced? You were put here for a reason and I don't think the person who signed your invitation had dying in mind; that comes from someone a bit lower. If you leave, someone else will be put in your place. Will they get as lucky as you have? Will there be a long line of agents die for whatever reason or are they just after you? Can you take this on?* **I don't know, I don't know, I don't know, I don't know,** I screamed at myself in my head.

****

There is a bit of a stigma attached to people who have to take the bus. I don't know if it's been this way as long as buses have existed but it is there now. They are labeled poor, mentally unbalanced, or poor *and* mentally unbalanced. Though I wasn't poor, I guess I'd reached the title of mentally unbalanced since the obnoxious, odoriferous, and rattle trap man sitting next to me gave me a worried look and moved to another seat. One small problem in my life solved.

I was the first one off the bus in Little Rock. I soaked up the sunshine and fresh air as soon as I could walk across to the small section of grass that was off to the side of the terminal. I had a half an hour wait for the bus to Hot Springs. I thought about getting my bags, finding a taxi and paying him to take me home, with all of the windows rolled down for the duration. Unfortunately, taxis are hard to find around bus stations and I knew it would be at least a forty five minute walk to the train station to find one. *Deal with it, Ced. You've made it this far only an hour and a half left.* I gulped in air and sunshine until I heard the call for my ride. Though this one had the same basic smell as the last one, there were a lot fewer passengers and no one sat within four seats of me in any direction.

Again I was the first one off the bus and into the sunshine of Hot Springs. I got my bags and went outside to sit in the fresh air. Now my only question was how to get home from here. If I hadn't had more than I could carry, I'd have walked it. But fifteen plus miles, two suitcases, and pillow was a bit much, even for a wheir to manage. I found a pay phone and a phone book. I flipped through it and found the number I was looking for. I opened my personal phone and dialed.

"National Parks Service, Hot Springs district, Lake Hamilton station," the voice answered.

"Yes. This is U.S. Marshal Cedwynne McKenzie. Is Bran Murray reachable?"

"Is this an emergency?"

"No. But it is important."

There was a moment of pause.

"Hold for a minute."

I heard the line click to hold. After a few minutes the voice came back on.

"Can you call back in about ten minutes?"

"Sure," I said and we both hung up.

I went and sat back on the bench I'd claimed. I needed sun and fresh air. I probably looked like some homeless woman sitting there with two suitcases and a pillow. No, wait; I was a mentally unbalanced homeless woman sitting on a bench with two suitcases and a pillow. I waited for about fifteen minutes and then hit the redial button. I listened as the voice went through the greeting.

"Bran Murray, please?" I asked.

There was a moment of wait.

"This is Bran Murray," Bran answered from the other end of the phone.

"Bran. This is Cedwynne."

"Hey, where are you?"

"Actually, I'm at the bus station here in town. I was wondering when you got off of work if I could bribe you to come pick me up and run me back to the house?"

"Yes, you could probably bribe me."

There was a short pause and he said nothing more. Finally, I remembered who I was talking to. Also, I realized I'd missed him.

"Will you come pick me up?"

"Sure."

"Sometime in the near future?"

"Sure."

"Can you give me a time you will get here, referenced in a basic way to the watch I am wearing?"

"I could."

"God dammit, will you?" I almost screamed the question.

I heard a chuckle.

"I get off here in about thirty minutes. It takes about ten to fifteen minutes to get there from here."

"Does that mean you will be here then?" I asked, covering my bases.

"Yes," he said, laughing.

"Thank you."

"You're welcome. Bye."

"Bye," I said as we hung up.

****

I found something to munch on, which I seemed to be doing a lot of now, and waited on my bench out in front of the bus station. My mind was still working on my endless loop when Bran's old beat up pickup pulled to the curb and Bran got out. He came around the front of the truck, looked at me and stopped. He stood there just staring.

"What?" I asked as I got up.

"What happened to you?" he asked a little shocked.

"Nothing really; no falls, no broken bones. Why?"

"You are different," he said as he came over and picked up my bags.

"Good different or bad different?"

"Not sure," he said distractedly.

"Thanks," I replied sarcastically.

"Don't misunderstand me, physically you look great. You're face looks like you have been lifting weights continuously for the last month and your hair is not the same as when you left, it's fuller and has more body. And, excuse my noticing, it looks like you got breast implants, which you really didn't need," Bran said as I followed him to the back of the truck.

"But?" I asked as he put my suitcases in the back.

"When you left you were ill and not doing so well. You come back and you are the picture of health and fitness. Just seems a little strange after only a week."

"Greta works wonders. And yes, these are the same boobs I left with, nothing more nothing less," I said as he walked me to the passenger door and opened it.

The ride to the house was a bit uncomfortable with Bran constantly checking me out and trying to make sense of what he saw. I took a good whiff of him and I suddenly realized what Greta had been talking about, slight human but very much a warm earthy flavor. I so wanted to ask him about it, but thought better of it as we started up the drive to the house.

"The place looks great," I told Bran as he pulled up and parked next to Bee.

"Thanks," he said.

He grabbed my bags out of the back while I took my pillow to the front door and opened it. I could smell them the moment the door swung in.

"God Dammit," I almost yelled.

"What is it?" Bran asked worried as he ran up the three steps and came next to me on the porch.

"Bent a fingernail back when I opened the door," I said quickly, trying to cover up my anger and fear.

"You scared the hell out of me."

"Sorry. Can I ask you for an unusual request? Could you wait out here for a minute or two?"

"Sure, why?"

"I left out something work related and I need to put it up right quick," I said.

"A little cloak and dagger don't you think?" he asked and set the suitcases down on the porch.

"Humor me."

"As you wish," he said, gesturing to the open door.

I smiled at him, went in the house, and closed the door after me. I took a deep breath. Two people--human. Something seemed familiar about one of them but I couldn't place it. I'd been so enthralled with my new senses that I hadn't asked anyone about the finer points of having them. Like how long does a scent linger? *Think about it, Ced.* I took another breath. Bran had been in here a week ago but I couldn't smell him. So they'd been here while I was gone. I walked through the house committing the scent to memory. They'd been in every room and it was strongest right next to the door down to the basement. I pulled my gun out and slipped my card in the slot above the door. I opened the door slowly, reached in and turned on the light. I listened intently but heard nothing. I walked a few steps down and lowered myself to peek below the ceiling of the basement. There was no one there. I walked down to the bottom of the stairs and took a deep breath. I could smell concrete, dust, paper, ink, plastic, and metal, but no humans. I figured I should be able to smell me but there was no real living scent down here. I walked upstairs and closed the door behind me. So they either didn't want to go down in the basement, or couldn't get down there. Maybe my office, at least, was secure. I put my gun back in the holster, walked back to the front door and opened it. Bran was leaning against one of the railings, waiting.

"Sorry about that," I said as I came out and grabbed my pillow and one of the suitcases.

"Everything safe?"

"Yep, nothing's going to jump out and get you," I said as I walked back into the house.

Bran followed me to the bedroom and sat my bag down where I asked him to.

"Would you care for a beer?" I asked.

"Don't mind if I do."

We walked back in the kitchen. I pulled two bottles out of the fridge and handed him one.

"Do you mind if we step outside? I've been cooped up in a box all day and could really use some fresh air and sunshine," I asked.

"Not at all."

We walked back to the front door, went outside and off into the yard.

"You seem a bit distracted and antsy. Are you okay?" he asked.

"Yes, I have a case on my mind. Have you noticed anything out of the ordinary this week while I have been gone?"

"You mean other than the nondescript dark gray sedan with tinted windows and a government license plate, USG 44-943, following me around from the time I got back from Russellville until I picked you up from the bus station?" he asked, smiling.

"What?"

"Did I stutter?" he asked, smiling wider.

"Bran, this is serious."

"Nothing is any more serious than we choose to make it."

"I'm worried about it and you," I said, stressing the "and you".

"I will take some extra precautions," he said, letting his smile fade.

"Did you see anyone out here this week?"

"No, but I worked a lot this week. And if someone was following me, there is nothing to say that they were not in contact with someone else."

"You are so good at easing my mind," I said sarcastically.

"Let me put it to you this way. Most people, who are in places that they don't belong, don't want to be caught."

"What are you talking about?" I asked, confused.

"May I see one of your ID cards?"

I pulled out my Marshal's credentials and handed it to him. He took it from me and headed back towards the house, getting his own wallet out of his back pocket. He went up the steps pulling something out of his wallet. I came up behind him and saw he had his driver's license out along with my ID.

"Watch closely," he said as he stuck my ID in and pushed the door open once the lock disengaged.

He pulled the door closed, then inserted his driver's license and pushed on the door, but it did not open.

"Okay, what did I just witness?" I asked.

"See the difference?" he asked, showing me the back of both cards.

"What--that one of them is a driver's license and the other is a U.S. Marshal's identification?" I asked.

"You can tell that from the backs?" he asked, looking at both of them.

"Well, no. But..."

"Without using your knowledge of what the fronts look like, what is the difference?"

I looked and to his credit there wasn't a lot.

"Nothing," I said.

"Look closer."

I looked closer at the two. I studied each of them and could not find any real difference other than maybe a slightly different color.

"I can't see anything," I said.

"Look closer," he said, tapping the magnetic strip.

"A magnetic strip, but both of them have it."

"Then look closer."

I got up on them and studied the strip, there was absolutely nothing different between them.

"I don't see any difference," I said, frustrated with the game.

"You might not, but a computer would."

It hit me. The card reader in the door was nothing more than a closed computer system that had been programed for the information on a particular card. So, somewhere was a way to check what magnetic strips would be allowed to access that small computer chip in the door.

"Why didn't you just say that from the beginning?" I asked a little frustrated with him.

"Ced, you are a very observant person. I have watched you figure things out step by step on more than one occasion. But sometimes you spend a lot of time in a loop worrying about theory and not noticing the practical. If I were to just explain it to you, then you would not break out of the habit of not noticing the obvious," he said, giving me a small smile.

"Bran, sometimes you can be a royal pain in the ass but today I think I love you," I said as I took my ID back from him and gave him a kiss on his cheek.

"Ced, remember: Fear, indecision, and doubt are in your head, not your heart."

"You are just full of riddles today aren't you?"

I expected some sort of esoteric answer out of him but all I got was a grin. It suddenly hit me who he reminded me of, Sam. I could remember Sam doing things like this to me. Though I'd usually get the big picture right, it was the small things that Sam would catch that would make the case. I think that was another reason why Sam and I made good partners, I would catch the crooks based on what I could figure out, and his ability to build the case would get them convicted. I wish I had him here as backup. He'd be the one who could make me understand how to proceed or tell me to drop it and run like hell.

"What are you doing Saturday evening?" I asked.

"Nothing. Why?"

"I figured I'd pay my debt and take you out to a good dinner for picking me up."

"Hamburger at the Dairy Diner?" he asked, chuckling.

"No, I was thinking something a bit more upscale. Do you know of a very good restaurant in town?"

"There are a few."

"Is there one that you prefer?"

"Not really. I don't tend to waste my money."

"Well, this one's on me. Pick one and give me directions."

"Do you have a piece of paper and a pencil?"

I pulled out my small notebook, flipped to an empty page, and handed him the pencil I kept with it. He wrote the name of the restaurant and directions to it and handed it back.

"I need to get going. I will see you tomorrow when I come out for the lawn," he said as he handed me his empty bottle and started walking towards his truck.

After I watched him drive away, I went back into the house and opened all the windows to try and air out the smells of people I didn't know. My brain started working on the magnetic strips. How to find out what the hell was going on at my house and in my life? My stomach gave out a large growl to remind me I hadn't eaten in a while. My food budget was going to be smashed if I continued to eat this way. I went in the kitchen searching for something to eat. Soup was just not going to do it. There was absolutely nothing substantial in my kitchen to eat. I'd have to do some significant grocery shopping tomorrow. I'd been cooped up all day and needed food before I started answering the newest puzzle that faced me. I locked the house back up, went outside and started walking towards the Dairy Diner that sat across the two lane highway from the road I lived on.

****

After a very large meal and the walk home, I opened the house back up, started a pot of coffee, unplugged my phone and turned it on. There was a message on the small screen of my phone saying I had missed calls. I flipped to my call log. I had one missed call from Burdock and three in the past two days from TTZ. I didn't find it interesting that TTZ had called me. What I found interesting was the number of calls in a short amount of time and when they were. He'd called me once Wednesday evening and twice today. Was he trying to force the meeting since he knew I'd been in the area? Well he'd have to wait, along with Burdock, until I could get some things straight in my head, especially after this past Tuesday night. I went back to my bedroom and retrieved the files I'd put together at Gary's office.

With coffee in hand, I sat down at the table in the center of the room to start working through the dangerous, nasty puzzle that had become my life. I opened up both files and spread them out so I could see everything. I pulled a larger notepad off of the desk and sat it in front of me. I made two columns; one titled professional and the other titled personal. On the personal side I wrote down my bullet points. If I wasn't human, what was I? If I wasn't a full wheir, why not? Had I lost any human feeling I ever had? Who was I? I circled the last one a couple of times.

On the professional side I started writing, knowing it would be a much longer list: Someone was trying to kill me. Someone was watching me, Bran and my house. Someone has been in my house. Were the first three related? Who was really pulling the strings behind all of this; Greyson, Zahn, or someone higher up?

I sat looking at the professional list and tapping my pencil lead against the paper making little dots as I thought about it. My brain was mush from everything I'd been through over the past couple of months and the amount of information that was stuck in there. Sam's voice came to me through the chaos: *Pick somewhere to start. Pick something that either looks like the beginning or something that you can reach out and touch easily.*

I circled "Someone has been in my house." How would I go about finding out what cards were programed into my system? Who would I ask?

IBI? Not on my life. Burdock? He probably wouldn't know. I wasn't sure I could trust any of the people on my phone, or they might not want to give me any information because of some stupid secrecy issue. I spun around in my chair and sat looking at the map hanging on the wall. Then it hit me. Another agent. But which one? Get as far away from your area and Washington City as you can. I looked out to the west coast. I picked the district that included Oregon and Washington. I picked up the phone, dialed, and waited while it rang. I was surprised by the female voice that answered the phone. Did I think I was the only woman working in this?

"Hello?" the voice asked.

"DTL District 24?"

"Who is this?"

"CAM District 5"

There was quiet from the other end.

"You can call me back on my phone," I said.

"And what would that prove?"

I thought for a second. She was absolutely right.

"I am not sure, but I need some information."

"I am sure you do. What's your code name?"

I had no clue. Zahn had played the game and was satisfied with his results.

"I have no idea."

"Then I think this conversation is over."

"Wait! I've only been on this job for just over a two months. No one said anything about code names," I said, pleading.

"Hold on a minute."

I heard the clicking of a keyboard in the background--God, you had to love wheir hearing.

"District 5 you said?"

"Yes."

A few more keystrokes.

"Are you near your safe?"

"Yes," I answered.

"Is it locked or unlocked?"

"Locked."

"Open it."

I got up from my desk, went to the safe and spun the tumbler; I cranked the lever, and pulled the safe open.

"Okay, it's open."

"Did you look through it thoroughly?"

"Sort of."

"Then the answer is no. There should be a couple of envelopes in there. Find the one that says 'Identify' and open it."

I found and opened the envelope, and looked at the printed page. Underneath each section number was a name. They looked to be characters from nursery rhymes and fairly tails.

"Okay."

"Anytime you call someone, you need to address them by their code name and refer to yourself by your own."

"Okay, so you are Mother Goose and I am...." I said as I looked for my district number and began laughing.

"What is so funny?"

"Out of all of the names in the world and I have to get Chicken Little."

I heard the rustle of a piece of paper.

"I see the humor. What can I do for you Miss Little?" she asked, chuckling.

"I have a couple of questions and I'm not sure where to go to get them answered. After the month I've had, I wasn't real sure about trusting any of the agents around me. So I picked a district far from mine. First do you hold IBI credentials in addition to any normal ones you held before you took your position?"

"Yes, as do we all."

"Not sure how your place is set up, but do you have extra security on your outer doors and to your office?"

"Yes, again, as do we all."

"Do both of your credentials open all the doors?"

"No. Why, do yours?"

"Both open my outer doors but only one opens my office."

"That is highly unusual; in fact it's unheard of. Your IBI credentials shouldn't open anything at your home or office. It is strictly for access to the IBI repositories throughout the country and as a second set of credentials should you need that cover while you're working. There are only three cards in the world that should open either door. Your original branch of service credentials open both, the director of that branch of service has a card that will open the front door, and the President has a card that will open the door to your office. The third card is your backup credentials." she explained.

"What backup credentials?" I asked.

"There should be another envelope in your safe that has a backup set of credentials for you. You need to take them and put them in a safety deposit box that you can get to in case you lose your primary or if they are stolen or destroyed. If you use your secondary one to open your door it will automatically disable the other one. You will need to guard your backup, if you use it; it will take them a couple of weeks to get you a new one. Also get a P.O. Box and give that address to your branch director, just for such purposes. Did an agent, with a district touching yours, not call you or send a letter explaining all of this?" she asked.

"No. Other than my liaison, I've had no real contact of any kind."

"This is bad. Hold on a second."

I heard a lot more keystrokes and some time went by.

"Not to seem rude, but can I ask a question?" she asked.

"Sure."

"How old are you? You sound rather young."

"I'm twenty-six."

"You're kidding! What the fuck were they thinking?"

"What do you mean?"

"I've never talked to or met an agent that was under forty. They seem to always want agents with seasoning. You must be extremely gifted or someone hates you a lot. Damn!"

"What?"

"You closed a case within your first month?" she asked, disbelieving.

"Kind of got lucky, I think. Though it's turned into something a bit more sinister."

The Water's Edge

"Can I give you some advice?"

"Please. I've gotten very little information and much less advice."

"Shelve anything you think you need to work on. Take at least two months to travel your district and get familiar with it. Start honing your skills at picking out the right stories from the papers. You're under no time line. Put your safety net in order then do cases. You should have gotten this advice the first or second day you were on the job."

"The safety net thing is what I'm working on right now which brings me back to the doors. Is there a way I can tell if someone other than me has accessed it? And is there someone I can call to change the fact that I can use either credential?" I asked.

"I am not sure how your computers are set up, but under your log in on the CS server you should have a folder that is specific to you. In it you should have a file with a technical adviser's number who can walk you through any questions you might have. Though he should warn you if you get near sensitive material, don't discuss anything that isn't related to your technological question."

"Okay got it. Thanks for your help."

"Sure, though you might be in for some hard times. It seems they've thrown you to the wolves."

If she only knew, I thought.

"Thanks again. I might be calling you in the future. Bye."

"Anytime. Bye."

I booted up the computers and waited. I found the file that Mother Goose had told me about. I opened it up and found the number and protocol for it. I picked up my private phone and dialed the number.

"Code Name, Please:" the voice asked.

"Chicken Little."

"One moment, please."

As I sat on hold I thought about how to hack the computers, find out who gave me this particular stupid code name, and hurt them badly.

"CS Tech Support, this is Jeremy, How can I help you?"

"I need some help with the card reader on the front door."

"Is your laptop up?"

"Yes."

"Shut it down and unplug it from the back of your main computer. Look for where you see the normal connection to the wall from your main computer. There should be some sort of plug-in like the one in the back of your desk computer where your laptop was attached."

I powered down my laptop, crawled under the desk, and unhooked it from the back of the desktop computer. I searched the wall until I found the square port.

"Okay, found it," I said from under the desk.

The Water's Edge

"Plug in the wire you unplugged from the back of your desk computer into the port in the wall. Turn you laptop back on and let it boot up."

I hit the button on my laptop and waited. Where normally it would go into my log on screen, it went to a different screen that was titled House and environs.

"Okay, I'm there," I said.

"Click on electromagnetic interfaces."

"Okay."

"Click on which item you wish to view."

I clicked on the front door. A list came up.

"Okay I have a list," I said.

"That should tell you who has accessed any particular door, what control number they used, and when they used it. You can change access on this if you would like. You can do that for any of the outside doors or outbuildings that you have. However, the reader for your safe room can't be changed unless you've had to use your backup credentials. If you're having problems with your card in the reader you might have to reenter it manually by your control number and name."

"How do I do that?"

"Click on the tab at the top that says access settings. Inside you can set up the outside readers to allow personnel such as housekeeping, gardeners, etc. You can set it up to read drivers licenses or any other identification card that has a magnetic strip. You can also delete anything listed, except yours and the director of your branch of service, and lock those out. At the bottom is an entry panel to set that up. It's fairly self-explanatory. If you highlight your own card it will allow you to reenter your information."

"Okay, thank you for your help."

"Will there be anything else?"

"No, I think that covers it."

"Have a good day," he said and hung up.

I went back to the list page and scrolled through the list. I kind of got a picture of what was going on. I clicked over to the access tab. Sure enough, there were three accesses granted. All I really knew about control numbers were that the first four digits was your branch of service and the second four was your clearance level. My Marshal Control number was USMS-1BaA-27546-BB0545-000488575. The control number on my IBI card was the same as my Marshal's credentials except that my IBI number started with IBIS as opposed to USMS. I knew that my clearance level had to be pretty fucking high since the president's started with 1AAA, when I checked mine against his on my safe room reader. On the outside reader I could see Director Perry's was programmed in but it had never been used. I looked at his clearance level; there was only one difference between mine and his. Mine was 1BaA and his was 1BAA. The control number for the identifier "I" that had been programed into the reader, was IBIS-**aA-

212

27***-BB05**-00*******. I remembered back to my basic computer classes in college that asterisks dealt with wild cards, and that it was meant to include everything within a parameter. I pulled out both of my credentials and studied the numbers. The IBI master number was more along the line of picking a set of numbers instead of one person's control number. Since everything lined up with my IBI control number, wherever the numbers or letters fell, that was why mine worked on the front door. I went back to the list of access. I printed off the list of every number that had accessed my house and what time and day.

I went through the list by hand and blacked out my numbers. I highlighted the ones prior to me moving in, in blue, and the ones after in red. From the beginning of the card reader log, I had five different numbers besides my own. Two of those ended before I took possession of the house; I figured they were whoever set everything up. The other three were scattered throughout, with one in particular being used the most. I wrote those three down and stuck them in the file on the center table with all of the things I'd taken off of the three soldiers who had tried to kill me.

I knew that I could probably go into a database and find the names and pictures that went with the numbers, but I would lay my life savings, which wasn't that much, on the fact that the pictures wouldn't match the men using them. And the moment I started searching, someone high up would be calling my phone and chewing on my behind. Better to wait until I had the proof of whoever was behind it before I lit up Washington City.

So what now? Do I just stop this in its tracks or do I catch the bastards with their hands in the cookie jar? What were people, IBI in particular, doing in my house? I had smelled them throughout the house but it was most concentrated by the door to my office. Was my house bugged? Was my office? Probably not my office since no one but me had accessed that reader. Okay then, my office was secure but the house wasn't. I thought about the fight with myself I had on the bus. Now was the time to decide if I would stay or go.

I could see seven year old me staring at the present me across time. *I'm sorry, Ced, but this isn't just about being scared and alone.* This wasn't about one bad man coming after me. But where was I going to go? I probably had two months' pay in my own bank account, and that wouldn't get me very far. What about my being, or not being, a wheir? What was I supposed to do about that without the help of the pack? Greta survived without a pack, until she met Willis. I wasn't Greta. *Come on, Ced. You've been self-reliant all your life.* Then what Bran had said to me earlier made sense: *Fear, doubt, and indecision are in your head, not your heart.* Fine. I turned off my head and listened to what my heart was telling me: **Catch the bastards!** I heard it loud and clear.

If I was going to stay and fight, I needed to know that I had a safe harbor here at my home and in Hot Springs. Greyson, Philip, and Zahn got moved very quickly to the back burner. Who was invading my home became the priority. I

213

shut down the computers, stretched, and went upstairs. Though it was only nine thirty at night, I was done with my day. I closed up the house, turned off the coffee pot, and went to bed.

Chapter 19
Friday June 9, 2248

I got up, went for my morning run, came back, took a shower, and started to get dressed. I found I had absolutely nothing that would fit me anymore. The only things I had were my tee shirts which were nowhere near as loose around the bust as they used to be, the couple of pairs of gym shorts Greta had bought me, my sweat shirts, and my shoes. Even my panties wouldn't stay up. I'd made the decision that I wouldn't leave my house unattended for more than the time of a run, so I would have to wait until Bran came out this afternoon to go do some shopping. I went into the kitchen to make some breakfast. All I really had to eat were a half dozen eggs and some sausage. Well, it would have to do until this afternoon.

****

I spent my morning drinking coffee and going through the papers that had accumulated. I found myself with nothing to do by eleven. I grabbed some water and went out on the porch to sit in the sun. I really needed to get something other than these folding lawn chairs to sit on. I pulled out my phone and decide to return the call Burdock had made earlier in the week.

"Burdock," his voice came through the phone.

"Hey, Captain. I saw you called earlier this week," I said, trying to sound upbeat.

"I hadn't heard from you and I was a little concerned after the last conversation we had."

"I'm fine. Just been real busy lately."

"Okay. I'm not really buying it but at least you're breathing."

"Yes, I'm breathing and I plan to continue doing so."

"Keep your head down, McKenzie."

"You too, Captain."

****

It was just a little after noon when Bran's tuck came bouncing down the drive. He pulled up behind Bee and got out.

"Waiting on me?" he asked as he shut the door of his truck.

"Not really. Just getting some sun," I replied from the porch.

He crossed over to the porch, grabbed the other chair, unfolded it and sat down.

"You seem to be craving the sun since you got home."

He was right. I hadn't really thought about it though.

"Riding a bus is no fun."

"I'm not real fond of it either."

"I'm going to make a run to town and do some shopping. I'll leave a newspaper in the door so you can get in and out to get water and use the restroom if you need it. Burgers or steaks this evening?"

"Burgers, I will let you off easy since we are doing the dress up thing tomorrow."

I hadn't forgotten that I was taking him out to eat tomorrow evening, but I hadn't realized that we would be going to some place nice and nothing I had fit. Okay, something to wear out needed to be added to my clothes purchases today.

"Burgers it is," I said, standing up as he did the same out of courtesy.

"I'll probably be gone for a few hours. If you decide to leave, would you lock the door knob?"

"If I leave, sure."

"Great. I'll talk to you in a little while."

I stepped off the porch, unplugged the car, got in and headed to town. I stopped at the bank, rented a safety deposit box and put my backup credentials in it, then headed to the main drag of town.

****

It took me two hours and a small fortune to do something I used to be able to do in less than thirty minutes and with much less money--buy clothes. I must have hit most of the clothing shops on the main drag in town. I noticed, much to my shock and surprise, that the clothing I was purchasing was picked to show off my figure, not down play it as my clothes in the past had. I even bought something I'd never owned before in my life; a purse. Not only that, I bought three of them, and a wallet. What were the world and my life coming to? *Come on, Ced, people are spying on you and trying to kill you and you're worried that you don't have a clutch to match your shoes? How about you save everyone some time and energy and shoot yourself? This is so not like you, Ced. What happened to Miss I don't care what the world thinks of me?*

With the back seat almost full, it was time to hit the grocery store. I pulled into the parking lot of the grocery store, found a spot, pulled in, and turned off the key. As I was getting out, I had a bit of an epiphany. I needed evidence on the people who were following me around and had been in my house. Bran had given me a license plate but I needed a bit more and now I knew exactly who to call, Mitch.

Mitch was one of those gizmo nuts. He worked in the files and information section in the Marshals office in Dallas. He and I had been friends almost as long as I'd been a Marshal. He was one of the few guys that could make me laugh on a daily basis and if anyone would or could help, it'd be him. We both used to come up with clue puzzles and brain teasers for the other one to solve just to entertain each other, so I hoped he'd understand the one I'd present him with today.

I moved off towards the store, pulled out my personal phone, punched in the number to his desk and waited. He didn't have a set schedule and it would be hit or miss on catching him. It rang about four times and I was ready to hang up when the phone picked up.

"United States Marshal Service, Information Section, this is Mitch," the familiar voice came over the small speaker.

"Don't say anything and listen. This is Tops," I said, making reference to the pet name he had for me that was a not so subtle reminder of how big my cup size was.

"Hey, how you doin'? I was just getting ready to leave, you almost missed me."

"I need some very; very discreet help. Can you manage that?"

"Sure."

"First. If I thought I had pests in my house and car. Could you recommend a good exterminator that could locate them and neutralize them?"

"I could send you instructions on how to do it yourself so you could save money, and it works as good or better than the chemicals the professionals use," he answered, picking up on the game.

"So where would you like me to send those instructions?" he asked.

"Send it to: Tops McBra, Care of, Sheriff Gary Benton, County Sheriff's Office, Barry County Courthouse, Cassville, Missouri. I can't remember the zip code though."

"I can handle that."

"You might want to make it from that address too so that if it happens to smudge, the post office will deliver it anyway. And you will take it *TO* the post office today?"

"I'll hand deliver it to the post master himself."

"Thanks."

"Anything else I can help you with?"

"I need something for this itch on my back, something that doesn't leave a trace."

There was dead silence on the phone.

"Gonna be a bit tougher."

"Do what you can and put it in the same package."

"Will try. But it might take a little longer to get to the post master."

"I can deal."

"Anything else?"

"Yeah, thanks much and forget about it all, just shred it from your memory."

"Okay, will do. Watch your ass."

I would need to call Gary this evening and tell him to expect a package addressed to Tops. But first, food.

****

After another small fortune in groceries, I was on my way home. Bran was off by the tree line doing something when I drove up into the carport and got out. I had most of my clothes in the house by the time Bran saw me and made his way over to help.

"Did you buy out the store?" he asked, looking in the small car with the bags of groceries filling the front seat and the portion of the back that hadn't been filled with clothes.

"A woman and her money are soon parted in a store."

He picked up a few bags and took them in the house.

I took me almost another hour to get all of the groceries and clothes put away. I started a load of laundry to wash my new underwear and began making hamburger patties. I took a beer out to where Bran had started making a fire for our normal Friday night meal.

"Would you like to take a shower or anything before we start cooking?" I asked, handing him his beer.

"That would be a plus. It was rather hot out here today."

"Do you have a change of clothes?"

"In the truck."

"I'll go through and open the front door for you. You can use the bathroom in the hall," I said and headed into the house.

While Bran was taking a shower, I picked up my personal phone and went outside to call Gary.

"Barry County Sheriff's office," the female voice answered.

"Sheriff Benton, please."

"Who may I say is calling?"

"Marshal McKenzie."

"Hold for a moment."

I waited for a few minutes.

"Ced?" Gary's voice came on the phone.

"Hey."

"You sound off. Is something wrong?"

"Things aren't necessarily right."

"You want to talk about it?"

"Can't really. I have a favor to ask."

"Sure, anything."

"First, you'll be getting a package there at your office addressed to Tops McBra, care of you. Call me when you do and keep it safe until I can get up there to get it."

"You in trouble?"

"Not yet. I may just be being paranoid but I'd rather be safe than sorry."

"I can take some time off and come help you."

"As much as I'd love that, we both know you can't."

"I'm worried about you, Ced," he whispered.

"Gary, I'll be fine for the next few weeks. I'm not going anywhere and I'm not doing anything out of the ordinary. I'm just doing research on cases. I promise, the most strenuous thing I'll be doing is lifting a coffee cup or bagel to my mouth."

"Are you lying to me?"

"You know I suck at lying. Do I sound like I am lying?"

"No, you don't."

"There are two things I need you to do over the next few weeks. One, keep an eye on Philip but don't confront him or treat him any different than you normally do. Second, pay close attention to anybody that comes into your territory, even if it's a family out camping."

"Ced. This is pretty cloak and dagger if you ask me."

"I will give you a little information if you promise me you'll sit on it until I get there."

"I promise."

"Don't go all Alpha on me. Promise me like you mean it."

"On the loyalty of the pack, I promise."

"Okay then. There have been people in my house while I've been gone. I think it is an extension of what's been happening up there but I'm not sure," I finished.

"You've got to be shitting me! Are you sure you don't want me to come down?"

"No I don't think that would be a good idea. Will you promise me you'll keep your head down? I so want to see those lovely green eyes again."

"Yes, Ced. I'll be level headed until you get here," he said very lowly and gently.

"Thank you," I said softly.

"I will call you in a couple of days."

"Be careful."

"You too. Bye."

"Bye, Ced."

It took a few moments of quiet air for both of us to hang up. For the few moments we'd been talking, I felt somewhat safe. I wasn't feeling safe now that I had hung up. I had to resist the urge to hit redial. I dumped the last call from the phone log and walked back into the house to check the laundry and get another beer.

Chapter 20
Saturday June 10, 2248

I'd bought a red skirt that was much shorter than anything I'd ever worn before. The matching top showed a lot of cleavage and a good two inches of skin between the bottom of it and the top of the skirt. I'd even taken it two steps further by going back into town this morning and having my fingernails polished a deep red and wore lipstick that matched my nails. I was even carrying one of my new purses, which was unheard of where I was concerned, but in my defense I needed somewhere to hide my gun and credentials. I will admit to the tube of lipstick I was carrying since there might be a need to touch up my one makeup indulgence. And yes the heels were a must with the dress, though I kept them low enough to not kill myself if I needed to run. The last thing like this I'd owned was a dress I had when I was in college. Though what I was wearing tonight would probably be considered rather conservative on a woman my age, it was quite form fitting, low cut and to me was very risqué. I almost felt slutty walking across the parking lot to the restaurant. I walked into the restaurant and saw Bran sitting at a table towards the back, he hadn't overdressed for the occasion, but he was wearing a nice button down, slacks, and nice shoes. He stood as the hostess showed me to the table.

"Geez, Ced. If I would have known this was a fancy dinner I would have put on a tie," he said as he pushed my chair in.

"Well, you cleaned up pretty good as it is."

We talked about generalities and life as we looked over our menus and ordered. He gave me an interesting look when I ordered the largest steak on the menu, rare, a baked potato, a double order of broccoli, green beans, and a large salad.

"Hungry?" he asked.

"You have no idea."

The top I'd worn this evening was of the summer variety and it had short sleeves. I'd worn long sleeves since I'd been bitten and this evening I'd been very good about keeping my left arm below the table or facing away from Bran so he couldn't see any of the damage. Though the scars had become very light since the moon, they were still noticeable if you looked close enough. And Bran, I'd found out on other occasions, was one to notice details. We were on our deserts and I was on my third glass of wine, when I finally slipped up.

"What happened to your arm?"

"Nothing really, just that tumble I told you about when I got back about a month ago."

Bran lightly grabbed my arm and pulled it over to him to get a better look at it. I saw a shadow cross over his eyes. He looked up and he seemed saddened.

"What?" I asked him.

"You should stick to the truth, lying is not your forte."

"What are you talking about?"

"Are you finished with your meal and desert?"

"Yes."

"Let's go for a walk."

"Okay."

I motioned for the waiter, paid the bill; we got up, and walked out into the warm early summer night. We walked in silence until we got to a small park a few streets over from the main drag of town. He motioned to a bench and we both sat. I knew he had questions but didn't know how to approach me with them, though I wasn't sure I'd answer them anyway.

"You hurried us out of the restaurant. What is it?" I asked.

"I should have figured it out on my own. You came back after the full moon. Fever, vomiting, and joint pain a few days before the next full moon. Then you come back with ripped muscles, fuller hair, and fingernails longer than I had ever seen on you. I should have put it together; you had been bitten," he said.

"What?" I asked with real surprise in my voice.

"I did not misspeak. You were bitten. I could have helped some."

Should I go on denying it? As of right now, I had not changed but I might next moon. He would know for sure when I left again.

"I was on a case; it was just a dog bite," I said, seeing if he would push it.

"Like I said in the restaurant, stick to the truth, you are a horrible liar," he said, smiling sadly.

He took my arm and pointed out some of the dimples in it.

"This is no dog. The configuration of the canines and molars, not a normal dog. You are wheir now. Aren't you?"

I was in a quandary. My brain was telling me to thank him for his concern but to politely tell him to fuck off, it was none of his business. But my emotions were looking for a friend and an ally around here.

"I don't know," I said, I guess my emotions won.

He looked at me funny.

"What do you mean you don't know? I think it would be fairly obvious."

"Bran. I am having a real problem here. I like you. I like you being around and talking with me. But my job is dangerous and the people who call me friend seem to be finding themselves in the same danger. I don't want to put you in that position. I can't talk about a lot of what I do, which puts people even that much more in danger that they cannot be prepared for."

"All of us are in danger from the moment we are born. You cannot protect me from any of it any more than I can protect you. Besides it is not up to you to decide what danger I can and cannot be exposed to."

"Then who is it up to?"

"Me."

I wasn't sure I was really buying the Taoist mumbo jumbo.

"Even if *not* getting you involved may save your life?"

"Are you responsible for me not paying attention and getting run over by a car when I am out walking?"

"It isn't the same."

"Sure it is."

"How?"

"I know the dangers of doing what I do. I cannot help the actions, malicious or benign, of others. All I can be is confident in me and my abilities. If I am not up to the challenge, then the end will come, as it shall for all of us at some time or another."

"I didn't change," I blurted out.

"What?"

"I went through all of the pain but I didn't change. When I woke up after the cramp, I was still in the same body."

"Did anything else change?"

"My hearing is incredible. I can smell a person from a hundred yards away if the wind is right and if they're right next to me I can tell you what they had for lunch and who they had sex with. As you've commented on, my body is hard as a rock now, my hair is full and thick, my fingernails are long and tough as railroad spikes. I think the best part is my period lasts all of about fifteen minutes now. But during the full moon, my skin is the same as it is right now and I still have opposable thumbs," I answered.

He sat next to me, thinking.

"I have never heard of that happening."

"Well, my friends say I still basically smell the same though now I have an overlay of wheir. Which reminds me. What are you?"

"I am not sure I know what you mean."

"I know that you've probably figured out that Greta is wheir. She told me, as we were riding up, that you smelled half human and half something else. Ironically enough, the same as half of my smell. I'd like to know what that is."

"Not being wheir, as you call it, I do not know what to tell you. I cannot know what you smell like."

I wasn't sure if he was being honest with me or being inscrutable.

"Well, since I've gotten home I know what she means. So if you will give me some clue as to what you are I'd at least know half of what my lineage is."

"You keep asking what I am. I was born human and I will probably die human."

"You're only half human."

"And what are you?"

"I have no idea, but I'm not human."

"You look human."

"So do wheirs except for one day a month."

"Okay, point taken," he conceded.

"Look, Bran, prior to this assignment I was blissfully unaware of anything worse than serial killers and mass murderers. In the past couple of months I have learned about things I'd always considered horror stories and fantasy. I remember reading the old tales about vampires, wheirwolves, elves, witches, fairies, and all sorts of creatures. I have always been told that there is a grain of truth in every myth... but.... I guess my question is: has this always existed but people did not know about it, or has it happened all of a sudden?"

"Yes."

"Now there's an answer for the ages," I said, frustrated.

"What I have been able to learn is this: some of it is what others have told me, some of it is what I personally believe, some of it could be nothing more than mere fairy tale and other parts come from personal experience. You can believe some of it, all of it, or none of it.

Back at the beginnings of life we, as the inhabitants of the earth, lived in closer harmony with the earth and sea. We also lived within the realm of the IS..."

"The IS?"

"The force of the universe. Some religions view it as God; others view it as the universal intelligence. I view it as the IS. The force that runs through everything and everyone. The ordered Chaos of the universe that is neither good nor evil, it just IS."

"Okay," I said to get him to continue.

"At one point in time, the world was shared by all number of beings including humans. There was a shift in something and the human population started expanding exponentially. With the human population explosion, the competition between the beings became intense.

For the Mythics, those not human, it became a question of personal survival. They hid their gifts as best they could and mated within the human population. Over time the only traits we saw of the old Mythics, for the most part, in the new human race would be someone that might have an overabundance of hair, preference for undercooked meats, longer canine teeth, you get the point. Though there were a few pure species still around, most stayed within their own communities and hid themselves even deeper out of the mainstream of human society.

This continued on for a lot of history until the bio companies introduced YU-233. Though the drug itself was not enough to change a millennium of evolution, it was the introduction of the genetically engineered seeds and food that flipped the switch. Something in the combination of the two made the Mythic traits start to reemerge in some of the human population. As those traits began to reemerge, the fall happened. A lot of the world reverted back to fundamental religions. Those that did not look, act, and believe the same way were ostracized and forced out of the community. Those that were different moved and found others that showed more of the traits that they themselves had and made their own communities; this included some of the pure species that had always existed.

In the first generation one in four emerged with all of the old genetic traits of those of ancient times and the more they mated the more it increased. Such as if one that showed all of the old genetic traits and one that carried the genes but did not show the traces themselves mated, every one of their offspring would be full blooded Mythic. Hence, reverse evolution in a way. As the populations and nations started to stabilize, the Mythics began mixing into the general population again. Now it is kind of like it was before, though the Mythics are not marrying into the human population to hide this time around and those marriages, as opposed to watering down the Mythic traits, are actually spreading them to an extent. The Mythic population is now growing where the human one is holding steady. I don't think the outcome will be the same this time around," he said.

"Why do you call them Mythics?"

"Because that is what they prefer to be called. Did that answer your original question?"

I sat in silence. I had never before tonight thought about where it all started. I was too busy worrying about the here and now.

"I'm not sure it totally answered the question, but it was a great synopsis."

"I do have one question for you."

"What's that?"

"Isn't that rather dangerous for you?" he said, pointing at my chest.

"What? My boobs?"

"No. The silver cross," he answered, chuckling.

I hadn't thought about it. I always wore it, as I was told to do.

"It's just a cross," I said.

"It has some fairly sharp edges on it and it is silver."

"Oh."

I hadn't thought of that. Would it kill me if it scratched me? I had no idea.

"I have to wear it and I can't dull the edges."

"I may be able to help with that. Do you have a pencil and piece of paper in your purse?"

"Yes," I said as I dug out my small notebook and handed it to him.

"May I?" he asked, pointing at the cross.

I unhooked the chain and handed it to him. He placed the cross on the paper, traced the edges of it, made some notes, tore out the page, and handed both the cross and the notebook back.

"Are you afraid of me?" I asked as I put the cross back around my neck.

"What?"

"Are you afraid of me?"

"Do I have a reason to be?"

"No. I mean does this make a difference to our friendship?" I asked, pointing at my arm.

"What makes or breaks a friendship is *who* you are not *what* you are," he said.

"I think I've lost some of who I am," I said as a couple of tears rolled down my cheeks.

"Why do you say that?" he asked quietly as he produced a handkerchief and handed it to me.

"I think I've lost my ability to care."

"Because of the bite?"

"Not directly," I answered as the tears continued to flow.

"Then what?"

"Because I can kill without feeling."

"Do you mean your first partner's killer?"

I shook my head no as I tried to stem the flow of tears with his handkerchief.

"You're being rather cryptic here. I am afraid I don't understand," he said.

"Do you have any idea what my job is?"

"U.S. Marshal with IBI credentials on special assignment, working cases from home, cases that bring you in contact with Mythic beings... My guess would be Counter Section."

I looked hard at him.

"Why is it the beings I meet know more about my job than I do?" I asked, crying openly now.

"Because Counter Section, for those that want to look closely, is one of the worst kept secrets in the country. Especially to the Mythics and those that have Mythic friends. Does all of this have something to do with the government cars that have been at your house and following me around?"

"Yes."

"Can you tell me about it?"

"Not supposed to." I sniffled.

"I am not supposed to know you are Counter Section either."

He had a very valid point. But what did I really know about him? Not a lot other than he'd dropped what he was doing to take me to Russellville, been someone nonthreatening to talk to, and never even approached menacing. Was he one of my allies? Was this what Burdock meant? I took good look at him with my sight. His aura was as it always had been other than it seemed a little more active. *Ced, only you can make the call as to whether you see him as an ally or not.* What did my heart say? Though I thought it might be colored with the fact I felt he reminded me of Sam, my heart told me that I could trust him with my life. I took the plunge.

225

"Bran, I need to tell you something but it may be a bit disjointed since I need to protect others in the process."

"Are you sure?"

"If you don't want to hear, I understand. It's not your problem," I said, a little hurt.

"I didn't mean it that way. I know how seriously you take your job and that you are very ethical about it. I don't want you to say anything that you feel you will regret later. If that is not the case, then I am here all night if you need me."

"The night you and I met, I'd been on this job for a total of twenty four hours. The night I was bitten, I closed my first case. Though there were a couple of unusual loose ends, I thought that was the end of it. During that, I was befriended by a pack of wheirs. When you took me to meet Greta, it was that pack I went back up to be with so they could help me with my turn. When I didn't turn I went back to where we were supposed to meet at the end of the night. A trap had been laid. Not for the pack, but for me personally. Two men with sniper rifles were waiting with a third down the road a little bit as backup. I killed all three of them before they knew what hit them. No remorse, no feeling, no nothing...," I said, letting the last of my sentence trail off.

"And you're sure they were after you?" he asked.

"I have proof."

"Then what were you supposed to do?" he asked in a way that told me I did what I had to do.

"And now you think that because you have felt no remorse you are a bad person. It is called shock, Ced," he continued.

"What?"

"It is called shock, it is a defensive mechanism. You are faced with a traumatic incident and you do what you have to do to survive it. Feeling absolutely nothing that you think you should feel is your brain doing what it needs to do to cope and protect you. The effects can last for months or years, but at some time in the future you will hit that wall and it will crumble. I have seen it in the war and with accident survivors; really anyone that has faced something traumatic."

"But I've killed people before, even in revenge," I objected with a hiccup.

"Let's take a look at your life for the past few months. You take a job that you know nothing about, you have no backup that I can see, you are thrown out here to try and take care of what someone else sees as a problem, you are faced with things that you don't even believe in, are now one of the things that you did not believe in, with people watching you and trying to kill you while you try to get a handle on not only what you are and who you are, but what the hell you are doing out here. That is enough for anyone to deal with after years of experience and decades to learn, much less someone as young as you are trying to do it in a mere three months. Give yourself a chance, Ced. However, just that you are worried about it tells me that you might want to put a bottle of Scotch back for the day the wall comes down," he said with a small smile starting.

I thought about what he said. He was right. I had to give myself some leeway. I wasn't perfect and I needed to try not to make my life and job something it couldn't be; perfect. The doubt was still with me but I understood it now. I dabbed my eyes with the piece of fabric and tried to return his smile.

"I think we have had enough information exchange for one evening," Bran said as he got up and offered me a hand.

****

We walked, not saying much, back to where I'd parked my car.

"Thanks for tonight," I said as I opened the door and handed him back his handkerchief.

"Ced. You can always talk to me if you need to. This is not going to go away overnight but knowing what you are dealing with should help over time"

"Thanks, Bran," I said as I stood on my tiptoes to give him a small kiss on the cheek.

"What was that for?"

"For being my friend."

He smiled back at me as I got in the car, closed the door, and headed home. I got home, took a shower, crawled into bed, and waited for sleep to come.

Chapter 21
Friday June 16, 2248

I had spent all week making myself get into a routine. I made sure that, rain or shine, I did the same things at the same time on the same days of the week. I wanted to make sure that whoever was watching me was getting into the habit of watching my habits. The more I could make them bored the more likely they were to make a mistake. I was counting on their complacency.

I'd gotten back from my morning run and was just about to go take a shower when my personal phone rang. I looked at the number; it was Gary's office. I picked up the phone and answered it, while I headed for the front door.

"To what do I owe the honor of this call?"

"I have a packaged for a Miss McBra. Do you know her?" he asked, giggling like a little girl.

"Giggling is so unbecoming for an Alpha," I said, laughing at him.

"I thought I would call and tell you it got here."

I looked at my watch; it was just now ten in the morning. If I left soon, I could get up there and back by midnight.

"Are you going to be around this afternoon?" I asked.

"Well, I did have an orgy to go to this evening but I guess I could skip it if I had to."

"You're not endearing yourself to me."

"Hey, I'm a warm blooded male. What do you want?"

"No comment."

"Are you pleading just the fifth or all of Directive One?"

"Yes."

"One of these days, Ced, I am going to call your bluff."

"Is that a threat?" I asked, chuckling.

"More like a......Okay, it's a threat."

"Oh goody." I laughed.

"So are you coming up today?"

"I need to take a shower, and then I'll be heading your way."

"Spending the night?"

"Doubt it."

"You're going to really piss off Greta if you don't stay."

"How about I eat dinner with everyone?"

"I think I can arrange that."

"Good. I should be there no later than four. What time do you get off?"

"Call me when you get to Greta and Willis' and I'll be out after I change."

"Okay. See ya' in a few hours."

"Drive safe," he answered and we hung up.

I took a shower, threw a change of clothes in Bee, left Bran a note apologizing for missing our Friday and promising we would have steaks next week, not burgers. I backed Bee around and headed down the drive. I would've taken the car but I wasn't sure I could get up there and back without an eight hour charge in between. Though if I took the car, I'd have a reason to stay. But I needed to get back and work on my routine. This little side track would give my enemies too much of a rest as it was.

****

It was a little past four by the time I got to Greta's. I parked Bee in the drive, went up on the porch, and knocked but got no answer. Greta's car was there, so I headed around the house towards the back yard. Greta was busily working away in her garden towards the back fence. She was in her normal outdoor attire: cut off tee shirt, shorts, and tennis shoes. I stood and watched her for a few moments. I'd never really noticed how pretty she really was, with her blonde hair glowing in the afternoon sun, soft facial features, and the tanned skin over tight muscles. I hopped over the fence and moved towards the other side of the house, wanting to be upwind of her so she would smell me and I wouldn't startle her. It only took a couple of seconds for my scent to reach her on the breeze. She looked up from her work, found me, and smiled broadly. She met me about half way through the back yard.

"Hey, sweetie," she said, wrapping me in a hug.

"Your self-invited dinner guest has arrived." I smiled at her as she let me go.

"Don't be silly. You always have a place at the table," she said as we started back towards the house.

I flipped open my phone and gave Gary a call to tell him I was here. By the time I finished that conversation, we were in the kitchen and I had a glass of lemonade in front of me at the table. I got up to help her fix dinner but mostly I kept her company while she cooked. She'd just put all of the chickens in the oven when Gary knocked, stuck his head in, and asked to come in. He made a beeline for me, took me in his arms, and gave me a long kiss without saying a word.

"Hello to you to." I smiled as he let me down to flat footed.

"I feel like I haven't seen you in a long time."

"It's only been a week," I laughed at him.

"That is seven weeks in dog years."

"Gary, do you have that package for me?" I asked.

"In the trunk of the car, I'll go get it here in a bit. I was more interested in seeing you. Besides, the longer I hold on to it the longer you'll stay around."

I gave him a quick kiss for the thought.

****

The Water's Edge

After dinner I helped Greta clear the table and wash dishes. We were sitting around the table, with coffee, when Gary went outside, got my package, and handed it to me. It was probably about eight inches square, three inches deep, and heavy. I smiled; Mitch had come through for me big time. I pulled the package over to me and opened it. I picked up the letter that had been placed on top.

Hey Tops,

I went one step further. I had an old sweeper around that had been replaced with a newer model. I went through it and cleaned it up. I was able to widen the bandwidth some and it should work for anything you need. There is some documentation with it to help. Also, you might want to check for visual surveillance before you use this. I typed up some things to search for and how to take care of it.

The other item you asked for is so off the beaten path you'll be fine. I also included two clips for it; the ammo will have to be your responsibility.

Ced, I'm worried about you. Please stay safe and call me when you can.

Keep your head down,
Mitch.

I so owed Mitch. I put the letter down and pulled out the sweeper he sent and it looked like a small transistor radio with a set of small earphones. I sat it to the side and pulled out the gun. It was an off brand nine millimeter. I'd probably need to make sure that I didn't put power loads in it. In the bottom of the box were the directions for the sweeper. I put Mitch's letter and the sweeper back in the box. I looked the gun over to make sure it was in working order.

"What, now I'm your arms dealer?" Gary asked.

"I thought you already had more guns than you could carry?" Greta asked.

"I have a need for something that's not traceable to me. And don't worry Gary, you won't be getting large shipments of automatic weapons," I answered.

"I better not be getting *any* shipments of automatics," he said, laughing.

"Do you have a bug problem?" Willis asked, pointing at the box.

I was a bit surprised that Willis would be the one to pick up on what it was.

"I think so," I answered.

"Is that one of those sonic bug repellents? I thought it was a radio," Greta asked.

"Wrong type of bugs, Grets," Willis said.

It took her a few seconds. I'd never heard her called that before. But then again I'd never really heard Willis address her by name, other than a couple of times when they first met me.

"You mean someone is spying on you?" she asked, openly frightened.

"Yes, but I have it covered. This is just to get the proof I need to have them arrested."

"How long have you known?" Gary asked.

"Once I got back after the full moon, though I had my suspicions before then."

"Aren't you frightened?" Greta asked.

"I was at first but all they want is information, not my death. I don't give them a lot of information and I have a plan to get to them."

"Really?" Gary asked.

I nodded at him. I placed the gun back in the box, put the lid on it, and set it aside. We sat and talked for a while longer. I glanced at my watch and saw that it was a little after seven; I needed to get back on the road.

"I really do hate to eat and run, but I have to get back home."

"Are you sure you won't spend the night?" Greta asked me.

"I really need to be heading."

I said my good-byes to Willis and Greta, picked up the box, and Gary walked me back to Bee.

"Are you coming back up this moon?" he asked, opening my door.

"I'll probably be up here around July fourth, if I'm still welcome."

He pulled me to him and wrapped his arms around me.

"I'd be very upset if you didn't come," he said, smiling down at me.

"Heaven forbid that I make the Alpha of a strong wheir pack mad at me," I said, smiling back.

He kissed my lightly.

"Have you been keeping an eye out around here?" I asked.

"Diligently. I haven't noticed anything out of the ordinary, not even with Philip."

"Can you find a way to let him know that I'll be coming back in July?"

"Yes, but why?" Gary asked, looking confused.

"I'm testing a theory. I want to feed him some information that I control for a change."

"Okay. I'll make sure someone leaks the information. There is something you should know though," Gary started.

"What would that be?" I asked.

"I've let my duties as Alpha go a bit over the last three months. I'll be running with Thomas and his portion of the pack this next moon. I didn't figure that you'd want to widen the circle of knowledge about your change."

"No, I wouldn't. Who usually goes out with Willis?"

"Greta, Casey, Albert, Mary, and Don. I rotate around for the change; then we all meet up."

"Last month I know you told them we were going out in a smaller pack since it was my first change. What are you going to tell them this month?"

"I've been working on that some. Haven't got a complete excuse for it yet, but I will before the moon."

"This is going to get difficult, isn't it?"

"There is a chance of it. We should be fine for a few months. No one will get too suspicious, especially with Willis, Greta, and Casey adding to the story," he answered.

"I hope so. I don't want you to have any problems in your pack and I certainly don't want to quit coming up here," I said, putting my arms around his neck and pulling him down to my lips.

"Me either," he said as we broke our embrace.

He smiled at me, picked me up by my waist, and sat me in the driver's seat of Bee.

"You be careful driving. Stop for coffee."

"Don't worry, the coffee is a must," I said, smiling at him as he closed my door.

I set the package from Mitch in the passenger seat, started the engine, and headed home.

****

I stopped for coffee in Russellville and put the battery back in my official phone. I had another missed call from TTZ. I'd been ducking him for almost two weeks now. I was going to have to take care of this pretty soon. My only question was which problem did I deal with first? TTZ or the people watching my house? TTZ and Greyson seemed to be more life threatening to me and the pack but the spies at home were probably doing more damage. I knew somewhere down the line that the paths of TTZ and the spies crossed, but the thing that was throwing me was that no attempt had been made on me at home, only up in Missouri. So which way did the pipeline run and which end could I cut first to be able to get the other end also? I thought hard about it as I drove down the winding road of highway seven. My gut was still telling me that home needed to be first. I just needed a definite plan.

Chapter 22
Saturday, June 17, 2248

Even though I got back rather late, I made myself get out of bed and go for my morning run. I came back, showered, got a cup of coffee, and went down to my office. I pulled over the box Mitch had sent me and opened it. I took out the sweeper and set it aside. I pulled out the printed pages Mitch had put together on visual surveillance and what to look for. I studied the notes on how to find them. Since I was in the basement already, I started looking around. I checked vents, lights, and wall switches. I found none. I turned on both computers and searched through the hidden files and programs to see if anything was being run through the system, nothing. I checked the case and monitors to see if any lenses had been hidden in them. I turned on the sweeper. It was actually very easy to use. I had to sweep through two sets of band widths but the basement came up clean, which I was kind of expecting. I swept both of my phones just to be on the safe side. Nothing came up on either phone, though I figured if they were listening in on that, they would be doing it at the cell towers since they had my frequency and number.

I went upstairs, grabbed the cleaning supplies out, which took me awhile to find since I used them so often, and began house work. I cleaned the house top to bottom, checking mirrors, paintings, and wall hangings to make sure that everything came off the walls and nothing was attached. I cleaned vents and everywhere that might hide a visual device. I found nothing, even in the spare bedrooms. That, in itself, took me the better part of two hours. Okay, maybe I'd been paranoid for no reason. I put away all of my cleaning supplies. I was good for another six months or so before needing them again.

I stood in the kitchen and started my sweep. It went off like a Geiger counter on both bands. There was not a room in the house that didn't show some sort of bug, even the hall. Okay, now there wasn't any doubt about my paranoia; it was real.

I followed the directions to find the exact hiding places. I found plenty of them in every room and the hall was worst of all, which seemed to have plenty of them around the door to the basement. One was even in my coffee pot. Is nothing sacred for Christ's sake? I wasn't really afraid, just pissed all over again. Okay, I knew the house was bugged but the basement wasn't. I'd guessed right about my office, they hadn't had access to it so nothing could be planted.

I took the sweeper back down to my office and put it on the center table. *So, Ced, how are you going to do this?* I asked myself, looking at the topo map I'd drawn the outline of my property on. As I stared at it, thinking, my brain started to work on its own. I pulled the map closer to me and really studied it. There was a state park not more than five miles away from me. Off of the park was a fire road that led back into the state forest and came within a half mile of my house on the north side of the property before it took a curve to its north. Having walked that section of my land, I knew it would only be about a thirty minute walk from the fire road to the house.

I knew I could probably pull in the U.S. Marshals, show them the bugs and my door access list, and let them handle it, but what good would that do if the people watching me had time to get out of town? Who would we catch; a couple of low level scape goats? Geez, I was becoming very jaded about my own government. I really wanted to catch them with their hand in the cookie jar, but how to do that? Who could I call to help? Burdock? His hands were tied where it came to me. One of my direct supervisors? Which one? I thought about the three men I answered to. I didn't know how high this went and Director Pinter was definitely out. Director Perry? It wasn't that I didn't trust him—I didn't know him well enough to trust him. The President? Yeah, like the President of The United States of America was going to pick up a gun and watch my back. *Look, Ced, they put you out here on an island. You're going to have to deal with this on your own.*

Wait a minute. I'd answered my own question just a few thoughts ago; the U.S. Marshal Service! I had to switch modes a little bit. I was a full U.S. Marshal now. I remember many a time Burdock getting on the phone to call in backup from another district. Why couldn't I do the same? I had no idea what hoops I'd have to jump through but it was worth a shot. I pulled my calendar over and opened it. My PMS hell would start around July first which was a Saturday. I had almost two weeks to set a trap. I gave some thought as to how I could draw them back into the house. Disabling a bug would do that. How could I work it so that I could be in the house when they arrived to catch them red handed? I looked at the calendar again. I did nothing special every week that would keep me out of the house but give me time to get back before they got here.

Mondays! Bran came out to do yard work every Monday and every other one he came out in the mornings instead of the afternoons. I always saw him before I started my run and he was usually gone by the time I got back. I was sorry to use Bran as a cover like that, but if it kept both of us safe he would probably understand. I knew he would be here in the afternoon this coming Monday. That would leave the following Monday, the twenty sixth, as my next morning opportunity. Could I pull this together in a little over a week? All I could do was try.

I pulled the notebook I kept business cards in out of the desk, and flipped the plastic pages until I found the one I was looking for. I hoped that the person I was looking for would be working on a Saturday morning. I opened my personal phone and dialed.

"U.S. Marshal Service, Arkansas district. How may I direct your call?" the woman asked.

"Is Marshal Hillis in today?"

"Who may I say is calling?"

"Marshal Cedwynne McKenzie."

I heard the phone click to hold and waited.

"Hillis."

"Marshal Hillis, Marshal McKenzie. We met a couple of months ago."

"Yes. Cedwynne, isn't it?"

"Yes, sir."

"What can I do for you today, Marshal?"

"I'm closing in on an arrest of some suspects for infractions of Directive One, section seven. Being on special assignment, I don't have the resources to handle the arrest and transportation of the suspects and would like to ask your assistance in this."

"What sort of time frame are we looking at?"

"One day at the most. A week from Monday."

"Whose budget will this come out of?"

Now there was a question I wasn't prepared for.

"I'm not sure yet, probably mine. I'll have to call the Director and find out. Regardless, you'll be credited with catching a government agency with their hand in the cookie jar."

"Which agency?"

"IBI," I answered. Though I wasn't sure if they would really be IBI, I was sure they'd be carrying IBI credentials.

"Are you kidding me?"

"No, sir."

"Let me start some paper work."

"Okay."

I wasn't sure where this was going but I guess I should hold on for the ride.

"Control number?" he asked.

"USMS-1BaA-27546-BB0545-000488575."

I heard the keystrokes of his computer and then a very long pause, followed by an almost inaudible, even for wheir hearing, Holy shit!

"Yes, ma'am. How many Deputies, when, and where?"

What was with the change in tone? And what, now no more paper work?

"Two will be fine, one with a camera, and the other with a rifle and transportation to a holding facility."

"How many suspects are you expecting?"

"Not really sure; three or four at the most."

"Are you sure that two Marshals will be enough, ma'am?" he asked.

What is it with all this ma'am shit?

"Yes, I'm pretty sure that will be enough."

"Where and when?"

"I'll give you a call next Friday to finalize all of that."

"Can I at least have a town name?"

"Sure. Hot Springs. Oh. A couple of more things."

"Yes?"

"If you have a male and female agent that could work together on this, that would be a plus. Have them drive a personal vehicle and not get out of the car when we meet so it looks as if they're just asking me for directions."

"Are you being followed?"

"I'm not sure but I don't want to take any chances."

"Yes, ma'am. I'll pass these instructions along."

"Marshal?"

"Yes, ma'am?"

"Please, Marshal McKenzie or Cedwynne is fine. I'm probably many years your junior and you have many more years in the service than I do. Please, no more ma'am."

"Yes M..... Marshal."

I had to mentally shake my head at that.

"Thank you."

"You're more than welcome. I'll have agents ready to meet you on Monday, June twenty-sixth."

"That will be wonderful. What time may I call you next Friday?"

"The afternoon would be best. I should be at my desk then."

"I'll talk to you then. And again Marshal, thank you for the help."

"Anytime Marshal."

We signed off and hung up.

I now had most of a plan and backup, I just needed to work out the details, but I'd have the rest of the week to do that.

Chapter 23
Friday June 23, 2248

I had spent the better part of the past week sticking very much to a schedule. Though I always went running in the early morning, I made sure that I varied the start time some. I'd get up and get dressed in running shorts and tee shirt, drive out to the park I'd picked, jog for three hours through it, and down the fire road that was close to my northern property line.

Over the last month, I made sure I kept doing the things I'd always done. If someone was following me, they got to waste their time watching me do my banking, shopping, and spending time in my favorite coffee shop. I'd seen a dark gray sedan a couple of times over the past month, but it had always been too far away to really get a good look at it or its occupants.

This morning I doubled back to the front of the park, as I was running, to make sure my "friends" had tailed me. Sure enough, there was a dark sedan sitting by the front entrance of the park. Though it gave me a case of the willies to know someone was following me, it also made me comfortable that they only came to the park to wait until I drove home.

I got back to the house, showered and changed, got some coffee and lunch, and sat outside reading the papers until Bran showed up for his weekly maintenance on the lawn. Once Bran had started work, I went back inside to my office, picked up my phone, and dialed the Marshals office in Little Rock. I was put on hold and I waited for Marshal Hillis.

"Marshal," Hillis said cheerfully.

"Have you had a good week?"

"Fairly good. Do you have the particulars for Monday?"

"Yes."

I gave him directions to the park I was jogging in.

"There is a building with restrooms in it about a quarter of a mile in from the front gate. Have them stop across from it. I will approach from the passenger side wearing running attire. I'll give them directions from there. What sort of vehicle will they be driving?" I asked.

"A fairly new Vantage smart car, blue, Arkansas tag; TGG-907. The male agent will be driving."

"I really want to thank you for your help Marshal Hillis."

"If this is what you say it is, you'll make my career. So it's me who should be thanking you."

"Let's hope this comes off without any hitches."

"The agents will be there on Monday. Have a good weekend Marshal."

"Thanks, you too," I said as we both hug up.

****

I handed Bran another beer as he tended the steaks on the grill.

"Are you still coming out Monday morning?"

"That's my plan."

"I need you to do something for me Monday."

"I was planning on trimming the hedges anyway," he said, laughing.

"That isn't it. You know, I couldn't care if the hedges get trimmed or not."

"Then what is it?"

"I need you serious for a moment. No Buddha, just straight talk."

"Okay. I will try," he said, smiling.

Why was he always this difficult and why did I seem to like it?

"I need you to get here at nine in the morning sharp, rain or shine. I need you to work exactly three hours and leave regardless of if you are finished or not. Can you do that for me?"

I knew it was killing him to not ask me which time zone I was using as a reference or some such thing, but he stayed within the guidelines I'd asked for.

"I can do that but what is this all about?"

"I'm going to take care of a certain dark gray sedan."

"Oh, really?"

"Yes, and when you leave, Monday, I want you to continue on with your day as you normally would—no deviation."

"Okay, but wouldn't it be simpler just to blow their car up?" he asked, smiling again.

"Would be for the immediate problem, but I want to cut down on future problems at the same time."

"Is there anything I should watch out for while I am out here?"

"Nope, do your normal things. Keep to the three hour window, no more, and specifically no less."

"Can do. Do you have a piece of paper?"

I pulled my notebook out of my back pocket and handed it to him. He pulled the small pencil out of the ring, flipped to a page, and wrote something down.

"I stay in one of the cabins in the park. I made the deal to renovate it over the summer in exchange for living quarters. That is the phone number there. Call me if you need anything," he said, handing me back my notebook.

"Thanks."

I flipped to another page and wrote down my personal cell number, tore it out, and handed it to him.

"This is my personal cell number if you need it," I said as he took the paper, folded it, and put it in his shirt pocket.

We sat on a blanket out in the yard, ate, and talked well into the night. As was usual with our conversation, I learned many things about the stars, the latest book he was reading, and how I could predict weather patterns, but nothing about who he really was. I stood on the porch and waved as he left, went back inside, and went to bed.

Chapter 24
Monday June 26, 2248

It was finally Monday and time to find out who was watching and listening. Though I'd been very intent on the problem here at home, I hadn't let my normal work go downhill. I'd been keeping an eye on the other case my predecessor left me but there had been nothing new on it since I'd taken over the district. There were, however, some interesting articles from around New Orleans over the past two months. I wasn't sure if it was in my purview or just a couple of satanic rituals that had a human sacrifice. I started a new folder for that one.

I got up, rinsed my cup out, and put it away when I heard Bran's truck pull up outside. It was time to start springing the trap. I picked up the coffee pot, still plugged in, and dropped it in the sink, with a real live "Shit," as it shorted out and sent sparks flying from where it was plugged in. After the electrical short I took off the faceplate of the receptacle, found the bug, made sure it was well toasted, and reapplied the faceplate. I knew the one in the coffee maker itself was toast since I left the coffee pot and maker in the sink of water, but unplugged. The back door of the house, which was in the kitchen, was a solid type with no windows. As a third line of defense, behind the normal locks and electronic one, a heavy metal bar had been fitted across it so that even if the other locks failed, it would take a lot of brute force to get it open. Though Bran and I used it on Friday nights, anyone who had been in my house while I was gone would know that I always kept it locked and the bar in. Today I pulled the bar, quietly from its position, and placed it next to the door.

I went downstairs and signed in to the house interface. I locked out the IBIS wild card number that had been used to enter my house. In its place I granted access to the two IBIS control numbers that had accessed the house most since I had moved in. This way I could only be surprised by one person today. I'd be the one to surprise the first one and I figured he'd just be a flunky sent to fix the problem.

****

I filled up a glass of water for Bran and took it to him. We spoke for a bit then I got in the car and drove to where I was going jogging. I left everything in the car I didn't need, especially my official phone, and headed out into the park. I'd planned this jog for a week and knew exactly how long it would take me to get back.

I saw the car next to the bathroom building and made my way by it. I leaned over into the passenger side window as it was rolled down. I was surprised to see Marshal Hillis in the back seat along with the two other agents. I got some strange looks from all in the car.

The Water's Edge

"You'll find a fire road to your right a little more than a quarter mile up this road. Take it and drive for a mile and a half. I'll meet you there on foot," I said and stood up.

I watched them drive away then went into the restroom. Nature waits for no one. I came back out and started jogging for the fire road. I saw the parked car and the three Marshals standing next to it. I jogged up and stopped.

"Marshal Hillis, you decided on joining us?" I asked, smiling.

"Thought you might be able to use the extra hand."

"That's an unusual wardrobe for a bust," the female agent said.

"I work better half naked," I laughed.

"So what's the plan?" Marshal Hillis asked.

"First, who am I working with?"

"Deputy Marshal Ken Taylor and Deputy Marshal Rita Simmons," he said, introducing them.

"I am Marshal McKenzie or Cedwynne, not ma'am," I said as I shook their hands.

"Where are we heading from here?" Marshal Hillis asked.

"We'll cut through the woods to the back of my house," I started.

"You're the victim?" Marshal Hillis asked.

"Yes. That's one of the reasons this will be your bust. I want no mention whatsoever of my name except where you absolutely have to."

"I can do that Marshal," Hillis replied.

"My house sits in a clearing ringed with trees. When we get there, I'd like to have the three of you fan out, staying within the tree line and hidden. Whoever has the camera needs to have a good view of the front door. Take pictures of anyone that comes to the front door, any vehicles that drive up, or anything else that looks suspicious. When we get there, the man that does my lawn may still be there; he's not a threat and will leave shortly. Don't worry about covering the back side of the house, there shouldn't be any threat from that direction. There should only be, at most, two people who will enter the house. I have them; if anyone else shows up they are yours. Consider them armed and dangerous. When I get the information I want, I will bring anyone in the house out and supply you with all the information you need for the arrest and prosecution. Any questions?" I asked.

"Where will you be?" Deputy Taylor asked.

"I'm going in the back entrance. Also, if anyone comes out without me, detain, or–if you feel the need–shoot them," I said.

Everyone nodded. I led them up the fire road for a bit until I found the spot I had marked. We went into the woods. The trees here were rather old and there was a nice lush canopy above me that cut down on the amount of underbrush. The walk through the forest was quite invigorating and I was a bit sad that I had to stop at the tree line behind my house. I searched the tree line that circled most of my house with my sight. I could see no auras hanging about that might be attached to someone I couldn't see. I waved the other Marshals out and gave them some time to make it to their positions. I took a deep breath and tried to smell anyone, but the wind wasn't quite right to catch the part of the house and yard to my left. I listened intently for a few moments to see if I could hear a car or vehicle coming up my drive. Bran had probably been gone for about five minutes by my calculations. I ran the short distance between the tree line and the backdoor. I slid my identification card in, heard the buzz, and opened it quietly. I closed the door slowly and gently slid the bar back into place without making a sound. I reached up in the cabinet and pulled down my normal side arm and the one that Mitch had sent me. I clipped my holster on the belt I wore with my shorts and held the other gun in my hand. The one in my hand was loaded with normal rounds and my normal side arm with silver. I figured if I needed the silver, I had it as a backup. I crept into the hall and stood, just out of sight of the windows and the front door, past the opening into the living room. The twenty minutes that passed felt like an eternity. I was about ready to walk out the front door and call everything off when I heard the buzz of the front lock and the door start to open. I stayed where I was until I heard the click of the door closing. I came out from behind the opening, gun aimed at chest height. I was surprised, but not shocked, at the man standing just inside the front door.

"Agent Gray! I always did think we had something going the last time we spoke, but you know it's customary to call before you drop by. "

I saw the tense body language of shock, though he recovered quickly. I took a quick look at his aura and a sniff, all human, at least I had the right gun aimed at him. I watched his hand twitch as he thought about going for his weapon.

"I can guarantee you that if you try, it will be the last thing you will ever do" I said and he relaxed his arm.

"Marshal McKenzie, I don't think you realize exactly what you're doing. I can..." He started talking while taking a step in my direction.

The bullet shattered the left earpiece on the annoying sunglasses he was wearing, creased his temple, shut him up, stopped his forward progress, and lodged in the drywall behind him.

"Move again and the next shot will be dead center of your head," I told him.

He was standing there with his left hand on his temple, testing the wound I had inflicted.

"May I say something?" he asked.

"Unless you tell me exactly what this is all about, then no."

He didn't say another word.

"Agent Gray, you will slowly move to your left until you are standing in front of the window."

He moved slowly to where I had directed him.

"Well, since the puppy is out peeing on the lawn it must mean that the master is not far behind. Special Agent Wallace, would you like to join us for tea?" I asked, speaking loud enough that anyone listening could hear.

"While we wait, how have you been Agent Gray?" I asked.

"Like you really want to know," he spat at me.

"Really. If you just wanted a date, flowers would have worked better."

"You won't live through this."

"Then neither will you. Please raise your hands, palm out, to about shoulder height please."

Agent Gray raised his hands. I heard the buzz of the lock on the door. I moved more to my left to keep everything in my vision. Special Agent Wallace oozed his way in, not quite shutting the door as he entered, and stood in front of it.

"Close the door all the way," I instructed.

"Marshal McKenzie. We need to....," Wallace started.

The next bullet shattered the right temple of Agent Gray's sunglasses, creasing his right hairline and making the glasses fall to the floor.

"You don't take direction well," I told Agent Wallace.

I heard the door click shut.

"Now that we're sort of alone we can have a chat," I said.

"What would you like to chat about?" Agent Wallace asked, giving me his smarmy smile.

"First, why me?"

"I'm afraid you will have to be a bit more specific. That's an all-encompassing question," Agent Wallace answered.

"True. Sorry. Why was I ever chosen for this assignment?"

"Truthfully, I don't know why. I have nothing to do with who is chosen or why. I thought that those above me were a little nuts in choosing you. Though, after just a few months on the job I have to admit you are one surprising and resourceful young woman."

"Second, why all this spying crap? Don't I have a hard enough job as it is to not add fighting off people who are supposed to be on my side?"

"Again. I don't know. I only take orders."

I fired another shot creasing Agent Gray's shoulder.

"I am sure, Agent Wallace, you have read at least some of my file. I can play the lie detector game all day, though, if I continue to shoot parts of Agent Gray away for every lie or direction not followed; there's not going to be much of him left when we leave," I said to Agent Wallace and pointed my gun at Agent Gray's crotch.

"Marshal McKenzie, what are you trying to prove here?"

"That I am tired of my life and my home being invaded and it is going to stop. Now, answer my question"

I saw Agent Gray's hand start slowly moving down.

"Special Agent Wallace, would you please tell your friend here that if he continues to move that I will run out of patience very quickly," I said.

"Bobby. I've told you, you need to read the background more thoroughly. She will empty that entire clip into you before you ever get anywhere near your weapon. I can also guarantee that she will have her backup weapon out and unload another clip into you before your body reaches the floor," Agent Wallace said to his partner.

"Nobody's that good," Agent Gray said.

"You willing to bet your life on it? There are reasons she was chosen for this job and not you," Agent Wallace said and waited for a beat.

"Didn't think so. Now just stand there and don't be stupid," Wallace said, before turning his attention back to me.

"Now, where were we?" Wallace asked.

"You were in the middle of lying to me."

"Marshal, just as you will not tell others about your assignment, I can't tell you about mine. So we seem to be at a standoff that will not resolve itself. So what are you going to do now?"

"Either shoot you here or take everything I have and turn it over to the Marshal Service."

"You don't have anything to take," he said, smiling larger.

"Really? I have you red handed in my house for starters, not to mention the twenty eight bugs that are planted in this house, which I'm sure will lead right back to someone's doorstep. Then there's the report of who has accessed my house and barn, and when, from the card readers on both buildings."

"My, you have been a busy young woman," he said, but his smile only faded a little bit.

"But really Marshal, what do you have? What will you even begin to try and charge us with, other than simple breaking and entering?" he asked.

"Directive One, section seven as a start. As we both know, that could carry a penalty of death for someone."

"Like you should talk about Directive One," he laughed.

"You think you have me on some infraction of it?"

"Hmmm. A clip emptied into a suspect shortly after the death of your partner a few years ago? Or maybe the three bodies found in the back of a government vehicle?" he asked, still smiling.

I felt like shooting him just to wipe the smile off his face.

"What bodies?" I asked.

He didn't say anything; I hadn't let his goading get to me.

"As far as the other suspect; it was a justifiable shooting," I said, not giving him anything.

I was getting tired of the game. Agent Gray decided to be stupid. I shattered his elbow with my fourth shot. He cried out in pain as he fell to the floor. I moved more into the room to keep him in my view.

"Agent Gray, understand me. I have nine shots left in this weapon. I have another thirteen in the one sitting in a holster at my lower back. Agent Wallace was right, I did take out the killer of my first partner, and I have also killed much better men than you. Dammit! Don't make me shoot limbs off of your body.

Agent Wallace, slowly remove Agent Gray's weapon and backup and toss them on the couch. Then you may put him in a more comfortable position because I know that has to hurt," I said.

I heard some movement from outside. Though Wallace or Gray wouldn't be able to hear it, I knew something was happening. I hoped that my side was stepping up. I watched as Wallace took out Agent Gray's weapons and tossed them on the couch.

"Now yours," I said.

Agent Wallace removed both of his weapons and tossed them on the growing pile of armament.

"Now, any identification you have. On the couch," I said.

Both wallets and flip identifications were added to the pile.

"We're getting nowhere. Agent Wallace, I will ask again. Why was I targeted for this?" I asked, as I aimed dead center of Wallace's eyes.

I saw the first crack in his exterior.

"You were new, had very little experience, and were over the most powerful CS district in the country."

"Great, next you'll bring up the fact that I'm a woman."

"You have no idea the real power you have or the danger you are in."

"Then explain it."

"That's for someone much higher than me to explain. Like I told you, I have people I answer to and take orders from. As much as you may think otherwise, I don't have all the answers."

"Then who did you get your orders from?"

He stood there, silent. I heard the doorknob jiggle and a small curse from outside, again so muffled that the two in here with me wouldn't be able to hear it.

"Then I guess we're pretty much done here. Agent Gray, Agent Wallace, you are under arrest for illegal surveillance by a government agency and four other sections of Directive One. Agent Gray, you will also be charged with attempted murder of a U.S. Marshal. Do I need to read you your rights or do you already understand them?"

"Like you really think you'll get us off this property?" Agent Wallace asked.

"Regardless, I asked you a question. Do you want me to read you your rights or do you already understand them?"

"Of course I understand my rights."

"Agent Gray?"

"Yes, I know my rights," he answered, gritting his teeth together in pain.

"You know this is for naught. There will be more firepower coming though that door in a minute and it will be moot," Agent Wallace said.

"By the time they get the charges planted to blow open that door, you will be dead and your operation will be over anyway."

"They don't need charges," Wallace grinned.

"If you mean your IBI identification cards. I reprogrammed the locks. The only two from IBI that will work are lying on that couch," I said, indicating the pile of hardware.

I watched the grin fade.

"Still you have to get us past anyone out there before you can make any of this stick," He said.

"Are you trying to say that you brought armed IBI agents on U.S. soil for an offensive strike?"

"Don't be so naïve, Marshal."

"I asked a question. Yes or no are your only options"

"Of course I brought backup."

"Close enough. In that case I will add another infraction of Directive One along with hindering a federal officer in the performance of their duty."

I reached into my shorts pocket, pulled out my personal phone, and opened it. I dialed Hillis' number and waited.

"Hillis," I heard after the rings.

"Everything okay out there?" I asked.

"Yep. Interesting stuff I've been hearing."

"I don't think I want to know. We'll be coming out in a bit."

"We're waiting."

"Later," I said and hung up.

I saw Wallace looking at me with the fear of what just might happen begin to register on his face.

"What? You think I came to this party alone?" I asked rhetorically.

"Get him up and help him to the door," I said to Agent Wallace.

"Do you know the political turmoil you're about to create? Your ass won't last through this either if I have my information right," He said as he helped Agent Gray to his feet.

"I don't give a fuck about political turmoil and what sort of information could you really have that would mean my ass?"

"Does May seventh mean anything to you?"

So he was going to hold the fact that I had been bitten over my head. I smiled.

"And how do you think you could prove any of your information?"

"It will only take one night," he said, and I understood what he meant.

"I'll take that chance," I said, laughing.

He looked at me in disbelief.

"Now go to the door and open it up," I instructed.

They moved to the front door and opened it.

"Out," I said.

I followed a short distance behind them. I could see a gray sedan and a van parked in my yard. Marshal Simmons was standing over four kneeling men with a rifle, three of them in armored vests, and the other in shirt sleeves. Marshal Taylor had his side arm pointed at the two coming out the door and Marshal Hillis was stepping down out of the back of the van. Agent Gray stumbled as he started down the porch steps. I saw his left hand go to his jacket pocket instead of going out to stop his fall. He spun towards me as he stumbled, the pocket in his blazer exploding. The bullet ripped through the outside edge of my left arm. It burned like hell, but I took aim and placed two rounds in his left shoulder and arm, but Marshal Taylor's round found it's mark in his head. Agent Gray didn't get off another shot. Agent Wallace stood over the body of his partner a little shaken.

"Some guys never learn," I said as I walked over to Marshal Hillis and offered my hand.

He shook it warmly.

"Are you okay?" he asked, looking at my left arm.

I looked at the outside of my upper arm. The bullet had only laid open some skin; in fact, it had already started to quit bleeding. Must be the wheir healing.

"Yes, a bandage and I'll be fine."

"Do we need to get you to a hospital?"

"No. Really, I'll be fine. Nice bust."

"Your bust, I was just backup."

"Your bust. I'm just the victim," I said staring hard at him and moved him further away from everybody.

"How much did you hear?"

"Pretty much everything after Agent Wallace entered. But they have a pretty complete setup in the van, everything was recorded."

"Good, then you know I pretty much stayed within the book."

He nodded his head at me.

"Interesting setup you have here. Sound proof walls, electromagnetic locks, bullet proof reinforced windows, and seclusion. What are you up to?"

"Special assignment. Though I'll have to warn you, the slugs that you pull out of Agent Gray won't come back to either of my registered side arms."

"I bet they will," he said, smiling.

I smiled back at him and nodded my head.

"Do you really have twenty eight bugs in that place?" he asked.

"At least, and that is not even counting the barn, anything outside, nor my two vehicles. Speaking of which, when you are collecting evidence can you go through my vehicles and phone and check for tracking devices?

"Sure, we're going to have the team out here anyway. They're on their way; should be here within the hour."

"I have a file of my front door access records that you're going to need, though you'll have to treat them as top secret and some of the control numbers will probably be redacted, but it should still leave you enough for prosecution. Also, you *will* be getting calls from the director of IBI and Director Perry. Tell them exactly what happened, not the official version. You don't need the hassle of the can of worms I just opened up."

"Yes, ma'am," he said, smiling brighter and nodding his head.

"We both know that even if we're lucky, we'll only get a person or two higher than Wallace. I'll do some research this evening to see if I can find out anything else that I can pass along, but I doubt there will be much. I owe you one Marshal and if there's anything I can ever do for you, please call. Especially if you have any strange cases that you don't know what to do with, I'm your girl."

"You have done more for my career in this one bust than you will ever know."

"I may have just ended it," I replied, laughing.

"Oh. Could you do me two more favors?" I asked.

"Sure, if I can."

"If you can have your team clear my bedroom and master bath first I would really appreciate it. I have been running this morning, I would like a shower, and to get into some clean clothes. Then if someone could take me back over to the park, my car is there along with my official phone, which you will want to sweep also."

"No problem."

I watched as the suspects were taken away and the crime scene techs arrived and started sweeping the area. I went back to my bathroom, cleaned up my arm, and put a bandage over it so that no one would ask why it was already beginning to heal. The thing that really pissed me off today, out of everything, was the demise of my good coffee pot. Now, if I wanted any coffee, I would have to pull the small one out of Bee.

They finally finished my bedroom and allowed me in to take a shower. It felt a lot better to be clean and clothed. I finished drying my hair and went out into the house, which was teaming with people. I sidestepped a couple of techs and noticed there were two standing in front of the door leading to the basement trying to figure out how to open it. One turned and saw me.

"Excuse me," he said politely.

"Yes?"

"We were told to sweep the house but we can't get this door open."

"No need, that's clear."

"But, we were..."

I pulled my credentials and showed them to him.

"That one is fine trust me." I smiled.

"Yes ma'am," he said and moved to another part of the house.

I walked outside, found Marshal Hillis, who had someone drive me back to the park. I picked up my car and drove home so they could go through it.

****

It was about two in the morning when I finally handed the information over that I had for the bust to Marshal Hillis, and he and his crew left. They had found monitoring devices all over the house, throughout the yard, and in the barn. They also found two tracking devices in the car and one tucked away deep in my official phone. The thing I found odd was that they found nothing on or in Bee. I went to bed that night comfortable in the fact that no one would be listening to me snore. I turned out the light and fell blissfully asleep.

Chapter 25
Tuesday June 27, 2248

The phone started ringing at six in the morning. I fielded two, very angry, calls from two directors that were ready to roast me over a spit. Luckily, Director Perry was just pissed because I failed to notify him before I went after another agency. Other than that, he was quite complimentary of the whole operation and hung up with a "Good job".

Director Pinter, on the other hand, had a lot more to say about cooperation between agencies and my secrecy. Being the well behaved Marshal I was, I more than politely pointed out that his agency's secrecy had not only banged up against Directive One, it had broken right through it, where my secrecy did nothing more than expose it and keep my butt safe. Director Pinter did not hang up with a "Good job" and I found out Director Pinter doesn't like to be corrected.

I'd just sat down with my breakfast of six sausage links, five eggs, three pieces of toast, and coffee when my phone rang again.

"Hello," I said.

"You just love pissing higher ups off don't you?" Burdock asked, laughing.

"Good morning to you too, Captain. Though I'm not sure what you are talking about."

"I know that at my pay grade most of the report was redacted, but with the victim's last name being McKenzie, and the location being redacted, I could think of no one else that would want to throw a hand grenade directly in the middle of Washington City. You know, Ced, I'm glad you are not under my command today. I wouldn't want the ass chewing I'm sure you have gotten by now," he said, still chuckling.

"Though I don't know what you could be talking about, I still have a third of my ass left. The President has yet to voice an opinion so I figure I'll be losing that before the day is over. So how are you doing?"

"I'm doing fine. Just thought I'd call and check on you."

"I had one of the best night sleeps since I took this job. I still have a lot of loose ends out there. But, for the moment, I have a bit of a respite from people targeting me."

"Well, work calls."

"And I have breakfast waiting."

"Later," we both said at the same time and hung up.

As I ate my breakfast I thought about all of the loose ends that were still out there. TTZ now topped the list; I needed to call him back and set up a meeting. But it would definitely wait until tomorrow. Today was mine to do as I wanted and I wanted to stay as far away from a schedule as I could.

Chapter 26
Friday June 30, 2248

After buying a new coffee pot and a quiet week at home, I was approaching happy with my life. I knew that it was about to come to an end with the call I was about to make. I picked up my official phone and dialed.

"Hello?" he asked.

"TTZ? This is CAM," I said.

"You are one hard agent to get a hold of. How was Louisiana?" he asked, with a tone in his voice that said he knew I hadn't been there.

"Sorry about that. You should know about leg work and stakeouts. But all in all, Louisiana is still there."

"I guess that's a good thing, but if it fell in the Gulf, your District would get a lot smaller."

"True, but then I'd have to take a boat to get to lower Mississippi. I was looking through my schedule and found I'm going to be up near your area on the seventh, if you would still like to get that file to me."

There was silence for a few seconds.

"Really? The seventh?"

"Yes. Is there a reason I shouldn't be available on the seventh?"

"No. It's just that a lot of our cases are pretty active that time of the month."

"Don't have anything that active."

"Then would Joplin be close enough for you?"

"Sure."

"There's a coffee shop on the southeast side of town called George's. I can't get there until about six that evening. Would that be convenient for you?"

Of course it was George's. George's was the string of coffee shops that were owned by George Greyson.

"Yeah, that will be fine. Friday, the seventh, at six in the evening. Got it. How will I know you?"

"I'll be wearing an old army cap with captains' bars on it. And you?"

"I'll be the least lethal looking girl in the place."

"That's not much of a description."

"For now; that's the best I can give."

"Okay, I will look for the least lethal looking girl in the place."

"See you then."

"Will do," he answered and hung up.

I was going to feel real foolish if all of this had been nothing more than a coincidence and TTZ had nothing to do with Greyson and wasn't Terrence Zahn. Deep down though I knew what I was getting into.

Chapter 27
Monday July 3, 2248

I had Bee loaded and ready to head north. Though the PMS from hell had started yesterday, it had nothing on last month. I was a bit surly but, with the help of Bran's tea, I was at least upright and functioning. I'd decided that if I left today I would be able to drive myself and not have to worry about taking the bus; that was something I never planned to do again in my life. I waited to say good-bye to Bran and ask him to keep an eye on the house. After Bran started to work, I hit the road.

The drive was pretty uneventful, and as I drove my symptoms seemed to worsen. I was never so happy to be someplace than when I pulled up into Greta's drive. She was sitting on the porch waiting for me as I drove up and came to meet me with a hug and a smile as I got out of Bee.

"Though it's not as bad as last month, this is still a royal pain. Please tell me this gets better over time," I said as I opened the back of Bee and we got my suitcases out.

"Yes, sweetie. It gets better. At least you're standing up this month and you're not near as feverish. It's already better," she said, taking the larger suitcase and leading me in the house.

We put my suitcases in the corner and I sat down on the bed.

"Why don't you go ahead and crawl in bed," she suggested.

"It is only five. That wouldn't be very social of me."

"Willis won't be home until around six and Gary is working the night shift tonight. You have no need to be social this evening."

"Are you sure you don't need help with something?"

"Hush and lay down if you want to. If you feel like it later, you can get up and do something," she said.

I wanted to argue more but my body was listening to Greta, not me, and I curled up in the bed and closed my eyes.

Chapter 28
Tuesday July 4, 2248

The sun was bright through the window of my room when I woke. All of my cramps were hitting me and I felt a little sick at my stomach. I went to the restroom then got my bottle of herbs and went in search of the kitchen. Greta and Gary were sitting at the table with coffee as I stumbled in. I grunted at both of them. Greta had already sat the teakettle on the stove in anticipation of my need. A mug and spoon awaited my tea next to the stove. I spooned in the mixture and waited on the water. Evidently, Greta had been keeping the water warm for me since it took very little time for the kettle to sing at me. I poured the water in my cup and stirred as I went to the table to take a seat.

"Rough night?" Gary asked me.

"The night was fine, it is the morning that is killing me," I replied and took a sip.

"What time is it?" I asked.

"Eleven thirty," Greta answered.

"I slept eighteen hours?"

"If my math is right, that would be about right."

"Damn, I'm sorry."

"It's okay, really. Would you like some brunch?"

"No, I don't think so. My stomach's not up to it right now."

"Would you like something for it?"

"Maybe in a little while, let me kill one thing at a time," I said, pointing at the tea.

"How long have you been here?" I asked Gary, leaning over to give him a quick kiss.

"Only about a half an hour. I didn't get off work until three this morning. I came by to see you since you got in last night."

"Not much to see today," I said.

"You might be surprised," he said, smiling at me.

"Normally I'd be ready to sit on your lap and smooch away, but right now the innuendos are a bit lost on me."

"I can see that," he said, still smiling.

"Really could you turn off the white teeth until the tea takes effect?"

"You must really be fun with a hangover," he said, laughing.

"It's less pretty than this, that's for sure."

Over the next hour my cramps got better and Gary stayed to talk until he had to head home and get ready for his shift. I was starting to get hungry and helped Greta get dinner ready. It was a quiet night around the table with just Greta, Willis, and I. Even through my cramps, I took special note of the interaction between Greta and Willis. I knew that Willis cared for Greta, I'd seen it the night

The Water's Edge

I was bitten, but I wasn't sure it was reciprocal on Greta's part. I felt like she was ordered around like a slave and it bothered me. That was one of the things about wheir life that I wasn't keen on. I didn't care who it was, if someone were to treat me that way I would be walking out the door with a dead body left behind. I stayed up later than I had the night before, but I was still in bed asleep by eight thirty.

Chapter 29
Thursday July 6, 2248

I slept, off and on, most of the day until I heard Gary come in and ask about me. Greta informed him I was in my room and a few moments later I heard the light knock on my door.

"Come in," I called from my curled up position on the bed.

Gary came in and sat down on the bed facing me.

"Hey, sunshine," he said as he leaned over and gave me a kiss.

"I feel more like an eclipse."

"A few more hours and you'll be fine."

"I know, I'm just ready for it to be over with. Though, I don't feel even half as bad as I did last month."

"I just wanted to check in with you before I headed over to meet up with Thomas."

"So what's the plan for me tonight?"

"I've told everyone that you still aren't up to running with the pack, that you're a little shy about where you fit in. Tonight just stay around here. I told everyone that you'll meet up with us at the restaurant for breakfast around nine."

"What if I do change?"

"Stay as calm as you can. Howl for me, we will be close enough to hear you. I'll answer and you will know instinctively which way to go. Don't worry, I'll find you," he said.

I moved over in the bed a little and patted the pillow. He lay down next to me and gathered me in his arms.

"Even though I know what will probably happen, I'm still scared."

"You'll be fine, Ced. Just don't leave the backyard unless you change. Otherwise enjoy the night and get in the house if you hear any of the pack getting close."

He kissed me gently and we laid there until the sun started to sink.

"I've got to get going. I'll see you in the morning if not sooner," he said as he started to get up.

I wrapped my arms around him and pulled him back down to me. I let him know I would miss being with him this evening with a very long hard kiss. He gave me one last kiss and got up.

"The restaurant's name is Becky's. It is right off the square in Cassville. You can't miss it," he said as he walked to the door.

"See you in the morning," I said as he smiled at me and walked out.

I heard him walk through the house, say Good-bye to Willis, and leave. I forced myself out of the bed and went into the living room where Willis and Greta were getting ready to leave.

"Are you going to be okay by yourself?" Greta asked coming over to me.

The Water's Edge

"I'll be fine," I said, but I wasn't very convincing.

Greta cupped my cheek with her hand.

"Just let happen what is going to happen. There is a ham in the refrigerator to eat when you get hungry. We'll see you tomorrow morning," she said as she kissed me on the cheek.

"You two have fun. Kill a deer for me," I said, trying to stay light.

I got a small laugh out of Willis as they were heading out the door. I stood alone in the house as I heard their car drive away. I couldn't imagine what Greta had gone through by herself before she met Willis. I didn't know what I would have done without her and the pack the past couple of months. I went into the bathroom, grabbed a couple of towels, and went to the back porch to wait for sundown. As the light faded in the west I felt the beginnings of the change as the cramps started to get stronger. I took off my clothes, spread the towels out, laid back on them, watched the evening stars above, and waited. I felt it start; I looked at the time on my watch. I closed my eyes and let it come.

****

When I came to I immediately looked at my hands. Same hands that I saw every day. I sat up and looked down at my watch. In total it had taken a little less than four minutes. I could smell the dying warmth of the day around me and could even hear the rustling of small animals out in the field beyond the fence. I heard the first howls off in the distance. I knew each and every one of them. I could hear Gary call to his pack and I felt a little sad that I was not out among them. My stomach called to me. I got up from where I was sitting, picked up my clothes, and the soiled towels. I wiped off my thighs and headed into the house.

****

Freshly washed and clothed I found myself on the back porch with a large slab of ham and a beer. I took a seat in one of the chairs on the porch and began my meal. After my second helping of ham and another beer, I was at least stated but very restless. I could hear the pack occasionally off in the distance and I so wanted to run. Gary had told me to stay within the fence line and I was intent on doing that but the wheir inside of me was really railing against it. Last month I hadn't needed to run since I was, for lack of a better term, hunting. I got up from the chair and started walking the fence line, then started running it. Though I thought that I would tire soon, it seemed the more I ran the more I wanted to keep running. I must have spent an hour crisscrossing the yard before I finally hit a point where I thought I could sit down again. Most of my night was spent, in rotation, sitting for a while and then running the backyard.

Just like last month, I felt the need to find someone and basically fuck their brains out. I needed to be close and connected with someone, and I was neither. Greta had told me that in her wheir form she thought mostly about two things; sex and hunting. Or was it hunting and sex? Either way, both were very much in the forefront of my mind. I knew I could do something about the sexual side of it, but I couldn't do anything to sate my need for closeness. I sat in the chair frustrated and mad that I couldn't be out with the rest of the pack. Though I'd been wonderfully surprised by the traits I had received without turning, I wasn't sure I was happy with this particular heightened sense. I'd never been that interested in sex before now. It wasn't that I didn't enjoy sex; it was that I never found an overwhelming need for it. Now, not only was there a need, it seemed like an insatiable urge that would drive me to do almost anything to get it.

Okay, Ced, get up and run some more. After a few more turns around the yard, I remembered something the guys I used to work with would say about taking a cold shower in situations like this. *Take a cold shower. Couldn't hurt.*

I don't know what a cold shower is supposed to do. It might be different for a man, but for me it just made me cold, wet, and even more frustrated that I didn't have anyone around to hold me, get me warm, and yes–screw me for hours. It was about three thirty in the morning when I dried off and went to bed, still frustrated.

Chapter 30
Friday July 7, 2248

Though I wasn't really ready to get out of bed when the alarm woke me, I at least felt good and wasn't tired; still horny, but not tired. I took a page out of Greta's fashion book when I got dressed. I put on very short hiking shorts, a cut off tee that showed from just below my breast down to the top of my shorts and, as is a must in her system, no bra. I slid a very light cloth blazer on that would hide my gun and headed into town.

I got to the restaurant and entered. It was fairly busy for a Friday morning at nine. I saw a large table that a few of the pack had gathered at and headed over. Most of the ones that were there were from Craig's portion of the pack. I said good morning to everyone and started to take a seat.

"Wrong seat, Ced," Craig informed me as I sat.

"We have assigned seats?" I asked, giggling.

"No, but you do," he said smiling.

"Do I have to eat in my camper?"

"No, but you do have to sit next to Gary. His seat is at the head of the table and yours is just to his right."

"Can I stay here until people arrive; it looks awful lonely on that end?"

I was craving the companionship and interaction that I had missed last night.

"Of course you can hang here."

I sat for the next twenty minutes talking with Craig and the others until Gary arrived. I got up and took my seat. Gary came by and put his arms around me from behind. I leaned my head back, took a deep sniff of him, and looked into his bright green eyes. He leaned over and kissed me from above.

"Did you survive last night?" he asked as he sat down.

"Yes, but God I am frustrated," I answered, stealing another kiss after he was seated.

"It happens," he said chuckling, knowing exactly what I meant.

I felt sorry for the restaurant. Twenty odd wheirs; sitting at the same table and ordering enough food each to get full. That was a tall order.

"How was your night?" Gary asked seriously.

"Went pretty much like the last time, only this time I had nothing to hunt and no one around. I don't know how solitary people do it."

"It can be hard but over time it becomes more manageable."

"I don't know how. It was a good thing nothing male was around last night. I would have used them for my wants then let them run and used them for dinner."

"This is a new side of you," he said, grinning at me.

"Yes it is and it scares me to death," I said seriously.

"Why?"

"This is not like me. It's new and I don't know what to do with it."

"I can help you with that," he snickered.

"Not before you and I have a talk."

"A talk? About what?"

"About everything involved with that, where the two of us are concerned."

It was then I noticed that the noise level had dropped at our table. Damn wheir hearing and inquisitiveness.

"What are you doing today?" I asked, changing the subject away from what should be discussed in private.

"I have to go to the office for a while but I'll be done by one or so this afternoon. Then we're having a get-together around eight tonight."

"Am I going to see you between that?"

He just looked at me, like I'd said the stupidest thing in the world.

"Sorry, dumb question," I said.

"What are your plans?"

"I have something I have to do in Joplin at six this evening, but other than that...."

"How long are you going to be there?"

"An hour at most."

"What's in Joplin?"

"Can we talk about this when you get off work?"

"Sure."

It was almost ten thirty when the meal wound down and every one started drifting out and home. Gary walked me out to Bee.

"I like this new look you have going," he said, gesturing to my clothes.

"Thought I'd steal from Greta for a day," I said, smiling.

"I very much approve of the theft."

"I will see you about two this afternoon," he said as he opened Bee's door for me.

"Damn skippy you will," I said smiling, kissed him, and jumped up in the cab before he could really get a hold of me.

"Playing hard to get?"

"I thought that's what all good girls were supposed to do," I said evilly and closed the door.

He shook his head laughing as I started Bee and backed her out of the parking space.

****

I'd thought I would be exhausted when I got back from breakfast but I was wide awake and needed to do something. I followed Greta into the back yard. As the sun beat down on my shoulders, I started helping her in her garden. I had never been around country life growing up; hell I'd never even had a house plant.

Though I would probably never be a country girl, there was something therapeutic and relaxing about the manual labor and the fresh air. Greta and I talked about our childhoods, she about growing up in west Texas and me in foster homes from Colorado to Kansas. Greta seemed unusually saddened by my stories of my early life in foster homes and she informed me that I would be up here to spend Thanksgiving and Christmas with her and Willis, and *no* was not an answer.

"Greta, what should I do about Gary?"

"What do you mean, sweetie?" she asked as she pulled another weed out of her garden.

"I know he wants more than just a goodbye kiss, and for that matter so do I. But our relationship is so much more complicated than just boy meets girl."

"So much more," Greta replied, almost sadly.

"What is that supposed to mean?"

"If you go down this path then you'll be walking through a mine field. I'm not saying do it or don't do it. All I am saying is there are many missteps you can make and many ways to make things harder on both of you. Though I find Gary to be a fair and strong Alpha and a very considerate and polite man, he is still a man; and a man that is single and doesn't really want to be," she said.

"So you're saying unless I'm ready to start a close relationship and accept all things wheir, I should get in my car, leave, and not look back?"

"No. What I'm saying is that the two of you need to make sure that your goals, wants, and needs aren't going to collide sometime in the near future. Nothing would make me happier than to see you and Gary have a happy life whether it's apart or together. If you don't think you can handle the day to day hassles of dating, and maybe mating with, a pack Alpha then don't string it along for either one of you. He will need to mate at some point in time, and probably in the very near future. Even if he doesn't mate I know, as a man, he wants to get married. I think the best scenario for him would be to marry someone that isn't wheir or doesn't change."

"Because if he marries outside of the pack it would mean more years of stability in the pack," I finished her thought.

"I can see you've at least thought about it," she said, smiling.

"So you and Willis would challenge him if he mated?"

"I don't care if he mates or not. Willis, however, has other ideas."

"What does Willis want?"

"He's content with the way things are right now. He's next in line for pack leadership which suits him as it stands. It is the fact I would lose status, should Gary mate, that has him ready to fight."

"He cares about you a lot."

"No. He cares about what my status brings to both of us," Greta corrected me.

"What are you saying?" I asked a little shocked.

"I find it ironic that everyone considers me the "Alpha" female since, unless you are screwing the Alpha of the pack, it doesn't carry much weight with anyone but the other females and the lesser wolves. But as long as I'm the Alpha female and Willis is number two in the pack, our positions pretty much guarantee him a large say in how things will run. If Gary mates, my status will be nothing more than that of any of the other females in the pack and Willis will have less clout if that happens. Willis doesn't like to play second fiddle to anyone and I know he won't with a female. Right now he isn't going to challenge Gary for the pack, but if Gary marries a wheir he would break from the pack and form his own. If he does that, I know three of the five females, maybe four, would follow him. That in itself would be attractive to other males in the pack.

Gary would be left with maybe six to eight members with maybe one sub-Alpha and one or two females...God, I hate this posturing...."

I turned and looked in her eyes.

"Greta, do you remember that morning before we went out looking for the Alpha? You were sitting at the table doing needlework and we were talking about why you should trust me."

"Yes why?"

"I had a realization that morning. Before, I'd seen you as just another person I had to deal with. Until that conversation, I hadn't taken into consideration that they were using you as bait and you didn't want any real part of it. I haven't made that mistake again and I'm not going to make it now. What is it *you* want, Greta?"

"Not to ever have been bitten would be a good place to start. Like I told you I just became resigned to the fact that I was wheir, I've never accepted it. I want things out of life, just like anybody else. I want a family someday, but I don't want to have to raise my children as wheir. If I could guarantee that my kids would be human, I'd have my three and enjoy the hell out of it. But as it is I won't be having offspring no matter what Willis says about it, which just might cost me. Where you and Gary are concerned, I have a fight going on inside me."

"How so?" I asked.

"If you and Gary were to get together, it would be a calming curve thrown at the pack. Since you don't morph, you would be most unusual. In all ways, especially if you married, Gary would be mated but the female alpha position would be happily blurry. Gary wouldn't be open to advances by other females, thereby assuring me my position and in turn Willis'. But since you couldn't go out with the pack, it would fall to someone else—me. Willis would probably be satisfied that I still held power over the other females and my position would be relatively recognized. Having you in the pack, even be it as an unusual member, would mean everything to me because you won't bow down to any of the Alphas. I'm sure that would cause Gary and the rest of them headaches to no end.

261

Do you know how much I would love to see that?" she asked, smiling.

"Seems to be a lot. That was half of it what is the fight?" I asked.

"That was from the selfish standpoint of having to be a female wheir and being stuck here. The other side of me, because I have grown very fond of you, says that you need to run like hell. Get away from this bullshit. You don't have to worry about one day a month. Five minutes out of your month and you're still who you are. Enjoy that, Ced, and don't let anyone try and take that freedom from you."

"Greta, I've become more than just fond of you. You're like the sister I always dreamed about but never had. Someone that cares about me and wants the best for me. You've helped me in more ways than you can imagine, even beyond dealing with being a wheir. I've had someone to call and talk to about things I've never been able to talk about with any of the men in my life. I'm not going to lose that."

I walked over to her and pulled her to me in a hug.

"I am amazed at how quickly I've become attached to you and I will never put you in danger again, I don't care what all of the Alphas in the world want."

She smiled at me, cupped my face in her hands, and kissed me on the lips. She pulled back and I could see the tears rolling down her cheeks.

"Will you be the family I never had?" I asked.

"On one condition."

"What would that be?"

"That you become the family I lost."

I smiled at her. She pulled me into a hug and nuzzled me. I felt the warmth of the closeness I had craved last night.

"Enough working in the yard. It's lunch time."

"I hope you're cooking because I suck at it," I said, laughing.

She grabbed me by the hand and led me up to the kitchen.

"You keep me safe and I'll do the cooking."

"Deal."

****

As Gary drove up, I rose from the porch chair I had been siting in. He kissed me gently, then broke our kiss and stared hard at me.

"Something wrong?" he asked.

"We need to talk."

I took his hand and led him around the house. We walked down the path to the tree line. It was the same path I had traveled to find them a few months ago. We walked quietly until we got to the stream. I took my shoes off, sat on a rock, and dangled them in the cold running water. Gary took a seat a little up the bank.

"Okay. Talk," Gary said without preamble.

"You really know how to woo a girl," I said, laughing.

"I don't date much," Gary replied, smiling at me.

"What I have to say may make you angry, can you deal with that?"

"Are you leaving and not coming back?"

"I don't want to."

"As long as that's not part of the discussion, I promise I won't get angry."

I thought for a moment, took a deep breath and continued.

"Over the past month I've thought more and more about you and I," I started.

"So have I," he interrupted.

"Have you thought through what it would mean if you and I started having an intimate relationship?" I asked.

He shrugged his shoulders at me.

"You are part of my pack," he said.

I smiled at him.

"I know I'm a part of the pack, but I don't belong to the pack. Since it looks like I'll never morph, what does that leave us with?"

"In some ways it makes things a little easier."

"Yes, it probably does but you know I'll never be subservient to anyone, or at least I hope you know that. I'm not sure where I fit in."

"I don't really care about that. All I know is I want you," he answered.

"Honestly, have you thought about whether you want to just have a relationship or if you want to mate? Since I don't morph, mating is a bit out of the question and I am not even considering marriage."

"I haven't asked you to marry me."

"That's all you got out of that question?"

"No. But we are not talking about marriage so why even bring it up?"

"I guess being female, it's where our thoughts wind up. So the point of this is that you want to screw me but not marry me?" I asked, grinning evilly since my mind was kind of running in that direction also.

"There's no winning here is there?" he asked, hanging his head.

"I have a friend that tells me there is no winning or losing, there is only knowledge," I said channeling Bran.

"Are you really going to be this difficult?"

"That is exactly the point I'm trying to make. Yes, I am always going to be this difficult. That's just the way I am. If we got together, at best I would be a thorn in your side, and at worst I could cost you your pack. I have a job and a life outside of this area that I'm not going to give up, at least not anytime in the near future. I plan to be up here when I can but I can't guarantee anything. I'm not going to move up here and you can't move your pack to where I am. Anything we have will be long distance most of the time and there may or may not be a future in it. Right now I can honestly say I like you, a lot, and want nothing more than to jump your bones but I don't want you or the pack to think that it means more than it does. Do I care if they think or know that I'm exclusive to you? Not at all. What I don't want them, or you, to think is that I hold some position in the pack other than the one I now hold."

"And how do you think your position in the pack will change?"

"I understand that how I view it won't change unless I change how I perceive it. What I worry about is how the others will view it. This brings me to the thing that will probably piss you off to no end."

"I told you as long as you aren't leaving and never coming back I won't get mad. So what is it you view as such a touchy subject?"

"Greta."

"What about Greta?"

"I'm not challenging you for the pack or anything like that," I started.

"But?" he asked, smiling.

"I've become very, very, very attached to and fond of her. If at any time she comes back from a moon hurt or I hear of anyone trying to harm her, I don't care whose door it leads back to, there won't be enough left of them to identify," I said, looking him straight in the eye.

He actually laughed.

"You find that funny from someone that carries two guns loaded with silver?" I asked.

"It just means you've made a bond. I think it's the best thing that could have happened for either one of you. Especially Greta. All of the other females in the group are biological. I've known for years that Greta has been.... hmmm, what's the word... unhappy, isn't it.... unsatisfied is the closest I can come. She has longed for someone to trust and be with that understands some of what she has to deal with. She, like you, didn't ask for what was done to her. I would expect nothing less out of the two of you. If packs were not singularly patriarchal, I would worry more about the two of you then any of the other sub-Alphas in the pack. I will even admit it plays into my hands."

"How's that?"

"I'm the Alpha; I want to stay the Alpha. If you and Greta have an alliance this deep, then neither Willis nor I, for that matter, will be able to really move against the other without pissing you two off. I've seen both of you fight and you're both quite formidable on your own. Do you think either one of us wants to face off against two bitches, one with teeth and one that is a crack shot on a full moon?"

"I hadn't thought of it like that."

"I have. I've known Greta for about eight years now. Though I know I could take her, I'd pay a dear price for it. For that reason I'm extremely wary of getting on her bad side. I've seen how you work. I know that you are a much better shot than I am. Even unarmed, I'm sure both of us would need a doctor or undertaker if we got into a fight," he said honestly.

264

"So you don't feel I am challenging you?"

"Some, but not in the way you think. Every pack has its own way of doing things. I've never known of a wheir that doesn't change so ours is just that much more unique. How is it going to work for you? I have no clue, but the pack has worked well the way it is, so I'm sure it'll be able to adapt to whatever is thrown at it."

"Gary, I know I don't understand all of the ins and outs of the pack and since I don't shift, I probably never will understand them. If you can approach this from a mostly human viewpoint, then we might have a chance at something."

"What would that mean?"

"I am not, and never will be, owned by the pressure of some hierarchy that I do not understand or necessarily agree with. I'll do whatever I can to not embarrass you or knowingly put you in a bad position, but I won't bow down to anybody."

"I would expect nothing less from you," he interjected.

"To be honest, I really don't know you that well and I'm not sure what you think or really want out of this or life. I've had basically twenty-six years that had nothing to do with you or the pack. Before a few months ago, you and the pack only existed in fantasy stories for me. I have a past and a history that I know nothing about that may, at some time in the future, catch up with me. Before I met you, I didn't know that there was anything different about me than any other woman in America. You have a job and a pack to run. I have a job and things to learn about myself. I guess what I am trying to say is, if you can live within these very gray and blurred lines, I'm all for seeing where it goes," I said.

I looked at him as he thought about what I said. He didn't say anything, got up, and offered me a hand up. I took my feet out of the water and slipped my shoes back on and got up. We walked in silence up the path for a bit.

"What do you have to do in Joplin this evening?" he asked.

I was surprised that the subject had changed.

"Something for work. I have to meet someone that has a file for me."

"You want some company?"

"As long as you understand that this is work related and you will have to sit in the car."

"I can live with that," he said, smiling.

I smiled back at him. I felt a jerk on my arm as he pulled me into the thick underbrush along the path. I knew this place, it was the opening I had tracked Greta and Willis to the day I came looking for them. His hands went down to my lower back, pulled me roughly to him, and kissed me. He broke our kiss and laughed.

"What?" I asked.

"Don't you ever take that thing off? I bet you even wear it in the shower."

I reached around, unclasped the holster from my belt, and tossed it gently onto the grass. I felt Gary's hands as he searched my lower back and ass. I pressed myself against him as I felt all of the wants from last night return. My knees went a little weak as he started to lay me down in the grass. I felt his teeth in my neck as he bit down hard. I slapped him upside the head, which made both of us laugh and him bite harder. I couldn't get him out of his clothes fast enough, or he mine.

****

I lay there with my head on his chest looking at the sky through the break in the trees. I had scratches, bruises, and a sense of being sexually sated for the first time in my life. I rolled over to look at him. He had a very pronounced hand print across his cheek and a series of pretty deep scratches across his chest that were already healing. I bent down to kiss him.

"That was fun," I said, quietly laughing.

"Have you always been this rough?"

"To an extent, yes. But I thought it was always like this with wheirs," I answered and lay my cheek back down and listened to the heart beating in his chest.

"Not after a moon. Leading up to it, yes, but it usually lessens after."

"Then we might want to not do this before," I giggled.

"I don't know, it could get quite interesting," he laughed.

"Could," I agreed.

"If we're going to Joplin, we might want to get moving," he said, looking at his watch.

I pouted at him, but sat up. We got redressed and walked hand in hand back to the fence around the back yard of the house.

Greta gave me a small knowing smile as I jumped over the fence.

"I'm going to go change. I will be back in about an hour," Gary said from the other side of the barricade.

"Okay. I'll see you in a bit," I said as I kissed him and watched him walk towards the side of the house.

"So you've made your decision?" she asked.

"I don't know if it was a decision as much as we came to an agreement, but I guess some things are settled–at least for now."

"I guess he took it rather well?" she asked, fishing.

"He even took me challenging him with a laugh."

"You challenged him?" Greta asked, shocked.

"Not for the pack. Only on one issue."

"What was that, if I may ask?"

"You."

"Me? What about me?"

I turned to her and placed my hands on her shoulders so I could look her in the eyes.

"If you are hurt at any time, be it on a moon or otherwise. I don't care where the blame rests, that person will not live to see the next moon. Even Gary," I said seriously.

"And he didn't tear you to shreds?" Greta asked, openly worried about me.

"No, he laughed at me," I said, smiling.

"He laughed at you?"

"He told me he'd expect nothing less out of me or you when it came to that."

"He actually told you that?"

"Greta, Gary may be the Alpha but he is not stupid or unfeeling. He's known for years that you feel the way you do. He's happy that you and I have formed the bond we have. And so am I. In a way it was the only thing that allowed me to do what I just did."

"I'm glad you're here," she said, pulling me to her.

"Me too."

"Well, I have to go get ready to head to Joplin," I said as we let go of each other.

"Why are you going to Joplin? Are you going to be back for tonight?"

"I have a quick meeting to pick something up and, yes, I'll be back in time for the get-together," I assured her.

"Are you going alone?"

"No. Gary is taking me."

She seemed a little more placated with that.

"Good, your job worries the hell out of me," she said, smiling.

"It doesn't do much for my emotions sometimes either," I agreed with her as I walked towards the house.

I went to the bathroom, looked at myself in the mirror, and knew exactly why Greta hadn't needed a whiff of me to know what I'd been up to. My hair was a wreck, flying in all different directions, with leaves and grass matted in it. My shirt was dirty and grass stained, as were my shorts. I went to the bedroom ran a brush through my hair and put on clothes that were a bit more appropriate for public viewing.

I reached in my suitcase and pulled out the gun Mitch had sent me, my official phone, and the file I had started on Zahn's transgressions. Loaded down, I went to the porch to wait for Gary and try to figure out some way to level the playing field in Zahn's territory.

Chapter 31
Friday Evening, July 7, 2248

Greta joined me on the front porch as I waited. Though we didn't say much, I knew she was worried about where I was going and what I was going to do when I got there. Gary drove up in his cruiser and pulled to a stop in front of us. He got out and came up on the porch as Greta and I rose from our seats.

"You ready?" he asked.

"Yes. Are you?"

"I'm here aren't I?" he asked, smiling.

"Gary. You take care of her," Greta spoke up from beside me.

"I promise Greta. I'll bring her back safe and sound."

"We will see you in a couple of hours," I told her as I gave her a quick hug.

"You be careful," she said as I walked down the steps.

"I will. I promise."

Greta watched us until we had turned out of the drive onto the secondary road.

"See what you've already started?" Gary asked, laughing.

"What?"

"Before you got here Greta would never have dared to tell me to do anything," he said, smiling at me.

"Well, if it's any consolation I am proud of the way you handled it."

"So what aren't you telling me about tonight?" he asked, changing the subject.

"What makes you think....?"

"Ced, give me a break."

"The person I am meeting tonight has the district above mine. I believe him to be in bed with Greyson."

"So what you are saying is that you're walking into a trap."

"There is a real possibility of that."

"Don't do it, Ced."

I told Gary, without too much detail, about the last few weeks at home and the IBI bust.

"You busted IBI?" he asked, shocked.

"Yes and I believe that the Alpha I killed, the three mercenaries, IBI bugging my house, Philip, Zahn, and Greyson are all tied together somehow. I'm not sure I will ever know the intricacies of it, but I'm going to cut as many heads off this snake as I can."

"So, you're eliminating this guy?"

"No. Nothing so bold. I'm going to give him a copy of everything I have linking him to all of it and I'm hoping he will be smart and back off. I am nowhere near brave enough to take out a Counter Section agent, especially one that's been established for as long as he has. I think this one is going to have to go through more formal channels than the others. I'm going to give him the choice of backing down or going with me to our supervisors."

"I thought you said you didn't have any real supervisors?"

"No, I think I said that I was somewhat autonomous, not that I didn't have supervisors. He and I both answer to three people. Mine is the Director of the Marshal Service, The Director of the IBI, and The President of the United States. His will be the same except he will answer to the Director of his original branch of service instead of the Director of the Marshal Service."

"You really answer to the President directly?" Gary asked, a little surprised.

"Yes, though I've never talked to him."

"So, someone would probably be very interested if one of you came up missing?"

"Let's put it this way; there has never been an unsolved case where an Agent died."

"Then why have they been after you?"

"That's the question that still has me a bit stumped," I said.

We had been talking for a good while and were about forty-five minutes out of Joplin.

"Can you take the next exit?" I asked.

"Sure," Gary said as he hit his signal and took the exit a few hundred yards from us.

"Just pull over for a minute."

Gary pulled to a stop. I grabbed my official phone, stuck the battery in it, and hit the on button. I waited a few seconds for it to find a local cell tower. I noticed I had three missed calls. I pulled them up. They were all from TTZ; the last one having been earlier in the day. I punched redial and waited.

"Hello?" he asked.

"TTZ? This is CAM. I saw I missed a couple of your calls. Was there something that you needed?"

"I had a few things come up and I was going to see if we could meet a little later."

"I'm already on my way to Joplin. I was planning on being there shortly after six."

"That's okay; the things I needed to take care of fell through. Six is fine."

"Great. I'll see you there."

"Yes." he said and hung up.

"How well do you know Joplin?" I asked Gary.

"Somewhat. What are you looking for?"

"I need a second hand clothing shop."

"Okay," he said as he put the car back in gear and got back on the freeway.

I looked through the racks until I found what I was looking for. A fairly large, man's, light coat and a nondescript baseball cap. I paid for my items and walked out to where Gary was in the car waiting.

"Do you know the area around George's Coffee shop on the southeast side of town?"

"Yes."

"How long to get there?"

"About ten minutes."

I looked at my watch it was about five twenty five.

"Okay, head in that direction. Stay off of the street it's actually on and park downwind of it," I directed.

"Are you really going through with this cloak and dagger shit?" he asked.

"I will do what I have to," I answered.

He gave me a bit of an angry face. He had shown great restraint and patience with me on this so far, but I got the feeling that would run out pretty soon. He drove and circled the area until he found a public parking lot downwind of the coffee shop and parked. I put on the old coat I'd bought then tried to pile my hair up and stick it under the ball cap. I ended up putting it in a ponytail and sticking it through the little hole, above the sizing snaps, which was no small feat considering how full my hair had become.

"My meeting is going to be around six. I'm going to go check things out beforehand. The meeting shouldn't take more than thirty minutes. If I'm not back by six forty-five. Leave; go home and start getting ready for a few bloody battles or think about relocating your pack."

"You expect me to just sit by and not do anything?" he asked with some disbelief.

"Yes. I need you to. You told me once that your first responsibility was to the pack. Don't forget that."

"But you are part of my pack."

"Maybe, but I'm an expendable part of your pack," I said, smiling at him.

He just looked at me. I leaned across the front seat and pulled him towards me with my hand on the back of his head. I looked into his eyes and kissed him. I pulled back and got out of the car.

"Please. Think about your pack. I would hate to think Greta was put in danger because the Alpha was thinking with his crotch and not his brain," I said as I closed the door.

I walked out of the parking lot and made my way to the street the coffee shop was on. I kept a hand on the gun Mitch had sent me that I was keeping in a side pocket on the coat. I walked until I was downwind of the coffee shop on the opposite side of the street. I came down to where I was diagonally across from the big windows that lined the front of the shop. There were seven or eight people scattered around inside. I turned on my sight. At a table, one at each side of the entrance sat two large wheirs; a lot of black streaks there. All of the others in the cafe were normal humans. The one I figured was him sat in the back corner facing the front wearing an old army hat and halfway reading a newspaper. Though his aura was rife with black, it seemed more like it was stained as opposed to the active streaks in the wheirs. I surveyed the restaurant layout. There was the seating area with a bar area behind to order at. Behind the bar was a kitchen area that I could barely see through the small pass window. To the right of the bar, which was on my left, there was a door that led to the restrooms.

I walked back up the street, crossed, and continued on down the cross street I had come in on until I got to the alley that led behind the row of buildings that the coffee shop was part of. I sniffed and almost threw up with all of the garbage and urine that met my nose. I sifted through the scents and found no active life other than a few rats. I gave the alley a once over with my sight; nothing seemed to be in the ally or above me in the windows or on the rooftops.

Keeping close to the side that the coffee shop would be on, I made my way down the alley to the back door of the shop. I tried the door knob and it turned, I cracked it and looked inside. There was a cook and a dishwasher talking but no one else. I looked at my watch; it was five after six. I took a deep breath, which almost made me retch again. I pulled my shield from my waist and held it in my right hand. Opening the door with my left, I made it in the door before the dishwasher noticed me. I put my finger to my lips to tell him to hush and showed him my badge. He nodded his head. I went to the door that led to the hall across from the bathrooms. I got through that door and into the hall without the cook seeing me. I walked up the hall to the door that led to the seating area proper. I would be at a little disadvantage since the door swung open towards the table where TTZ was sitting. But at least the lookouts were facing the front, watching the street and the front door. I put my shield back on my belt and opened the door just enough to slip out, then quickly took a seat right next to the man at the back reading the paper. I could see the surprise on his face as I sat down.

"TTZ, I presume?" I asked, not much above a whisper, and held out my hand.

"CAM?" he asked, taking my hand.

"The one and only. Though; some people seem to know me as a Clair McDuff."

I saw a little color drain from his face. I also noticed that his voice had caught the attention of the two wheirs sitting up front. I knew they caught my scent from the confused and surprised looks on their faces.

"I found that a little insulting. Do I really look like a Clair to you?" I asked rhetorically.

"Are you always this brash?".

"I find it's the last thing most people expect out of someone like me."

"I'll give you high marks on the description. I would have to admit that you look to be the least lethal girl in the place," he said with a small smile.

"Right now I'm the only girl in the place. So what do we do now?" I asked, letting him make the next move in a very tense situation.

He pulled a folder out of the folded newspaper and slid it towards me. I accepted it and pulled it in front of me. I watched as one of the wheirs got up, threw a tip on the table, and left following another patron out. I figured this would happen when they realized their mistake. I would have to force my way out regardless of the way I left.

"I hope that this will help you," he said.

I was surprised at the earnestness I thought I heard in his voice.

"I hope so too. By the way, I have something you might find helpful," I said as I reached for the folder I was holding under the coat.

I watched the wheir in front go for the inside of his blazer.

"You can tell your guard dog I don't keep my weapon where I'm reaching," I said to him, loud enough that the wheir could hear.

I saw TTZ give his head a nod and the wheir relaxed, but he was still pissed at me for calling him a dog. What the wheir didn't know was that I had kept my hand on the gun in my left pocket the whole time. Though a shot from it wouldn't kill him, unless I got lucky or it was well aimed, it would definitely slow him down. I pulled the folder out and slipped it across the table to him. He looked at me quizzically. He pulled it in front of him and opened it up. He flipped the couple of pages and closed the file slowly.

"Interesting," he said, though I could tell I had fired a shot across the bow.

"Let's not beat around the bush, Terrence. I have a proposition for you."

"What would that be, Cedwynne?"

So I wasn't a nameless entity to them.

"You stay out of my district, leave me and the people I was sworn to protect alone, and that..." I started, pointing at the file.

"...will never see the light of day," I finished.

"I wish it were really that simple."

"And why can't it be that simple?"

"Cedwynne, both of us are just pawns for others who hold the strings, no matter which side either of us are on."

"And a pawn has been known to checkmate a king."

"Not without backup," he said and I got both meanings.

"I guess it depends on who has the more powerful king," I said, shrugging my shoulder.

"Maybe. Though, I was impressed with your little IBI bust. There were a lot of people, on both sides that were surprised by that one," he said, chuckling.

"Thank you, I guess."

"You know, Cedwynne, I've had the pleasure of reading your file. You're a very interesting and promising young woman. It saddens me to see someone so young in your predicament."

"And what *is* my predicament?"

"Caught between two masters and not being able to serve or trust either one."

I wasn't really sure what he meant by that, but I have to think about it later, now I needed to extract myself from the situation and get my ass out of here without getting shot.

"Aren't you tired of being a pawn?" I asked.

"I gave up caring years ago."

"So, this is going to continue?"

"Probably."

"I won't be taken lightly, Terrence."

"No one is taking you lightly anymore, I assure you. But now the game has changed and you are sitting on the wrong square of the board. You won the first round, though I am not sure that will be much comfort to you in the future."

"I don't really have a clue what you are talking about."

"Then that file just might help you. Provided you are as sharp as I think you are," he replied, pointing at the folder in front of me.

"Just as that file might just save your life," I responded, nodding at the one in front of him.

"Is that a threat?"

"If I ever find you in my district, outside the dictates of your CS appointment, I will hunt you down and kill you. That simple."

"You really think you can back that claim?" he asked, somewhat amused.

"I've surprised myself with what I have been able to accomplish in the short amount of time I've been on the job. True, you may kill me or have me killed this evening. But if the wheirs couldn't do it and the three mercenaries you sent couldn't, what makes you think that it will be any different tonight Special Envoy Zahn?"

He openly paled.

"Because you are in my district now," he finally said.

"Maybe, but you'll be the first one to die," I said and started to get up.

"Are you sure you wouldn't like to walk out with me? There is someone that's interested in meeting you and I can guarantee your safety that way," he said, not moving.

"No. I would prefer to go out the way I came in."

"Out the back?"

"Alive."

"If that's what you believe, then please—feel free," he said and gestured towards the door to the hall.

I picked up the file he'd given me, stuffed it under my coat, stood up, and took a couple of steps back so I could get to the door handle. I watched the wheir in front start to reach in his coat. I flung the door open and ran in the hall. I heard the sound of the silencer right before the wood on the door splintered at the spot where I had been standing. I put my shoulder into the kitchen door and opened it. I ducked down to be out of the sight of the little window between the kitchen and the front. I flipped the lock on the hall door and ran towards the door to the alley. I didn't bother to turn the handle; I kicked it open and flew through it. I was brought up short by the prone body of the wheir that had left the front earlier laying on the ground. He wasn't dead but he would be out for a while. I looked up and was met by those wonderful green eyes.

"I thought I told you to not get involved," I said quickly.

"I'm not one to take orders," he said and held out his hand.

I took it and we ran down the alley. I couldn't hear anything yet but I knew it was coming. We had about another twenty feet to the end of the alley when I heard the door of the coffee shop bang open. I pushed as fast as I could run, which was pretty quick I found out. I was working through my head if I could get my gun out and aim before getting shot, or if I had a better chance making it to the end of the alley. The end of the alley won out.

I heard the hammer being pulled back on a revolver. I pushed Gary towards the other side of the alley and I broke to the left about the time the bullet whizzed between us. Neither one of us stopped running; we had about three more feet to go. I knew whoever was shooting at us was now running also, which meant that he would be hard pressed to get off an accurate shot. Gary hit me with a full body tackle from the right side sending me and him flying towards the left corner of the ally. We hit the ground just past the corner as another bullet sent shards of brick flying. I rolled up on my feet to see Gary a few feet ahead of me running towards his car a few feet down at the curb. I ran to the passenger side and got the door open about the time he started it. I jumped in and heard another shot, but didn't hear it hit anything. The tires spun before I got the door closed and we shot out on the street into what little traffic that existed. Gary reached down and hit the switch for the lights and the siren. We flew through the streets and hit the entrance ramp to highway seventy-one south as cars pulled to the side to let us through. We had to have been doing over a hundred until we flew through Neosho and Gary turned off the siren and lights and slowed to a normal speed.

"That was fun," I said sarcastically.

"Never a dull moment with you around, that's for sure."

I pulled my phone out of my pocket, turned it off, and pulled the battery. Gary flipped his phone open and dialed.

"Greta?"

"Yes, we're both fine."

"We'll see you in about an hour."

"Okay. Later." He ended the conversation and hung up.

"You know you're worrying Greta to no end," he said.

"I would cook Greta a good meal to apologize but my culinary skills suck."

"You could always just shoot a cow and bring it to her."

I stuck my tongue out at him as I took off the hat.

"Now, that's a cute side of you," he said, smiling at me.

I slid across the seat and settled in next to him. He put his arm around me and kissed me on the top of my head. We drove for the rest of the way on two lanes and back roads until we got to Willis and Greta's.

Both of them were sitting on the front porch as we drove up. I knew that they were waiting on us since I counted almost fifteen cars already here. Gary parked and shut the engine down. He got out and I slid under the steering wheel to get out on his side. He took me by the hand and led me up on the porch.

"Here, Greta. She is safe and sound," He said, showing me to her.

My new overprotective big sister got up, came over, hugged me, and took a big sniff to make sure Gary wasn't lying to her. Once she was sure I was fine, I could tell; she let out a large emotional held breath.

"I smell gunpowder on you," she said accusingly.

"I promise I didn't fire my gun. For once I have come up here, around a moon, and not killed anybody," I said, smiling.

"Then go get changed so we can eat. That coat does nothing for you," she said as she pushed me towards the door.

I changed into something a bit more conservative than earlier; pretty much fashion a la Greta, but this time with a bra.

I helped Greta get the rest of the food out on the tables as the rest of the pack milled about. As I moved about I noticed the sniffs and the cocked eyebrows, especially from the females, and I knew what they could smell. I could feel the tension from the women as they were waiting to see how the hierarchy would change for them. I also noticed that Gary wasn't glued to my side this evening as I moved about the pack. I caught Greta as she was passing by me to sit down at a table.

"Greta, you are my friend, sister, and my only family. Absolutely nothing changes in the pack or with us," I said very lowly, staring hard at her.

She smiled down at me, put her arms around me, and kissed me on the lips. I felt the tension from the females dissipate some. In that display, they saw I refused my status over Greta. I squeezed her hand as she left to take her seat beside Willis. We ate our meals with good conversation and laughter. I got up to get Gary and I another beer and was stopped by Thomas.

"I need a beer, Ced," he called out to me.

I stopped in my tracks. I knew what he was doing and I didn't like it. He was already testing Gary, through me, and his control over me and the pack. I bit my tongue hard and looked over at Gary. I was not going to do anything to put him in a bad position tonight, but I'd warned him about situations like this. He smiled at me and gestured with his hand to have fun. I smiled back at him and walked to the table where Thomas was sitting. Conversation had stopped and everyone seemed glued to the event about to happen. I had out maneuvered Thomas by acquiescing to Gary first and now I had the permission of the Alpha to rip Thomas apart and Thomas knew it.

"I beg your pardon?" I asked as sweetly as I knew how with the smell of hypothetical blood in the air.

"I said I need a beer," Thomas said, sticking to his guns since he already opened his mouth. I unclasped my holster and laid it, with gun in it, on the table. I also placed my credentials on top of it.

"Are you going to threaten me with your position?" Thomas asked.

"As a government agent? No, that is why I removed those trappings. As a member of this pack yes," I answered as I placed my hands on the table and leaned towards him.

I made sure I kept eye contact with him as I leaned closer.

"I am not your bitch. If I could be confused as anyone's bitch it would be Gary's. If you need more refreshment then I suggest that you get up and go get some. However, if I am up and you wish to pose your request for libation in a polite way, I will be more than happy to oblige your thirst," I said as calmly as I could.

"I guess that Greta and I will need to have a talk about her females," He said, getting almost nose to nose with me.

He was trying to do an end around and I knew it.

"Thomas, I want you to understand this very clearly. Anybody, and I do mean anybody, touches a hair on Greta, they will not see the next moon. I killed the last Alpha that tried to hurt her and I will do it again in a heartbeat," I said, making sure I touched noses with him and he could smell there was no fear in me.

We had not been having a private conversation and everyone in the place heard every word. I knew I had him cowed, but I needed to give him some small out so he wouldn't lose status for being cowed by a female.

"Now, Thomas. I was getting up to get Gary and I another beer. Can I get you anything?" I asked trying to be sweet again, though it wasn't really working.

I stood up, still looking at him, and started to put my gun and credentials back on my shorts.

"A beer."

I looked hard at him again.

"If you wouldn't mind," He added quickly.

"Not at all," I said as I walked over to the porch, grabbed three beers, opened them, and headed back.

I put Gary's in front of him as I passed and sat the new one down in front of Thomas. I even bussed the empties as I left. I threw the dead bottles in the can Greta had out for them and took my place next to Gary. It wasn't until I sat back down that the conversation even began to start back up again.

"Nice play," Gary whispered to me.

"Sorry. I knew what he was doing and it pissed me off," I apologized.

"You have nothing to apologize for. He brought it on himself. He also lost something tonight."

"What was that?"

"Because I didn't get involved, everyone understands that I found the whole thing quite inconsequential. He lost a little status in the pack since I just let my bitch, no offense, handle him," he answered.

"No offense taken on the bitch remark, but I didn't want anyone to lose standing," I said, feeling a bit bad about it.

"That is one of the things about the pack. If you're going to make a run at the Alpha, no matter how small or trivial you better be prepared to back it up. He was testing the waters and found them too hot. Don't worry he will be fine, that's just how it is. All will be forgotten by the third or fourth beer he asks you to get tonight."

"What?"

"If you think he's not going to take you up on your offer to get him a beer every time you get up, you miscalculated badly," Gary laughed.

"Shit. Fucked by my own mad."

"Afraid so. At least he'll ask nicely," Gary replied, still laughing.

I kept an eye on Philip the whole time we ate; I still had one loose end to try and take care of before I left.

"When are you going home?" Gary asked, breaking my concentration.

"I need to head back tomorrow. I still have a job I have to take care of."

"Where are you sleeping tonight?"

"Wherever someone will let me," I answered, smiling at him.

I pulled back after the kiss and smiled as sweetly as I knew how which lately, especially with him, was pretty fucking sweet.

****

With the meal over and the dishes carried back into the house, the real party began. As Gary predicted, anytime I was up Thomas would loudly ask me to bring him another beer. And the more beers I brought him the louder he would ask the next time. Gary had been right, it turned into fun and games by the third or fourth beer. Gary, Willis, Greta, and I were sitting around the table talking and I informed Greta that I wouldn't be sleeping here tonight, but I would come back out for breakfast with her before I left tomorrow. I could tell that she was split on

277

the issue, but she smiled and told me that would be great.

"I have one more thing I need to take care of for the pack tonight before we leave. Please let me do this my way," I said as I started to get up.

"Why are you so intent on doing it this way?" Gary asked.

"Because you have too much of an association and I have some information that you don't," I answered.

"Be careful," he said as he let go of my hand and let me rise.

I mingled with the pack for a little while until I made my way to where Philip was talking with a few of the others. I listened to the conversation for a bit and watched as most of the people around him drifted to other conversation elsewhere. I lightly touched him on the shoulder, smiling, and moved him further out into the back yard. I took a look at him with my sight to read him. Though the anger was still there, it had lessened. It was the fear I could smell that overshadowed anything else.

"Philip, we need to talk," I said once I had moved him far enough away that even wheir hearing would not pick up our conversation.

"What do we need to talk about," he asked, trying to stay calm.

We had managed to get to the split rail fence and I leaned across it.

"Philip, I do not know why you're so angry and intent on the path you are traveling but personally, after the past couple of months, I don't care. All I know is that I am tired of people trying to kill me and your informing on us to Zahn and Greyson is going to stop."

I could see that I had struck a nerve with at least one of the names I had mentioned.

"The way I see it, you have one of four choices. One; you can close up shop, give a valid reason to your partners, and move far away from here, maybe California, before the next moon. Two; you can go before Gary plead for your life and try and make him see you are going to change and break ties with your current master. Three; run back to Kansas City and hope that your master puts a quick end to you before I get to you. Four; stay here as if nothing is going on and be ripped to shreds. If you choose one of the first two, I'll help you in any way I can, but if I hear of one indiscretion I will find you and kill you, that simple."

"You think you have all the answers, don't you?"

"No, Philip. The only answers I have are the ones I can think of. These are just the ones I have that makes sense for all of us."

"You have no clue what you're up against," Philip said.

"Then explain it to me."

"You personally have never been the target."

"Then who has been?" I asked, remembering my picture on the mercenaries.

"It isn't who, it is what. Any agent holding your district would have been the target. They didn't know who the hell you were before I told them. They don't give a shit about you, just like they don't give a shit about me. If it isn't me that's here, they will find someone else to be here."

"How did you know anything?"

I could see him smile in the darkness.

"It is amazing what people will talk about to their accountant," he said, laughing.

"Who were you getting your information from?" I asked, pushing it.

"That is something that you will never know, Marshal."

I believed him, or at least I believed I would never get any more information from him.

"I didn't choose this," Philip said sadly.

"None of us do. Not even the biological wheirs. I know I didn't," I replied.

"Aren't you furious about it?" he asked.

"Why? What good will it do me? What good has it done you, other than to put you in the position you are now? You have to deal with one day a month. You have a strong pack around you that would have helped. Isn't that enough to be thankful for?"

He stood there looking out over the back field and the tree line behind, not answering me.

"Philip, I have a serious question for you that I would like for you to answer. Will you answer it?"

"Maybe. It depends on the question."

"From the moment you met me you've hated me. Why?"

"Because, part of you smells just like him and in some ways you act just like him."

I was speechless for a second. He had smelled someone like me? Of all the answers he could have given, that was the least expected.

"Who do I smell and act like?" I asked, not sure I wanted the answer.

"Greyson."

Was I related to him? Was he a long lost relative? My God, this was getting weirder by the moment.

"How do I act like him?" I asked.

"You both have a way of getting people to do exactly what you want. And you seem to get what you want regardless of others."

"What did Greyson do to make you hate him so much?"

"He made me this."

"He's a wheir?"

"No, but he has people who work for him that are. In fact, the Alpha you killed was the one that did it at his bidding. All of you are bastards," Philip spat.

I thought I'd been reaching him but now I knew I couldn't. Maybe someone could, but it wouldn't be me.

"So, what choice are you going to make?"

"What, you want an answer this minute?"

"Before I go back to sit with my friends, yes."

"Then I guess you will be waiting a long time to sit down," he said, laughing at me.

"Fine, it is your life," I answered and moved away from him.

"You call this a life?" he asked as I backed away.

"It is the only one you had," I answered and walked back in the direction of the party.

I got back to where Gary was talking to Willis and Greta.

"How did it go?" Gary asked.

"I don't think it went well at all. I'm afraid that you're going to have one hell of a mess on your hands," I said sadly.

"Well... you tried," he said and put his arm around me.

I watched Philip as he started back towards the party and pretty much made a beeline for Mary. I saw the flash of light on metal just before he grabbed her from behind. I flew out from under Gary's arm and over other people's tables before anyone else knew what was going on. I found myself face to face with Philip. He had a knife to Mary's throat. Mary had been able to get one hand around his wrist but she wasn't quite strong enough to do anything other than keep it off of her. It was then I saw the serpentine ridges along the blade of the knife. It was as if someone had just melted the silver and poured it down the blade. It was a split second later I heard Gary charging forward.

"Gary! The knife has silver on it," I shouted to keep him off.

"Marshal. Keep your hands where I can see them," Philip spat at me.

"Okay, they're right here," I said, keeping them out and at waist height.

I felt Gary move behind me. Gary positioned himself so that he was standing just to my right side. I felt him put his hand on my back.

"Gary, stay where you are," Philip yelled.

"Okay, Philip, I am not moving," he said as he raised his right hand.

I could feel him unsnap the strap on my holster and tuck it between the holster and my back. I hoped he would think to switch the safety off before he drew it. I heard the small click of the safety and smiled.

"Philip. What is all of this about?" Gary asked.

I was a bit surprised that Gary only pulled the weapon out part of the way then took his hand away from my back. I glanced over at him with a questioning expression as he moved more to my right and showed his hands to Philip.

"You'll never have any idea what this is about," he said and smiled sadly.

"But, Philip, we can talk about this and work something out," Gary said as he took another couple of steps away from me.

I finally realized what he was doing. As he kept Philip talking, I put both my hands on my hips so my knuckles were against my hip bones.

"Philip, this isn't helping you at all. I gave you choices that would give you a shot at a fresh start," I said, taking the focus off of Gary so he could get a few more paces away from me.

"Philip, this isn't what any of us want. I don't want to see anyone in my family to get hurt. Not even you," Gary said.

I knew that I had one shot and one shot only at this. If I fucked up Mary would have a very slow and nasty death. *Don't focus on the hostage*, I reminded myself. While Gary was talking, I zeroed in on the space just above the ridge of Philip's nose. I knew where my gun was and knew where my arm would end up. I just had to line that up in my mind. Out of the corner of my eye I saw Gary take a small step forward. Philip took the knife and pointed it at Gary.

"Gary, don't take another step you piece of Alpha..."

That was all Philip got out before his head exploded. I watched as he dropped to the ground, letting go of Mary. Mary screamed and ran towards me. I held out my hand and pulled her to me, threw my arms around her, and pulled her into a hug.

"I thought I was dead," Mary sniffled into my shoulder.

"Not on my watch," I said and hugged her closer.

Greta came over and pulled Mary away and made her sit down at the nearest table. I flipped the safety back on and shoved my weapon back in the holster, snapping the strap back in place. I walked over to where Gary, and most of the higher males of the pack, stood around Philips body.

"Are you okay?" Gary asked me.

"Yes. But why did you make me take the shot?" I asked.

"I knew without a rifle I could never have made that shot and not hit Mary. You could."

"So Willis, was it justified?" Gary asked.

"Yes, according to nineteen other witnesses it was all *you* could do Sheriff. By the way, Gary, that has to be one of the best shots I've ever seen you make. Do you want to call the coroner or should I?"

"If you could I would appreciate it. I think I need to talk to Ced for a minute," Gary said as he walked over to me and led me to the back of the yard.

"I can't keep your name totally out of the report, but it will only list your name not your title and only as a witness," he said, looking at me.

I nodded that I understood.

"I'll be back in a minute, okay?" he asked.

I nodded again. He walked away towards the house. I took a few steps toward the back of the yard and the fence. I stood looking out over the back field, deep in thought. I had killed more people in the last three months than I had in my three years in Dallas as a Deputy Marshal. It was beginning to be a habit that I didn't like. I thought I was going to make it through a full moon without someone dying. Wrong. Maybe I should take up smoking; it couldn't be any more deadly for those around me. I felt a hand wrap around my waist.

" Are you okay sweetie?" Greta asked.

"No," I answered honestly.

"What else could you have done?" Greta asked as we both stared out towards the tree line.

"Nothing, I guess. I was just wondering why it came down to me. I've killed a lot of people since I took this fucking job."

I laid my head down on my arms, on top of the fence, and cried. Greta gathered me into her arms, placed my head on her shoulder, and smoothed the back of my hair as I cried myself out. This was becoming a habit with me. *Kill someone; cry, kill someone; cry.*

I saw Gary come back out of the house. He walked over to me pulled my holster and credentials off of my belt and handed them to Craig, who had followed him over. I watched as he walked to a fence post, figure distance and angle, walk away, then fired his own weapon. He walked over to where the bullet entered the post and dug it out gently with his knife. He walked back over to the body, dropped the bullet into the mess that used to be Philip's head, picked up a small stick and flipped the bullet in a straight line out into the grass. He re-holstered his weapon and came back over towards us.

"Ced?" he asked.

I looked up at him with red, swollen eyes.

"Anne," I said.

"What?"

"List my name as Anne McKenzie. Anne is my middle name."

"Okay. We need to go back towards the house," he said as he held out his hand.

I took his hand but still kept Greta's in my other. We walked back to one of the picnic tables and they sat me down next to Mary.

"Mary, you know what happened. Anne kept Philip talking until I could get a shot. Got it?" Gary asked.

Mary and I both nodded our heads. Greta got up and I watched as she and Willis made the rounds of the guests to make sure the stories matched. I heard the sirens off in the distance.

"I'm sorry, Gary. I was trying to keep this out of your hair," I said.

"This is probably the best outcome we could have hoped for. We had twenty witness that saw him take a hostage and that both of us tried to talk him down. It ties up the end fairly easy. Especially for me and Willis."

"Why Willis?"

"Willis is the prosecuting attorney for the county."

"Really? Willis is an attorney?"

Gary nodded his head. I knew Willis had a day job but I would never have pegged him for a lawyer.

It didn't take long for the place to be invaded by two Deputy Sheriffs and a coroner. Pictures were taken of the body and statements were taken from the witnesses. I was relieved when Gary directed the Deputy, who was taking my statement and asking for my address, to go do something else. Gary came over and sat down next to me.

"Can I have a rain check on tonight until next month?" he asked.

"Sure, why?" I asked, not really caring where I slept tonight or if I would sleep.

"I'm going to be gone most of the rest of the night and I have a hunch that you aren't going to be up for anything but some sleep."

"If that. Will I see you before I leave tomorrow?"

"Hopefully, if you don't leave too early."

I pulled him to me and kissed him, then laid my head on his shoulder to cry a bit more.

"Where did my gun get off to?" I asked as I finally pulled myself together some.

"Craig put it in your room. There needed to be no question of who had the gun."

"Okay."

I guess I was still a little shell shocked. I was not being much of a conversationalist.

"I have to go to the office," he said as he kissed me again.

"I'll see you in the morning."

I watched him walk up the back steps and disappear into the house. I sat at the picnic table with my head in my hands.

"Ced?" Greta asked.

I raised my head and looked at her.

"You did what you had to do," she said.

"That's little consolation when someone loses their life."

"Maybe, but it's the reason you are who you are. It is the reason you have nineteen people that would stand next to you and not flinch. You do what you have to do to save those around you. It is the reason you are loved here," she said, touching my face gently.

I smiled sadly at her.

"I'll survive. I always have and I always will. It just saddens me, even Philip."

"Come on sweetie, let's go to bed," she said, getting up.

"I can really stop a party can't I?" I asked as I stood up, noticing that everyone was gone, including Philip's body.

"I can honestly say you knocked em dead," she said, smiling.

"Oh great, We are down to black humor now."

"Looks like it."

I let Greta lead me into the house. While she turned off lights, I went to the bathroom and took a shower. When I got out, the house was dark. I ran naked across the hall to my room, pulled down the covers, and went to bed. It didn't take long for me to start crying again. I felt like I was in pain. I heard the door open and close. The covers lifted on the other side of the bed, I felt the body weigh it down. I smelled the aroma that was Greta and felt her reach out for me and pull me to her as she snuggled into my back. She held me and let me cry.

"Why do I always seem to fuck up the best days?" I asked.

"You didn't hold a knife to someone's throat. He wanted to die, Mary didn't. So both of them got what they hoped for."

"Though I don't begrudge Mary her life, I do begrudge Philip his death because I pulled the trigger and gave him an easy way out at my expense," I said, sniffling.

"You know how much I hate killing but he needed to die," she said and pulled me closer.

I laid there in the dark with Greta's arms around me, as my sobbing became the occasional sniffle. I looked at the clock that Greta had bought and put in the room for me. It read three in the morning. It was as if something snapped inside. I needed to be in my own home and alone. I worked my way free of Greta and rolled over. I gently touched her face to wake her.

"Something wrong?" she asked sleepily.

"I need to turn the light on. Why don't you go back to your bed?" I asked as gently as my scratchy voice would let me.

"I don't want to leave you alone," she answered, waking up some.

"I'm going home."

Greta sat up, wide awake.

"It's late, stay until you are more rested," she pleaded.

"I'm not sleeping, Greta. I don't know if you'll understand this or not but I need to go home, be by myself, and work some things out."

"I'm worried about you. You are not acting like yourself."

I sat up and cupped her face with my hands.

"Greta, you are all the family I have and I love you, but I need to be by myself. I need to work this out and it's not going to be pretty. I won't be able to be nice around Willis or Gary and they wouldn't understand why."

"I can't let you just leave like this."

"Really, Greta, I need to do this," I said as I swiveled around and turned on the bedside lamp.

Greta watched as I got dressed and threw my things in the suitcases. I knew she was hurting for me and at a loss as to how to help me. Once I had my bags packed, I sat back down on the bed with her.

"I want you to know that I would never have made it through the last few months without you. I meant it when I said you are my sister and my family. Right now I need you to let me do this my way. I will be back; I just have to go right now."

"Do you want me to make you some coffee or something to eat to take with you?"

"No, I'll get something on my way home. Would you tell Gary that I am thinking of him and I will call him in a few days to explain?"

Greta nodded her head, tears of her own starting to form.

"I love you, Greta," I said as I kissed her, picked up my bags, and headed out the door.

I threw everything in the back of Bee, cranked the engine over, moved her out on the road and stepped down on the accelerator and headed south.

Chapter 32
Tuesday, July 11, 2248

Bran had been right. When the wall crumbled, it fell hard. I spent the rest of the weekend in bed with Mister Scotch-and-Water to drown my guilt, and a roll of toilet paper for the tears. I woke up Monday and realized I had some unfinished business and took the first train out I could get. I think I stared at the scenery and nothing else the entire trip between Little Rock and Lexington Kentucky.

****

I stepped off of the train early Tuesday morning and grabbed a cab to take me down to the little town of Keene just southwest of Lexington. I stopped at a small flower shop and picked up a single rose to take to the local cemetery.

The cabbie pulled up to the entrance of the graveyard and rolled slowly through until I found what I had been looking for. I got out, asked him to wait, and walked out among the graves. A few rows back was one of the plain rounded headstones that denotes a military grave. There were still a few bare spots where the grass seed had not yet taken over the grave. I went up to it and placed my rose on top of the headstone. I looked down at the epitaph that was written.

Major William A. Strathmore
US Army retired.
c. 2170 – June 29 2248
Loving Father and Husband.
He shall be missed.

"Major, I'm sorry," was all I could say.

****

I smelled her before she spoke.

"Were you a friend of my husband?" the voice asked from behind me.

I turned to see a very pretty woman with blue eyes and dark hair. She was probably in her late eighties.

"I met him once and he made an impression on me. I didn't get a chance to come to the funeral, but I wanted to pay my respects. I'm very sorry for your loss."

"You don't seem military. Where did you two meet?" she asked, coming up beside me.

"I am a U.S. Marshal. I was working a case and had the opportunity to spend an hour or so with him not long ago. He struck me as someone I would have been proud to have on my side."

"Thank you for your thoughts and the flower," she said as she bent down to put her own bouquet at the base of the stone.

"Missus Strathmore, I truly am sorry for your loss. I wish I had some magic word or action that could help you in some way."

"It is enough that his friends have called and come by."

"I must get back to the train station in Lexington; I wish you a long and comfortable life," I said as turned to go.

"What's your name?"

"Marshal Cedwynne McKenzie."

"Thank you again, Marshal."

I smiled at her and went back to the cab that was waiting to take me to the station. I could have gone my whole life without seeing; much less talking to, the wife of the man I had killed. Though talking to her didn't do my emotional state any good, I had made my peace with what had happened that night. I still had guilt and I was still sad when I thought about those three men, and even Philip, but I knew now that even though they died by my hand, I did not kill them. One promise I made, quietly, to Missus Strathmore was that the people responsible for all of their deaths would pay a price before I died.

I picked up some coffee in the dining car and headed back to my own berth. I perused the papers at the small table near the door of my own car. The closest thing to my area was this past Sunday's paper out of Kansas City. I picked it up and carried it back to my little room. I sat down, placed my coffee on the small table near the window, found the front page of the paper, and began reading to pass the time.

The paper was incomplete, someone had stolen the funnies, but there was enough of it there to at least keep me occupied for a while. I found it on the second page in a section called the State Round-up.

Joplin - A failed robbery attempt at a George's Coffee shop on Kerry Avenue, Friday, July 7, cost the life of one patron in the establishment. A Mr. Terrence Zahn lost his life when he tried to intercede in the robbery. One suspect has been arrested but State and local police are still searching for his accomplice. A spokesman for the company said that they sent their heart felt sympathies out to the family of Mr. Zahn and have offered a reward of five thousand Credits for the capture of the second assailant. Funeral is set for Saturday, July 12, at 1:00 P.M. At Ceder Creek Cemetery in Wheeling West Virginia.

Zahn was dead? That simplified some things, but it also started another scary thought. Had Zahn gotten in the way of a stray bullet or just gotten in the way? If

Greyson had Zahn killed, that meant he had larger fish protecting him, which would mean his benefactor was pretty high up or at least well connected. I was back to the question of who could I trust?

I continued to read the paper, after I cut out the article about the robbery, and had saved my least favorite section for last–The Business Section. I should have read it sooner; a small article at the bottom of the page was of real interest.

Kansas City – Saturday, July 8, George Greyson owner of the George's Coffee and Backwoods Restaurant chains, released a statement that his company would be moving its home offices to Omaha, Nebraska at the beginning of next year. Their statement indicated that Mr. Greyson wanted to expand further into the upper Midwest and that since his business interests were well established in Missouri and Illinois he wanted to be closer to the newer stores to make them as strong and successful as his present ones were. Continued on 5-D.

I flipped to the continued article and finished reading, though it really gave me no more in-depth information. I cut out that article and placed it on the seat beside me with the one about Zahn. I looked out the window as the scenery sped by. Maybe Zahn had been right and I had won this round. God, I hoped so. I could use a break from this.

****

I looked at the decaying skyline of the Dead Zone of Memphis as the train passed the northern edge of it and crossed the river into Arkansas. As we were heading to West Memphis and the station where I would have to switch trains to the one heading to Little Rock, I could see the skeleton of the old sports arena called the Pyramid. I had been told that when it was built it was covered in black mirrored glass; I could just imagine what it had looked like. Now it sat, a rusted, overgrown, metal outline of its former grandeur in the hot summer sun.

I switched trains and got comfortable in my little berth as the train pulled out of the station heading for Little Rock and ultimately, home. I watched the delta slide by as I thought about what I wanted to do next. I remembered Mother Goose's advice about taking some time to get to know my District and the people in it. I think it was time I grew up a little and started taking some of the advice I'd gotten. So as long as a snake didn't rear its ugly head and try and bite me, I was going to do exactly as she had suggested.

I'd basically had both of my phones off for over a week now. I knew that I should probably get back to the land of the living and call the people who were probably worried about me. I turned both phones on and waited for them to find towers. I had numerous missed calls from both Greta and Gary on my personal phone and three missed calls on my official one. I scrolled through the numbers on my official phone. Two calls from Burdock and one from Director Perry. Greta and Gary would have to wait a few minutes. I hit the pre-programed number on my phone, waited for the beeps, and hit the key that sent my control number.

"Director Perry," the voice said.

"This is Marshal McKenzie. I saw that I had missed your call and was returning it."

"Do you not answer your phone?"

"Sorry, sir. I needed a few days to decompress. It's been an eventful few months for me."

"Which brings me to why I was trying to reach you."

"What would that be sir?"

"I need you in Washington City on the third of August."

"Really? Why, if I may ask?"

"We feel a debriefing would benefit everyone. Especially after the death of an agent on your northern border, your run in with IBI, and closing your first case so quickly after your appointment," he answered.

He said *we*. There were only three people that could constitute that "We". I remembered all the times I'd been called into Burdock's office. I always felt like I was going to see the Principal. I guess I would have to reevaluate that. Burdock had been the Vice-Principal. I would be seeing the real Principal now.

"What about my cases?"

"They will wait. This is not a request, Marshal."

"Yes, sir."

"Call me and tell me how you are getting here and I will meet you when you arrive."

"Yes, sir. I will make my arrangements when I get home today."

"Good. I expect to hear from you by tomorrow afternoon."

"Yes, sir. Anything else?"

"No. I think that about does it."

"I'll talk to you tomorrow."

"Good day, Marshal," he said and hung up.

I had a funny feeling that there was more to it than a simple debriefing, but I had no one I could call to get more information.

****

I spent the rest of my trip to Little Rock making the three other calls I had to return. Out of all three of the calls, only the one to the female of the group garnered me an inquiry as to how I was doing. The two men were just upset that I hadn't called them. For Gary, I soothed his ruffled feathers. For Burdock, I apologized for not keeping in touch and not letting a friend know how I was doing. But I also pointed out that I had a job that was way out of his purview and that he was my liaison not my boss.

I thought of one other call I needed to make after I got on the commuter train from Little Rock to Hot Springs. I opened my phone and punched in the number.

"Hello," the female voice answered.

"Mother Goose, Chicken Little," I said.

Though I didn't know the woman on the other end of the line, she had given me good advice and information.

"Hello, Miss Little. You seemed to have been a busy little girl."

"How so?"

"Closing a case, taking IBI down, and all within three months. Do you ever sit still?" she asked, laughing.

"I was going to; starting today, but I have a question."

"What's your question?"

"I've been called to Washington City for what they are calling a debriefing. Is that normal?"

"It isn't unheard of with new agents. In a way it doesn't surprise me with the death of an agent in a bordering district."

"Okay. Thanks. I needed an answer I thought I could trust."

"I wouldn't worry too much about it. Enjoy the break and the trip to the Capital. I hear they're making wonderful progress with the buildings and landmarks there."

"Thanks again. Have a good day."

"You too, Miss Little."

Chapter 33
Thursday August 3, 2248

Who and what was I? What had my life become? Those questions repeated themselves, over and over, as I packed for my trip to Washington City.

To add the topping on the cake, the full moon was only a couple of days away; I was right in the middle of my new Brobdingnagian PMS from hell. To punctuate everything, I'd run out of the herb mixture Bran had given me for my normal cramps. To say that I was in a bit of a grumpy mood would be a small–okay, not so small–understatement. Luckily, Bran was going to meet me at the station with a new supply before my trip.

August fifth would be the third moon since my bite. I was hoping this debriefing would be over in time for me to get down to Cassville to be with the pack. Though I hadn't morphed, I found it helpful to be around Greta, Gary, and the pack at that time, especially for the sex with Gary after. Though Gary and I had only started being intimate after the last moon, I had made a few trips up to just see him. Our sexual encounters were quite the strenuous exercise and very fulfilling.

The last time, we'd rented a room in Springdale and had to pay a fairly stiff fee for the lamps and tables that got broken in our reverie. Yep, I needed to be in Cassville in a couple of days. If this went longer than that it would mean; I would have to face this alone for the first time and I wasn't thrilled about that scenario.

I picked up my suitcases and headed out to the car to load them, then ran back inside to grab my purse and lock the house up. I sat down behind the wheel, stuck the key in the ignition, and tossed my purse in the passenger seat. Another change over the past four months: Never before in my life would I have been caught dead wearing form fitting clothing and carrying a purse. Now, much to my practical chagrin, I dressed, more than occasionally, in tight shirts and pants and always had my purse, usually including lipstick. Yes, my life had gone downhill quickly.

****

I pulled into the parking lot of the train station and got out. I saw Bran approaching me with a smile on his face and the large, square, brown jar complete with cork stopper that contained the remedy for my cramps. He came over to me as I was getting my bags out.

"To make sure we do not have a government overthrow," he said, smiling and handing me the jar.

"If I wasn't so grateful, I would come back with some pithy retort," I said, taking the jar and putting it in one of my suitcases.

The Water's Edge

"So, why are you going to Washington City so close to the moon?"

"I got called in for a debriefing and I couldn't really say no."

"Well, make sure they don't pull your panties down too far," he said, smiling.

"Really? You went there? I am sorely disappointed in you, that would've been something I would have said," I picked at him, smiling.

"You have been a bad influence on me," he replied, grabbing my largest suitcase.

"Shall we?" he asked as he gestured to the steps of the station.

I took off in the direction of the lobby to get my ticket and wait for my train. I checked my bags with the platform porter and said Good-bye to Bran since he needed to get back to his job at the State Park. I waited until my train number was called and went to find my private berth. I produced my ticket and the conductor showed me to my cabin.

I felt the train jerk as it started out of the station. I'd taken the early train out of Hot Springs even though it was a commuter to Fort Smith and would be stopping a lot. Once I switched trains in Fort Smith I would be on an express to Washington City, only stopping in Fayetteville and Joplin. I should get to Washington City by about five thirty or six this evening. Once the train had reached its top speed, I found the dining car for some hot water to mix my herbs in and make my tea. I also grabbed a couple of egg sandwiches to tide me over until lunch and returned to my cabin.

I switched trains in Fort Smith and got comfortable for the rest of my journey. I found it odd that I had lived my whole life in this area of the country and never made it to visit Washington City.

When the U.S. was reformed in 2192, the leading Unions insisted that the capitol be moved to a more central location and a spot was picked, just south of Kansas City, to become the nation's new capital. A square, roughly seven and a half miles by seven and a half miles, was set aside on the Kansas-Missouri border for the city, including what used to be called La Cygne Lake, in Kansas. The lake had been renamed to Jefferson Lake when the City was founded.

After the reformation of the nation, the Dead Zone of Washington D. C. was the first to start being reclaimed. It had taken almost twenty years to dismantle the White House, the Capitol building and the Washington monument, move them to Washington City and reassemble them. It was still an on-going process as the government continued to move all of the monuments and national buildings. It was decided that all of the historic buildings and monuments that could be saved would be moved and the rest would be razed and allowed to revert back to wilderness.

Two of the most notable attractions in the old capital, Arlington National Cemetery and The Smithsonian Institution, would be left and restored to their old grandeur. The cost alone of moving all the graves in a national cemetery helped make the decision of leaving it.

The decision on the Smithsonian, however, came later in the process. As the work of the new reclamation companies continued over the years, new businesses and small towns started to pop up in support of the reclamation companies. Hotels, restaurants, and new citizens started moving to an area that had been one of the hardest hit by The Fall. It was at that time the government decided to renovate and leave The Smithsonian as a tourist destination to help the local economy after the reclamation companies finished their work in the area.

One of the major reasons that the reclamation of a dead zone was such a time consuming task was the lessons the nation had learned about recycling over the past one hundred and fifty years. Everything that could be recycled, would be. Though it was estimated it would take another thirty years to reclaim the old capital, the newspaper reports and pictures of the process showed the great strides already made. With over six hundred major and minor dead zones in the country, most economists believed that the future base of our economy, over the next two hundred years, would be in the hands of the reclamation companies.

To head off the problems that the original capital had encountered with its population, no permanent residents were allowed to live in Washington City proper. Only elected officials, their families, and household help were allowed to reside within the city limits of the capital. *Allowed to reside inside Washington City* might be the wrong term; all elected officials were required to reside within the city limits for the duration of their term.

The police force for the city was made up of a mixture of the military police from all of the branches of service who served a normal four year assignment. It fell to the director of the U.S. Marshal Service to be responsible for the police force of the city. Inside the city there were five precincts, each commanded by an appointed commander from one of each of the branches of service. This allowed for the continued protection of the Commander in Chief by the soldiers he commanded, yet kept the U.S. Marshal Service the law enforcement arm of the nation.

As a self-proclaimed student of political history and law, I'd always been amazed that the government under the old constitution ever got anything accomplished. With all the problems that still existed in our country, thankfully, professional politicians weren't among them anymore. Now every elected official to a national office had term limits. Representatives were limited to one eight year term, Senators to twelve years, and the President and Vice-president to a ten year term each. Even the Supreme Court, though appointed, had term limits of thirty years for each Justice.

Though a politician was not something I aspired to, I always thought First Citizen would be an interesting job to have. The First Citizens were elected to staggered, six year terms but did not vote on laws, or on domestic or international policy. They were the citizens' representatives in Washington City as a reminder to the other elected officials that they worked for the population as a whole.

Just as any company had an owner that set the hours of operation and deadlines, the government had this tribunal to do the same. Their jobs were strictly defined. They were responsible for setting the hours the government would be in session, setting deadlines for votes on bills, and laws once they reached the floor of the House or Senate and doing yearly, publicly published, reviews on all elected officials, including the President. Those yearly reviews were not on how a Congressman or Justice might vote, but that they were at their post when they should be and voting. The First Citizens could not remove an elected official from office. They could, however, force a vote of no confidence in a special election for any elected official other than the President. Though they did a review on the President, impeachment was still in the hands of congress.

As we gained speed out of the depot in Fayetteville, my stomach started telling me I hadn't had anything to eat since the herb tea, two egg sandwiches, and three cups of coffee on the train from Hot Springs. I picked up my purse and went looking for the dining car, locking the cabin door on my way out. I got the normal looks from the male population as I found a seat and picked up the menu that had been preset on the table. I ordered a large rare steak and a beer and looked into the early afternoon that lit the world outside. By the time we had reached Joplin I had finished my meal and most of my second beer. I ordered a third and just sat as I waited for the train to leave the station. As the train began to move I felt a little sad that I had left Joplin and not taken Gary up on his offer for an afternoon delight as I passed through.

****

I collected all of my things as the train slowed and entered the station in Washington City. A porter came to my door, as the train stopped, to collect my luggage and move it to the platform. I followed him out into the lessening heat of the evening and onto the brightly lit deck. I was just transferring my bags to a small public flat car when I was approached by Director Perry, another man in a suit and tie, and a member of the Washington City police force. The cop was a tall, probably around six feet, African American woman that was about my age. I could tell that she was all human and in very good shape.

I had probably met Director Perry a grand total of about three times: Once when I took my oath office, and then at a couple of the Marshal's Ball and Awards Banquets over the past five years. None of those meetings amounted to more than a handshake of congratulations or a hello. Even after my appointment our interaction had been confined to a few phone conversations and all of those were business related.

"Marshal McKenzie?" Director Perry asked, a bit unsure.

"Yes, sir."

He stood looking at me for a few seconds like he was trying to put something together in his own mind.

"Is there something wrong sir?" I asked.

"Ah... No, Marshal. I was trying to marry what I know about you with the person I am meeting."

"Did I forget to put on matching shoes today?" I asked, smiling.

"Not at all, it's just... I was expecting someone a bit different." he said, matching my smile.

"I have my credentials if you need to verify them."

"No, Marshal, it isn't that. All we have on file is the photo from your credentials. After reading your stats I thought some mistake had been made where your height was concerned. I was expecting you to be a little taller and bigger, quite frankly."

"Sorry to disappoint."

"No disappointment, just a bit of a curve."

"I guess I'll take that as some sort of compliment."

"I hope you will since I butchered it anyway," he said, laughing.

"Marshal, this is Deputy Marshal Davis, my aid and driver; and Lieutenant Suzanne Grimes, Washington City Police Department," he said, introducing the two with him.

"Pleased to meet both of you," I replied, shaking both of their hands in turn.

"Lieutenant Grimes will be your driver and companion for the next couple of days."

"Do I really need a bodyguard?"

"Not as such, but she'll get you from one place to the next without you having to be worried about finding your way around."

I wanted to ask him where she'd been when they dropped me in the middle of nowhere with a monstrosity of a vehicle, and I had to find my way to my new home by the registration in my new car.

"Also, I need your weapon," he said, holding out his hand.

"Am I under arrest?" I asked feeling, now, that this was not a plain debriefing.

"No."

"Am I being relieved of duty or put on administrative leave for some reason?"

"No."

"Then, with all due respect, I will not relinquish my weapon."

"I beg your pardon?" he asked, rather forcefully.

"Section two, paragraph seven of the rules and regulations governing the United States Marshal Service and the Marshals on active duty: Under no circumstances shall a fully empowered Marshal of the United States relinquish their weapon for any reason except those listed below. One: being in the White House or Capitol building of the United States of America, and only then when asked to do so by a ranking member of the Secret Service. Two: in any Federal Court when asked to do so by the Judge presiding over that particular court. Three: when placed under arrest but not until the Marshal's full rights are spelled out under the Constitution of the United States and Directive One. Four: when put on administrative leave, relieved of duty, or terminated from the Marshal Service, and then only to their direct supervisor. Five: when in situations where the Marshal feels the loss of life would be greater than acceptable and the only foreseeable way to avoid said loss of life is to put down their side arm.

Section one, paragraph five, of the same rules and regulation: A Marshal is to keep their weapon within reach at all times on or off duty for the duration of their appointment unless the requirements of Section two, paragraph seven, prevents them from complying with this order.

In no way do I mean any disrespect, but unless you can point out to me that there will be a larger than acceptable loss of life, I see nothing in those rules and regulations that will allow me to comply with your directive."

I stood waiting for the barrage. What I got was a laugh.

"Davis, pay close attention to what just happened. Welcome to Washington City, Marshal McKenzie," he said, extending his hand and smiling.

"So, we're testing my knowledge of the rules and regulations?" I asked, taking his hand and smiling back.

"Not really. Marshal Davis needed an object lesson and after reading your yearly reviews by Marshal Burdock, I thought you might be the perfect person to give it to him."

"I see my reputation precedes me."

"You have no idea, Marshal. Shall we get you to your quarters?"

"That would be great but, not to seem rude, is dinner included anywhere in here?"

"Your staff will prepare you something when we get there."

"I have a staff?" I asked, a little shocked.

"Not a big one. You have the Lieutenant here and you will have a cook and housekeeper at your billet."

I reached down to pick up my luggage but they were quickly taken from me by Marshal Davis. Director Perry led us through the lobby of the station and outside where a long black car with dark windows waited for us. Lieutenant Grimes opened one of the back doors and Director Perry waited by it for me to get in. I got in the door, sat down, and slid across the seat so he could enter. I felt the trunk close after Marshal Davis stowed my luggage. The other two entered the front, with Davis driving. He started the car and pulled out into traffic. Once we were rolling, Director Perry hit a button and a dark glass window rolled up separating the front seat from the back compartment.

"Marshal, I want to apologize now for the next couple of days," he said, breaking the silence.

"What's going to happen?" I asked, feeling my apprehension rise.

"In Counter Section any one of an agent's three supervisors can call an agent in for debriefing on any excuse. Neither the President nor I called this debriefing." He said letting me do the math.

"Director Pinter must be exceptionally pissed at me," I said, looking out the window.

"That would be an understatement."

"So, basically this is a witch hunt."

"I have no idea. He didn't give me much; other than the reasons you and I spoke about earlier."

"I'm not buying it."

I thought about the timing of it and something Agent Wallace had said to me when I was arresting him: *Do you know the political turmoil you are about to create? Your ass won't last through this either if I have my information right.* Pinter was going to try and pin me up with a full moon. Fine, then he would get to deal with my PMS.

"How long is this supposed to take?"

"He said he wanted you here for a couple of sessions. You should be out of here no later than Sunday."

"That son of a bitch," I said under my breath.

"What?"

"Nothing, sir."

"I don't think you realize how much dirt you stirred up. Director Pinter is on very thin ice right now."

"Nothing personal, sir, but he should be."

"Can't argue that point, but he's going to do everything within his power to take down anyone he thinks is a threat to him or his position."

"Director, I hope you won't be disappointed in me if I defend myself with everything I have."

"I would expect nothing less from a trained Marshal."

I felt the car pull to a stop. Even though the glass between the compartments was thick, I could hear Marshal Davis being asked for his credentials and his business in the neighborhood. After few moments the car continued on with a few turns, went slowly over a bump, and came to another stop.

"I hope that your accommodations will be acceptable. All we had open was one of the smaller houses."

"I'm sure it will be fine as long as it has a bathroom, kitchen, and a bedroom," I said.

"And a coffee pot." I added quickly

"I'm sure it will meet those requirements," he replied, smiling.

A few seconds later my door opened and Lieutenant Grimes offered me a hand out. I took it, got out of the car, and stood looking at a fairly large two story house in a neighborhood of large two story houses.

"I would hate to see the large ones," I said to Director Perry as he came around to my side of the car.

He smiled and gestured towards the front door with his hand. I walked up to the door and Lieutenant Grimes rushed in front of me to open it. I walked in and was met in the fairly large foyer by a tall slender woman in a uniform dress.

"Marshal McKenzie, this is Bella Clark. She is the housekeeping staff and cook for your visit." Lieutenant Grimes introduced the woman who was around forty.

"Marshal McKenzie," Bella said, stiffly nodding her head in my direction.

"Where can I put these?" Marshal Davis asked, indicating the suitcases he held.

"Follow me," Bella said as she moved towards the staircase with Marshal Davis following.

"I hope that you'll find everything you need. If not, the Lieutenant will be more than happy to procure it for you," Director Perry said.

"Thank you, sir."

"Lieutenant Grimes has your itinerary for tomorrow. I will see you at the meeting," he said, extending his hand as Marshal Davis came back down the stairs.

"I should be just fine," I said, as Director Perry went to the door.

"Have a good evening," he said as both he and his driver left.

"Marshal. If you would care to freshen up, I will start dinner. Is there anything in particular you would like?" Bella asked as she stood stiffly at the bottom of the stairs.

"For starters, unless there are other people here and you feel the need to keep up formalities, my name is Cedwynne, not Ma'am, Marshal, or any version of that, and I will address you as you wish to be addressed. I absolutely hate to eat alone so if I sit down to eat I expect the same out of both of you. If I sit to read the paper or a book, I don't expect either of you to stand at attention to wait on me hand and foot. I work for a living the same as you. As for dinner I would like a steak—very rare, baked potato, a vegetable, and a salad if that is in the house. If not, then whatever you feel like cooking is fine with me," I started.

"But, ma'am...." Bella started to say.

I gave her a hard look.

"Ah...ma... Miss Cedwynne, we are not allowed to eat with the visiting dignitaries."

"May I address you as Bella, or is there something else you would prefer to be called?"

"No, Miss Cedwynne, I prefer Bella," she answered.

"Fine. Bella, I am not a visiting dignitary. I am a U.S. Marshal and I usually fix my own soup. I am not at a restaurant and for the next few days this is my home. I don't want, and can't stand, the servant thing. Nothing that is said or done in this house over the next few days will be scrutinized by anyone but me. Do we have an understanding?"

"Yes, Miss Cedwynne," she said, though she did not smile.

I just shook my head and turned to Lieutenant Grimes.

"And how do you prefer to be addressed?"

"Suzanne will be fine."

"Great. Now was that so hard?" I asked the room.

I got no response.

"I can see I have a lot of work to do. Where can I freshen up?"

"I can show you your room," Suzanne said.

"Thank you," I said as I followed her up the stairs.

Bella fell in behind us and followed up to a door that Suzanne opened and let me enter. I was given the master suite which, to my shock, was as big as all three of my bedrooms at home, and the bath was as big as my own master bedroom. Bella opened my suitcases and started putting my clothes away.

"Really, Bella, you don't have to do that."

"You have your job, I have mine," she answered giving me a little bit of a smile.

"May I ask a question?" Suzanne asked.

"Sure."

"You seem very young to be a full Marshal. What district are you over?"

"I'm not in charge of a normal district; I'm on special assignment and one of the perks was a promotion," I answered.

Suzanne gave me a real once over as she stood there looking at me.

"Do you have any special dietary needs, Miss Cedwynne?" Bella asked, changing the subject.

"Other than having a high metabolism and needing to eat often, no."

"Are there any particular foods you would like me to stock for your stay?"

"I eat a high protein diet. Eggs, bacon, sausage, ham, steaks, salads and potatoes are my foods of choice when I have to cook for myself. I like my eggs over very easy, with very runny yokes, and there is never a wrong time of day to have coffee. If you find you'd like to cook something special or have a favorite dish you prepare, I am always open to new foods."

"Thank you. I will go start dinner," Bella said and started to leave.

"Thank you, Bella."

"I'm going to have to get her to loosen up some," I said more to myself, after she left.

"Don't blame her. The service staff in the city goes through an exhaustive background check and extensive training," Suzanne offered up.

"I guess I've been in the field too long."

"I can't believe that you disregarded a direct order from your supervisor."

"He knew I couldn't comply with the order when he gave it. I don't know what object lesson Marshal Davis needed, but I know what my duties are and even if the President asked me, I could not have complied."

"In the Army that's a court martial offense."

"Good thing I am not in the Army," I said, chuckling.

"Yes, probably a good thing," she agreed smiling.

"Well, I'm going to take a shower and get into something a lot more comfortable so if you would like an opportunity to change out of your uniform, now would be the time."

"Will we be going anywhere else this evening?"

"Not unless we just have to, no."

"Then I'll leave you to your shower," she said as she left the room, shutting the door behind her.

****

I emerged out of my bedroom and started towards the stairs. I had gone for home comfort with flannel pajama bottoms, baggy sweatshirt and my pink, fuzzy slippers. I had just reached the top step when Suzanne emerged from her bedroom and was at my side before I could start down.

"Really? Are you going to go to the bathroom with me also?" I asked sarcastically.

"If I have to; yes. You are my responsibility while you are here and I take my responsibilities seriously."

I started chuckling as I started down the stairs.

"What do you find funny about that?" Suzanne asked, hurt.

"I find nothing funny about that. What I find funny would be the reaction of some of the other Marshals I used to work with if they found out I had a bodyguard, especially around my time of the month. It would amuse them for months on end."

"Oh," Suzanne replied, placated.

"Where is the kitchen in this place?"

"Just off of the living and dining rooms."

I guess I should have known this place had a dining room. I reached the bottom of the stairs, turned to my left and I was in the dining room. There was only one place setting on the table.

"Does this place have a table in the kitchen area?" I asked.

"Yes."

I went to the dishes on the table, piled them all together, and headed for the door that I guessed to be the kitchen. Bella was shocked as I entered the large kitchen and sat at the table in the breakfast nook next to a bay window.

"But, Miss Cedwynne..." Bella started.

"I told you two; I don't wish to eat alone. If you refuse to sit down to a meal with me, I'll eat in here so I can have some company," I said as I started to replace the dishes and silverware on the table in front of me.

"This isn't right, Miss Cedwynne," Bella said.

"You know, Bella–I visited Right once but they wouldn't let me stay. Which was fine with me since I didn't like it there anyway," I said, putting the last touches on my place setting, which in itself was laughable since I wasn't sure which fork went where.

"Bella, I think you are going to lose this argument," Suzanne chimed in, came over to the table, and sat down.

"But I could lose my job."

"Trust me Bella, you won't lose your job. Now finish what you're doing and make sure there's enough for all three of us," I said.

"Yes, Miss Cedwynne." Bella said, defeated.

I got up from the table and went to the refrigerator to see if there was any beer. I'd just reached for the door when Bella turned.

"Miss Cedwynne! You may make me sit and eat with you, you may engage me in conversation, and totally disrupt the way a house is supposed to run. But, you will not come in my kitchen," she said, looking straight at me holding the large knife she was using to cut up vegetables.

Though in a fight I could probably take her easily, I'd learned a hard lesson about women and their kitchens from Greta. Don't fuck with them or you just might get fucked up. I backed slowly out of the kitchen area, with Bella keeping the point of the knife aimed at me from across the room. When I had sat back down, Bella came around the end of the counter, plastered a smile on her face, and spoke.

"Was there something I could get for you Miss Cedwynne?" she asked sweetly.

"I was just wondering if there happened to be any beer in the fridge."

"Regular lager or dark ale?"

"Regular, please."

In just a few seconds a bottle and chilled glass were set before me. Bella went back to the kitchen and I started pouring my beer. Suzanne sat in her chair, quietly laughing.

"What are you laughing at?"

"The big bad Marshal that isn't even afraid of the director of the Marshal Service gets kicked out of the kitchen by the cook. I can just read the headline in the paper," she answered, grinning.

"Just for that we're going for a midnight run."

"Bring it on," she said, calling the bluff.

I took a swig of my beer and scowled at her until the food arrived. I had two dinner companions, though one of them was uncomfortable throughout the entire meal. With the meal over and Bella not allowing me to help clean up, I ordered some coffee and moved to the living room.

The living room here had to be at least two and a half times bigger than my own. It had a couch, loveseat, two chairs, full book shelves, a fire place, and a television. I plopped down on the loveseat with the novel I was reading and Bella brought in a tray with a coffee service on it. She put the tray down on the coffee table in front of me.

"For future reference I take my coffee black so, unless the two of you take cream or sugar with yours, I don't need the accoutrements," I said to Bella.

Bella poured me a mug and handed it to me. I began to take a sip. It became hard for me to read when I noticed that both Suzanne and Bella were standing watching me.

"This won't do!" I exclaimed.

"Something wrong with the coffee, Miss Cedwynne?" Bella asked.

"No, it isn't that. If the two of you are going to insist on following me and waiting on me, you will sit down with me. Otherwise, go to bed because you are wasting your time standing there," I said.

Both Bella and Suzanne sat down stiffly.

"I am going to have to get the two of you to let your hair down. Please, have some coffee and kick your shoes off," I laughed.

Suzanne took me up on the offer of coffee but Bella remained seated.

"No coffee for you, Bella?"

"No, thank you. A little too late in the evening for me."

"I respect that," I said as I took another sip.

"So, what is the schedule for tomorrow?" I asked Suzanne.

"You have a meeting at ten thirty. I don't know how long that will last, but as far as I know there's nothing planned for the afternoon or evening."

"Okay, thanks," I replied and tried to go back to my novel.

After a few minutes of being conscious of the scrutiny I was receiving, I closed the book and looked at my two companions.

"Bella, do you have anything else to do this evening other than wait on me?"

"Other than turning down your bed, no Miss Cedwynne."

"Then go turn down my bed and do what you want to do the rest of the evening. I'm only going to be drinking coffee and reading," I said.

"But the coffee is in the kitchen," Bella responded, as if I was incapable of getting it myself.

"Bella, if you will allow me in the kitchen to get my own coffee, I promise that I will only refill my cup. When I get ready to go to bed I will rinse out my cup, leave it in the sink, and turn off the pot. Can we do that?"

"As long as if you need something you ring my room."

"I promise I will ring your room if I need anything other than a cup of coffee."

"As you wish. What time would you like breakfast tomorrow morning?" she asked as she stood.

"Around eight would be nice. I'll need some hot water for a tea I brought, if you don't mind."

"Yes, Miss Cedwynne," she said as she left the room taking the milk and sugar from the coffee service back towards the kitchen.

I saw her, a few minutes later, crossing to the staircase and heading up.

"I would have to kill myself if I lived here all the time."

"She's just doing her job."

"I know but, geez, the woman needs to laugh a little. Are you much of a reader?"

"I kill a book now and again."

"Well there are shelves of them over there. You're doing your duty by sticking by my side but there's no reason you can't enjoy your time sitting," I said, pointing to the two bookcases on the wall.

Suzanne shrugged her shoulders, got up, went to the cases, found a title, and returned to her seat.

Other than the occasional run to the kitchen for coffee, my evening was spent very quietly. I finally had enough of my day and stood up. With Suzanne basically glued to my side, I put my cup in the sink, turned off the coffee pot, and headed up to my room.

Chapter 34
Friday August 4, 2248

It took all the will power I had to get out of the bed. Thankfully, my full moon cramps and fever were much less painful than last month. However, they were still starting to build towards tomorrow, compounded by my normal cramps since I hadn't had any tea this morning. I took a shower, got dressed for the day, and went downstairs to find some hot water and breakfast, in that order.

****

Suzanne drove us through the streets of Washington City as I sat and let the trepidation and wheir cramps build as we neared our destination. She pulled around an unassuming three story building, down the ramp, to an underground garage. I followed her through the parked cars to an elevator that took us up to the third floor. She led me down a couple of hallways to a room that had the definite look of a small court room. There were a couple of pew type benches behind a small knee wall and a raised desk opposite. A table had been set up in front of the knee wall, facing the desk and a longer table had been set up on the floor in front of the desk, facing the gallery. At the long table there were three chairs and one of the newer speaker type phones in the middle. Suzanne pointed to the small table facing the desk. I went through the little doors in the short wall and took a seat behind it. Suzanne took a seat directly behind me, behind the knee wall. Director Perry and Deputy Marshal Davis entered from the same doors I had. Director Perry said good morning to me and took a seat to my right at the table facing me. Davis sat in a seat behind him. A short time later Director Pinter entered through the same door followed by his own assistant. I didn't know Director Pinter personally, other than from phone conversations, but I'd seen his picture numerous times. He reminded me a lot of Agent Wallace though he'd taken a bit better care of himself so his stomach didn't stick too far over his belt. He walked to the table facing me, sat his briefcase down, and sat at the chair on the other end from Director Perry, leaving the center seat open. A few moments later the door in the back of the room that I figured led to the judge's chambers, opened. All four of the men in front of me stood. I did nothing until Suzanne leaned forward and told me I needed to stand.

Great, I have a judge and no representation, I thought as I stood. I'd seen pictures of the man that entered in every federal building and post office in the country; President Bradley, himself. He was followed by a very muscular, tall, and dark Secret Service agent. The President nodded his head at everyone and motioned us to take our seats. It was then I caught a whiff of him and had to open up my sight on the room. It seemed everyone in the room was human but me and the fucking President of the United States. I had no clue what he was. He wasn't wheir and he wasn't like Bran. I'd never smelled this smell before. It was like honeysuckle in the forest after a summer rain. His aura was also something I'd never seen before–it was shiny silver and gold; it had the silver base but a very pronounced gold corona. From the look on his face he must have been as confused and surprised as I was.

"Do you two know each other, Mister President?" Director Perry asked, indicating me.

"No. She just reminds me of a friend of my daughter's," he answered, taking his seat.

Everyone in the room followed the President's lead and sat.

"Well then, straight to business. Director Pinter, this is your meeting please begin," the President directed.

"Thank you, sir. By regulations Agent McKenzie is allowed a witness for these proceedings. Agent, do you have someone that you would prefer to be here for this?"

I looked at everyone in the room.

"Lieutenant Grimes will be suitable for my witness."

"Lieutenant, what is your clearance level?"

"Three, lowercase 'a', one, one," Suzanne said from behind me.

I saw a moment of indecision on Pinter's face. The President said something in the ear of Pinter and then Director Perry. All three of them looked at each other for a second, then all of them nodded their heads. Pinter called his aid forward and said something in his ear. The aid nodded his head and went back to his own briefcase. The aid walked out from around the table went up to the knee wall and handed Suzanne a piece of paper and a pen.

"Lieutenant. Please read over the document and sign it. If you feel you cannot, then I would ask that you remove yourself from the room," Director Pinter instructed.

We waited for a few moments as Suzanne read the document, thought for a moment, and then signed it and handed it back to Pinter's aid. The aid took the document back to the table, placed it in front of Pinter, then retook his seat.

"Lieutenant, if you would move to the table next to Agent McKenzie," Pinter instructed.

Suzanne got up and installed herself next to me at the table.

"Lieutenant, did you understand the document you just signed?" he asked.

"Yes, sir."

"You also realize that any information that is disseminated here is not to leave this room, and if you are found to have broken the terms of the document at any point in the future you may be charged with treason, and that a crime of treason can carry a sentence of death?"

"Yes, sir."

"Agent McKenzie, for the record, when did you start your current assignment?"

"Do you want the day I accepted this position, or the day I arrived at the residence that was provided for me?"

"Both, if you don't mind."

"Wednesday, March 29, 2248 I accepted the assignment from an Agent Wallace of IBI through Marshal Terrance Burdock who was my supervisor at the time. I arrived at my residence the morning of Tuesday, April 4, 2248."

"Were you involved in an altercation the night of Tuesday, April 4, 2248 at the Horse Barn Bar and Grill?"

"Yes."

"You drew your weapon during the altercation."

"Yes, after I was outnumbered four to one, but my side arm was never fired and there was no loss of life."

"You identified yourself as a U.S. Marshal?"

"Yes, sir."

"Did you identify yourself before or after you drew your weapon?"

"After."

"Why did you wait until after?"

"It was my first day in my assignment and I had been required to keep my assignment secret. I did not draw my weapon or identify myself until I knew there was no other way to calm the situation."

"But yet the local police were still called to the scene."

There were a few beats.

"Are you not going to answer the question?" Director Pinter asked.

It was out before I could stop myself.

"You made a statement, you did not ask a question."

I heard the small snort out of Director Perry.

"You closed your first case, by your report, on Monday, May 8, 2248?" Pinter asked, moving on.

"I believe that is right, though it probably should have read Tuesday, May 9, 2248 since it was after midnight. An oversight on my part."

"Did you draw and fire your weapon on that night?"

"Yes, sir. In the process, killing four suspects."

"And how do you feel about that night?"

"I am not sure I understand your question."

"Were you upset, happy, unfeeling, depressed.... You get the picture Marshal."

"I am never happy about the loss of a life. That night was no different."

"How did you feel about closing your first case?"

"To this day I don't consider it my case. It was one of two that my predecessor left me. To be honest, I was happy to close it."

"Could you please walk us through, in a general nature, how you went about choosing that case to begin with and how you choose that place and time?"

"After reading the old case files that were suggested by my predecessor, I chose to actively pursue the one that had most of the initial investigation completed. Using my knowledge of the myths surrounding those you call shape-shifters and the dates of the murders, I surmised that all of them took place around full moons. The first full moon I went out on, nothing at all happened. After further investigation and becoming aware of some other cases that were located in the next district, I found that my first stakeout had been too far south. After re-interviewing a few of the leads the former agent had listed, I found credible information that led me to that place and time."

"Did you know that there were four suspects when you went out?"

"No, sir. I was under the impression there was only one."

"So you were surprised by the others?"

"Yes."

"You were faced with a shifter on a full moon and yet you had enough wits about you to also take on the other three, even though they surprised you?"

"Yes, sir."

"You were the driving force behind the original arrest of Agent Wallace, Agent Gray, Agent Dean, Agent Simmons, and Mr. Collier, a technician for IBI?"

"I am not sure about all of them but I was the arresting agent of Agent Wallace and Gray. I never knew the names of the other three until now."

"Tell me, Agent McKenzie, what led you to believe that your house had been entered?"

"There should only be two people who are able to enter my house; myself and Director Perry. Since I was fairly sure that Director Perry was not rearranging my curtains, I deduced it had to be someone else."

"Rearranging your curtains?"

"When I returned from closing my first case I noticed that the curtains, which I never close, in my living room were closed. I decided to take a deeper look into it. I found, through our tech support, that I could access the readers on my door locks. I found an odd IBI control number had been programed in. Once I looked at the list of who accessed my front door I deleted the old IBI number with the asterisks and programed in the three control numbers that had used the lock. I laid a trap and caught them."

"Did you draw your weapon during that?"

"Yes."

"Did you fire your weapon?"

"Yes."

"How many times?"

"Six."

"How many of those shots would you say were in self-defense?"

"Four."

"Would you please explain those four?"

"The first stopped Agent Gray's advance towards me. I creased his hairline. The second was into his right elbow when he went for his gun and the last two were into his left shoulder and arm when he tried to shoot me with a concealed weapon in his pocket."

"You mean to tell me that you purposely did not take a kill shot, even with him shooting at you, and all of your shots landed where you wanted them? You are trying to tell me you are that good of a shot?"

I started to answer when I was interrupted by Director Perry.

"I will answer that one for Marshal McKenzie; yes, she is that good of a shot, I have studied her scores. Jeremy, this is getting away from a normal debriefing. You are making this sound more like an investigation than a meeting to get information and to help our agent cope with it. What is your point?"

"From the information I have received, I believe that Agent McKenzie is no longer capable of performing the duties to which she has been assigned. I am just determining if that is the case."

"What information?" the President asked.

"Tips from other agents and their informants. It is my contention that she has been affected by the first case she closed."

I saw the look of concern for me in the Presidents eyes. If I hadn't already killed Philip, I would do it now.

"Are you trying to relieve her of duty?" Director Perry asked.

"If it is within my power; yes."

"This is a witch hunt because she caught your boys so far off the reservation it isn't funny. Get a grip Jeremy," Director Perry said, red faced.

"Nonsense, besides; it will be quite easy to prove. Won't it, Agent McKenzie?"

I so wanted to slap that smile off his face and if it wasn't for the cramp that grabbed my attention, I would have.

"I'm not sure I understand what you mean," I said, gritting my teeth through the pain.

"I guess you have the choice of just telling us the truth right now or showing everyone in this room the proof later."

"Marshal, do not say another word. Jeremy, you are not going to railroad this the way you want it to go. If you have evidence of her doing something that constitutes removal, you need to produce it. We will go through the proper procedures and she will have the right to rebut that in an official hearing," Director Perry said.

"Jake, why waste the money when it can be answered so easily?" Pinter addressed Director Perry but looked directly at me.

"Not on my watch. Bring your evidence and we will do this in an official manner. Marshal McKenzie, you are free to go. I will get in contact with you once Director Pinter has produced his evidence," Director Perry said.

"May I say something?" I asked.

"Of course," the President said.

"I would like to hear what Director Pinter has in mind."

I think I took everyone off guard with that.

"I would suggest that you come clean. If not, then just a small get-together at your billet tomorrow evening, say.... between nineteen hundred and twenty two hundred."

"I have no problem with a get-together, but I'll need fifteen minutes in there somewhere to take a quick shower."

"I'm sure you will," Pinter said, smiling.

"Are there any other requirements?"

"Yes," Pinter answered.

"What would that be?"

"Starting right now, you will be in the presence of someone else at all times."

"I am not going to have someone going to the bathroom or sleeping with me. I'm sorry, Director Pinter, but I have to draw the line there," I said, standing up.

"Then you will be confined to quarters with an armed detail outside."

"Okay, I can live with that."

He seemed shocked that I agreed.

"Director Pinter?" I asked.

"Yes?"

"Tomorrow night is BYOB. I will not share my Scotch," I said, smiling.

He looked hard at me.

"Director Pinter, are we through for the day?" the President asked.

"Yes, sir. We will reconvene at nineteen hundred tomorrow at Agent McKenzie's quarters."

"I hope you know what you are doing, Director Pinter," the President said and rose.

The room rose with him. He left the room and Pinter made sure he was gone as soon after as possible. Suzanne was eying me suspiciously as Director Perry made his way to the table where I was at.

"Marshal, you don't have to go through this charade. We can make him produce his evidence."

"I really don't care what evidence he thinks he has. I have nothing to hide but severe PMS."

"But he's accusing you of being a shifter."

"Director, I have never had fur or walked on four legs in my life and I won't start tomorrow," I said with authority.

The Director laughed. I had never considered that the truth could be so funny.

"Well then, I will see you tomorrow at seven in the evening. Don't worry, I'll bring my own bottle," he said, smiling.

"Don't worry, I'll share my Scotch with you and the President. Director Pinter, however, is on his own."

"Good day, Marshal," he said as he left the room with Marshal Davis following.

"I bet Bella will love the hell out of this. She'll get to be all prim and proper for the President," I said to Suzanne.

I was a bit surprised that she wasn't taking the bait.

"This way," was all she said, nodding towards the door.

****

It was a very quiet and tense ride back to where I was staying. Once we were back in the house I asked Bella to fix some lunch and motioned Suzanne up to my room. I closed the door behind her and turned to look at her.

"What's the problem?"

"You're Counter Section."

"I can't confirm that."

"But you won't deny it."

"No."

"So, all of it is true."

"All of what?"

"Everything I've heard."

"Not knowing what you have heard, I will not even venture to guess if it's true or not."

"There are things out there like wheirwolves and vampires."

"If you have any inkling of Counter Section, you know I can't answer that."

"How did you get chosen to do that?"

"Honestly, I don't have a clue. One day I was a Deputy Marshal, the next....."

"Aren't you scared?"

"Of Pinter? No. He is the least scary thing I've met in awhile."

"No, of everything else."

"I am afraid of my own shadow some days."

"How do you do it? You are so...."

"Young? Petite? Female? I haven't found any of those to be a detriment yet. Though I've found all of them to be an asset at times," I answered, finishing the statement for her.

"Is it true you have an unlimited budget?"

"I wouldn't say it is unlimited; expansive would be a better word. I have found, though, that the budget isn't what opens doors for me. Being a Marshal does that better than any amount of money ever could."

"Do you really work alone?"

"Yes."

"God....." she said, shivering.

"Most of my days are spent at home in my comfy clothes reading the paper and drinking coffee. You got a taste of it last night. It is not near as glamorous or as exciting as it might appear."

"But still...."

"There are two sides to that 'but still'."

"I guess. But to know the things you know must be incredible."

"Maybe, but right now my cramps are killing me, I want to take a shower, and change. I'll meet you downstairs for lunch."

"Oh. Okay."

She started walking towards the door.

"Suzanne?"

"Yes," she answered and turned.

"I have a friend that told me something once: it is not what you do or don't know that will kill you, it's the things you think you know that will."

"What is that supposed to mean?"

"Don't go off halfcocked thinking you know what you are after; know all about it before you do or let it come to you, and find out about it in your comfort zone."

"Oh," she said as she walked out the door and closed it after her.

Chapter 35
Saturday August 5, 2248

My temperature had risen steadily throughout the day, along with my bad mood. My wheir cramps were hellacious and I'd spent most of the day curled up on the couch trying to read. I knew that the actual time of the full moon had been around nine in the morning, but nothing was going to happen until the sun went down. As the time came nearer for everyone to arrive; my temperature started to spike. I didn't feel like getting dressed in anything but comfy clothes. I knew that I should put a better foot forward since the President was going to be here this evening, but I felt like a caged animal on display and everyone was going to get me as I was–comfy and bitchy. The first knock on the door came a little before seven. I got up to answer it but Bella beat me to the door. Director Perry came in alone. He was a little shocked at my appearance.

"Marshal are you okay? You look a little flushed," he said.

"Are you married?" I asked him as he came in.

"Yes."

"Are there a few days a month that you would rather be anywhere but around your wife?"

"Oh..." he said, understanding.

"Come in," I said as I wandered back into the living room.

We had just sat down when the doorbell rang again. This time I let Bella handle it. The President walked into my living room with two Secret Service agents this time. One of them was the same one I had seen yesterday and the other one, if he hadn't been white, could have been the first's twin. I could also smell that both of them were armed with silver. I guess I couldn't blame the President. I stood with Director Perry.

"Mister President. Please have a seat. You must excuse my attire for the evening, but I'm not in an entertaining mood," I said, pointing to a chair.

"I quite understand," he said and sat in the chair offered.

I could see the concern on his face as his detail took up places behind him. Director Pinter arrived a little after the President, though it was one of the Secret Service agents that answered the door, not Bella. He entered the room, followed by his aid.

"Director Pinter. I have allowed this farce but your aid must wait outside in the car. I understand the President and his detail, but you do not get the same right in my house."

"But..." he started to say.

"Your host has made a request of you, Director Pinter. I would suggest you abide by it," President Bradley said.

"John, wait in the car," Pinter said to his aide.

The man walked back outside and I heard the door close after him. I was hit with a cramp that almost doubled me over.

"Is there a problem?" Director Pinter asked in a knowing way.

I just looked at him and let him think what he wanted. Bella served some hors d'oeuvres and drinks. I'd meant it when I told Pinter that it was a BYOB but Bella refused to let me be a bad hostess.

I could feel my fever and cramps building as the sun started to sink into the west. I so wanted the main cramp to get here so I could get this over with. I felt the first of the major cramps start. I knew I had about ten minutes to get to a bathroom.

I stood and all of the men in the room who were not already standing, stood with me.

"If you gentlemen will excuse me for about fifteen minutes, I will get my act together and we will eat dinner," I said as I started towards the stairs.

I noticed Pinter was following me.

"Where do you think you're going?"

"With you. I'm not letting you out of my sight."

"Like hell you are. I'm going to the bathroom to take care of a female problem and take a quick shower."

"You think I believe that?"

"If what you think is going to happen, does. Do you really want to be in a locked room with me?" I asked in a whisper that only he could hear.

I saw in his eyes he hadn't thought of that. Director Perry and the President joined us at the bottom of the stairs.

"Really, Jeremy?" Director Perry asked.

"Yes, really."

I was hit with a massive cramp that doubled me over and I bent at the knees. The President reached over to steady me.

"Are you all right, Agent?"

"Just a woman thing."

I turned and started to step up on the first step and was hit with another one. Shit, I'd misjudged. There would be no way I would make it to the top of the stairs much less my bedroom or bath. I sat down on the bottom step as another cramp came. Now not only did I have the cramps going, but I had the embarrassment of having five men watching the beginning of my period. On my last moon the cramp had lasted a little less than four minutes, I hoped it would be shorter this time. I felt the beginning of the big cramp. I snuck a look at my watch and closed my eyes. I tried to push the situation out of my mind and let come what was coming anyway. I heard the beginnings of my own scream.

I opened my eyes to see five very worried men looking at me. Four of them were concerned about me and one about himself. I looked quickly at my watch and did the math, three minutes that time. I found my focus and began to stand up. I could feel the wetness in my sweatpants and running down my leg. Now there was no more pain, just anger and embarrassment. I looked hard at Director Pinter.

"Are you happy now? Not only have you just embarrassed me, you have embarrassed every woman in the world. Director Perry, Mister President, if you will excuse me for a few moments to clean up, I would appreciate it."

"By all means, Miss McKenzie," the President said gently.

I was struck by his not using my title. I smiled as best I could at him, turned, and went up the stairs. I was almost to my room when the conversation at the bottom of the stairs started.

"Director Pinter, I don't know what you thought you were going to prove tonight, but I can't see you proved anything that all of the women in the world haven't known since the beginning of time. I expect to see a report on my desk by eight, Monday morning, detailing what you thought you knew, evidence you thought you had, your sources, and a written apology to Marshal McKenzie. And so help me, Director, you keep this vendetta going against a promising young agent, I will have your head on a platter. Do I make myself clear?" the President asked and I could hear the anger in his voice.

"Jeremy, I'd suggest that you take this opportunity to leave," Director Perry added.

There was a pause in the conversation as I reached the door to my room.

"Now, Jeremy." the President almost yelled.

I heard the front door slam about the time I closed my bedroom door.

****

After my shower, I put on the clothes I had laid out; a light summer blouse, knee length skirt, and some strap sandals. For as hard as I tried, my hair would only be partially tamed and there was nothing I could do about the wild look in my eyes. I took a look at myself in the mirror as I applied some lipstick to make sure I was at least presentable.

I found the President, his two agents, and Director Perry in the living room when I returned downstairs. Director Perry and The President rose when I entered the room.

"Gentlemen, I would like to apologize for my behavior earlier. I assure you I am feeling much better and will be a better host."

"Marshal, there is no need to apologize for anything," the President said.

"Would you like to join me for a late dinner?"

"Though I could think of nothing better, I have other duties I need to attend to. Would you walk with me to the door?"

"Yes, sir," I said, smiling.

As he started moving towards the door his scent came back at me. I needed to get some food in me pretty soon because I felt like I was stalking my prey in a forest full of honeysuckle. I do so love the smell of honeysuckle. He stopped at the door and turned to his detail of agents.

"Gentlemen, would you please wait for me right outside the door?"

"But, sir..." his agent started, looking at me.

"Bill, if she wanted to assassinate me she could have done it ten times over. If she wants me dead, you couldn't stop her anyway. I'll be fine."

Bill looked hard at me as he ushered the other agent out, followed him, and closed the door.

"Mister President?" I asked.

"What happened tonight?"

"I'm not sure I understand the question."

"I am sure you do," he said, looking down at me since he was almost six foot five.

"Didn't I already have enough of my secrets exposed tonight?"

"I guess you did. I apologize."

"No need to, sir. If we'd met on the street and you weren't the President then this conversation might be different."

"I'm sure it would," he replied, smiling.

"But to attempt to answer your question; your guess is as good as mine or my friends."

I watched his smile fade.

"You haven't a clue do you?"

"No, sir. I don't."

"You are a very unusual young woman."

"Thank you?" I said, not really sure it was meant as a compliment.

"That didn't come out right did it?" he asked, laughing.

"I'm not sure. But I will take it as a compliment."

"Please. I hope that we will meet up again and have a better chance to talk in private."

"That would be something I would like to do."

"Good evening, Marshal Cedwynne McKenzie," he said, holding his hand out.

"And you, President Bradley," I replied, taking his hand.

He turned, opened the door and the agents rushed him to the car waiting in the drive. I closed the door and returned to the living room where Director Perry was still standing.

"Marshal, I want to apologize again. If I would have realized this was what he was up to, I wouldn't have allowed you to accept his demands," he said.

"Though I am really mad and embarrassed, I'm almost glad it happened."

"How is that?"

"He can never cry wolf again, even if next time he's right," I said, smiling.

"He may never get the chance, if he's not careful."

"How's that?"

"The President's made Counter Section a bit of a pet project for the last three years of his term. He wants an agency strictly for CS and Director Pinter has been dead set against it. Your little sting operation last month gave The President some ammunition to not only move Counter Section out of Director Pinter's jurisdiction, but to maybe even clip the wings of IBI, at least here in the States."

"I never meant it to go that high. I just wanted people out of my house."

"I don't blame you."

"Are you joining me for dinner?"

"If the invitation still stands, I would be delighted. My wife is away visiting family and I would be eating alone tonight anyway," he answered.

"Good. I'm starving and I hate to eat by myself," I said as I started walking towards the dining room.

"Bella?" I called.

She came out of the kitchen door.

"Director Perry will be joining me for dinner, could I ask you to set him a place?"

"Yes, Miss Cedwynne," she said, smiled at me, and went back into the kitchen.

I went to the place that was already set. The Director pulled out my chair for me then took a seat across the table. It wasn't long before his place was set and we were starting our salads.

"So, where do you go now?" the Director asked.

"I'm going to take some advice for a change."

"That being?"

"I had an agent tell me to quit working on cases, take a couple of months to get to know my district and the people in it. I think I'm going to take a bit of a working vacation for a few weeks."

"You probably should have done that to begin with."

"What and miss all of this fun?" I asked, laughing.

"Marshal Burdock said you were a handful."

"The Captain would know."

I noticed that he was smiling at something going on in his head.

"What?" I asked.

"I hope you won't take this the wrong way, but I would have paid good money to see a shifter in pink fuzzy slippers. Now there would be a fashion statement."

"I hope you and the President understand my wardrobe choice this evening."

"I don't think you need to ever mention it again."

Bella came in and sat our steaks down.

"Bella, have you and Suzanne eaten?" I asked.

"Yes, Miss Cedwynne. We ate earlier."

"Good. Thank you," I said as she returned to the kitchen.

"When will you be leaving?" Director Perry asked.

"Nothing personal, but I plan to be packed and on a train first thing tomorrow."

"No offense taken. If it were me I'd be on one tonight," he said, smiling.

I'd thought about it but I knew that once everyone left, I would be doing a stroll around the neighborhood or maybe a run; Suzanne was really going to hate me since I knew she wouldn't let me go alone. My tolerance for being in the house was coming to an end and I could already feel the draw of the fresh air and night.

****

Finally, everyone had left the house but the people who were supposed to be there. I ran up the stairs and knocked on Suzanne's door. I waited a few moments until it opened. Suzanne gave me an odd look once she saw my eyes.

"Cedwynne. What can I do for you?"

"I'm going to go for a jog. I don't expect you to go along but I wanted you to know where I was."

"Let me get changed."

"Really, Suzanne, you don't have to go. I am going to be up and on a train early tomorrow, you might want to go for the rest instead."

"No. If you leave the house, I am with you."

"Suit yourself. I'll be ready in about ten minutes."

"I will be too," she said and closed the door.

****

The night was very warm and I was sweating before we'd been out more than twenty or thirty minutes. I found myself laughing.

"What are you laughing about?" Suzanne asked.

"I was just thinking about something one of my foster mothers once told me. I was about thirteen or fourteen and I'd been outside doing some chores. I came in to take a shower and I was complaining about being sweaty and she admonished me to remember that women glisten they don't sweat. I guess I'm not a woman because I've always sweated. Are you glistening yet?" I asked, still chuckling.

"I passed glistening when I entered the army." She laughed.

"Though I don't know how you've kept your humor this evening," she added.

"Why?"

"I really didn't let you out of my sight this evening. I saw what they did to you from the top of the stairs. I would have killed that little jackass Pinter."

317

"Don't worry, he's on my figurative death list."

"Why do you have to put up with him? I thought he was IBI and that Director Perry was your supervisor?"

"I have three supervisors and all of them were here tonight."

"That must be a pain."

"The only pain is the man that arranged this witch hunt. As far as Director Perry or President Bradley go, I rarely hear from Director Perry and this was the first time I'd ever spoken to the President. Normally they can only reach me by phone. Needless to say, I'll be conveniently working when Pinter calls now."

I decided I'd had enough of the jogging pace so I started pushing it. After about an hour of running I could tell that Suzanne was starting to labor, and after another fifteen minutes she was slowing way down. I stopped and jogged in place as she bent over and put her hands on her knees.

"Really?" she asked, looking up at me.

I just smiled at her.

"Will you let me out of your sight for a little bit?" I asked.

"How much of a little bit?"

"I want to do my sprints. I'll use this block to sprint around. You'll be my start-finish line."

"You're nuts. Fine," she said, panting and pointed down the street.

I took off at a dead run. After my third time passing her spot on the street I told her one more time around. I slowed as I came up to her the fourth time and dropped into a walk as I approached.

"I would kill for your endurance. What's your mile time?" she asked as I came to a stop.

"If it's just one mile and I'm going all out about four minutes thirty seconds."

"Do you run marathons?"

"The only marathon I ever ran was the endurance marathon when I was in training."

"What's the endurance marathon?"

"It is one of the last tests that the Marshal Cadets go through. They set up a course and you run, on all different types of terrain until there's only one left. I won," I said, smiling at her.

"How long did it take you?"

"I stopped after twenty six hours. I figured two hours after my last competitor dropped was enough."

"You *are* nuts."

"Maybe. But if it will make you feel any better it took me almost two days to be able to walk again," I laughed.

"Not much of a consolation," she answered as we started walking back towards the house.

Chapter 36
Sunday August 6, 2248

I got off of the train in Joplin a little after noon, rented a car, threw my bags in the trunk, and headed south. I flipped open my personal phone and dialed.

"Barry County Sheriff's Office," the voice answered.

"Is Sheriff Benton in today?" I asked.

"No, he's off until Monday," the man answered.

"Thank you. I'll call back later," I said as I hung up and dialed Greta's number.

It rang a few times before Greta picked up. Thankfully, I hadn't woken her.

"Hey, Greta."

"Ced. It's good to hear your voice. I missed you last night."

"I missed you too. Is Gary there?"

"No, he's looking at a house he is thinking about buying, Willis went with him."

"Is there some sort of meal planned for tonight?"

"Of course."

"Would you mind an extra body for the evening?"

"Really? You're coming?" she asked, excited.

"I'm about thirty minutes out of Joplin. I should be there in about an hour. Don't tell anyone."

"My lips are sealed."

"Good. See you in a bit."

"Drive careful."

"I'll try."

Greta was waiting on the porch for me as I drove up. I parked the car under the trees in the front yard so it would be out of the way when everyone got there. She came over and hugged me tightly then helped me take my bags to my room.

"You were missed last night," she said as we sat the suitcases down in the corner.

"I thought I would go nuts by myself. It took running for almost three hours last night to get to where I could settle down and sleep. I don't know what you are cooking, but it smells wonderful," I said as I sat on the bed.

"A large number of hams: One of them even has your name on it," she smiled as she sat down next to me and nuzzled my neck.

God, I'd missed this closeness. I threw my arms around her and pulled her back down on the bed with me. We lay close, talking about my trips over the last month. She was especially interested in how I was doing after the way I had left last month. Though Gary and I had met at places in between, since then I hadn't been up to Cassville in a month. I assured her I was much better and wouldn't be leaving in the middle of the night. She kissed me gently and disentangled herself from my arms to get up.

"I have some things to do. Why don't you take a shower and change into something a lot more comfortable."

"Do I smell that bad?"

"No, but you do smell like a train and everything associated with it. Clean it off and smell like you," she said, smiling and walking to the door.

"You don't smell like anything but you. I've missed you."

She smiled at me and left the room. I did as Greta suggested. Though I really liked the place where I lived and had found a home there, I'd come to think of Willis and Greta's house as my second home. It wasn't so much the building or where it was located as it was the people. I felt safe and loved.

Freshly showered and dressed in shorts and a tee shirt, I found Greta in the kitchen working on the evening meal. I didn't know how she did it. She would basically cook the entire meal for twenty hungry wheirs and that was a feat. I found a beer in the fridge and leaned up against the counter where she was working.

"When is everyone getting here?"

"Around five."

"Did everyone have a good moon?"

"Yes, I believe we did. Though I think Casey has a bit of a dilemma going."

"What's up?"

"Seems he's fallen in love," she answered.

"Is it serious?" I asked.

"Serious enough that Casey proposed and she accepted," Greta answered.

"Wow, Casey married."

"Small problem though."

"What is that?" I asked.

"He got permission from Gary to tell her about himself. Gary figured that if she didn't believe him she'd think he was nuts and break it off, or if she did believe him she would want nothing to do with him."

"And?"

"She believed him and wants someone to turn her," Greta answered, setting down her knife and looking at me.

"She doesn't have a clue does she," I said sadly.

"Not in the least."

"Have you tried talking to her."

"Not yet. I was thinking maybe you could say something to her also."

"Why me?"

"You and I are the only ones that have gone through that."

"How old is Casey?"

"Thirty-one."

"I thought he was younger. How about her?"

"Twenty-nine."

"Ouch. She's not even old enough to make her decision about children," I said, more to the room than Greta.

"Will you help me with her?"

"Of course, but I don't know how much help I'll be."

"I think both of us relating what we went through and how hard it was and is, not to mention that if she does this she can never go back, might make her see things differently."

"How hard is she pushing this?"

"Not that hard yet and I know that Casey has told her that if she insist on becoming wheir, he wouldn't allow it until closer to the wedding."

"When are they planning on getting married?"

"Sometime next spring."

"So this isn't something we have to ruin tonight over."

"No, I guess not but the sooner we start the better chance we have of talking her out of it."

"True, but could I have one month up here where I didn't have to do anything like having massive wheir PMS, ruining people's lives, or killing someone? Just one month can I eat and have a good time?"

"I guess you're entitled," Greta laughed.

"Has Gary weighed in on this?"

"I think he is a bit torn on the subject. On his human side he sees the real pitfalls for her, but on his animalistic side he sees a new member of the pack and a female to boot. I think he would like for this one to go away so he doesn't have to deal with it."

"Sucks being the Alpha," I laughed.

"You're horrible, Ced."

"I have been accused of that on more than one occasion."

We talked for a little while longer. I was feeling the need for a nap before everyone got there. I kissed Greta on the cheek and went to lay down for a while. It was a little before three when I flipped off my shoes and lay down, pulling the afghan up over me.

****

"Greta! Where the fuck is she?" I heard Gary's shout.

I smiled as I woke up more.

"She was laying down taking a nap but I'm sure she is awake now," I heard Greta respond, laughing.

I rolled on my back and waited. I heard the footfalls down the hall. There was no knock and the door flew open.

"You little shit," Gary said, smiling from the door way.

"Hello to you too," I said from the comfort of the bed.

I was surprised at the speed in which he closed the door, had most of his clothes off, and was in the bed next to me searching for my mouth with his.

"Why didn't you call?" he asked when he came up for air, pulling my tee shirt off with the question.

"Surprise."

"If I would have known, I wouldn't have gone out to look at the house today," he said, working my shorts off.

"Where would the fun be in that?" I asked, snaking him out of his underwear.

Since it was in the middle of the day and we were at someone else's house, we tried to keep it down to a dull roar. I'm sure that Greta and Willis were still getting an earful but I didn't care. I hadn't seen him in almost two weeks now and it was after a full moon. Though I hated the term horny, that was the only word that could describe what I was. I rolled him on his back and looked into those green eyes. I slung my leg over him and lowered myself, feeling him slip in. It didn't take long before I felt him explode within me. I smiled down at him and continued my ride until the sparkles fired off behind my own eyelids. I collapsed down into him and giggled.

"It is so good to see you," I said into his chest.

For once both of us had gotten out of a sexual encounter without any bruises, cuts, or scratches. In a funny way I felt a little cheated. I could hear a number of voices out in the house. People had started arriving around our climax. I was sure I'd get some knowing looks this evening. I rolled off of him and lay down.

"We might want to join the others," he said, laughing.

"You first, I need to clean up a bit."

He raised up on the bed and started finding his clothes. I lay there watching the rippling muscles in his back and sides. God, he was beautiful.

"Come on," he said, holding out his hand.

I took it and rose to a seated position.

"You go on out. I am going to use the rest room," I replied, as I collected my clothes and weapon.

He left the room and I snuck across the hall to the bath. I cleaned up, put my hair in some sort of order, and went out to join the party.

****

Most of the people had already migrated to the back yard. A few of the females eyed me and smiled as I grabbed a beer out of the fridge. I said hello and walked out the back door into the light of an early evening of summer. I found Gary sitting in a chair on the back lawn next to Willis. I walked over and sat on the arm of his chair.

"Hey, Willis. How have you been?"

"Doing well. And yourself?"

"If I never see Washington City again, I could live with that."

"Bad visit?"

"The worst."

I saw Greta and the women in the yard head to the house. I handed Gary my beer and followed them in to help get all of the food out and on the tables. Though I didn't agree with the women having to wait on the lazy asses sitting out waiting to be fed, I wasn't going to revolt against the system by not helping them.

I sat down next to Gary after everything had been laid out. Gary began to dish up his plate as did the rest of the company. As I was picking up my first bite I heard Thomas shout to me from his table.

"Hey, Ced. I need a beer," he said, laughing.

I knew he was still picking at me from last month. I picked up my own half empty bottle and sent it in his direction, with a hard overhand toss. He ducked and came up looking at me.

"If you want a beer you better learn how to catch," I laughed back at him.

He smiled at me and raised his own in salute.

The meal was uninterrupted by disgruntled wheirs holding knives or me shooting anyone. I thought all of that was a real plus. I had a chance to really visit with the pack for a change and I had nothing pressing except a sort of a vacation and a lot of papers to read. I was actually happy and enjoying myself among people that accepted who I was and needed no other reason to be around me.

Chapter 37
Monday August 7, 2248

I'd decided to drive back to Hot Springs instead of returning the car in Springdale and catching the train. It wasn't any longer and I wouldn't have to deal with the odors and people. I gave some thought to getting a third car. Something like Greta's that would give me a vehicle to take a trip in that wasn't Bee. The small car I had was good for short trips to Little Rock, but an extended vacation wasn't in the cards. Bee was a wonderful companion when I was working and camping but taking it into a city was an experience I really didn't like. City streets weren't made for something that size and parking was a whole different problem. This week I'd go car shopping. Maybe I had enough money in my personal account to buy a good used one. I hadn't checked my personal account in a while since I rarely used it anymore. There would have to be a few months pay built up.

****

I was already a bit tired by the time I took the exit in Russellville to head south. Though I'd stayed the night in Cassville; neither Gary nor I got much sleep. I wish I could blame it all on him but I was probably more guilty about the lost sleep than he was. I had just hit the two lane highway out of town when my official phone rang. I glanced at the number. *Burdock calling me?* That was unusual. I picked up the phone and flipped it open.

"McKenzie," I said.

"Ced. I'm glad you answered," Burdock replied.

I could hear something in his voice that I didn't like.

"What is wrong, Captain?"

"It's Sam."

I felt my heart sink into my stomach.

"What about him?"

"Sam has been shot."

"Is he....." I asked, not being able to say the word.

"No. He will recover but he's going to be laid up a while."

"What the fuck happened?"

"We had a raid this past weekend. Sam's partner froze, almost got three teams killed. Sam kept his head about him and drew fire until the others could get out of harm's way. Sam took a slug in the hip. Fractured it pretty good."

"Did you kill that weaselly little fuck of a partner?"

"Not yet."

"How is Chandra?"

"She's okay. Really hasn't left the hospital for two days now."

"I suppose it is a big no-no for me to come down and see him isn't it?"

"Yes. But there's nothing that says you can't call and check on him."

"It wouldn't make a difference to me if there was."

"I figured as much," Burdock said, chuckling.

"Burdock, tell me straight. Is he out of danger?"

"Yes, though he'll probably walk with a limp from now on. The doctors have him on bed rest for the next few weeks until the bone heals, but he should be up and at 'em soon enough."

"Thank you, Terry."

"I didn't want you to hear about this secondhand."

"I appreciate that. I'm going to get off of here and call Sam and Chandra. What is going to happen to his partner? I can come kill him for you if you need me too."

"No, Ced. I'll take care of that problem."

"You better. And you better damn well make sure that Sam gets a good partner next time."

"I will. I don't need you down here in the middle of my ass. I got rid of you once I don't need to go through that again. Especially since I don't outrank you anymore," he answered lightly.

"Damn skippy," I chuckled.

I spent the rest of the drive to Hot Springs on the phone talking with Sam and his wife to make sure that they knew I missed them and was wishing for his speedy recovery. I pulled into the parking lot of the train station and threw my bags in my own small car. I checked the rental car back in and hoofed it back to where I'd parked.

****

Bran was working in the yard when I pulled up. He stopped what he was doing and came over to help me with my bags.

"Did you survive?" he asked as he grabbed my bags.

"I'll have to tell you about it sometime. I just don't think now is it," I said as I opened the door to the house and let us in.

"Bedroom?" he asked, indicating the bags.

"Please," I answered as I went to the kitchen, started a pot of coffee, and made Bran a large glass of water.

I sat my purse on the table and lowered myself into a chair.

"I made you a glass of ice water," I told Bran as he came in kitchen.

"You seem a little preoccupied. Something wrong?" he asked as he took a drink.

"My old partner got shot this past weekend."

"Is he alright?"

"As alright as you can be with a bullet in your hip."

"You going there to see him?"

"Can't, against the rules."

"Sorry, Ced."

"I talked to him and his wife. They seem to be doing okay."

"Not the same."

I nodded my head and got up for some coffee.

"I'm going to be out of town awhile and I wanted to ask you to come out throughout the week to check on the place, eat the food that's here so I don't have to throw it out. That is if you wouldn't mind."

"Sure. But I can't get in."

"I'll program your driver's license into the reader for the house and barn. I should have done that a while ago."

"When are you leaving?"

"Probably next weekend. I will be in and out over the next two months but mostly out."

"A case you are working on?"

"Not really. I dove right in when I got here. There's a large part of my district I haven't even seen and I'm going to rectify that. Sort of a working vacation; without cases."

"Lucky you," he replied, smiling at me.

"Let's hope so."

Bran finished his water and headed outside to finish the yard. I unpacked, did laundry, and started reading through the papers that had accumulated over the past few days. Before Bran left for the day, I programed his identification into the readers. I would need to get keys made before Friday when he would come back for the maintenance on the lawn.

I went down to the office to file the few leads I had culled from the papers. I looked at the file folder sitting on my desk that Zahn had given me a month ago. For some reason I just hadn't wanted to look at it. I pulled it too me, drumming my fingers on the outside of it. Did I really want to waste this much time today? I decided if I wanted to fuck up a day, I would wait for a Wednesday and shoved the file back towards the edge of my desk.

I thought about this past weekend and the good and the bad of it.

Good: Pinter was on very shaky ground right now and was being watched closely by others. Maybe he would leave me alone for a while.

Bad: Before this past weekend the only person that had ever witnessed my near change had been Greta. Having others watch had been embarrassing and a bit demeaning. Also, until this weekend there were only five special beings or Mythics as Bran called them, in the world that knew I never morphed; now, counting the President, there were six.

The Weird: The fucking President of the United States wasn't human. I hadn't seen that one coming. But, what was he? Vampire? Fairy? Troll? Okay, I was reaching now. Witch? Who's to say.

I had another sobering thought. Were his intentions toward the Mythic community good or bad? What if he was out to destroy every other type of Mythic but his? Could he be pulling the strings behind Greyson and TTZ? God, I'd hate to think that he was the one after me. How in the hell do you fight the entire federal government? *Okay, Ced, get a grip. If the President was after you, you'd be dead by now.* Maybe I was supposed to be. *Really, Ced, you're going here? I'm sure the President had something to do with your appointment. Why go to the trouble of filling a vacancy then creating a new one?* Finally, something I had no answer for.

I so needed to get out of town and get away from the cloak and dagger.

Next subject, Ced. New car now or when you get back from your vacation? Well, I'd probably be doing some camping so I'd be taking Bee on the whirlwind tour of my district, so I guess when I got back I would go shopping for new wheels.

I closed the folders lying open on my desk, grabbed a couple of road maps, turned off the light, and headed upstairs to plan out my trip.

Chapter 38
Thursday October 5, 2248

When planning my trip the only rule I made was that every stop kept me moving in a pattern that would be representative of an area without revisiting a section I had already been in. I also made sure that I bypassed the larger cities because I figured that the majority of my investigations would take me to them soon in the future. In fact the most prominent cases I was following right now were in New Orleans and that would be the next place I would be heading to when I got "back to work".

I took time off of my tour to make sure I was in Cassville for the moons. I also blackmailed Gary into taking a week off and meeting me in the middle of nowhere for a small vacation from everything. Though, if the truth be told, it didn't really take a lot of effort to get him to agree. He and I spent most of the week holed up in Bee doing nothing but eating and staying in bed. Okay sure we hiked some and went sightseeing but for the most part it had been a carnal holiday.

I'd been surprised by my time out and about. Though there was not much social-economic difference between lower Missouri, Arkansas, and Louisiana; lower Mississippi was a bit of an eye opener for me. The gulf coast of Mississippi had made a comeback from The Fall but the rest of it was still steeped in what I would consider poverty. Where the poorer portions of the other states just seemed to have less money, the people in lower Mississippi seemed destitute. I found that part of my trip heartbreaking.

The only personal disappointment in the trip was that every time I found myself on the Gulf and near a beach, it had been storming and I was never able to go swimming in the ocean. I had this wonderful new bikini Greta had picked out for me that I never got the chance to show off.

I ended the last leg of my trip in Cassville for the last moon. I'd been with the pack for the last couple of moons; nobody died and I didn't have to kill anyone. Both a real plus. Gary and I had really started to bond but for some reason I just wasn't ready to take the next logical step. Maybe I knew I wasn't ready or just maybe I was thinking too much about how complicated that sort of relationship would make the rest of my life.

Though I'd dropped by Hot Springs a couple of times to spend a night in my own bed, I hadn't really been home for a long time. I knew I would miss the people standing on the porch waving Good-bye, but I was ready to get back to Hot Springs and my own home. I watched Willis and Greta's driveway recede in my rear view as I headed home. I found it a bit odd that out of all of the people that had seen me off; it was Greta that I seemed to miss the most, not Gary.

It had been a restful and educational two months. I'd had time to see the part of the country that made up my district, meet people in it and get my head on straight for the first time in a long time. I even came to some sort of grips, in my head, about my life after taking over this district as a Counter Section Agent. Though the question of what my lineage was still bugged me, I'd made my peace with what I was doing for a living and having the traits left over from the wheir bite. I think some of that came from finally giving up the mental fight of analyzing it to death.

****

I pulled onto the freeway in Fayetteville, after a coffee stop, and headed south and finally toward home. I hadn't gotten more than a mile or two down the road when my government phone rang. I looked at the number and wondered what new little hoop Director Perry wanted me to jump through.

"McKenzie," I said as I picked up the phone from the seat beside me.

"Marshal. How are you doing these days?"

"I'm doing fine. And yourself?"

"Doing well."

Okay this call was a little too upbeat for my comfort.

"What can I do for you?" I asked.

"Do you have anything that you can't break away from on the thirteenth of October?"

"That all depends."

"On what?"

"If it's another debriefing, I am in the middle of five cases and can't get away. Other things could be negotiable provided it doesn't include a trip to Washington City."

"Nothing quite so sinister," he said, laughing.

"Does it include Director Pinter?"

"Not anywhere near," he answered, still laughing.

"Then shoot. I'll probably be open."

"The District Eight Ball and Awards will be held on the thirteenth and your old partner is receiving the Marshal's Medal of Valor."

"Sam is getting the award?" I asked, happy to hear Sam would be recognized.

"Yes and Marshal Burdock and I felt it would be appropriate if you awarded it to him."

"Me? I would be honored but I thought that I was supposed to stay away from Dallas."

"Marshal, after your first few months on the job and the embarrassment and indignity you suffered at the whim of Director Pinter, I felt you had earned the right to honor him. Burdock told me how close the two of you were and I feel you should be there."

"Sir, I would be honored."

To present this award to Sam would be a treat for me. I owed Sam so much and this would be something I could give back.

"One caveat," he said.

"I have to do it over the phone?" I asked, almost scared of what he would say.

"Nothing quite so prohibitive," he laughed.

"You can't tell anyone you are going down there. No one will know you are there until that evening. Can you live with that?"

"Yes, sir. I can more than live with that."

"Great. I'll send you the confirmation on your hotel reservation when the details are finalized. And Marshal, please keep your presentation speech under five minutes."

"I'll do my best sir."

"Then I'll see you in about a week. Keep your head down."

"Thank you, sir. And you too," I said as we hung up.

Wow. I get to go and give one of the few people in my life I truly cared about something that would honor him. Damn, that meant I had absolutely nothing to wear. *Really, Ced? Do you want a new purse too? Don't forget the new shoes.....*

Chapter 39
Friday October 13, 2248

The superstition about Friday the Thirteenth had survived for hundreds of years. It had survived The Fall and the Bio-war. As far as I was concerned it was the luckiest day of the year. It wasn't a Wednesday and I was back in Dallas.

As I sat in the beautician's chair, I fingered the cross that hung around my neck and smiled. Bran had made me this wonderful wooden holder that left the cross portion open and gleaming but kept the sharp points away from my skin. He'd made it out of an exotic wood called Bloodwood that was a deep red and he had polished to a high sheen. Bran had many hidden skills I was still finding out about.

It took almost two hours for the beautician to finally tame my hair to her liking. I paid and tipped her and walked the short distance to the hotel I was staying at to get ready for the banquet.

****

As I stood in front of the mirror putting on my–God, help me–makeup, I had to hang my head in a bit of shame. Seven months ago you would never have caught me dead in a form fitting tight dress much less makeup. Since my first moon I had done a one eighty on the femininity front. I'd tried to pull in the reins but there was something in me that kept overruling my sanity and self-respect. My last foray into the realm of clothes shopping should have tipped off my utilitarian side, though I'd really needed a new wardrobe. Besides, I needed someplace to hide my side arm when I went out in a dress. Why else would I carry a purse? *Really, Ced? Keep telling yourself that especially since there was always lipstick in there too.* Then there was the page I took out of Greta's fashion book when I was up in Cassville. Of course I wanted to fit in. *This is going downhill, girl. What about the bikini you took with you on vacation? You always wore a one piece before. Hey it was Greta that picked it out and I didn't want to hurt her feelings. Then let's talk about the tailored red satin dress you bought for tonight, the four inch heels and matching purse.* I had to have a nice cocktail dress if I was going to present an award, I needed the height to be able to see over the lectern I would be standing behind, and the purse matched the dress; besides, I bought it for the same reason I bought any purse–to hide my side arm. *Don't forget the lipstick.* Half of me felt vindicated and the other half was not buying any of it. My utilitarian side was just smiling at me, waiting for me to have to run in the heels.

I slipped the dress on and zipped it up. It was low cut, making it look as if I was bringing two bald friends to the dance with me, and stopped a couple of inches above my knees, hugging me all the way down. It showed everything I had. My utilitarian side almost won out on changing until I put on the heels and looked in the mirror. God, I was cute. The only thing that looked slightly out of place was the odd wooden encased silver cross that lay at my cleavage. But hey, it was red and matched the dress.

I put my thirty-eight and credentials in my purse, picked up the gun I usually wore on my back, and walked out of the room. I stopped by the front desk, had them put my normal gun in the hotel safe, found a taxi out front, and had it take me to the hotel where the Awards Banquet and Ball was being held. I had the driver let me off at the back dock as I was instructed to do where I was met by Deputy Marshal Davis who took me upstairs to the service corridor of the ballrooms.

I was seated in an unused, smaller banquet room to eat my meal and wait my turn at the lectern. I'd finished my meal, which wasn't near enough rubber banquet chicken, and made my way into the service corridor behind the ballroom. I watched the servers moving about taking food and coffee into the room and returning with used dishes and cups. I found an extra chair and moved it, and myself, into the room itself behind the curtain that had been put up to hide the service doors from the attendees. I sat as the speakers started with their speeches. National District Eight was the district that covered Texas, Oklahoma, New Mexico, Old Mexico, Arizona, and Colorado. Needless to say, there were a lot of people in the room, most of whom I didn't know. I knew that Sam's award would probably be towards the last since it was one of the highest awarded that wasn't awarded posthumously. I waited as the last of the keynote speakers ended their presentation and handed the mike over to Director Perry. He began to hand out all of the awards throughout the district. I could smell the coffee as it was being taken past me to refresh the waiting cups on the tables. God, I could use one now.

"Now we have one more award to give. Normally I would give all the citations and medals out, but I thought tonight it would be much more fitting to have a special guest present the last one," Director Perry started.

I perked up my ears.

"Most of you in the audience will not know our next presenter. But I would like for all of you to know this Marshal has made all of us proud by her dedication to the job, her tenacity, and most of all her willingness to enforce the laws of this union regardless of the personal cost. To present this next award my I introduce, Marshal Cedwynne McKenzie."

I rose from my seat and made my way over to the side stairs and up to the stage. Most of the applause in the room was the polite type for anyone that would be introduced. Though the six or seven tables, just to the right of the stage, of the people I used to work with, applauded with more gusto that soon turned to catcalls as I hit the stage in my dress. I walked to the lectern, shook hands with the Director, who offered me the mic. I installed myself behind the lectern and looked out on the large sea of faces waiting on me to instill something profound into the evening. I seriously doubted that was going to happen.

"First, I would like to thank Director Perry for allowing me this honor. Thank you, sir," I said in the direction that the Director was sitting on the dais.

"A wise man once said to me, and I quote: If you would shut your mouth occasionally, kid, you might be able to hear what the fuck is going on. That was the first day I met my new partner. He didn't say it loudly to get my attention nor meanly to rattle my cage. He said it as a profound truth. It wasn't until a year after that I understood what he meant. Though most days I don't do a good job of following that advice, it's the days that I do that tend to keep me safe. I know only a small portion of you here tonight and I know that all of us, in thought and intent, would take a bullet for anyone else around us. It is a rare, and maybe unlucky, minority that turns that thought into deed. For the men and women here that I worked closely with, I knew every day that they would be there for me regardless of what I was facing on the job. However, there was only one that did that for me off the job. The man that I am here to honor tonight; Sam Gresham was not only my partner he was, and is, my friend. Every month he would face the horrors than no one else in our department would—my PMS. I'm sure that he would tell everyone right now that taking a bullet was nothing compared to that," I said and paused for some chuckling to quiet down.

"For the time, affection, and patience that Sam showed me, it is my honor to present the U.S. Marshal's Medal of Valor for bravery and courage in the line of fire to; Deputy Marshal Samuel T. Gresham, Texas District One," I said, pulling the case and citation off of the top of the lectern and waiting for Sam to come on stage.

Sam still had a bit of a limp as he made his way from the table he was sitting at to the stage. He came up, I handed him his award, and wrapped my arms around him in a hug. He kissed me on the cheek then acknowledged the applause that was for him. The Director rose and came over to shake his hand, pointed me to his vacated seat on the dais and began his closing remarks as Sam made his way back to his seat. I sat and listened as the banquet and awards portion of the night came to a close.

Since this year's banquet was being held in Burdock's district, he was the emcee for the evening. After the Director finished his speech; Burdock took the microphone and ended the ceremony, directing everyone to the next ballroom for the dance and open bar. I rose as the house lights came up and made my way to where the Director and Burdock were talking next to the lectern. I waited as they finished.

"Director Perry?" I asked as they finished talking.

"Yes, Marshal?"

"I wanted to thank you for allowing me that. It meant a lot to me," I said, offering my hand.

"You are more than welcome. I felt you needed that after the past few months you've had," he said smiling and taking my hand.

"May I ask you a question and not seem rude?" he asked.

"Sure."

"Where are the pink slippers?" he asked, smiling.

"They clashed with the dress. I had to go with something a little more in the same color pallet." I answered, smiling back.

"Well, your choice does you credit."

"Thank you, sir."

The Director was pulled in another direction and left me alone with Burdock.

"God, Ced. You look incredible."

"I'll take that as a compliment," I said, blushing.

"Very much so. I am glad you didn't dress this way when you worked here. Our squad would've never gotten anything done," he said, chuckling.

"I can still be pretty lethal when I want to be."

"So I've heard."

"I want to thank you for all of the help over the last few months."

"Any time, Ced," he replied, still staring at me.

"You keep this up and your wife is going to have your hide," I said, smiling at him.

"I just can't get over the way you look."

"Well then, you get to buy my first drink," I said as I slid my arm in his and let him lead me down the front steps of the stage.

Burdock walked me through the emptying banquet room, across the hall to another room complete with orchestra, dance floor, and open bars.

"What would you like?" Burdock asked, as we walked towards one of the crowded bars.

"Double Scotch, rocks, splash."

Burdock made his way to the bartender as I waited at the edge of the crowd. One of the things I wasn't prepared for this evening was the amount of cologne and perfume that assailed me. Now that I had the senses I did, I was amazed at the need people felt to take a bath in stinky stuff. My hearing was also a double edged sword; though I could hear things that others thought I couldn't, there were times I wish that I hadn't. Burdock returned shortly with drinks in hand. He offered mine to me and I took it.

"I need to find my wife. Can I escort you anywhere?"

"Nah, I'm going to mingle, find Sam and some of the guys. If I don't catch up with you again, say hello to Sally for me."

"Sure. Oh, I almost forgot," Burdock said as he pulled an envelope out of the breast pocket of his suit coat.

"This came for you, here, about two weeks ago. The Director told me yesterday you would be coming so I brought it along," he said as he handed it to me.

"What is it?"

Burdock shrugged his shoulders.

"I'll talk to you later," he said loudly as the band started playing.

I nodded my head and looked down at the envelope. It was addressed to me but had no qualifiers, such as Marshal or Deputy Marshal. It just read Cedwynne A. McKenzie. There was no return address and the writing looked feminine. I looked at the post mark. It was from somewhere in North Carolina. I folded it up and stuck it down in my purse. I'd found, in my short life, that anything unexpected would pretty much ruin a good day. This was a good day, even if it was Friday the thirteenth and I figured I would wait for one that was going badly to ruin further by opening it. I walked through the crowd until I found the group of tables that my old squad had commandeered for the evening.

"Is this a private party or can anyone join?" I asked coming up to one of the tables.

I got a lot of hellos, great to see yous, and wow look at yous.

"You know this table is just for us lowly Deputy Marshals," Sam said above the din and rose to greet me.

I walked around the table to where he was, next to his wife, hugged him again and gave him a very wet kiss on the cheek.

"It is so great to see you," I said with a tear falling down my cheek.

"You surprised all of us," he said, looking down at me smiling.

"When the Director calls you can't say no."

"Bullshit. I've heard you say no to everybody," he laughed.

"How are you really doing?" I asked concerned, indicating his leg.

"I'll be fine. I have more physical therapy to go through but they say I will be as good as new in a few months," he answered.

"You know if I catch up to your partner, he's a dead man."

"Ced, you were green once yourself."

"Not the point. If I thought that you were going to be put in danger by me taking this position, I would have never left."

"It could have happened to me anyway."

"Not on my watch."

"Look. I was the senior marshal, I knew he wasn't ready for it, but I didn't speak up."

"No you don't Sam. Don't you dare take the blame for someone else's fuck up. He screwed up. He needs to learn how to deal with that and find a way to make himself a better Marshal or resign," I said hotly.

I wasn't going to sit there and listen to Sam have to make excuses for an inept partner. Yes, he'd made excuses for me during my time of the month but he never had to make this sort of apology for me.

"If it helps, I'm taking my two year leave of absence starting now. I won't be going back into the field for a while," he said, trying to placate me.

"It helps a little. But if I hear of you going back out with an inexperienced partner, Director Perry and The Captain won't know what hit them."

"You talk like you have some pull now," he said, smiling at me.

"Let's put it this way. I have three supervisors now and I outrank Burdock so he isn't one of them. I'm also sure that I could bring the President on board for this one."

"Calling in the big guns?" he asked, laughing.

"I will if I have to."

"Not here anymore and still have my back. I do miss you, Ced."

"I miss you every day," I told him as I gave him another hug.

"Sorry, Chandra, I think I am hogging your husband," I said to his wife as we broke apart.

Chandra was about ten years younger than Sam and quite beautiful.

"Come over here and sit. Tell me how you're doing," she said as she got up and gave me a hug also.

I sat next to Chandra talking while most of the Marshals came by the table to congratulate Sam and say hello to me. Sam seemed to be looking well and I was happy that I had been here to present him with his honors and not here to give his award to his wife posthumously. I had eaten many meals at their house over the two and a half years we were partners and I kind of viewed them as the parents I never had. Chandra told me that they were moving to a new house and starting to work on a family. I knew that the two of them would have beautiful, smart and well behaved children. We had been talking about a half an hour when I remembered I had a debt to repay while I was here.

"Have you seen Mitch from information this evening?" I asked the Marshal sitting on the other side of me.

"You mean Miracle Mitch?"

"Yep."

"I think he's at that table near the corner with the rest of the geeks."

I was a bit put out by that. Though Mitch worked in the information section he, and all the people that worked in supporting posts, had been through a basic training and was graded out with proficiency in a hand gun, law, and hand to hand. If they went out in the field in support, they had to be able to handle themselves in an emergency and Mitch could. He was more than a geek.

I excused myself from the table and made my way across the room to where Mitch was sitting. He had his back to me deep in a conversation with others at the table. I came up behind him, leaned over and put my arms around his neck.

"What's a girl gotta do to get a dance in this joint?" I asked in his ear.

The conversation at the table stopped as Mitch turned in his seat to see who had accosted him.

"Tops! It's so good to see you," he said as he jumped up and gave me a hug.

Mitch was not the rough and tumble, ripped guy at the beach. He was of average height and build with a bit of a paunch and would never be confused with Adonis but he was nice, intelligent, and loyal, and most any girl would be lucky to land him.

"It's great to see you too. I came over because at the very least I owe the man that saved my butt a dance," I said.

"Sure, but I have two left feet," Mitch said, smiling.

"Then we'll make a wonderful couple since I have two right ones," I said, showing him my heels.

He offered me a hand and we walked to the dance floor. I realized he actually was a pretty good dancer as he waltzed me around the floor.

"Mitch, I want you to know that you saved my ass."

"You know I would do whatever you needed."

"Your little toy helped bring IBI down a few pegs."

"That was you?"

I nodded my head.

"You're lucky you weren't killed over that."

"You know it's going to take more than that to get to me," I answered, smiling.

"True. You were always an ornery one."

He smiled; we danced another song, and then walked back to the table. I reached up and put my arms around his neck.

"Mitch, I want you to understand I care about you very much and in a way I love you. Keep your head up and everything will happen for you," I said lowly so only he could hear.

I laid a very wet and sensual kiss on him for all of his friends to see.

He pulled back shocked.

"I've got to go back to my district. You saved my butt; if I lived around here anymore I would make you take me out to dinner," I said to him loud enough for the table to hear, especially the females.

I winked at him, smiled, and headed back to Sam's table swinging my hips as a show. I could hear the conversations starting as I got out of what they thought was earshot, silly them.

****

I hadn't waited for the morning to leave. It was just a little past midnight by the time I cleared the city limits of Dallas heading back to Arkansas. I was glad that Sam was beginning his leave and would be out of harm's way for a while. I so didn't want to have to come down here for a funeral. It had been great seeing everyone and I was split in my feelings. Part of me felt the night had been entirely too short, but a bigger part of me was happy to be returning to what was now my home. It's strange how things can change in such a short time. Though I would miss the few real friends I had in Dallas, I wasn't sad about leaving.

Although I'd worked and lived in Dallas most of my adult life, it had never felt like home. I never had the feeling of belonging that I now had in Hot Springs. I guess it was something I'd learned, but not realized over the past few months. I had put down roots. It was my home and I'd fought to keep it. I knew that it could come crashing down in a second if someone above me really wanted me out, but as far as I was concerned it would take an act of God or Congress to get me out of there now. I smiled, pressed down on the accelerator, and took the car way above the speed limit. For the first time in my adult life, I couldn't wait to get home.

www.ingramcontent.com/pod-product-compliance
Lightning Source LLC
Chambersburg PA
CBHW061322170626
46817CB00001B/268

9780989721301